The "Wednesday" literary circle, Moscow, December 1902. Seated left to right: *Andreev, Fyodor Chaliapin, Bunin, N. D. Teleshov, E. N. Chirikov;* standing left to right: *S. G. Skitalets (Petrov), K. P. Pyatnitsky, Gorky.*

Nicholas Luker (ed. & trans.)

AN ANTHOLOGY OF RUSSIAN NEO-REALISM: The "Znanie" School of Maxim Gorky

ARDIS

Library of Congress Cataloging in Publication Data:

An anthology of Russian neo-realism.
    1. Short stories, Russian—Translations into English.
2. Short stories, English—Translations from Russian.
I. Luker, Nicholas J. L. II. Title: "Znanie" School of
Maxim Gorky.
PG3286.A57   891.73'01'08   81-12758
ISBN 0-88233-421-2   AACR2

TABLE OF CONTENTS

ACKNOWLEDGEMENTS

I am deeply indebted to the late Max Hayward, Fellow of St. Antony's College, Oxford, England, who not long before his death very kindly read my translations in manuscript, made many useful suggestions and, as always, gave me much encouragement. No translator of Russian could have wished for a more exacting and knowledgeable critic than I had in him. I am only sorry that he did not live to see this book's appearance.

I also wish to express my gratitude to Dorothy Honniball of Nottingham University Library, England, for typing my manuscript with her customary diligence and skill. My thanks must also go to Dr. Sergei Hackel of the University of Sussex for kindly supplying me with information about St. Vera.

To my forbearing wife, Patricia, and my impish young son, Nathaniel, I owe a special debt of gratitude. While she created the peaceful domestic atmosphere that is so conducive to productive work, he provided the entertaining diversions that are so refreshing amid long hours of labor.

Nicholas Luker

Nottingham, England
September, 1979

To Lois, my mother, with love and gratitude

The "Wednesday" literary circle, photographed in Moscow, December 1902. Seated left to right: Gorky, Andreev, Bunin, N. D. Teleshov; standing left to right: S. G. Skitalets, Fyodor Chaliapin, E. N. Chirikov.

During the twenty years from 1895 to 1915, Russian realism under-
went a vigorous revival after the literary doldrums of the 1880s. In those
two decades a large group of prose writers brought the genre of the short
story to an eminence unprecedented in Russian literature. It is with the five
authors most responsible for that resurgence—Gorky, Andreev, Bunin, Kuprin
and Artsybashev—that this anthology is concerned. In their different ways all
of them won lasting reputations both at home and abroad. What was the
background to this extraordinary revival of Russian prose and how did it
come about?

I

The assassination by terrorists of Alexander II in 1881 triggered merciless repression of revolutionary organizations in Russia. The reign of Alexander III was a period of militant nationalism, social conformity, and public
apathy. As the iron grip of reaction tightened on all levels of society, medioc-
rity, passivity and tedium enveloped Russian life, with the result that for the
first decade of the new Tsar's reign revolutionary activity virtually ceased.

Alexander III had resolved to ensure the survival of Russian autocracy
and safeguard the status quo. But if he and his reactionary ministers could
coerce the people into a fearful silence with military courts and deportations,
floggings and pogroms, they could not check the spread of ideas. By the
early 1890s—and especially after the Tsar's death in 1894—resistance to the
repression initiated during the previous decade was becoming apparent. Beginning here, popular resentment was to grow until it erupted in the revolution of 1905. In 1891 and 1892 cholera and famine wreaked havoc in western
Russia, bringing untold suffering to millions. Mismanaged by the government,
these disasters caused violent unrest among both peasants and urban poor.
While 1896 and 1897 saw serious disturbances in the cotton mills of Petersburg, 1903 brought a wave of strikes that started in Rostov-on-the-Don and
spread through southern Russia, from Baku to Odessa. In many cases the
strikers were for the first time organized by Marxists—proof of the growing
influence of Russian Marxism as a movement.

Vital to the success of that movement was the enormous growth of
the urban working class brought about by the extraordinarily rapid development of Russian capitalism in the late 1800s. Between 1865 and 1890 the
size of that class had more than doubled, and by 1900 it had reached two and
a quarter million. Moreover, this was now a hereditary working class born and
bred in the cities, a factory proletariat generated by the expansion of Russian
industry. Living in appalling squalor in the new industrial centers, these

underprivileged masses were to be tinder for the spark of revolution.

By 1904, shaken to its foundations by unprecedented economic and social change, as well as by revolutionary propaganda and terrorist assassinations, Russian society was in serious ferment. The unpopular Russo-Japanese War of 1904-1905 only made things worse. A series of disastrous defeats—among them the loss of Port Arthur and the destruction of the Baltic Fleet at Tsushima—revealed the bankruptcy of the regime. As discontent at home rose still further, opposition elements turned the situation to their advantage, and demonstrations and mass strikes followed. But much worse was to come, for though smoldering, the fire of revolution was not yet truly lit.

What set the nation ablaze was "Bloody Sunday"—January 9, 1905—when a peaceful procession of 150,000 people marched to the Winter Palace in Petersburg to present a petition to the Tsar. When the crowd reached the Palace, soldiers opened fire, leaving a thousand dead and two thousand wounded. Immediately, revolt swept the country. There were demonstrations, strikes, and violent clashes with the police. The months that followed saw bloody peasant uprisings, barricades in several cities, and mutiny in both the army and navy. By October, when a general strike began, the country was paralyzed. Later that month the Tsar was forced to issue a constitutional manifesto, which guaranteed certain civil liberties and promised the election of a legislative parliament, the State Duma.

But the victory was hollow. In July 1906, the First Duma was dissolved by the Tsar, and early in 1907 the Second Duma suffered a similar fate. Though the months of upheaval had forced the government to make concessions, the masses remained as underprivileged as before. The Leviathan of autocracy had weathered the storm and the 1905 Revolution was essentially a failure. It would be over a decade before the Bolsheviks razed the ancient edifice of Tsarism to the ground.

II

If the 1880s and early 1890s were a period of stifling conformity in Russian life, in literature they were years of stagnation. After reaching its peak in the novels of Tolstoi and Dostoevsky in the 1860s, the great Russian realistic tradition was manifestly in decline. With the exception of Anton Chekhov, who won recognition during these years, the period is devoid of major writers. Two figures, however, deserve special mention. Vsevolod Garshin (1855-1888), a soldier in the Russo-Turkish War of 1877-1878 and a melancholic who took his own life, is remembered for his stories "Four Days" (1877), written after he was wounded, and "The Red Flower" (1883), set in a lunatic asylum. The radical writer and publicist Vladimir Korolenko (1853-1921) was very different. Exiled to Siberia as a student, he later became editor of the Neo-Populist journal *Russian Wealth*, a position which he used to campaign on behalf of national minorities and fight for the abolition of capital punishment. Among his best works are "Makar's Dream" (1886), the story of a peasant from the Yakut region of Siberia, and his unfinished autobiography, *The History of My Contemporary*, serialized from 1906 onwards.

Apart from Garshin and Korolenko, there was a handful of lesser writers who were not without talent. Perhaps the most prolific was the journalist Peter Boborykin (1836-1921). Influenced by both Turgenev and Tolstoi, and later by the French Naturalist school, his eighteen novels span fifty years (1860 to 1910) and reflect the changes seen by their author in the spiritual and social life of Russia. Among them are *New Men* (1887), in which he criticized reactionary trends of the time; *The Pass* (1894) and *Vasily Tyorkin* (1895), which show the triumphant rise of Russian capitalism; and *Craving* (1898), a portrayal of the young proletariat. In addition, Boborykin wrote many tales describing the life of the Russian intelligentsia, and towards the end of his career published his successful novel *The Great Collapse* (1908), a colorful account of the ways in which the 1905 Revolution affects a family.

Also important at this time were the regional writer Dmitry Mamin-Sibiryak (1852-1912), whose novels showed the damaging effects of capitalism in his native Urals; and the railway engineer Nikolai Garin-Mikhailovsky (1852-1906), the author of rural sketches and an autobiographical trilogy, *Tyoma's Childhood* (1892), *High School Boys* (1893), and *Students* (1895), a work notable for the elegant simplicity of its style. An even finer stylist was Alexander Ertel (1855-1908), an amazingly energetic writer of German descent who is remembered for his panoramic study of rural life, *The Gardenins* (1889), generally considered one of the best novels of the late 1800s. Rather different was Vasily Nemirovich-Danchenko (1844-1936), brother of Vladimir, the joint founder with Stanislavsky of the Moscow Art Theater in 1898. His novels reflected the debates on women's emancipation in the 1870s and 1880s. Less well known was Mikhail Albov (1851-1911), the author of gloomy stories about Russian ecclesiastics. Writing of a lighter kind came from the pen of Ignaty Potapenko (1856-1929), a Ukrainian-born author who wrote humorously of the philanthropic activity of heroic individuals. The prose work of Peter Yakubovich (1860-1911), who used the pseudonym Melshin, was much sterner stuff altogether. After serving a term of eight years' hard labor for militant revolutionary activities, he drew on his experiences for his best work, *In the World of the Outcasts* (1898), a description of convict life reminiscent of Dostoevsky's *Notes from the House of the Dead*.

None of these writers was outstanding, however, and by the late 1800s the realist tradition was considerably eroded. Though still the dominant genre in Russian literature, realism was now far from new, and many readers were growing tired of it.

There was, of course, another reason for the continuing decline of the realist tradition at the time: the extraordinary cultural phenomenon of Russian Symbolism (or Decadence as it was called in its early stages) that began in the 1890s and eventually brought about a renaissance of Russian culture.

In 1893, just a year after the appearance of Gorky's first tale, the poet and critic Dmitry Merezhkovsky (1866-1941) published his long essay "On Reasons for the Decline of Contemporary Russian Literature and On New Literary Trends," a work which became the manifesto of the Modernist movement. Setting his face against the utilitarianism of the 1860s and 1870s, Merezhkovsky asserted that beauty was the supreme virtue in art and maintained that instead of serving his fellow men the writer should reveal his original personality. Only estheticism and individualism, he believed, could regenerate Russian literature. From its small beginnings here, the Modernist movement was to move from strength to strength during the next two decades, inspired in its early years by the romantic revival in Europe in general and in France in particular. Its cultural impact was quite without precedent, for it brought about immense changes not only in poetry, fiction and criticism, but also in theater, ballet, sculpture, painting and music, changes which gave the movement a central place in the blossoming of Russian culture in the early 1900s. It was, in short, nothing less than the most significant artistic phenomenon seen in Russia since the Golden Age of the previous century, a brilliant but final efflorescence of pre-Revolutionary culture that has earned the early 1900s the name "Silver Age."

The Modernists no longer regarded literature—and poetry, their chief medium, in particular—in the way the majority of Russian writers had regarded it since the early 1800s: a didactic tool with which to instruct their readers and make them aware of political and social problems. Valuing refinement above personal duty, and preferring individualism to social obligation, the Modernists dealt a body blow to the radical Russian intelligentsia, nourished for decades on a diet of civic morality and public responsibility. Needless to say, such anti-social priorities were anathema to the majority of traditional realist writers, and the two literary trends soon found themselves in conflict. While the Modernists denounced realistic prose as obsolete and vulgar, the realists condemned their opponents' self-indulgent estheticism and disdainful neglect of actuality.

Towards the turn of the century the rivalry between the Modernists led by Valery Bryusov and Konstantin Balmont, and the traditional realists championed by Maxim Gorky became intense. In 1898 Sergei Diaghilev founded the Petersburg review *The World of Art*, designed as a forum for Modernist painters, writers and dramatists. The following year saw the establishment in Moscow of the Scorpion publishing house which printed work by members of the new school. In 1901, 1902 and 1903 Scorpion issued *Northern Flowers*, a literary almanac which brought together Moscow and Petersburg branches of the movement and published Modernist poets. In 1904

12

Scorpion began to publish its own review, *The Scales*, which was followed by two further journals, *The Golden Fleece* and *Apollo*, founded in 1906 and 1909 respectively. Associated with *The Scales* was another review, *The New Way*, founded in 1903 to cater to those on the religious wing of the Modernist movement. Greeting the appearance of *The Scales* as an ally of *The New Way*, the critic Dmitry Filosofov (who was violently opposed to Gorky) called upon its contributors to join the struggle against the "barbarians" of the realist camp.

Though by the late 1890s the cultural tide was running strongly against them, the realists were not altogether without resource. By the early 1900s their forces were consolidated in two literary groupings, the "Wednesday" circle and the "Knowledge" school, both of which served not only to sustain but also to revitalize the realist tradition in what amounted to a state of literary siege.

III

The "Wednesday" group of writers was formed in Moscow in 1899 by the writer Nikolai Teleshov, at whose apartment the circle met each Wednesday. An extension of a similar group, "Parnassus," set up by Teleshov in the mid-1880s, the "Wednesday" circle played an important part in Russian literary life in the years leading up to 1905. Though composed chiefly of realist writers of the younger generation, the group was in no sense an official body with rules and regulations, and so its membership was both numerous and diverse. Among those who attended regularly were: Teleshov himself, Bunin, Veresaev, Serafimovich, Goltsev, Belousov, Razumovsky, Timkovsky, Goloushev and Naidyonov. Writers from elsewhere paid periodic visits too: Korolenko and Gorky from Nizhny Novgorod, Chirikov and Kuprin from Petersburg, and Yelpatevsky and Chekhov from the Crimea. In addition, Rachmaninoff, Chaliapin and actors from the Moscow Art Theater would occasionally attend, while older writers like Zlatovratsky and Mamin-Sibiryak were sometimes present.

Meetings of the group were largely devoted to the critical discussion of members' new works—discussion often so frank that it was cruel to the author involved—and political and social issues were raised rarely and only with general reluctance. It was at a "Wednesday" meeting in late 1900 that Gorky introduced the young lawyer Leonid Andreev and then read out the latter's story "Silence," since Andreev was too nervous to read it himself. In his turn Andreev later introduced both Serafimovich and Veresaev to the circle. At a meeting of the group in September 1902, Gorky first read his well-known play *The Lower Depths* to fellow writers and to actors from the Moscow Art Theater.

By the late 1890s, with the appearance of collected stories by Gorky,

Bunin and Kuprin, the reading public was aware of the realist movement as a coherent literary school. In 1897 the monthly magazine *Life* was founded in Petersburg, and in late 1898 (the year which saw the first issue of the Modernist review *The World of Art*) Gorky's close friend, the Marxist Vladimir Posse, was appointed its editor. From then on until its suppression in mid-1901, the journal devoted its pages chiefly to work by the young realists. Among other periodicals which published the realists were the prestigious *Russian Wealth*, the versatile *God's World*, and the popular *Journal for All*, which were based in Petersburg. Kuprin in particular was closely connected with the latter two journals in the early 1900s.

Though it arose largely from the "Wednesday" circle, the "Knowledge" *(Znanie)* grouping was to prove a much firmer bulwark against the onslaught of Modernism. In May 1898, K. P. Pyatnitsky, V. I. Charnolussky, V. D. Protopopov and other former members of the Literacy Commission closed down in 1895, received permission from the authorities to establish in Petersburg the Knowledge publishing house, a cooperative in which participating authors would hold shares and enjoy the profits on their publications. In late September 1899, during his first visit to the capital, Gorky met Pyatnitsky and joined Knowledge as a shareholder. He soon began to play an important part in the management of the enterprise and became the main contributor to its publications. Posse, another shareholder, was also important in the administration and helped Gorky with editorial work.

Knowledge published predominantly work by the young realists, and reached the peak of its popularity with the reading public in the years immediately preceding the revolution of 1905. In March 1904, it issued the first of its famous green-backed "miscellanies" *(Sborniki)* of tales by contemporary writers. Printed in an edition of 41,000 copies and costing only one ruble, the volume contained work by Gorky, Andreev, Bunin, Veresaev, Garin-Mikhailovsky, Gusev-Orenburgsky, Serafimovich and Teleshov. Between 1904 and 1907 alone, no fewer than nineteen miscellanies were published, with a total printing of over 700,000 copies. In all, forty miscellanies appeared before the organization closed down shortly before the outbreak of World War I.

Though there were no direct links between the "Wednesday" circle and the Knowledge enterprise, Gorky's connections with both were obviously crucial. Thus the first Knowledge miscellany (dated 1903) was made up almost entirely of material which had been read at meetings of the "Wednesday" group, notably Gorky's poetic essay "Man" of 1903. Among other significant early miscellanies were number three, published in January 1905, and dedicated to the memory of Chekhov, who had died the previous July; and number six, published in May 1905, which contained Kuprin's sensational army novel, *The Duel*, and which sold over 40,000 copies in that year alone.

It is curious that almost all the realists who gathered around the

Knowledge enterprise were born during the decade 1860 to 1870, and that the four most significant of them published their first important works within a few years of each other in the 1890s: Gorky ("Makar Chudra," 1892); Kuprin (*Moloch*, 1896); Bunin (his prose collection *To the World's End*, 1897); and Andreev ("Bargamot and Garaska," 1898). Though most members of the school are now regarded as minor figures overshadowed by those above, they deserve mention as writers instrumental in the revival of Russian prose fiction during the early 1900s. While very few of them were as tendentious as Gorky, as a group they were characterized by an awareness of social problems, and several of them were radical in their views. However, what elements of protest there were in their writing became less marked after the debacle of 1905.

One of the most significant members of the group after its four leaders was the physician Vikenty Smidovich (1867-1945), who wrote under the pseudonym of Veresaev. A Marxist of provincial stock, he achieved popularity around the turn of the century with his tales that reflected the ideological development of the Russian intelligentsia. His first novel, written in diary form and symbolically entitled *Pathless* (1895), shows a young doctor struggling against the cholera epidemic of 1891-92 and battling both with loss of faith in himself and in the possibility of a radical transformation of life. In 1901 Veresaev created a sensation with the publication of his *Notes of a Doctor*, a book of revelations in which he sharply criticized medical training in Russia at the time. This was followed in 1902 by his tale "At the Turning Point," and in 1907 and 1908 by his notes *At War*, published in Knowledge miscellanies, in which he described his experiences as an army surgeon in the Far East during the war with Japan. After the 1917 Revolution Veresaev remained in Russia, winning acclaim both for his novels *The Impasse* (1922) and *The Sisters* (1933), and for his biographical studies of Pushkin and Tolstoi. Shortly before his death he completed fine translations of the *Odyssey* and *Iliad*.

A more committed Marxist than Veresaev but a much less gifted writer was his close contemporary Alexander Serafimovich (1863-1949), whose real name was Popov. Born into a military family on the Don, he was later exiled to Archangel Province for revolutionary activity as a student. His first tale, "On an Ice Floe," was published in 1889, and his first collection of stories in 1901. Two years later he joined Knowledge. A series of tales reflecting contemporary proletarian life followed, among them "The Funeral March" (1906), "The Glow of a Fire" and "At the Precipice" (1907). His first novel was *Town in the Steppe* (1910), which deals with the construction of a new industrial town and the struggle between capitalists and proletarians that accompanies it. Serafimovich's reputation was only well and truly established after 1917, when he became one of the first writers to support the Bolsheviks. His devotion to them was rewarded by expulsion from the "Wednesday" circle, a measure indicative of the anti-Bolshevik mood that prevailed among Russian writers immediately after the Revolution. His second novel, *The Iron Flood* (1924), one of the earliest works about the Civil War, has become a Soviet classic. Winner of the Stalin Prize and the Order of Lenin, Serafimovich is now regarded as a leading early Soviet writer.

Nikolai Teleshov (1867-1957), who came from merchant stock, was a rather more moderate member of the school, though he was strongly influenced by Gorky. His early tales, "In Troikas" (1895) and "Beyond the Urals" (1897), were inspired by a journey across Siberia suggested to him by Chekhov. In 1903 Knowledge published his first collection of stories, while the first miscellany issued in the following year contained his tale "Between Two Shores." Later works, such as "On a Dark Night" (1904), "Sedition" (1905), and "The Overseer" (1906), all appeared in miscellanies. Teleshov was also the author of several legends, fables and fairy tales. After the Bolshevik Revolution he remained in Russia and played an active part in the Writers' Union. Perhaps his most valuable work is his *Notes of a Writer* (1948), in which he recorded the acquaintances and experiences of his long literary life.

Evgeny Chirikov (1864-1932) was another member of the Knowledge group who had suffered for his revolutionary activities. Born in Kazan, the son of an excise official, in 1887 he was sent down from the university for his part in student demonstrations and banished to Nizhny Novgorod. He spent the next five years wandering southern Russia in the Gorkian fashion. Though his first story appeared in the provinces in 1886, it was not until the mid-1890s that he became widely known, with a series of tales about Russian provincial life, among them "In the Forest" (1895) and "Progress" (1896). More significant were "Tanya's Luck" (1901), the story of a prostitute, and his plays *The Jews* (1904) and *The Peasants* (1905), which mirrored social tensions in Russia on the eve of revolution. Chirikov's complete works were published in eight volumes between 1903 and 1909 by Knowledge. He was one of the first writers to desert the group, however, and his last separate work published by the enterprise was the tale "On the Threshold of Life" (1908), after which he left for the almanac *Land* and the new Petersburg publishing house, Sweetbriar (see below). Chirikov emigrated to Bulgaria in 1920 and lived in Sofia before moving to Prague in 1921, where he died in January 1932.

If any member of the Knowledge group was a faithful literary and political disciple of Gorky, it was Stepan Petrov (1869-1941), whose pseudonym "The Wanderer" *(Skitalets)* both reflected his Gorkian peregrinations and demonstrated his devotion to the master. Born near Samara of peasant stock, he was introduced by Gorky to the "Wednesday" circle, and in 1902 Knowledge published his first volume of collected stories. The author of poetry, sketches and tales, among them "Octave" (1900), "The Forest Has Caught Fire" (1906), and "Cinders," which appeared in the tenth Knowledge miscellany in 1906, Skitalets was one of the few writers who did not leave the enterprise after 1905. In 1921, however, he joined the Russian far eastern emigration, but after spending twelve years in Harbin he returned to Moscow in 1934. The years before his death saw the publication of several volumes of his work.

Sergei Gusev-Orenburgsky (1867-1963) was much less of a political animal. The son of a Cossack merchant from Orenburg, he became a priest and by the early 1900s was known for his tales about the provincial clergy. In 1903 Knowledge published his first collection of stories, and in the following year his tale "In the Parish," the story of a country priest, appeared in the first Knowledge miscellany. His most significant work, the tale "Land of Fathers," a broad canvas of Russian life spanning the turn of the century, was published in the fourth Knowledge miscellany in 1905. Like Skitalets, he remained faithful to Knowledge after 1905, and his tales—"In a Remote District" (1912), for example—continued to appear in miscellanies until the enterprise closed. After the 1917 Revolution, however, Gusev-Orenburgsky emigrated to New York where he lived until his death.

The oldest member of the group was Sergei Eleonsky (1861-1911), whose real name was Milovsky. Like Orenburgsky, he had a religious background. The son of a priest from Penza Province, he studied in a seminary and then taught in various church academies. His first tales about the life of the provincial clergy and the church school milieu appeared in the 1880s. Highly regarded by Gorky, he had volumes of stories published by Knowledge in 1904 and 1908. His end, however, was both premature and tragic. Hounded by the religious authorities for his unorthodox views, he fell prey to nervous illness and committed suicide.

The agrarian problem that played so significant a role in Russia during the troubled years between 1900 and the Bolshevik Revolution found particular expression in the work of Viktor Muizhel (1880-1924), the son of a Latvian peasant from Pskov Province and one of the youngest members of the Knowledge school. After youthful wanderings and a succession of jobs, in 1904 he won recognition with his tale "In Bad Weather." This was followed in 1911 by his most notable work, the two-volume novel *The Year*, which portrays Russian village life during the years of reaction after 1905. After the 1917 Revolution he remained in Russia, producing among other works the tale "Cook's Children" (1924). Muizhel died of consumption at the early age of forty-four.

Two more authors, both of Jewish origin and both dramatists as well as prose writers, enjoy a special place in the diverse group around Gorky. Semyon Yushkevich (1868-1927), a physician like Veresaev, is remembered for his pictures of Jewish ghettoes in provincial towns such as Odessa. His first work was the story "The Tailor" (1897), but it was his tale "The Collapse" (1902) that made his name widely known. Between 1903 and 1908 Knowledge published his collected works in five volumes. His play *Miserere* was successfully staged by Stanislavsky at the Moscow Art Theater in 1910, while his other dramas such as *In the City, The King,* and *Hunger* all appeared in Knowledge miscellanies. Yushkevich broke with Knowledge in 1907, however, and joined the Sweetbriar publishing house. In 1920 he emigrated to France, where he wrote several works, notably the novel *Episodes* (1923). He died in Paris.

David Aizman (1869-1922) was equally concerned with the problems of his own people. After studying fine art in Paris, he published his first tale, "A Little to One Side," in 1901. In a series of stories that followed before the first revolution he depicted the life of underprivileged Russian Jews. Perhaps the best of several works by him about the events of 1905 is the tragedy *The Blackthorn Bush* (1907), which deals with an armed rising by factory workers. This was followed in 1908 by his tale "The Bloody Flood" and his play *The Bright God*. In the same year Aizman left Knowledge and joined Artsybashev's almanac *Life*. He remained in Russia after the Bolshevik Revolution.

Though the Knowledge group did not include every Russian realist in the early 1900s, it did dominate prose fiction at the time, and so while they may have been only on its outer fringes, few authors remained totally unaffected by the school. Four significant prose writers of the period who did not strictly belong to the group deserve brief mention. The youngest of them, Boris Zaitsev (1881-1972), was introduced to the "Wednesday" circle by Andreev and had his first volume of stories published in 1906. After the first revolution his work appeared chiefly in Sweetbriar almanacs. Close to Bunin in his manner, he is remembered in these years for his first novel, *A Distant Land* (1913). In 1922 Zaitsev emigrated to France where, like Bunin, he wrote much of his best work. He died in Paris. With him belongs Ivan Shmelyov (1873-1950), known in the early 1900s for his short stories and first novel, *The Man from a Restaurant* (1912), the story of a waiter. He too left Russia after 1917 and continued to write in emigration. Much more prolific was Ivan Novikov (1877-1959), the author of poetry, prose and drama, and remembered at this time for his novel *Between Two Dawns* (1915), which deals with the events of 1905. Unlike his fellows, he remained in Russia after the 1917 Revolution. Last but not least was Sergei Sergeev-Tsensky (1875-1958), a writer whom Gorky much admired, but who occupied a position that set him essentially outside any literary grouping. While the realists rejected him, the Modernists refused to recognize him as their own. His early prose works, such as "Boredom" (1903), "Babaev" (1907), "The Sadness of the Fields" (1908), and "Movements" (1911), brought him fame. His tale "Forest Marsh," a somber story of peasant life, appeared in the first Sweetbriar almanac in 1907. Sergeev-Tsensky remained in Russia after 1917, producing novels such as *Transfiguration* (1923) and *The Ordeal of Sevastopol* (1939), a lengthy treatment of the 1854-55 Crimean War that became a best-seller.

Given the immense diversity of their temperaments, talents and backgrounds, it is surprising that the young realists connected with the Knowledge cooperative formed a cohesive group at all. But despite the connotations of the word "school"—they are often referred to as the "Knowledge" or Gorky school of fiction—they were never a truly homogeneous body, and fundamental differences between the members did not take long to emerge. While Andreev and Bunin, for example, eventually left the enterprise for ideological or artistic reasons, other members such as Serafimovich and Gusev-Orenburgsky remained faithful to it until it closed. Almost no member of Knowledge, however, was prepared to renounce his literary or political views in order to fall completely in line with the attitudes represented by Gorky.

IV

The failure of the 1905 Revolution caused profound changes in Russian society. The wave of punitive reaction that began in 1906 brought widespread disenchantment both with public ideals and with the very idea of revolution. The national disillusionment was greatly increased in 1908 when it was revealed that Evno Azef, head of the terrorist wing of the SR Party, was an agent of the Secret Police. This revelation not only accelerated the disintegration of revolutionary parties in general but also occasioned a wave of suicides among those who found their disenchantment in radical ideals intolerable. By the eve of World War I the revolutionary parties were to have lost much of their influence among thinking Russians, who now had little time for their traditional radicalism.

During the years of reaction, the Russian intelligentsia lost faith both in themselves and in the masses whom they had hoped to serve. As they succumbed to pessimism and gloom, their cherished ideal of civic responsibility fell prey to anti-political individualism and moral laxity. Strongly reinforced by Nietzsche, whose works had first appeared in Russian translation in the early 1890s, a cult of hedonism swept the educated younger generation, and the pursuit of sensual pleasure became their prime concern.

Literature was not slow in reflecting the pathological obsession with sex that gripped the intelligentsia. While European authors such as Wedekind and Strindberg who dealt with sexual problems were avidly read in translation, dozens of Russian writers set about producing erotic material to satisfy the national craving. They had not, after all, to look back very far to find suitable models; Andreev's tales "In the Fog" and "The Abyss" of 1902 had both been sensational excursions into the erotic. (His influence is clear, for example, in Potapenko's *A Story of One Youth*, serialized in late 1907 in the journal *The Contemporary World*.) While dubious publishing ventures mushroomed to cater to the prevailing social mood, secret Free Love clubs enabled young people to display their sexual prowess. With the immense vogue enjoyed by erotic literature went a preoccupation with morbidity and perversion that found its expression in societies devoted to Satanism and suicide.

19

Sex-oriented publications in the years 1906 to 1912 were legion. However, while purely pornographic works require no mention, several erotic writers were not altogether devoid of talent. Perhaps the best-known were Anatoly Kamensky (1876-1941), author of the tales "Leda" and "The Four" (1907); Anastasia Verbitskaya (1861-1928), whose melodramatic work in six volumes, *The Keys to Happiness*, published between 1909 and 1913, was a best-seller; and Evdokia Nagrodskaya (1866-1930), whose novel *The Wrath of Dionysus* (1910) examined sexual problems and preached the doctrine of free love in vigorous terms. Less popular was Nikolai Oliger (1882-1919), whose stories reflected the general preoccupation with eroticism. All four authors were influenced by the primitive Nietzscheanism of the time. Works by other writers followed the same trend, among them Kuzmin's much-discussed novel of homosexuality, *Wings* (1907), Sologub's story "Fairy Magic" (1909), and Vinnichenko's tale "Self-Honesty" (1911). It was writing such as this that made the years from 1907 to 1917 what Gorky called "the most impudent and shameful decade in Russian literature."

It is in this context of political indifference and moral collapse that Artsybashev's *Sanin* occupies pride—or notoriety—of place. The novel's reputation is, however, not altogether deserved. Though more than any other work of its time it both mirrored and fostered the epidemic of sexual licence that swept educated Russian society after 1905, the novel's success and influence were out of all proportion to its artistic merits. Much of the sensation it caused was due to its suggestive treatment of sex—outrageously immoral and decadent to the older generation, and invigoratingly daring and frank to the younger. Most readers and critics saw in its egotistical hero—who advises his sister to have an abortion, urges his friends to commit suicide, and satisfies his lust for a young schoolmistress by practically raping her—the supreme embodiment of cynical amoralism, a voracious man-beast to whom carnality is all. But to see no further than this was to do Artsybashev a disservice. Indeed, he himself resented the fact that his would-be imitators—who flooded the bookstalls with pornographic trash—degraded in his readers' eyes what he had wished to express in *Sanin*. Interestingly too, he rejected the popular notion that his apology for individualism was strongly influenced by the then fashionable Nietzsche. Though he acknowledged the German as a brilliant thinker, he had no sympathy either for his ideas or for his bombast. He felt much more affinity, he once wrote, for the individualist anarchist philosopher, Max Stirner.

Whatever the literary shortcomings of Artsybashev's novel may be—and its tiresome philosophizing passages are perhaps the most obvious—its social and historical significance cannot be denied. Sanin is a hero of his time, when public ideals had lost their currency after the failure of 1905, and when educated young Russians sought an escape from their pessimism and disillusionment in hedonism and sensual gratification.

Artsybashev's historical importance during the first decade of this century is not, however, the only reason why his name appears in this anthology beside those of Gorky, Andreev, Bunin and Kuprin. Though he never actually belonged to the Knowledge group, he considered himself an "inveterate realist" and a disciple of the Tolstoi school. He had connections with many members of Knowledge and after 1905 several of them became contributors to his review *Land*. Besides, from 1907 onwards he himself contributed to several almanacs of the time, notably those published by the Sweetbriar house, which printed work by the realists. Furthermore, despite the sexuality and morbidity of much of his writing, the gap between it and work by several members of Knowledge—especially Andreev—is not as wide as may appear. Moreover, like many members of that school (Gorky and Andreev in particular), Artsybashev played an important part in revising the restrained treatment of physical things traditional in Russian literature. His writing furthered the lifting of nineteenth-century taboos on disease, death and sex, a process begun by Tolstoi in such tales as "The Death of Ivan Ilych" (1886) and "The Kreutzer Sonata" (1889), and continued, for example, in the early works of Gorky and Andreev. Finally, it must be said that though when he founded the almanac *Life* in 1907, Artsybashev set out to make it rival the flagging Knowledge, he remained a determined enemy of the Symbolists and cannot be counted among them. Like Andreev, that "Hamlet of Russian Literature," as he has been called, Artsybashev stood near the crossroads of two quite different literary movements.

V

The 1905 Revolution seriously weakened the cohesiveness of both the "Wednesday" circle and the Knowledge school. Until 1905 the "Wednesday" group was largely apolitical in composition and relations between its members were generally comradely and relaxed. But the events of 1905 and 1906—particularly the massacre on "Bloody Sunday"—brought to light the essential political incompatibility of many of its members, and the atmosphere at meetings of the circle could never be the same again. Though the group continued to exist until 1918, well before then several members had left what had once been a very vigorous and progressive literary society.

It is interesting to note that in 1907, after his return to Petersburg from Finland, Andreev organized "Wednesday" gatherings of his own along the lines of their Moscow counterparts. Though several well-known writers attended, among them Sergeev-Tsensky, Chirikov and Yushkevich, he failed to recreate the ambience of Teleshov's circle.

The effect of 1905 on Knowledge was infinitely more serious. Not only did it eventually prove fatal to the enterprise's survival, but it also jeopardized the continued existence of any effective form of the realist tradition in the face of Symbolist supremacy.

The relations after 1905 of leading members of the group with Knowledge in general and Gorky in particular illustrate the gradual disintegration of the school. Of Bunin especially it should be said that he had always kept aloof from his fellow members, despite the fact that he had belonged to the group for years. Though he had work published by Knowledge for almost a decade and though his writing often shows a concern for social issues, he did not share the progressive views held by many of his colleagues. During the years of reaction the gulf between him and more radically-minded members widened still further, and he drifted away from the enterprise.

Relations between Andreev and Gorky were complex. After 1905 symbolic and pessimistic elements became much more marked in Andreev's work, and in the summer of 1907 he broke altogether with Knowledge. Later he joined the editorial board of Sweetbriar, which published work by the realists in competition with Knowledge, but stood midway between that enterprise on the one hand and the Symbolist journals *The Golden Fleece* and *The Scales* on the other. In 1907 the house issued its first almanac, and twenty-three more followed before the enterprise closed down in 1916. Andreev's tale *The Seven Who Were Hanged* appeared in the fifth Sweetbriar almanac in May 1908. So complete was his break with Knowledge that in 1909 Sweetbriar published volumes five to seven of his collected works, the first four volumes of which had already appeared under the Knowledge imprint between 1901 and 1907. Among other realists who eventually contributed to Sweetbriar publications were Kuprin, Chirikov, Sergeev-Tsensky, Yushkevich, Aizman and Zaitsev. Andreev himself later edited several of the house's almanacs.

For his part, though not indifferent to social problems as both *The Duel* and *The Pit* indicate, Kuprin never wished to use his work as a political weapon in the way that Gorky did. After the 1905 Revolution, irritated by Gorky's insistence that he turn to social issues, he moved from Knowledge to the review *Land*, edited by Artsybashev, and contributed several pseudo-Utopian tales to it. In 1908 his already cool relations with Gorky became cooler still with the publication of his tale "Seasickness," whose Social Democrat heroine is raped aboard a Crimean steamer. Gorky considered the work a crude slur on the SD Party with which he was closely connected.

Though Kuprin, Skitalets and Chirikov went on contributing to Knowledge miscellanies until 1908, and Bunin and Gusev-Orenburgsky until after that, by 1910 the school had lost most of its prestigious members and was clearly failing. In 1906, however, the enterprise had introduced its successful "Cheap Library" series of small books designed for the mass reader and modestly priced at between two and twelve kopeks. Over three hundred titles eventually appeared, with a total printing of about four million copies. Meanwhile, the untiring Gorky demonstrated his abiding enthusiasm for the cooperative by contributing work of his own until 1911—notably his novel *Mother*, published in miscellanies 16 to 21. At the same time he brought several new, younger writers into the organization, the most significant of whom was Mikhail Prishvin (1873-1954), whose rural tales were published in two volumes by Knowledge between 1912 and 1914. In 1910 at Gorky's invitation the experienced journalist V. S. Mirolyubov, former editor of the *Journal for All* which had been suppressed in 1906, assumed overall responsibility for the miscellanies. But the publishing house still continued to decline. Moreover, as time went on, Gorky did not receive the effective help from Pyatnitsky that he might have expected, and after 1912, frustrated by his lone struggle as the guardian of the realist tradition, he ceased to have any connection with the enterprise. By then its days were numbered. In 1913, severely weakened by internal problems, Knowledge disintegrated altogether.

*   *   *

Though it had survived for little more than a decade, the Knowledge organization had proved of crucial importance for Russian literature. Despite its undistinguished later years when it was overshadowed by its Symbolist rival, the school had played a vital role in the maintenance of the realist tradition at a time when the literary odds were stacked heavily against it. However, while most of the credit for administering Knowledge and inspiring its members must go to Gorky, much of the school's artistic success was due to superb stylists such as Bunin and Kuprin, whose mastery of prose was second to none. In this sense, arguably perhaps, it is they rather than Gorky, Andreev or Artsybashev, who personify the lasting literary significance of the grouping and form the keystone of this anthology. Undimmed by time, the luster of their work gives it prominence in the rich artistic legacy left by Tsarist Russia on the eve of her annihilation.

23

Изданіе товарищества „ЗНАНІЕ" (Спб., Невскій, 92).

I.

СБОРНИКЪ

ТОВАРИЩЕСТВА „ЗНАНІЕ" ЗА 1903 ГОДЪ.

КНИГА ПЕРВАЯ.

СОДЕРЖАНІЕ:

Цѣна 1 рубль.

С.-ПЕТЕРБУРГЪ.
1904.

The front cover of the first Znanie (Knowledge) sbornik (anthology). It is called the Znanie anthology for 1903, and is dated "St. Petersburg, 1904." The contents listed include stories by Andreev, Bunin, Veresaev, Garin, Gorky, Gusev, Serafimovich, and Teleshov. The cost was one ruble.

Vikenty Veresaev in the early 1900s.

Leonid Andreev in the early 1900s, photographed in St. Petersburg.

LEONID ANDREEV (1871-1919)

Born in the town of Oryol, Andreev belonged to the provincial Russian intelligentsia. His father was a land-tax surveyor and his mother the impoverished descendant of an aristocratic Polish family. The boy attended the *gimnaziia* in Oryol from 1882 to 1891, and then entered the University of St. Petersburg to read law. After two unsuccessful years there—during which he attempted suicide because of unrequited love—in 1893 he was sent down, but managed to enroll at the University of Moscow instead. In 1897, despite two further attempts to kill himself, he passed his final examinations and began work as assistant to a Moscow barrister. But his legal career did not last long; later that year he began to write reports of court cases for a Moscow paper—invaluable experience which led directly to his emergence as a leading writer of the time. There followed links with prominent journals as well as with the Knowledge publishing house, and the start of a lifelong association with Gorky.

In February 1905, Andreev was imprisoned for a time after permitting the Central Committee of the Social Democratic (SD) Party to hold an illegal meeting in his Moscow apartment. Later that year, after his release on bail, he left first for Finland and then Germany and Switzerland. In late 1905 his youngest sister died suddenly at the age of twenty-one, and only a year later he lost the wife he had married in 1902. Though he remarried in 1908, Andreev never fully recovered from this double tragedy, and from 1906 onwards gloom became increasingly prevalent in both his life and work. Early in 1907 he left Russia to visit Gorky on Capri, then lived in Petersburg for a year before settling finally in Finland, where he built an extravagant house some forty miles from the Russian capital.

1908 marked the peak of Andreev's career and he reveled in the publicity and wealth his writing brought him. But at the same time he was subjected to systematic vilification by various newspapers, and by 1912 his health was on the verge of collapse because of overwork and stress. The outbreak of World War I awoke the patriotic publicist in him, and in 1916 he moved back to Petrograd, full of enthusiasm for a victorious war. In 1917, however, he became a sworn enemy of the Bolsheviks. As his material situation deteriorated and his literary reputation waned, he sank into profound melancholy before dying of a heart attack in Finland in September 1919.

Though tales by Andreev first appeared in provincial papers in 1895, his literary career is usually dated from the publication of the story "Bargamot and Garaska" in 1898. In 1901 Knowledge published an immensely successful collection of ten stories by him, among them "The Grand Slam," "Silence" and "Once Upon a Time There Lived." A second edition included new works such as "In the Basement" and "The Wall." The publication of

"The Abyss" and "In the Fog" (1902)—tales which treated sex in an outspoken fashion—caused an uproar in the conservative press and Andreev suddenly found himself famous. The next five years saw the appearance of his best prose works—"The Life of Vasily Fiveisky" (1903), "The Red Laugh" (1905; his response to the Russo-Japanese War), "The Governor" (1906), "Judas Iscariot" (1907), and *The Seven Who Were Hanged* (1908). After 1908 he concentrated on drama, and his last major prose work, *Sashka Zhegulyov* (1911), attracted little attention.

Andreev's first play was *To the Stars* (1906), and during the next decade a dozen more dramas followed it. Among them were *Savva* (1906), *Tsar Hunger* (1907), *Black Masks* (1908), *Anathema* (1909), *The Ocean* (1911), *Thou Shalt Not Kill* (1914), and the popular *He Who Gets Slapped* (1916).

During World War I Andreev wrote anti-German propaganda in support of Russia's war effort, and then during the Civil War produced anti-Bolshevik material. His last work, *S. O. S.* (1919), was an impassioned appeal to the Allies to intervene and save Russia from Bolshevik tyranny.

Leonid Andreev/THE SEVEN WHO WERE HANGED

Dedicated to L. N. Tolstoi

I

"At one p.m., Your Excellency!"

As the Minister was a very fat man prone to apoplexy, it was necessary to spare him all agitation, so they took every precaution in warning him that a serious attempt had been planned on his life. When they saw he took the news calmly and even smiled, they told him the details: the attempt was to be made the next day, as he left to make his report. Several terrorists—already given away by a provocateur and now under the watchful eye of police agents —were to meet at one p.m. near the entrance to the Minister's house armed with bombs and revolvers, and wait for him to come out. There they would be arrested.

"One moment," the Minister interrupted in surprise. "How on earth do they know I'll be leaving to make my report at one p.m., when I only found out myself the day before yesterday?"

The officer in charge of the bodyguard spread his hands in a vague gesture:

"At one p.m. precisely, Your Excellency."

Astonished but at the same time approving of the measures taken by the police who had arranged everything so well, the Minister shook his head, and a gloomy smile spread across his thick, dark lips. With the same smile, obediently and not wishing to hinder the police any further, he quickly got ready and drove off to spend the night in someone else's hospitable mansion. His wife and two children were taken away too, away from this dangerous house near which the bomb-throwers would gather the next day.

While the lights shone in the unfamiliar mansion and the friendly faces greeted him, smiled and expressed their indignation, the Minister felt a pleasant sense of excitement—as if he had just received or was about to receive a great and unexpected decoration. But the people around him went away, the lights were put out, and through the plate glass windows there shone on the walls and ceiling the spectral, filigree light of the electric lamps outside. A light that was alien to this house with its pictures, statues and the stillness entering from the street, a light that was itself silent and indeterminate, it provoked disquieting thoughts about the futility of locks, guards and walls. And then, in the night, amid the silence and solitude of this strange bedroom, the Minister began to feel insufferably afraid.

He had something wrong with his kidneys, and whenever he became extremely agitated his face, arms and legs filled with fluid and swelled, and this made him seem bigger, fatter and more massive still. Now, crushing the

29

springs of the bed under his bloated flesh, with the anguish of the sick man he was he felt his swollen face that seemed to belong to someone else, and thought incessantly of the cruel fate being prepared for him. One after another he recalled all the terrible occasions recently when bombs had been thrown at men of his high rank and higher still. The bombs had torn their bodies to shreds, splattering their brains over grimy brick walls and knocking their teeth from their sockets. Because of these recollections, his own obese, sick body spread out on the bed already felt like someone else's that was suffering the fiery blast of an explosion. It seemed as if his arms were being torn from his trunk at the shoulder, as if his teeth were falling out, his brain breaking up into fragments, his legs and feet growing numb and lying submissively on the ground with their toes turned up like those of a corpse. He moved urgently, breathing loudly and coughing so as not to resemble a corpse in any way, surrounding himself with the living sound of creaking springs and rustling bedclothes. To prove he was completely alive, not in the least bit dead, and indeed like everyone else far from dead, he said abruptly in a loud, deep voice amid the silence and solitude of the bedroom:

"Well done! Well done! Well done!"

He was praising the detectives, the police and the soldiers, all those who guarded his life and had so opportunely and cleverly prevented his murder. But though he stirred on the bed, praised his protectors, and smiled a wry, forced smile to express his scorn for the stupid terrorists and their miserable failure, he still could not believe he was saved, or that life would not suddenly desert him at one fell swoop. It seemed to him that the death people had planned for him—a death that was still only in their minds and their intentions—was already standing there beside him, would continue to do so, and would not go away till those people were arrested, had their bombs taken from them, and were put in a secure prison. Over there in that corner stood death, and it would not go away—could not go away, like an obedient soldier posted on guard at someone else's wish and command.

"At one p.m., Your Excellency!" came the spoken words, modulated in every tone of voice: first gaily mocking, then angry, then stubbornly obtuse. It was as if a hundred gramophones had been wound up and set going in the bedroom, and all of them, one after the other, with the idiotic diligence of machines, were shouting the words they were ordered to shout:

"At one p.m., Your Excellency!"

This "one p.m." the following day that till so recently had been in no way distinguishable from any other hour, and was merely the steady movement of a hand over the face of his gold watch—this "one p.m." had suddenly acquired an ominous persuasiveness, leapt from the watchface and begun to lead an independent existence, stretching upwards like a huge, black pillar that cut his whole life in two. It was as if no other hours existed either before or after it, and as if it alone, insolent and conceited, possessed the right to some special life of its own.

30

"Well? What do you want?" asked the Minister angrily through his teeth.

And the gramophones blared:

"At one p.m., Your Excellency!" And the black pillar fawned and smirked.

Gritting his teeth, the Minister raised himself on the bed and sat up, resting his chin on his palm. He could not possibly sleep on an abominable night like this.

Pressing his face between his plump, scented hands, he imagined with horrifying clarity how he would have got up the next morning knowing nothing about what was in store, would have drunk his coffee, still knowing nothing, and then would have dressed in the anteroom. Neither he nor the hall porter who helped him on with his fur coat, nor the footman who brought him his coffee, would have known that it was utterly senseless to drink coffee and put on a coat when in a few moments all this—the coat, his body and the coffee inside it—would be obliterated by an explosion and snatched away by death. Now the porter was opening the glass door... And it was he, that dear, kind, gentle porter with his pale blue soldier's eyes and his chest covered with decorations, it was he, who with his own hands was opening that terrible door—opening it because he knew nothing. And everyone was smiling because they knew nothing.

"Oh!" said the Minister suddenly in a loud voice and slowly took his hands from his face.

Staring far into the darkness before him, his gaze motionless and intent, with the same slow movement he stretched out his hand, felt for the lamp-bracket, and turned on the light. Then he stood up, and without putting his shoes on walked barefoot across the carpet, found another lamp-bracket on the wall, and lit that. The room became pleasant and bright, and only the rumpled bed with its quilt that had slipped to the floor told of some horror that was not yet completely over.

Dressed in his nightclothes, his beard dishevelled by his restless movements and his eyes full of anger, the Minister looked like any cross old man suffering from insomnia and severe breathlessness. It was as if the death being prepared for him had stripped him naked, snatched him from the magnificence and impressive splendor around him—and it was hard to believe that it was he who possessed such power, that it was his body, such an ordinary, simple human body, which was to perish so terribly amid the fire and thunder of a monstrous explosion. Without dressing and not feeling the cold, he sat down in the nearest armchair, propped his tousled beard on his hand, and in quiet, profound reverie stared intently at the unfamiliar stucco ceiling.

So that was it! That was why he had felt so afraid and anxious! That was why death was standing in the corner, why it would not and could not go away!

"Fools!" he said with weighty contempt.

"Fools!" he said again, only more loudly this time, turning his head

31

slightly towards the door so those to whom the word referred could hear. It referred to those whom a short while ago he had praised so highly and who in an excess of zeal had told him in detail about the attempt planned on his life.

"Well, of course," he said to himself, his thoughts suddenly resolute and fluent, "now they've told me and I know about it, I feel frightened, but after all, if they'd not told me, I wouldn't have known a thing and would have drunk my coffee quite happily. Well, afterwards, of course, I'd have been killed, but am I really so afraid of death? Here I am with bad kidneys, and I'll die someday, I know, but I'm not afraid because I don't know anything about it. But those fools said to me: 'At one p.m., Your Excellency!' They thought I'd be glad about it, the fools, but instead death has come and stood in that corner and won't go away. It won't go away because it's me thinking about it. It's not death that's frightening but knowing about it, and life would be quite impossible if a man knew with absolute certainty the day and hour he would die. But those fools go and tell me in advance: 'At one p.m., Your Excellency.'"

Everything was so pleasant and easy now, as if someone had told him he was immortal and would never die. Feeling powerful and wise again amid this pack of fools who had intruded so impertinently and senselessly into the mysteries of the future, he began to think just how blissful ignorance could be, and his thoughts were the painful thoughts of an ailing old man who had experienced a great deal in his time. No living creature, neither man nor beast, can know the day and hour of its death. Now not long ago he'd been ill, and the doctors had told him he would die and had suggested he make final arrangements. But he hadn't believed them and had in fact remained alive. And in his younger days this had happened: things had been going very badly for him and he'd decided to do away with himself. He'd got the revolver ready, written some letters, and even fixed the time for his suicide, but at the very last minute he'd suddenly thought better of it. Always, at the very last moment, something unexpected might turn up, and for that reason no one can say when he will die.

"At one p.m., Your Excellency," those obliging asses had told him, and though they had only told him because his death had been averted, simply knowing its possible time had filled him with terror. It was quite possible he would be killed one day, but it would not be tomorrow—it would not be tomorrow—and he could sleep in peace like someone immortal. The fools, they didn't know what great law they had abused, what yawning chasm they had revealed when they had said with that idiotic amiability of theirs: "At one p.m., Your Excellency."

"No, not at one p.m., Your Excellency, but no one knows when. No one knows when. What?"

"Nothing," replied the silence. "Nothing."

"No, you said something."

"It's nothing, never mind. I said: 'Tomorrow, at one p.m.'"

With a sudden feeling of sharp anguish in his heart he realized he would know neither sleep, peace nor joy till this accursed, black hour torn from the watchface had passed. Only the mere shadow of something—something not a single living creature should know—was standing there in the corner, but it was enough to eclipse the light and envelop him in the impenetrable darkness of terror. Once disturbed, the fear of death crept throughout his body, taking root in his bones and thrusting its pallid head from his every pore.

It was no longer tomorrow's assassins that he feared—they had vanished and been forgotten, mingling with the multitude of inimical faces and events surrounding his life—but something sudden and inevitable: an apoplectic stroke, the rupture of some stupid, narrow artery that would suddenly be unable to withstand the pressure of the blood in it and would burst, like a glove pulled tight on plump fingers.

His short, fat neck felt terrible, and it was unbearable to look at his swollen fingers, to feel how short they were, how full of mortal fluid. If earlier, in the darkness, he had been obliged to move so as not to resemble a corpse, then now, in this bright, terrifying, coldly hostile light it seemed terrible, impossible to move, even to reach for a cigarette or ring for someone. His nerves were taut. Each one seemed like a bent wire standing on end, topped by a little head with crazed eyes staring in terror and a gaping mouth choking in silent convulsions. There was no air to breathe.

Suddenly, in the darkness, amid the dust and cobwebs somewhere beneath the ceiling, an electric bell sprang into life. Its little metal clapper beat in spasms of terror against the rim of the gong, fell silent, then shuddered again in incessant, sonorous horror. His Excellency was ringing from his room.

People came running. Here and there, in chandeliers and on walls, lamps flared into life—too few of them for bright light but enough for shadows to appear. They appeared everywhere: rising in the corners and stretching across the ceiling; clinging flickeringly to every projection and running along the walls; and it was hard to see where all these innumerable, misshapen, silent shadows had been before—these mute souls of mute things.

A deep, shaking voice said something loudly. Then they telephoned for a doctor: the Minister was ill. His Excellency's wife was sent for too.

II

Sentenced to Death by Hanging

Things turned out as the police had expected. Four terrorists, three men and a woman, armed with bombs, infernal machines and revolvers, were caught right by the entrance to the Minister's residence, while a fifth, another woman, was found and arrested in the conspirator's apartment, of which she was the owner. At the same time a great deal of dynamite, many half-finished bombs, and arms were seized there. All those arrested were very young: the eldest of the men was twenty-eight, and the younger of the two women only nineteen. They were tried in the fortress where they had been imprisoned after their arrest, tried quickly and in a closed court, as was the custom in those merciless days.

At the trial all five were calm, but very grave and thoughtful: so great was their contempt for the judges that none of them wished to emphasize his fearlessness by an unnecessary smile or a feigned expression of gaiety. Their calm was just sufficient to protect their souls and the great, mortal darkness within them from the malevolent, hostile eyes of others. Sometimes they would refuse to answer the questions put to them, and at others they would reply—briefly, simply and precisely, as if they were replying not to their judges but to statisticians filling in special tables of figures. Three of them, two men and one woman, gave their real names, but the other two refused, so their identity remained unknown to the court. Towards everything taking place at the trial they displayed that distant, subdued curiosity characteristic of people who are either seriously ill or possessed by a single, vast, all-consuming idea. They shot swift glances around them, took note of an occasional interesting word, then returned to their thoughts at the very point where they had left them.

Nearest the judges sat one of the accused who had given his name—Sergei Golovin, the son of a retired colonel and himself a former officer. He was still very young, with fair hair and broad shoulders, and was so robust that neither prison nor the expectation of inevitable death had been able to remove the color from his cheeks and the expression of youthful, happy naivete from his light blue eyes. He kept on tugging vigorously at his tousled little blonde beard to which he was not yet accustomed, and gazed fixedly at the window, narrowing his eyes and blinking.

The trial was taking place at the end of winter, when amid snowstorms and leaden frosts the approaching spring occasionally sent, like a harbinger, one clear, warm, sunny day or even just a single hour, but one that was so springlike, so sparkling and avidly youthful, that the sparrows in the street went mad with joy and people seemed intoxicated. Now, through the dusty upper window that had not been cleaned since last summer, a strangely beautiful sky could be seen. At first sight it seemed milky-gray and smoky, but if you looked at it longer, it turned blue, and the blue grew more and more bright, deep and boundless. And because the sky was not revealed at once in its entirety, but lay chastely hidden in a transparent haze of cloud, it became attractive, like a beloved woman. Sergei Golovin looked at the sky, tugged at his beard, screwed up first one eye then the other beneath their long, fluffy lashes, and pondered something earnestly. Once he even began to move his fingers quickly and his face wrinkled up with innocent joy, but he glanced around him and his joy was extinguished like a spark under someone's foot. Almost at once, almost before it could fade into pallor, the color in his

34

cheeks turned a sallow, deathly blue; and the soft hair torn painfully out by its roots was gripped as in a vice by fingers that had turned white at their tips. But his joy at the spring and at being alive was stronger, and after a few minutes his naive, youthful face was lifted up to the spring sky once more.

The pale, young girl whose identity was unknown but whose nickname was Musya gazed into the sky too. She was younger than Golovin but seemed older because of her gravity and the blackness of her proud, unflinching eyes. Only her gentle, slender neck and slim, girlish arms told of her age, together with that indefinable quality that is youthfulness itself. That quality sounded clearly with the flawless tone of an expensive instrument in her pure, melodious voice and in every simple word or exclamation that revealed its musical essence. She was very pale, though her pallor was not deathly but that peculiar glowing whiteness seen when a mighty fire seems to burn within a human being, making the body shine translucent like fine Sevres porcelain. She sat almost motionless, and only occasionally, with an imperceptible movement, fingered a deep mark on the middle finger of her right hand—the mark left by a ring she had taken off recently. She looked at the sky not with fond affection or joyful memories but only because in this grimy, official room that little patch of azure was the most beautiful, unsullied and honest thing—and unlike the judges it tried to elicit nothing from her eyes.

The judges felt sorry for Sergei Golovin, but they detested her.

Her neighbor sat motionless too, his hands between his knees in a rather stiff pose. His identity was unknown but his nickname was Werner. If a face can be locked shut like a heavy door, then he had shut his face like an iron gate and hung an iron padlock on it. He stared fixedly at the dirty plank floor, and it was impossible to tell whether he was calm or desperately agitated, whether he was thinking about something or listening to what the detectives were testifying to the court. He was not tall but his features were fine and delicate. He was so handsome and gentle that he reminded one of a moonlit night somewhere in the south, on the coast, where cypresses cast their dark shadows, but at the same time he gave the impression of immense, quiet strength, insuperable determination, and cool, audacious courage. The very courtesy with which he made his brief, precise replies seemed dangerous, accompanied as they were by a slight bow; and if on all the others their prisoners' smocks seemed an absurd piece of buffoonery, in his case there was no hint of this whatsoever, so alien did the garment seem to him. Though the other terrorists had been found in possession of bombs and infernal machines, while Werner had only been carrying a black revolver, for some reason the judges regarded him as the leader and addressed him with a certain respect, their words as brief and businesslike as his were to them.

Next to him was Vasily Kashirin, the whole of him consumed by the sheer intolerable terror of death and by the equally desperate desire to suppress that terror and conceal it from the judges. Since early that morning, as soon as they had been brought to court, he had begun to pant with the racing of his heart. Little drops of sweat kept appearing on his forehead, his hands were clammy and cold, and his shirt, wet with sweat, stuck to his body, hampering his movements. With a superhuman effort of will he forced his fingers not to shake, while his voice was steady and clear and his eyes were calm. He saw nothing around him, and the sound of voices reached him as if through a fog, while into that same fog he directed his desperate efforts to answer firmly and loudly. But having answered, he immediately forgot both the question and his reply, and wrestled with himself in silent terror once more. So clearly had death laid its hand on him that the judges tried not to look at him. It was as hard to guess his age as it is that of a corpse which has already begun to decompose. According to his papers, though, he was only twenty-three. Once or twice Werner touched him gently on the knee, and each time he answered briefly:

"It's all right."

The most terrifying moment for him was when he suddenly felt an irresistible urge to shout—with the desperate, wordless cry of an animal. Then he would touch Werner gently, and without looking up, Werner would reply softly:

"It's all right, Vasya. It'll soon be over."

Surveying them all with her solicitous, maternal eye, the fifth terrorist, Tanya Kovalchuk, was tormented by anxiety. She had never had any children and was still very young and red-cheeked, but she was like a mother to them all, so full of concern, so infinitely loving were her glance, her smile, her fear. She paid no attention whatsoever to the trial, as if it were something totally incidental, and only listened to the way the others replied: did his voice shake, was he afraid, should she give him some water?

She could not look at Vasya for anguish and only wrung her plump fingers quietly. She gazed at Musya and Werner with pride and admiration, her expression grave and earnest, and she kept trying to catch Sergei's eye with her smile.

"The dear one, he's looking at the sky. Just you look, just you look, my dear one," she said to herself. "But what about Vasya? What on earth's wrong? My God, my God!.. What am I to do with him? If I say something it'll only make things worse, and what if he starts crying?"

Like a still pool at dawn that reflects the clouds flying by above it, her kind, dear, plump face reflected every swiftly passing feeling, every thought of her four comrades. She paid no attention at all to the fact that she was being tried and would be hanged too—all that was a source of profound indifference to her. It was in her apartment that a cache of bombs and dynamite had been found, and though it was hard to believe, it was she who had greeted the police with gunfire and wounded one detective in the head.

The trial ended at about eight o'clock, when it was already dark. Before Musya's and Sergei's eyes the blue sky gradually faded, but it did not turn pink and smile softly as on summer evenings. Instead, it grew dull and gray, then suddenly became cold and wintry. Golovin sighed, stretched and glanced out of the window once or twice more, but outside the night was already cold and dark. Still tugging at his beard, he began to scrutinize the judges and the soldiers with their rifles as inquisitively as a child, and smiled at Tanya Kovalchuk. As for Musya, when the sky grew dim she calmly shifted her gaze, and without lowering her eyes looked into a corner of the room where a cobweb swayed gently in the imperceptible draught from the hot-air heating. And she remained thus till sentence was passed.

After the sentence they bade their defense counsel farewell, avoiding their helplessly dismayed, sorrowfully guilty eyes as they did so. The condemned then found themselves together for a moment in the doorway and exchanged a few brief words.

"It's all right, Vasya. It'll all be over soon," said Werner.

"But I'm all right, old fellow," replied Kashirin loudly in a calm, cheerful voice.

And in fact his face had turned a faint pink and no longer resembled that of a rotting corpse.

"To hell with them, they've gone and hanged us after all, you see," said Golovin, and swore.

"It was to be expected," replied Werner calmly.

"Tomorrow they'll pronounce sentence in its final form and then put us all in the same cell," said Tanya, consoling them. "We'll be together right till the execution."

Musya said nothing. Then she stepped forward.

III
You Mustn't Hang Me

A fortnight before the terrorists were tried, the same district military court, but with different judges, had tried and sentenced to death by hanging a peasant called Ivan Yanson.

Yanson had worked as a laborer for a prosperous farmer and had not differed in any particular way from other poor landless workers like him. He was an Estonian by birth, from Wesenberg, and gradually, over the course of a few years, by moving from one farm to the next, he had reached the capital itself. He spoke Russian very badly, and as his employer was a Russian —Lazarev by name—and as there were no other Estonians in the vicinity, Yanson did not say a word for almost the whole of his two years on Lazarev's farm. In general though, he was apparently not inclined to be talkative. He was silent not only with people but with animals too: he watered the horse in silence, harnessed it in silence as he moved slowly and lazily round it with little shuffling steps, and when the animal, disturbed by his quietness, began

37

to play up and be a nuisance, he beat it with his whip-handle in silence. He beat it cruelly, with cold, savage persistence, and if this happened when he had a bad hangover, he would go into a frenzy. Then the sound of the whip could be heard as far away as the farmhouse itself, together with the terrified, abrupt, agonized clatter of hooves on the plank floor of the barn. His master beat Yanson for beating the horse, but could not cure him of it, so he gave it up.

Once or twice a month Yanson would get drunk. This usually happened on days when he drove his master to the big railway station where there was a refreshment room. After dropping his master, he would drive half a verst away from the station and, plunging the horse and sledge off the road into the snow, would wait there till the train had gone. The sledge lay askew, almost lying on its side, and the bowlegged horse stood up to its belly in the drifts, lowering its muzzle from time to time to lick the soft, feathery snow, while Yanson lay in an awkward, half-sitting position in the sledge and seemed to doze. The loose earflaps on his shabby fur cap dangled limply like the ears of a setter, and under his small, reddish nose there was a patch of moisture.

Then he would drive back to the station and quickly get drunk.

He would cover the ten versts back to the farm at a gallop. Lashed mercilessly and filled with terror, the jade galloped at top speed like one possessed, as the sledge swerved from side to side, keeling over and colliding with telegraph poles. Letting go of the reins and almost flying off the sledge at every moment, Yanson half sang, half yelled something in Estonian in abrupt, indistinct phrases. More often than not though, he did not sing, but silently clenched his teeth in an access of mysterious fury, pain and ecstasy, and hurtled onwards like a blind man: he did not see anyone coming towards him, shout to them in warning, or slacken his furious pace either at bends in the road or when going downhill. How he did not knock anyone down or smash himself to death on one of these wild journeys was beyond comprehension.

He should have been sacked long ago, just as he had been sacked from other jobs, but he was cheap and other workers were no better, so he stayed two years. Yanson's life was devoid of all events. Once he received a letter in Estonian, but as he was illiterate and those around him knew no Estonian, the letter remained unread. With wild, fanatical indifference, as if he did not understand that it contained news from home, he flung it on the manure heap. Evidently longing for a woman, he even tried to make advances to the cook, but he had no success and was crudely rebuffed and ridiculed: he was short and puny with a freckled, flabby face and sleepy little eyes that were a dirty bottle-green. He regarded even this failure with indifference, and did not pester the cook any more.

But all the same Yanson was listening to something the whole time. He listened to the sound of the dismal, snow-covered fields with their mounds of frozen manure that resembled a line of small graves covered with snow; he

38

listened to the sound of the soft, dark expanse of distance, to the wind moaning in the telegraph wires, and to people's conversation. What the fields and telegraph wires told him he alone knew, but people's conversation around him was alarming, full of rumors about murder, robbery and arson. One night the little bell could be heard ringing from the chapel in the neighboring hamlet, its sound so thin and feeble that it resembled the tinkling of a harness bell, and flames crackled against the sky: some strangers had plundered a rich farm, killed the owner and his wife, then set fire to the house.

On their farm, too, life was uneasy: the dogs were let loose not only at night but during the daytime too, and the master kept a gun beside him when he slept. He tried to give Yanson one like it, a single-barrelled, old one, but Yanson turned it over and over in his hands then shook his head, and for some reason refused it. The master could not understand why he did so and cursed him, but the reason was that Yanson had more faith in his Finnish knife than in this rusty, old firearm.

"It'll kill me," he said, looking sleepily at his master with glassy eyes.

And the master waved his hand in a gesture of despair.

"Well, you really are a fool, Ivan! What a life it is with workers like you!"

Then one winter's evening, when the other laborer had been sent off to the station, this same Ivan Yanson who would not trust a gun, made a highly involved attempt at armed robbery, murder and rape. Somehow he did it with amazing simplicity: he locked the cook in the kitchen, then with the air of a man who feels extremely sleepy, went lazily up to his master from behind, and quickly stabbed him again and again in the back with his knife. The master slumped unconscious to the floor and his wife began to rush about the room screaming, while Yanson, baring his teeth and brandishing his knife, started ransacking trunks and chests of drawers. He found some money, then noticed the mistress as if for the first time, and without the slightest premeditation flung himself upon her. But because he dropped his knife, she proved to be the stronger, and not only resisted him but very nearly strangled him as well. Then the master began to toss about on the floor, the cook started breaking down the kitchen door with the oven fork, and Yanson ran off into the fields. He was caught an hour later, squatting behind a corner of the barn striking one sputtering match after another and trying to set fire to the farm.

A few days later the master died of blood poisoning, and when Yanson's turn came among all the other thieves and murderers, he was tried and sentenced to death. At the trial he was just the same as always: small, puny, and freckled, with sleepy little glassy eyes. It was as if he did not quite understand the meaning of what was happening, and seemed completely indifferent: he blinked his white eyelashes, looked vacantly and without curiosity around the imposing, unfamiliar room, and picked his nose with a stiff, hard, calloused finger. Only those who had seen him in church on Sundays might have guessed that he had smartened himself up a little: he had wound a dirty-red, knitted scarf around his neck and moistened his hair here and there. Where his hair was wet it was dark and smooth, while on the other side of his head it stuck up in light, sparse tufts, like wisps of straw in a bare cornfield flattened by hail.

When sentence was pronounced—death by hanging—Yanson suddenly became agitated. He turned a deep red and began to tie and untie his scarf, as if it were strangling him. Then he began to wave his arms in a confused way and said, addressing the judge who had not pronounced sentence and pointing at the same time to the one who had:

"She said I must be hanged."

"Who is 'she'?" asked the president of the court who had read the sentence, his voice a deep bass.

Everyone smiled, concealing their smiles under their moustaches and among their papers, while Yanson pointed at the president with his index finger and replied angrily and distrustfully:

"You!"

"Well?"

Yanson again turned his eyes to the silent judge with his restrained smile—someone in whom he detected a friend, someone with no part in the sentence whatsoever—and said again:

"She said I must be hanged. You mustn't hang me."

"Take the accused away."

But Yanson managed to say once more in an earnest, forcible tone:

"You mustn't hang me."

He looked so absurd with his outstretched finger and his angry little face to which he vainly tried to lend an air of gravity, that even the soldier escorting him broke the rules and said to him under his breath as he led him from the room:

"Well, old fellow, you really are a fool!"

"You mustn't hang me," repeated Yanson obstinately.

"They'll string you up with my blessing, and you won't even have time to twitch!"

"Come on, keep quiet!" shouted the other escort angrily. But he could not restrain himself either and added: "So you're a thief too! Why did you go and kill someone, you fool? Now go and hang for it!"

"Might they give him a reprieve?" asked the first soldier, who had begun to feel sorry for Yanson.

"What d'you mean? Reprieve ones like him?.. Now that'll do, we've done enough talking!"

But Yanson had already fallen silent. Again he was put in the same cell that he had already spent a month in and had had time to grow accustomed to, just as he did to everything else: to beatings, vodka, and the dismal, snow-covered fields strewn with round little mounds like a cemetery. Now he even felt glad when he saw his bed and his barred window, and when they gave him some food—he had not eaten since that morning. The only disagreeable thing was what had happened in court, but he could not think about it and indeed was incapable of doing so. And he could not imagine death by hanging at all.

Though Yanson had been sentenced to death, there were many others like him, and he was not considered an important criminal in the prison. So the warders talked to him without being wary or deferential, just as they would to anyone else not faced with death. It was as if they did not regard his death as death in the real sense. Hearing of the sentence, the warder said to him:

"Well then, old fellow! So they've gone and hanged you, have they?"

"But when will they hang me?" asked Yanson mistrustfully.

The warder became thoughtful.

"Well now, you'll have to wait a bit for that, till they've got a batch of you together. To do it first for this one, then for that isn't worth the bother. You'll have to wait till it gets busy."

"Well, when will that be?" Yanson asked insistently.

He was not in the least offended to hear that it was not worth even hanging him by himself, and he did not believe what the warder said, thinking it was an excuse for postponing his execution then perhaps cancelling it altogether. And he felt glad: that imprecise, terrible moment which he could not think about retreated into the distance somewhere, becoming wildly improbable and unbelievable, like every death.

"When, when!" The warder was angry now, dimwitted, morose old man that he was. "It's not like hanging a dog, you know: off behind the barn with it, hup! and that's that. But that's how you'd like it to be, isn't it, you fool!"

"I don't want to be hanged!" said Yanson suddenly, his face wrinkling in a cheerful grin. "It was she who said I must be hanged, but I don't want to be!"

And perhaps for the first time in his life Yanson laughed: a rasping, absurd but terribly joyful, gay laugh. It sounded like a goose cackling: ha-ha-ha! The warder looked at him in astonishment, then frowned sternly. This ridiculous gaiety on the part of a man who was to be executed was an affront to the prison and the execution itself, and made them into something very odd. Suddenly, for a single moment, for the very shortest instant, the old warder, who had spent his whole life in the prison, acknowledging its rules as if they were laws of nature, felt that both the prison and all his life in it were a kind of madhouse, in which he himself, the warder, was the chief madman.

"Oh, to hell with you!" he spat in disgust. "What are you grinning for? You're not in an alehouse here, you know!"

"I don't want to be hanged—ha-ha-ha!" laughed Yanson.

"You're Satan himself!" said the warder, feeling the need to cross himself.

No one looked less like Satan than this man with his small, flabby face, but in his goose-like cackling there was something that destroyed the sanctity and inviolability of the prison. He only had to laugh a little more, it seemed, and the walls would collapse with decay, the bars rusty with moisture would fall from the windows, and the warder himself would lead the prisoners out through the gates: "Please, gentlemen, do have a walk around town—but perhaps some of you might like a trip out into the country instead?" "You're Satan himself!"

But Yanson had already stopped laughing and just narrowed his eyes slyly.

"Well, you'll see!" said the warder in a vaguely threatening tone and walked away, glancing behind him as he did so.

All that evening Yanson was calm and even cheerful. He kept repeating to himself the words he had spoken earlier: "You mustn't hang me," and they were so convincing, so wise, so irrefutable, that it was not worth worrying about a thing. He had forgotten about his crime long ago, and only regretted sometimes that he had not succeeded in raping the mistress. But he soon forgot about that, too.

Every morning he would ask when he was going to be hanged, and every morning the warder would reply angrily:

"You've still got plenty of time, you Satan! Just you sit there and wait!" And he would walk quickly away, before Yanson had time to burst out laughing.

And because these words were repeated monotonously over and over again, and because every day began, went by, and came to an end just like the most ordinary of days, Yanson finally became convinced that there would be no execution at all. He very soon began to forget about the trial, and lay about on his bunk for days on end, dreaming dimly of the dismal, snow-covered fields with their little mounds, of the refreshment room at the station, and of something else that was more distant and bright. He was well fed in prison, and very quickly, in just a few days, put on weight and began to give himself airs.

"She'd like me now all right," he once thought, remembering the mistress. "Now I'm a stout fellow, just as good as the master!"

The only thing was that he felt very much like having a drink of vodka, then racing off on the little horse as fast as she could go.

When the terrorists were arrested, the news reached the prison, and one day to Yanson's usual question the warder suddenly gave the unexpected, strange answer:

"It'll not be long now."

He looked calmly at Yanson and said meaningfully:

"It'll not be long now. About a week, I'd say."

Yanson turned pale, and as if nodding off to sleep, asked with a glassy look in his lackluster eyes: "Are you joking?"

"First you couldn't wait and now you say I'm joking! We don't joke here. You might like joking but we don't," said the warder with dignity, and walked away.

Already by the evening of that day Yanson had grown thin. His taut skin that had been smooth for a while suddenly puckered into a multitude of little wrinkles, and in places even seemed to hang down. His eyes had become completely sleepy and all his movements had grown very slow and sluggish, as if every turn of his head, movement of his fingers, or step of his foot was an immensely complicated, cumbersome undertaking that had to be considered for a very long time beforehand. That night he lay on his bunk but did not shut his eyes, and though he was sleepy they remained open until morning.

"Aha!" said the warder with pleasure on seeing him the next day. "You're not in an alehouse here, my lad!"

With the agreeable sense of satisfaction felt by a scientist whose experiment has succeeded yet again, he examined the condemned man attentively and in detail from head to foot. Now everything would proceed as it should. Satan was shamed, the sanctity of prison and execution restored, and with condescension and even genuine pity for Yanson, the old man inquired:

"Will you be seeing anyone or not?"

"Why should I see anyone?"

"Well, to say goodbye. Your mother, for instance, or your brother."

"You mustn't hang me," said Yanson quietly, and shot the warder a sidelong glance. "I don't want to be hanged."

The warder looked at him and silently waved his hand in a gesture of hopelessness.

By evening Yanson was a little more calm. The day had been such an ordinary day, the cloudy winter sky had shone in such an ordinary way, footsteps and someone's businesslike conversation had sounded so ordinary out in the corridor, and the cabbage soup made of sauerkraut had smelled so ordinary, natural and usual, that again he stopped believing in the execution. But by nightfall he was terrified. Formerly he had regarded the night simply as darkness, as a particularly dark time when one had to sleep, but now he felt its mysterious, menacing essence. So as not to believe in death, he had to see and hear ordinary things around him: footsteps, voices, light and sauerkraut soup, but now everything was unusual, and the silence and darkness themselves already seemed like death.

The longer the night dragged on, the more terrifying it became. With the naivete of a savage or a child, who thinks everything is possible, Yanson wanted to shout to the sun: shine! And he begged, he implored the sun to shine, but the night steadily dragged her dark hours over the earth and no force possessed the power to halt her movement. This impossibility, becoming clearly apparent to Yanson's feeble mind for the first time in his life, filled him with terror. Still not daring to perceive it clearly, he now sensed the inevitability of approaching death, and numb with horror already mounted the first step of the scaffold.

The day reassured him, then the night frightened him again, and so it went on till the night when he both sensed and realized that death was inevitable and would come in three days' time, at dawn, as the sun was rising.

He had never thought about what death was, and for him it possessed no form, but now he clearly felt it, saw it and sensed that it had come into his cell and was searching for him. To escape from it, he began to run about the room.

But the cell was so small that it seemed to have not sharp but blunt corners, and they all pushed him back into the middle. And there was nothing to hide behind. And the door was locked. And the cell was light. He collided silently with the walls several times, and once banged against the door with a muffled, hollow sound. He ran into something and fell flat on his face, then felt death seize him. Lying on his belly and clinging to the floor, he buried his face in the dark, grimy asphalt and screamed in terror. He lay there yelling at the top of his voice till someone came. Even when they had lifted him from the floor, sat him on his bunk, and poured cold water over his head, Yanson still could not bring himself to open his tightly shut eyes. He would open one a fraction, catch sight of a bright, empty corner of the cell or someone's boot in the wide expanse of the floor, and start shouting again.

But the cold water began to take effect. Things were also helped by the fact that the duty warder, still the same old man as before, hit Yanson across the head a few times by way of a remedy. This sensation of being alive really did drive death away, and Yanson opened his eyes and slept the rest of the night soundly, though with a thick head. He lay on his back with his mouth open, snoring in loud, quavering tones, and between his half-open eyelids one flat, dead eye gleamed white, its pupil invisible.

From then on everything in the world—night and day, footsteps, voices and cabbage soup—became sheer horror to him, plunging him into a strange state of incomparable stupefaction. His feeble mind could not connect these two notions that were so monstrously contradictory: the ordinary daylight and the smell and taste of cabbage soup that went with it, and the knowledge that in two days or perhaps only one day, he must die. He did not think or even count the hours, but simply stood in mute horror before this contradiction that tore his brain in two. He turned an even, pale color that was neither red nor white, and appeared calm. But he ate nothing and stopped sleeping altogether: he either sat on his stool all night with his legs drawn up fearfully under him, or walked quietly and stealthily around the cell, looking drowsily around him. His mouth was half open the whole time, as if in continual, immense astonishment, and before picking up the most commonplace object, he would examine it vacantly for a long time then pick it up with mistrust.

Once he had become like this, both the warders and the guard who watched him through the peep-hole ceased to pay any attention to him. His state was normal for the condemned, and in the opinion of the warder who had never experienced it, it resembled the condition of a beast at the slaughter, when it is stunned by a blow with an axe-butt on the forehead.

"He's dazed now and won't feel a thing right till he dies," said the warder, scrutinizing him with practiced eyes. "Ivan, d'you hear me? Eh, Ivan?"

"You mustn't hang me," answered Yanson in a flat voice, and his lower jaw dropped once more.

"But you shouldn't have killed anybody, then they wouldn't be hanging you," said the chief warder in a didactic tone. Though still a young man, he was very imposing, with decorations on his chest. "But you went and killed someone, and now you don't want to be hanged for it."

"You took it into your head to kill a man for nothing at all. You're stupid, very stupid, but you're a crafty devil as well!"

"I don't want to be hanged," said Yanson.

"All right, my friend, so you don't, but that's your business," said the chief warder indifferently. "Instead of talking nonsense, you'd do better to get your things in order—you must have something, after all."

"He hasn't got anything. Just a shirt and some trousers. Oh, and a fur hat too, the dandy!"

So the time passed until Thursday. On Thursday, at midnight, a lot of people came into Yanson's cell and a gentleman with shoulder-straps said:

"Come on, get ready! It's time to go."

Still moving just as slowly and sluggishly as he always did, Yanson put on all the clothes he possessed and tied the dirty-red scarf around his neck. Watching him dress, the gentleman with shoulder-straps said to someone as he smoked his cigarette:

"How warm it is today! Just like spring!"

Yanson could hardly keep his eyes open and was nodding off, moving so slowly and with such difficulty that the warder shouted at him:

"Come on, come on, get a move on! You're half asleep!"

Suddenly Yanson stopped.

"I don't want to be hanged," he said limply.

They took him by the arms and led him out, and he stepped forward obediently, squaring his shoulders. Outside he immediately felt a breath of moist spring air, and a wet patch appeared under his nose. Even though it was night it was thawing more quickly still, and with a ringing sound merry drops of water fell steadily onto the paving-stones. As he waited for the policemen to climb into the unlit, black carriage, rattling their swords and stooping as they did so, Yanson idly wiped his wet nose with his finger and adjusted his badly-tied scarf.

IV
Us Folk from Orel

During the same session the district military court that had tried Yanson sentenced to death by hanging a peasant from the Elets district of Orel Province, one Mikhail Golubets, nicknamed Mishka the Gypsy, alias the Tatar. His most recent crime, one with precise evidence to prove it, was armed robbery and a triple murder, but before that his shadowy past was wrapped deep in mystery. There were vague rumors that he had taken part in a whole series of other robberies and murders, and one sensed that the years gone by were full of bloodshed and somber, drunken revelry. With complete frankness and total sincerity, he called himself a robber and referred ironically to those who fashionably styled themselves as "expropriators." He spoke readily and in detail of his last crime, since denying it had gotten him nowhere, but to questions about his past he only grinned and whistled softly:

"Try to find the wind in the fields!"

But when people badgered him with questions, the Gypsy assumed a dignified, serious air.

"All us folk from Orel, we're all hotheads," he would say soberly and gravely. "Orel and Kromy, they say, that's where the best thieves live. Karachev and Livny, they're marvelous for thieves too. But as for Elets, it's father to all the thieves on earth. There's no doubt about it!"

He was nicknamed the Gypsy because of his looks and his thievish tricks. He was extraordinarily black-haired and lean, with yellow patches of burnt skin on his prominent Tatar cheekbones. He rolled the whites of his eyes like a horse and was forever hurrying somewhere. His glance was swift but terrifyingly direct and full of curiosity, and the thing on which it rested seemed to lose something, surrendering part of itself to him and becoming something else. The cigarette he had glanced at was just as difficult and unpleasant to smoke as if it had already been in someone else's mouth. Some perpetually irrepressible force lived within him, first twisting him up like a tightly coiled braid of hair, then flinging him out like a broad sheaf of swirling sparks. And he drank water almost by the bucketful, just like a horse.

To every question at his trial he leapt up and replied briefly and firmly, apparently even with pleasure:

"Correct!"

Sometimes he would emphasize the word:

"Correct!"

Then quite unexpectedly, when the questions concerned something else, he sprang up and asked the president of the court:

"Allow me to whistle!"

"Why do you wish to do that?" asked the judge in astonishment.

"The witnesses say that's how I signalled to my friends, so I'll show you how I did it. It's very interesting, you know."

Rather at a loss, the president agreed. The Gypsy quickly put four fingers in his mouth, two from each hand, rolled his eyes ferociously—and the still air of the courtroom was rent by a real, wild, robber's whistle that deafens horses, makes them twitch their ears and rear, and turns men pale despite themselves. The savage joy of the killer, the mortal anguish of the slain, the sinister shout of warning, the wild cry for help, the darkness of a foul autumn night, and the sound of empty solitude—all this was in that piercing shriek which seemed to belong to neither man nor beast.

The presiding judge shouted something, then waved his hand at the Gypsy, and the robber obediently fell silent. Like a singer who has triumphantly performed a difficult but always successful aria, the Gypsy sat down, wiped his wet fingers on his prison smock, and surveyed those present with a self-satisfied expression.

"There's a robber for you!" said one of the judges, rubbing his ear.

But another, with a broad, Russian beard and Tatar eyes like the Gypsy's, gazed somewhere over the thief's head, smiled and said:

"But it really is interesting, you know!"

And with peace in their hearts, without pity or the slightest pang of remorse, the judges sentenced the Gypsy to death.

"Correct!" he said when the sentence was read out. "A good gallows in an open field. Correct!" And turning to the soldier escorting him, he flung out with bravado:

"Well let's go, shall we, you ugly devil? And hold on tight to your gun, or I'll take it away!"

The soldier glanced at him sternly and warily, caught his fellow escort's eye, and fingered the bolt on his rifle. His companion did the same. And all the way to the prison the soldiers felt as if they were not walking on the ground but flying through the air. So preoccupied were they by their prisoner that they were unaware either of the earth beneath their feet, the time, or their own selves.

Like Yanson, Mishka the Gypsy had to spend seventeen days in prison before his execution. All seventeen days flew by as quickly for him as one, filled as they were with the single, undying thought of escape, freedom and life. The irresistible force that had hitherto possessed him but was now cramped by the walls, bars and blind window of his cell, channelled all its fury inwards and set his mind ablaze, as when a live coal is flung down on a wooden floor. As if in a drunken frenzy, vivid but incomplete images swarmed, collided and mingled in his head, whirling by in an irrepressible, blinding blizzard, and all were directed towards one thing—escape, freedom and life. Flaring his nostrils like a horse, the Gypsy would sniff the air for hours on end and imagine he could smell hemp and the pale, pungent smoke of a fire. Then he would spin round his cell like a top, quickly feeling the walls, tapping them with his fingers, planning how to escape, piercing the ceiling with his gaze, and sawing through the bars in his mind's eye. His indefatigability had exhausted the soldier watching him through the peephole, and several times now, in desperation, he had threatened to fire. The Gypsy would make some coarse, derisive retort, and things only ended peaceably because the wrangling between them soon turned into a torrent of ordinary, harmless peasant abuse, amidst which talk of shooting seemed impossible and absurd.

At night the Gypsy slept soundly and almost did not stir, lying motionless but alive, just like a temporarily inactive spring. But as soon as he leapt to his feet, he began to circle round and round his cell, feeling the walls and thinking. His hands were constantly hot and dry, but his heart was sometimes filled with sudden cold, just as if a lump of solid ice had been placed in his breast and was sending a slight, chill shiver through his whole body. At these moments the already swarthy Gypsy turned darker still, becoming the dark bluish color of cast iron. He acquired a strange habit: as if he had eaten too much of something that was excessively and unbearably sweet, he kept licking his lips constantly, smacking them and with a hissing sound spitting out through his teeth the saliva that constantly filled his mouth. And he could not finish what he was saying: his thoughts were moving so fast that his tongue could not keep up with them.

One afternoon the chief warder came into his cell accompanied by an escort. He looked askance at the floor bespattered with saliva and said gloomily:

"Look how filthy you've made it in here!"

The Gypsy retorted swiftly:

"You've covered the whole world with filth, you swine, but I haven't said anything to you! What have you come crawling in here for?"

In the same gloomy voice the warder offered him the job of hangman.

"So you can't find anyone, eh? That's smart! Here you are, he says, go and do a bit of hanging, ha-ha! There's necks and ropes all right, but nobody to do the hanging. That's smart, it really is!"

"It'll mean you'll stay alive, though."

"I should think so, too! I won't be doing any hanging for you if I'm dead, will I? That's a good one, you fool!"

"What do you say, then? Take it or leave it: yes or no."

"And how do they hang folks here? I bet they strangle 'em on the sly!"

"No, they do it to music," snapped the warder.

"Well, you're a fool all right! Of course you've got to have music! Like this!" And he broke into a rollicking song.

"You've gone right off your head, old fellow," said the warder. "So what do you say then? Talk sense."

Baring his teeth, the Gypsy grinned:

"You're in a hurry! Come back later and I'll tell you."

Into the chaos of vivid but incomplete images overwhelming the Gypsy

48

with their racing torrent, there came bursting a new one: how grand it would be to be the hangman in his red shirt! He vividly imagined the high gallows and the square filled to overflowing with people, and how he, the Gypsy, would walk about on the scaffold in his red shirt, carrying his little axe. The sun shines on the heads of the crowd and sparkles merrily on the axe, and everything is so luxuriant and gay that even the man who is about to have his head cut off is smiling too. Beyond the crowd can be seen carts and the muzzles of horses—peasants have driven in from the countryside—and further away still can be seen open fields.

"Ts-akh!" The Gypsy licked his lips, smacked them, and spat out the saliva filling his mouth.

Suddenly it was as if someone had pulled a fur cap over his face and right down over his mouth: everything became dark and airless, and his heart was a lump of solid ice sending a slight, chill shiver through his whole body.

The warder came once or twice more, and each time the Gypsy said, baring his teeth in a grin:

"You're in a hurry! Come back later."

In the end the warder shouted through the peephole in passing:

"You've missed your chance, jailbird! They've got somebody else!"

"Oh, to hell with you, do your own hanging," barked the Gypsy. And he stopped dreaming about being a hangman.

But towards the end, the closer the execution came, the racing torrent of broken images became too swift for him to bear. He wanted to stop, plant his feet wide apart and come to a halt, but the whirling torrent swept him on and there was nothing to grasp hold of: everything was afloat around him. His sleep had already become fitful. New visions appeared, as distinct and weighty as painted wooden blocks, racing by even more swiftly than his thoughts. It was no longer a torrent but an endless cascade hurtling down from a mountain so high that it had no summit, a wildly spinning flight through all the colors in the world. Before his arrest the Gypsy had only sported a rather dandyish moustache, but in prison he had grown a short, black, bristly beard, and it gave him a terrifying, mad look. At times he really did go out of his mind, and circled quite senselessly round and round his cell, though he still went on feeling the rough, plastered walls. And he drank water like a horse.

One day towards evening, when the lights had been turned on, the Gypsy got down on all fours in the middle of his cell and began to howl, making the trembling cry of a wolf. He did this particularly earnestly, howling as if carrying out some important and necessary task. He filled his chest with air then slowly expelled it in a long, quavering howl, narrowing his eyes and listening attentively to the sound he made. The very way his voice shook seemed rather contrived, and he did not howl at random, but carefully sounded every note in that wild beast's cry which is so full of unspeakable terror and sorrow.

Then all at once he cut short the howl and without getting up remained silent for a few minutes. Suddenly he began to mutter softly into the floor:

"Good friends, dear friends... Good friends, dear friends, have pity... Good friends!.. Dear friends!.."

And again he seemed to listen to what his words sounded like. He would say a word, then listen.

Then he leapt up and without pausing for breath swore foully for a whole hour.

"Oh, you bastards, to hell with y-y-y-you!" he yelled, rolling his blood-shot eyes wildly. "If I must be hanged, then hang me, instead of... Oh, you bastards..."

White as a sheet and weeping with anguish and terror, the guard banged on the door with the muzzle of his gun and shouted helplessly:

"I'll fire! D'you hear me? I tell you I'll fire!"

But he did not dare fire: unless there was a real revolt, they never fired on prisoners who were sentenced to death. And the Gypsy ground his teeth, cursed and spat. Poised on the extremely fine dividing line between life and death, his mind was crumbling like a lump of dry, weathered clay.

When at night they came to his cell to take him to execution, the Gypsy began to bustle about and seemed to revive. The taste in his mouth had become sweeter still and his saliva streamed down in uncontrollable amounts, but his cheeks had turned faintly pink and his eyes sparkled with their former rather fierce slyness. As he was dressing, he asked one of the officials:

"Who's doing the hanging, then? The new fellow? He can't be very good at it yet, can he?"

"There's no need to worry about that," replied the official drily.

"But why shouldn't I worry, your Honor? It's me who's being hanged, you know, not you. Just don't be sparing with that prison soap on the old slip knot!"

"All right, all right, be quiet, please."

"It's him there who's used all your soap up," said the Gypsy, pointing to the warder, "just look how that mug of his shines!"

"Be quiet!"

"Well, don't be sparing with it!"

The Gypsy began to laugh, but the taste in his mouth was growing sweeter and sweeter. Then his legs suddenly began to go strangely numb. All the same, as they went out into the courtyard, he managed to shout:

"Carriage for the Count of Bengal!"

V

Kiss Him—and Keep Quiet

The sentence on the five terrorists was pronounced in its final form and confirmed the same day. The condemned were not informed when the execution would be, but from the way things were usually done they knew they would be hanged that same night or, at the very latest, the following night. When they were offered the opportunity of seeing their relatives the next day, that was on Thursday, they realized the execution would be on Friday at dawn.

Tanya Kovalchuk had no close relatives, and what relatives she had were out in the wilds somewhere in the Ukraine, and hardly knew about her trial and impending execution. Since Musya and Werner had refused to reveal their identities, they could not see any relatives at all, so only two of the condemned, Sergei Golovin and Vasily Kashirin, were to see their families. Both thought of this meeting with anguish and horror, but could not bring themselves to deny their parents a few last words, a last kiss.

Sergei Golovin was particularly worried at the prospect of this meeting. He was very fond of his mother and father, had seen them only a short while ago, and was horrified now at the thought of what the meeting would be like. The execution itself, in all its monstrous singularity, its mind-shattering insanity, was easier to imagine and did not seem as terrible as these few brief, incomprehensible minutes that existed as it were outside time, outside life itself. How should he look, what should he think, what should he say? His brain refused to tell him. The most simple and ordinary gesture: taking them by the hand, kissing them, and saying: "Hello, father," seemed utterly frightful in its appallingly inhuman, insane falsity.

After sentence had been passed, the condemned were not imprisoned together as Tanya had expected, but were each left in solitary confinement. Sergei Golovin spent the whole morning till eleven, when his parents came, furiously pacing his cell, tugging at his beard, screwing up his face pitifully, and muttering something. Occasionally he would stop his pacing, fill his lungs with air, then blow it out like someone who has been under water too long. But he was so full of vigorously youthful life that even at these moments of cruellest suffering the blood coursed beneath his skin, coloring his cheeks, and his eyes were a bright, innocent blue.

However, everything went much better than he had expected.

The first to enter the room where the meeting took place was his father, Nikolai Sergeevich Golovin, a retired colonel. Everything about him was white—his face, beard, hair and hands, as if a snowman had been dressed in human clothes. He was wearing the same little frockcoat he always wore, old but well cleaned with brand new, crisscrossed shoulder-straps and smelling of benzine. He came into the room firmly, as if on parade, his steps brisk and precise, and stretching out his dry, white hand, said loudly:

"Hello, Sergei!"

Behind him came his mother with her short steps and a strange smile on her face. But she shook his hand too and repeated loudly:

"Hello, Sergei!"

She kissed him on the lips and sat down without a word. She did not fling herself on his neck, burst into tears, cry out, or do anything terrible as Sergei had expected—she just kissed him and sat down without a word. And she even smoothed her black silk dress with shaking hands.

Sergei did not know that the colonel had spent all the previous night shut away in his little study pondering this ritual with every ounce of strength he possessed. "We must not burden our son's last minutes but make them easier for him," he had resolved, and carefully weighed every possible word, every gesture, of the conversation the next day. But sometimes he became confused, forgetting what he had managed to prepare, and wept bitterly on a corner of the oilcloth sofa. But in the morning he had explained to his wife how they should behave during the meeting.

"The main thing is to kiss him—and keep quiet!" he instructed her. "You'll be able to talk later, after a short while, but when you've kissed him, keep quiet. Don't start talking straight after you've kissed him, d'you understand? Or you'll say the wrong thing."

"I understand, Nikolai Sergeevich," replied the mother, weeping.

"And don't cry. God forbid that you should cry! You'll kill him if you do!"

"But why are you crying yourself?"

"Looking at you makes me cry! You mustn't cry, d'you hear?"

"All right, Nikolai Sergeevich."

In the cab he meant to repeat his instructions once more, but forgot. And so on they rode in silence, both of them bent, old and gray, thinking their thoughts while the city bustled gaily around them. It was Shrovetide and the streets were noisy and crowded.

They sat down. The colonel adopted his prepared pose, his right hand behind the lapel of his frockcoat. Sergei sat still for a moment, then saw his mother's lined face close beside him and sprang to his feet.

"Sit down, Sergei," begged his mother.

"Sit down, Sergei," said his father, echoing his wife.

No one spoke for a while. The mother was smiling strangely.

"How we've pleaded for you, Sergei!"

"It's no use, mother..."

"We had to try, Sergei, so you wouldn't think your parents had deserted you."

Again no one spoke for a while. It was terrible to utter a word, as if every word in the Russian language had lost its proper meaning and now meant only one thing: death. Sergei looked at his father's clean little frockcoat that smelt of benzine and thought: "He's got no orderly these days, so he has to clean it himself. How on earth is it I never noticed him cleaning that coat before? He must do it in the mornings." And suddenly he asked:

"How's my sister? Is she well?"

"Ninochka doesn't know a thing about this," replied his mother hastily. But the colonel stopped her sternly:

"Why lie about it? The girl's read the papers! Sergei must know that all... his loved ones...were thinking and..."

He could not go on and stopped. Suddenly, all at once, the mother's face crumpled, quivered and broke, becoming wild and wet with tears. Her pale eyes stared madly and her breathing grew more and more loud and rapid.

"Se...Ser...Se...Se...," she said again and again, without moving her lips. "Se..."

"Mother!"

The colonel stepped forward, shaking all over with every fold of his coat and every wrinkle on his face. Without realizing how dreadful he looked himself with his deathly pallor, he said to his wife with desperate, forced firmness:

"Keep quiet! Don't torment him! Don't! Don't! He's got to die! Don't!"

Frightened, she had already fallen silent, but he still kept on shaking his clenched fists in a restrained way close to his chest and saying again and again:

"Don't torment him!"

Then he stepped back, put one trembling hand behind the lapel of his coat, and with an expression of forced calm asked loudly with white lips:

"When?"

"Tomorrow morning," replied Sergei, his own lips equally white.

The mother was looking down, biting her lips, and apparently did not hear what was said. And still biting her lips, she uttered the strange, simple words:

"Ninochka sends her love, Sergei."

"Give her mine," said Sergei.

"I will. And the Khvostovs send their regards."

"What Khvostovs? Oh, yes!"

The colonel interrupted:

"Well, we must go. Get up, mother, it's time!"

Together the two men lifted the mother who was weak with sorrow.

"Say goodbye!" ordered the colonel. "Give him your blessing."

She did everything she was told. But as she made the sign of the cross over her son and kissed him with a brief kiss, she shook her head and said senselessly over and over again:

"No, that's wrong. No, it's wrong. No, no. What shall I say afterwards? What shall I say? No, it's wrong."

"Goodbye, Sergei!" said the father.

They shook hands and kissed briefly but firmly.

"You..." Sergei began.

"Well?" asked the father abruptly.

"No, that's wrong. No, no. What shall I say?" said the mother again, shaking her head. She had already managed to sit down again and the whole of her was rocking to and fro.

"You..." Sergei began again.

Suddenly his face crumpled up pitifully like a child's and his eyes immediately filled with tears. Through their sparkling film he saw his father's white face close before him with tear-filled eyes just like his own.

"You're a fine man, father."

"What? What?" said the colonel, startled.

And suddenly, as if collapsing, he fell with his head on his son's shoulder. Once he had been taller than Sergei, but now he had grown shorter, and his soft, dry head lay on his son's shoulder like a small, white bundle. Each avidly kissed the other without saying a word: Sergei his father's soft, white hair, and the father his son's prison smock.

"And what about me?" said a loud voice suddenly.

They looked around: the mother stood there with her head flung back, watching them with anger and almost with hatred.

"What did you say, mother?" shouted the colonel.

"What about me?" she said in an insane voice, tossing her head. "You're kissing each other, but what about me? The men can do it, can they? Well what about me? What about me?"

"Mother!" Sergei threw himself into her arms.

What happened then is something one cannot and should not tell.

The colonel's last words were:

"I give you my blessing for your death, Sergei. Die bravely, like an officer."

They left. Somehow they left. One moment they were there, standing and talking, then suddenly they were gone. The mother was sitting here, the father standing there, then suddenly they were gone. Returning to his cell, Sergei lay down on his bunk with his face to the wall so the guards could not see him, and wept for a long time. Then, exhausted by weeping, he fell fast asleep.

Only his mother came to see Vasily Kashirin—his father, a wealthy merchant, had not wanted to come. When the old woman came in, Vasily was pacing up and down and shivering with cold, though it was warm and even hot in the room. Their conversation was brief and painful.

"You shouldn't have come, mother. You'll only torment both yourself and me."

"Why did you do it, Vasya? Why did you do it? My God!"

The old woman burst into tears, wiping her eyes with the ends of her black, woollen shawl.

Accustomed like his brothers to shouting at his mother because she was a simple woman, he stopped, and shaking with cold, said angrily:

"There we are! I knew it! You don't understand a thing, mother! Not a thing!"

"Well all right, all right. What's wrong—are you cold?"

"Yes..." snapped Vasily, and began pacing the room again, looking at his mother angrily and askance.

"Have you caught a cold, perhaps?"

"Oh, mother, what have colds got to do with it when..."

And he waved his hand in a gesture of despair. The old woman meant to say: "Your dad's been telling me to make some pancakes since last Monday," but she took fright and began to wail:

"I says to him: he's your son after all, you know, so go and give him your blessing. But oh no, he dug his heels in, the old devil..."

"Well to hell with him! What kind of a father is he to me? He's been a bastard all his life and he's still one now!"

"Vasya, how can you say that about your own father?" The old woman drew herself up in reproach.

"I can."

"About your own father!"

"A fine father he is to me!"

It was ridiculous and absurd. Ahead of him lay death, while here something petty, futile and useless had arisen, and the words cracked like empty nutshells underfoot. Almost weeping with anguish at the perpetual lack of understanding that had stood like a wall between him and his family all his life and that now, in the last few hours before death, had appeared again in all its terrible absurdity, Vasily shouted:

"But don't you see, I'm going to be hanged! Hanged! Do you understand or don't you? Hanged!"

"But you shouldn't have harmed anybody, then they wouldn't have..." shouted the old woman.

"My God! What is this? Even wild animals don't do this! Am I your son or aren't I?"

He began to weep and sat down in the corner. The old woman began to weep in her corner too. Incapable even for a moment of coming together in a feeling of mutual love and setting it against the horror of imminent death, both wept the chill tears of loneliness that fail to warm the heart. The mother said:

"You say I'm not a mother to you, you reproach me. But I've gone really gray these past few days, I've turned into an old woman! And you say things like that and reproach me!"

"All right, all right, mother. I'm sorry. Now it's time for you to go. Give my brothers my love."

"Aren't I your mother? Don't I feel sorry for you?"

Finally she went away. Weeping bitterly and wiping her eyes with the

55

ends of her shawl, she could not see which way she was going. The further she went from the prison, the more bitterly she wept. She retraced her steps then, absurdly, lost her way in the city where she was born, had grown up and grown old. She wandered into a deserted little park with a few old, broken trees in it, and sat down on a wet bench where the snow had thawed. And all of a sudden she realized that tomorrow he would be hanged.

The old woman sprang to her feet and tried to run, but her head suddenly began to swim and she fell down. The icy path was wet and slippery, and she could not get up at all: turning round and round, she raised herself on her elbows and knees, but then fell over on her side again. Her black shawl had slipped to reveal a bald patch among the dirty gray hair on the back of her head, and for some reason she imagined that she was at a wedding feast: her son was getting married, she had drunk some wine, and now she was very tipsy.

"I can't. Really, I can't, I swear it!" she said, shaking her head and refusing more wine, and crawled over the icy wet snow. But still they kept pouring her more wine, pouring and pouring.

Already her heart was beginning to ache with the drunken laughter, the food and drink, and the wild dancing—but still they kept on pouring her more wine. Pouring and pouring.

VI
The Hours Fly

In the prison where the condemned terrorists were held there was a steeple with an old clock. Every hour, every half hour, every quarter hour rang out with a slow, mournful sound that gradually died away high above, like the distant, plaintive cry of birds of passage. During the day this strange, sad music was lost amid the noise of the city and drowned by the hubbub of the big, crowded street that ran past the prison. Trams went rumbling by, horses' hooves clopped on the roadway, and swaying automobiles blared far ahead. Many peasant cabbies had come into the city from the surrounding districts specially for Shrovetide, and the little bells on the necks of their small horses filled the air with tinkling. There was the sound of voices too, the gay, slightly tipsy voices heard at Shrovetide, and in perfect harmony with all these very different sounds were the young spring thaw, the muddy puddles on the pavements, and the trees in the public gardens that had suddenly turned dark. A warm wind blew off the sea, its gusts sweeping and humid, and it was as if one could see with the naked eye the minute, cool particles of air whirling away together in friendly flight into the boundlessly free expanse of distance, laughing as they went.

At night the street grew quiet, flooded with the cheerless brilliance of its big electric lamps. And then the immense prison, without a single light in its sheer walls, was sunk in silence and darkness, separated from the perpetually busy city by a barrier of silence, immobility and gloom. Then the striking of the clock became audible, the slow, mournful birth and death of a strange melody alien to this earth. Again it was born, and deceiving the ear it rang out softly and plaintively, suddenly stopped, then rang once more. Like great, limpid drops of glass, the hours and minutes seemed to fall from an unknown height into a bowl that was ringing softly. Or it sounded like the cry of birds of passage.

Day and night this sound alone was heard in the cells where each of the condemned sat in solitude. Through the roof, through the thick stone walls it came, making the silence quiver, then retreated imperceptibly, only to return just as imperceptibly once more. Sometimes they forgot about it and did not hear it; sometimes they waited for it with despair, living from one stroke to the next, no longer trusting the silence. This prison was reserved for important criminals and it had its own special rules, strict, harsh and rigid like a corner of the prison wall itself. If there is nobility in harshness, then the profound, dead, solemnly mute silence in which every rustle and breath could be heard—that was noble.

In this solemn silence, broken only by the sad sound of the minutes ebbing away, five people, three men and two women cut off from every living thing, waited for nightfall, dawn and execution, and each prepared for it in his own way.

VII
There Is No Death

Just as throughout her life Tanya Kovalchuk had thought only of others and never of herself, so even now she worried only about the rest and felt profound anguish for them. She imagined death insofar as it was something agonizing that was imminent for Sergei, Musya, and the others, but as for herself it seemed not to concern her in the slightest.

As though recompensing herself for the control she had shown at the trial, she wept for hours on end as only old women who have known much sorrow or young, compassionate, good people can weep. The idea that Sergei might not have any tobacco, or that Werner might perhaps be going without the strong tea he was used to—and all this added to the fact that they must die—tormented her no less perhaps than the thought of the execution itself. The execution was something inevitable and incidental that was not worth even thinking about, but if a man who was in prison and what's more awaiting execution had no tobacco, then that was quite intolerable. She recalled and went over the fond details of their life together, and felt weak with terror at the thought of Sergei's meeting with his parents.

She felt particularly sorry for Musya. For a long time now she had thought that Musya loved Werner, and though this was completely untrue,

57

she still hoped fervently for something fine and joyous for them both. Before her arrest Musya had worn a little silver ring engraved with a skull and cross-bones surrounded by a crown of thorns. Tanya would often look at that ring with a feeling of pain, seeing it as a symbol of doom, and half seriously, half jokingly would beg Musya to take it off.

"Give it to me," she implored her.

"No, Tanechka, I won't. Anyway, you'll soon have a different ring on your finger."

For some reason they all thought she was sure to get married before very long, and this offended her, for she had no wish for a husband what-soever. Recalling her half-serious conversations with Musya and knowing that now she really was doomed, she choked with tears of motherly pity. Each time the clock struck she lifted her tear-stained face and listened, wondering how this long, insistent call of death was being received in the other cells.

But Musya was happy.

With her arms behind her back in the prison smock that was too big for her and made her look strangely like a man or a teenage boy dressed in some-one else's clothes, she paced the cell with even, untiring strides. The sleeves of the smock were too long for her so she had turned them back, and her thin, slender, almost childlike arms emerged from the wide sleeves like the stems of flowers protruding from the mouth of a crudely made, grimy jug. The coarse cloth irritated and chafed her slim, white neck, and from time to time with a movement of both arms she would free her throat and carefully feel with her finger the place where the chafed skin was red and smarting.

Back and forth she paced, and growing agitated and blushing, tried to justify herself to others. She justified herself by the thought that she, who was so young and insignificant, who had accomplished so little and who was not in the least like a heroine, would suffer the same honorable, beautiful death that real heroes and martyrs had suffered before her. With an unshak-able faith in people's goodness, in their sympathy and love, she imagined how worried they felt about her now, how troubled and sorry they were—and she felt so ashamed that she blushed. It was as if by dying on the gallows she were committing some enormous blunder.

At their final meeting she had asked her defense lawyer to get her some poison, but had suddenly thought: what if he and the others think I'm doing it out of bravado or cowardice, and instead of dying humbly and inconspicu-ously want to create more of a sensation? And she had added hastily:

"No, it's all right, you needn't."

Now she desired only one thing: to explain to people and prove clearly to them that she was not a heroine, that it was not in the least terrifying to die, and that they should not feel sorry for her or worry about her. She wanted to explain to them that she was not at all to blame for the fact that she, who was so young and insignificant, was suffering such a death, and that so much fuss was being made over her.

Like someone who is actually being accused, Musya searched for excuses, trying to find something at least that would ennoble her sacrifice and lend it real value. She said to herself:

"Of course, I'm very young and might have lived a long time yet, but..."

As a candle fades in the brilliance of the sunrise, so her youth and life seemed dim and pale beside the magnificent, resplendent halo that was to illumine her humble head. There was no excuse.

But perhaps that special feeling she had in her soul was infinite love, infinite readiness for heroism, infinite disregard for herself? After all, it was not really her fault that she had not been allowed to do all she could or wished—she had been slain on the threshold of the temple, at the foot of the sacrificial altar.

But if that was so, if a person was valuable not only for what he had done but also for what he had wanted to do, then...she was worthy of a martyr's crown.

"Am I really?" she thought with embarrassment, "am I really worthy of that? Worthy enough that people should weep for me or worry about me when I am so small and insignificant?"

And she was filled with ineffable joy. There was no hesitation, no doubt, for she had been received into the bosom of her peers, she had stepped as if right into the ranks of those sacred souls who from time immemorial have passed through fire, torture and execution to ascend to the heights of heaven. There they enjoy serene peace, rest and boundless, quietly radiant happiness. It was as if she had already left this earth and was drawing near the mysterious sun of life and truth, soaring incorporeal in its light.

"And this is death! How can one call this death?" she thought blissfully.

If all the scholars, philosophers and executioners in the world had gathered in her cell, laid their books, scalpels, axes and nooses before her, and begun to prove that death exists, that men die and kill one another, that there is no immortality—they would only have astonished her. How could there be no immortality when she was now already immortal? And how could one speak of immortality, how could one speak of death, when she was already dead and immortal at this moment, alive in death as she had been alive in life?

If they had carried a coffin into her cell with her own body decomposing in it and filling the room with its stench, and said:

"Look! This is you!" she would have looked and answered:

"No, that's not me."

And if they had begun trying to convince her that it was she—she!—attempting to frighten her with the sinister sight of decay, she would have replied with a smile:

"No. It's you who think that *this* is me, but *this* is not me. How can I, the woman you are talking to, how can I be *this*?"

"But you will die and become this."

59

"No, I shall not die."

"You will be executed. Here's the noose."

"I will be executed, but I shall not die. How can I die when I am already immortal?"

And the scholars, philosophers and executioners would have stepped back, saying with a shudder:

"Do not set foot on this spot, for it is sacred."

What else did Musya think of? She thought of many things, since for her the thread of life was not broken by death, but went on being calmly and evenly woven. She thought of her comrades, both those far away who felt pain and anguish at the imminent execution, and those close at hand who would mount the scaffold together. She was surprised at Vasily. Why was he so frightened? He had always been so brave and could even trifle with death. Last Tuesday morning, for example, when Vasily and she were strapping around their waists the explosive devices that in a few hours' time would blow them up, Tanya's hands had been shaking with agitation and the others had been obliged to stop her helping them. But Vasily had joked and played the fool, spinning round and round and behaving so carelessly that Werner had said sternly:

"You shouldn't take liberties with death."

So why was Vasily frightened now? But that incomprehensible fear of his was so alien to Musya's soul that she soon stopped thinking about it or seeking the reason for it. She suddenly felt a desperate urge to see Sergei and have a laugh with him about something. She thought for a little, then felt an even more desperate urge to see Werner and convince him of something. And imagining Werner was walking beside her with his precise, measured tread that drove his heels into the ground, Musya said to him:

"No, Werner, my dear, that's all nonsense, it doesn't matter a jot whether you killed X or not. You're clever but it's just as if you're always playing that chess of yours: take one piece, then another, and the game's won. What matters here, Werner, is that we ourselves are prepared to die. Do you see? After all, what do these people think? They think there's nothing more terrible than death. They themselves have invented death, they're afraid of it themselves so they try and frighten us with it. Now this is what I'd like to do: walk out by myself in front of a whole regiment of soldiers and start firing at them with a Browning. There'd be just one of me and thousands of them, and I mightn't kill a single one of them. But that's what matters—there are thousands of them. When thousands kill one it means that the one is the victor. It's true, Werner, my dear."

But this too was so clear that she did not want to try and prove it any longer. Anyway, Werner probably understood now himself. Or perhaps her thoughts simply did not wish to dwell only on one thing, like a lightly soaring bird that can see boundless horizons and reach the whole expanse and profundity of the sky, all the joyously caressing, tender immensity of azure. The clock struck again and again, making the dead silence quiver. Into that harmonious, distantly beautiful sound flowed her own thoughts, they too beginning to ring, and the images slipping rhythmically through her mind themselves became music. Musya felt as if she were driving somewhere down a wide, smooth road on a still, dark night, with the soft springs of the carriage giving gently and the little harness bells jingling softly. All her anxiety and agitation had receded, her weary body had dissolved in the darkness, and in its joyous fatigue her mind calmly brought forth vivid images, revelling in their bright colors and quiet peace. She recalled three friends of hers who had been hanged not long ago, and their faces were serene, joyful and dear to her—dearer even than those of the living. So in the morning a man thinks with joy of his friend's house which he will enter that evening to find a welcome on smiling faces.

Musya was very tired of walking up and down her cell. She lay down carefully for a while on her bunk and went on dreaming with her eyes barely closed. The clock struck again and again, making the mute silence quiver, and between the banks of its ringing sound radiant, melodious images drifted gently by.

She thought to herself:

"Is this really death? My God, how beautiful it is! Or is it life? I don't know, I don't know. I'll watch and listen."

For a long time now, ever since her first days in prison, her ears had been playing tricks on her. She was very musical, and her hearing had become more acute with the stillness. Against the backdrop of scant, fragmentary sounds coming from the reality around her—the footsteps of guards in the corridor, the striking of the clock, the whisper of the wind on the iron roof, the creaking of a lantern—her ears created entire musical tableaux. At first she was afraid of them, driving them away as delusions of a sick mind, then she realized she was quite well and not ill at all, and began to give herself to them quite calmly.

Now, suddenly and with total clarity, she caught the sound of martial music. She opened her eyes in astonishment and looked up—outside the window it was night and the clock was striking. "Again!" she thought calmly and closed her eyes. And as soon as she had closed them, the music began to play again. She could clearly hear soldiers—a whole regiment of them—coming around the corner of the building to the right and marching past her window. Their feet beat regular time on the frozen ground: left, right! left, right!, and she could even hear a leather boot squeaking occasionally and someone's foot suddenly slipping then immediately righting itself again. The music came nearer: it was a completely unfamiliar but very loud, briskly festive march. There was evidently some special occasion in the prison tonight.

Now the band had drawn level with her window, and the whole cell was filled with cheerfully rhythmic yet discordant sound. One trumpet, a big brass one, was playing shrilly and badly out of tune, first lagging behind the others then racing ahead in a ludicrous fashion. Musya could see the earnest expression of the little soldier playing it, and she laughed.

Everything moved away into the distance. The footsteps died away: left, right! left, right! From a distance the music was even more beautiful and gay. The trumpet shrieked once or twice more in its loud, brazen voice that was so happily out of tune, then everything faded away. Once again the clock rang out slowly and sadly from the steeple, making the silence quiver very slightly.

"They've gone!" thought Musya with sadness. She felt sorry for the departed sounds that were so funny and gay, sorry even for the departed soldiers, because those earnest men with their brass trumpets and squeaking boots were quite different from the ones she would have liked to fire at with her Browning.

"Well then, more!" she begged in a caressing voice. And now more images come. They bend over her, surround her in a transparent cloud, and lift her up to where the birds of passage are flying by and crying like heralds. To left and right, above and below, they cry like heralds. They call, announce and proclaim their flight far and wide. They spread their broad wings and the darkness supports them as the light does too; and on their chests thrust out as they cleave the air the shining city gleams blue with light reflected from below. Musya's heart beats more and more steadily and her breathing grows more and more calm and gentle. She is falling asleep. Her face looks tired and pale, there are dark shadows under her eyes, and her slender, girlish arms are so very thin, but there is a smile on her lips. Tomorrow, at sunrise, this human face will be distorted by an inhuman grimace, her brain will be flooded with thick blood, and her glazed eyes will start from their sockets—but today she sleeps quietly and smiles in her great immortality.

Musya has fallen asleep.

But in the prison life goes on, a life of its own that is deaf yet quick to catch every sound, blind yet ever vigilant, like perpetual anxiety itself. There is the sound of footsteps somewhere. Whispering can be heard. A gun rattles. Someone gave a shout, it seems. But perhaps no one shouted at all—one only imagines it because of the stillness.

Now the grating in the door falls open without a sound, and a swarthy face with a big moustache appears in the dark opening. For a long time it stares at Musya in surprise, then disappears as soundlessly as it came.

The striking clock rings out its melody for an agonizingly long time. It is as if the weary hours are climbing a high mountain as the hands creep towards midnight, and the ascent grows more and more difficult and painful. They suddenly stop, slip, fall back with a groan, and crawl agonizingly on once more towards the dark summit.

There is the sound of footsteps somewhere. Whispering can be heard. And the horses are already being harnessed to the black carriages that bear no lights.

VIII
There Is Death and There Is Life

Sergei Golovin never thought about death, looking upon it as something incidental that did not concern him at all. He was a strong, healthy cheerful young man, endowed with that calm, serene *joie de vivre* that makes any evil thought or feeling injurious to life rapidly disappear without trace in the organism. Just as any cuts, wounds or stings he received healed quickly, so everything painful that injured his soul immediately rose to the surface and faded away. To every undertaking or even pastime, whether it was photography, cycling or preparation for an act of terrorism, he would bring the same calm, cheerful earnestness: everything in life was gay, everything in life was important, and everything had to be done well.

He did everything well: he handled a sailing boat magnificently and was an excellent shot with a revolver; he was as steadfast in friendship as in love, and believed fanatically in one's "word of honor." His friends laughed at him, saying that if a detective, an agent, or a notorious spy gave him his word that he was not a spy, then Sergei would believe him and shake hands with him as a friend. He had just one failing: he was convinced that he had a good voice, whereas he had not the slightest ear for music, sang abominably and was out of tune even in revolutionary songs; and he was offended when people laughed.

"Either you're all asses or I'm an ass," he would say in a serious, injured tone. And after thinking for a moment they all concluded in a tone that was just as serious as his:

"It's you who's the ass, you can tell by your voice."

But as is sometimes the case with good people, they loved him perhaps even more for this failing than for all his good qualities.

So little did he fear death, so little did he think about it, that on the fateful morning of the planned assassination, before they left Tanya Kovalchuk's flat, only he ate a proper breakfast and enjoyed it: he drank two glasses of tea half diluted with milk, and ate a whole five-kopek loaf. Then he looked sadly at Werner's untouched bread and said:

"Why aren't you eating? Go on, eat, you've got to keep your strength up."

"I don't feel like it."

"Well I'll eat it then. All right?"

"You've certainly got a good appetite, Sergei."

Instead of replying, with his mouth full of bread Sergei began to sing in a voice that was muffled and out of tune:

" 'Cruel blizzards are blowing o'er our heads...' "

After his arrest Sergei began to feel sad: they had made a bad job of it and failed, but then he thought: "Now there's something else that must be done well—dying," and he cheered up. However strange it may seem, even

63

from his second morning in prison he had begun to do gymnastic exercises according to the unusually efficient system of a German called Müller that he was very keen on: he stripped naked, and to the amazement of the guard anxiously watching him, conscientiously performed all eighteen prescribed exercises. The fact that the guard was watching him and was evidently amazed by what he saw was gratifying for Sergei as a propagandist of the Müller system. Though he knew he would get no reply, he still said to the eye peering at him in astonishment through the peep-hole:

"It does you good, old fellow, it gets your strength up. This is what they should start making you do in your regiment," he added in a loud but gently persuasive voice so as not to frighten the guard, unaware that the soldier simply thought he was mad.

The fear of death began to manifest itself in him gradually, in fits and starts somehow: it was as if someone kept taking hold of him and with their fist jolting his heart from below with all their might. It was pain he felt rather than fear. Then the sensation would fade, and a few hours later it would return, growing more and more prolonged and marked each time. It was already clearly beginning to assume the dim shape of immense, even intolerable, fear.

"Can I really be afraid?" he thought in astonishment. "What nonsense!"

It was not he that was afraid, but his strong, young, vigorous body that could not be deceived either by Müller's gymnastics or by sponging down with cold water. And the stronger and fresher his body became after being rubbed down, the more unbearable was the momentary sensation of fear. Precisely at those moments when, before his arrest, he used to feel a particular upsurge of strength and *joie de vivre*—in the mornings, after a sound sleep followed by physical exercise—it was then that he felt this acute, seemingly alien fear. He noticed this and thought:

"You're stupid, Sergei, old fellow! So it's easier for your body to die, you should make it weaker, not stronger. You're just stupid!"

And he gave up his gymnastics and cold sponge-downs. By way of explanation and justification he shouted to the guard:

"Don't you worry about me giving it up! It's still a good method, my friend. Only it's no good for people who are going to be hanged. It's fine for everyone else though!"

And in fact things seemed to get easier. He tried eating a little less too, so as to grow even weaker, but despite the lack of fresh air and exercise, his appetite was still enormous and hard to satisfy, and he ate everything he was brought. Then he began to do this: before beginning his food he would tip half of it into the waste bucket. That seemed to help—a dull, sleepy lassitude took possession of him.

"I'll show you!" he said, threatening his body, but then ran his hand tenderly and sadly over his soft, flabby muscles.

But soon his body became accustomed to this regime too, and the fear of death appeared once more—not as acute or as searing as before, it is true, but even more achingly wearisome, like nausea. "It's because they're taking a long time over it," he thought, "it would be better to spend all the time till the execution asleep," and he tried to sleep as much as possible. To begin with it worked well, but after a while, either because he slept too much or for some other reason, he began to suffer from insomnia. With it came painful, vigilantly wakeful thoughts, and with them a longing to live.

"Am I really afraid of it, damn it?" he asked himself, thinking of death. "It's losing my life I regret. It's a magnificent thing, whatever the pessimists say. What would a pessimist say if he were being hanged? Oh, I feel sorry about losing my life, very sorry. And why's my beard grown since I've been in prison? It wouldn't grow for ages, and now suddenly it has. But why?"

He shook his head sadly and heaved a few long, heavy sighs. A silence—then a long, deep sigh; another brief silence—then again an even longer, heavier sigh.

So it went on till the trial and the terrible last meeting with his old folk. When he woke in his cell with the clear realization that life for him was over and that before him were only a few hours of empty waiting and death, he felt strange. It was as if he had been stripped completely naked, stripped in an unusual way—not only had they taken off his clothes but had also snatched sun and air from him, together with noise and light, actions and the power of speech. There was no death yet, but there was no longer any life either. There was something new and staggeringly incomprehensible though, something half devoid of all meaning yet half possessing meaning, but it was so profound, mysterious and superhuman that it was impossible to discover it.

"My God!" said Sergei in agonized amazement. "What is all this? And where am I? I...what I?"

He examined the whole of himself attentively and with interest, beginning with his big prisoner's shoes and ending with his belly that protruded in his prisoner's smock. With his arms spread wide, he walked up and down the cell, continuing to examine himself, like a woman in a new dress that is too long for her. He turned his head around and around and found that it did in fact turn. And this thing that for some reason was rather frightening was himself, Sergei Golovin, and soon it would no longer exist.

And everything became strange.

He tried walking about the cell, and it seemed strange that he was walking. He tried sitting down, and it seemed strange that he was sitting. He tried drinking some water, and it seemed strange that he was drinking, swallowing and holding the mug, strange that he had fingers and that those fingers were shaking. He choked, began to cough, and as he coughed, thought: "How strange that I'm coughing."

"So am I going out of my mind, then?" he wondered, turning cold. "That would be the last straw, damn them!"

65

He wiped his brow with his hand, but that seemed strange too. Then, without breathing, he sat motionless for what seemed like hours on end, suppressing every thought, stopping himself from breathing loudly, and avoiding all movement—for every thought was madness, every movement was madness. Time ceased to exist, as if it had been transformed into space, transparent and airless, into an immense expanse that contained all things, earth and life and people. All this could be seen at a glance, all of it to its furthest limits, to the brink of that mysterious abyss—death. The agony of it lay not in the fact that death was visible, but that both life and death were visible at the same time. A sacrilegious hand had drawn back the curtain that from time immemorial had hidden the mystery of life and death, and they had ceased to be mysterious. But they had become no more comprehensible than a truth written in an unknown language. There were no concepts in his human brain, no words in his human tongue capable of encompassing what he saw. And the words: "I am afraid" sounded within him only because there were no other words, and because there neither was nor could be any concept in keeping with this new, superhuman condition. So it would be if a man, remaining within the bounds of human understanding, experience and feelings, suddenly saw God himself—saw him and did not understand, even though he knew that this was called God. And he would shudder in an unprecedented agony of unprecedented incomprehension.

"There's Müller for you!" he said loudly with extreme vehemence, and shook his head. With that sudden complete change of feelings of which the human soul is so capable, he began to laugh sincerely and gaily: "Oh, Müller! Oh, my dear Müller! Oh, my splendid German! All the same, you're right, Müller, and I, my friend Müller, am an ass!"

He walked quickly up and down the cell several times, and to the renewed, supreme astonishment of the guard watching through the peep-hole, quickly stripped naked then cheerfully and with extreme diligence performed all eighteen exercises. Bending and stretching his young body that had grown rather thin, he squatted on the floor, breathing in and out, then stood on tiptoe and flung out his arms and legs. After each exercise he said with pleasure:

"That's right! That's the way, Müller my friend!"

His cheeks became flushed, beads of hot, agreeable sweat emerged from his pores, and his heart beat strongly and steadily.

"The point is, Müller," Sergei argued, sticking out his chest so his ribs were clearly visible under the thin, taut skin, "the point is, Müller, that there's a nineteenth exercise—hanging by the neck in a fixed position. And that's called execution. Do you understand, Müller? They take a live man, let's say Sergei Golovin, swaddle him like a doll, and hang him by the neck till he's dead. It's stupid, Müller, but it can't be helped—it has to be done."

He leaned over onto his right side and said again:

"It has to be done, Müller my friend."

IX
Terrible Solitude

To the same striking of the clock and separated from Sergei and Musya only by a few empty cells—but just as desperately alone as if he were the only man in all the universe—the wretched Vasily Kashirin was living out his life in anguish and terror.

Covered with sweat, his wet shirt sticking to his body and his once curly hair now straight and dishevelled, he rushed convulsively and hopelessly about his cell like a man with an excruciating toothache. Sitting down for a moment, he began to run about again, pressing his forehead to the wall, stopping and looking for something, as if seeking a remedy for the pain. He had changed so markedly that he seemed to have two different faces: the former, youthful one had disappeared, and in its place was a terrible, new one that had emerged from the darkness.

The fear of death had manifested itself in him straightaway and taken complete possession of him. On that fateful morning, heading for certain death, he had trifled with it, but by evening, when he was imprisoned in his solitary cell, he was whirled away and overwhelmed by a wave of mad terror. While he himself, of his own free will, was going to meet danger and death, and while his death, terrible though it seemed, lay in his own hands, he felt calm and even gay: in this sense of boundless freedom and the firm, bold assertion of his audacious, fearless will, the wrinkled, almost old-maidish shred of fear within him was lost without trace. With the infernal machine strapped around his waist, he seemed transformed into an infernal machine himself, containing within him the brutal reasoning of dynamite and conferring on himself its lethal, fiery power. Walking down the street amid bustling, everyday people preoccupied by their own affairs and hurrying quickly out of the way of cabs and trams, he felt like a stranger from another world, where fear and death were unknown.

Suddenly, all at once, there was an abrupt, preposterous, stupefying change. He no longer went where he wanted to go, but was taken where others wanted him to go. He no longer chose where he wanted to be, but was put by others in a stone box and locked up like a mere object. He was no longer able to choose freely between life and death, like everyone else could, but was doomed to inevitable, certain destruction. Having been for an instant the embodiment of will, life and strength, he had become a pitiful example of unique impotence, a man transformed into a beast waiting for the slaughter, a deaf and dumb thing that could be displaced, burnt or broken at will. Whatever he said, they would not listen, and if he began to shout, they would stuff a rag in his mouth; even if he tried to walk himself, they would still take him away and hang him; and if he began to resist, throwing himself about and lying on the ground, they would overpower him, lift him up, tie him up, and carry him like that to the gallows. The fact that it was people who would perform this mechanical task on his person, people just like himself, lent them an unusually novel and sinister appearance: half apparitions, specters of something illusory, and half mechanical dolls on a spring that would take him, lay hold of him, lead him away, hang him, and pull him by the feet. Then they would cut the rope, lay him in a coffin, take him away, and bury him.

From his very first day in prison people and life became for him an incomprehensibly frightful world of apparitions and mechanical dolls. Almost out of his mind with terror, he tried to imagine that these people had tongues and could speak, but he could not, for they seemed dumb. He tried to recall their speech, the meaning of the words they used in their dealings with one another, but he could not. Their mouths opened and sounds came from them, then they dispersed by moving their legs, and there was nothing more.

So a man would feel if, at night, when he was alone in the house, all the things around him came to life, began to move, and acquired over him, a human being, unlimited power. Suddenly a wardrobe, a chair, a desk or a sofa would begin to pass judgement on him. He would shout and rush about the room, imploring them and crying out for help, but they would say something to each other in their own tongue and then the wardrobe, the chair, the desk and the sofa would take him and hang him. And the other things around him would look on.

To Vasily Kashirin, a man sentenced to death by hanging, everything began to seem toylike and small: his cell, the door with the peep-hole in it, the striking of the clock, the neatly designed prison, especially the mechanical doll with a rifle who stamped his feet in the corridor, and the other dolls who frightened him by glancing at him through the peep-hole and handing him his food without a word. What he felt was not terror in the face of death, for he even wished for death: in all its age-long mysteriousness and incomprehensibility it was more accessible to the intellect than this world that had been transformed in so preposterous and fantastic a way. Moreover, death seemed to have been completely destroyed in this mad world of apparitions and dolls, losing its great, mysterious meaning and itself becoming something mechanical and only for that reason, something terrible. They would take him, lay hold of him, lead him away, hang him, and pull him by the feet. Then they would cut the rope, lay him in a coffin, take him away, and bury him.

A man would have disappeared from the face of the earth.

At the trial the nearness of his friends had brought Kashirin to his senses, and for a moment he again saw people as they really were: they were sitting there trying him and saying something in a human tongue, listening and apparently understanding. But already during his meeting with his mother, with the horror of a man who is beginning to go out of his mind and realizes it, he distinctly felt that this old woman in her black shawl was no more than a skillfully fashioned, mechanical doll like those that say: "da-da" and "ma-ma," only a better made one. He tried to talk to her but thought with a shudder:

"My God! But she's just a doll too! A mother doll. And that's a soldier doll over there, and at home there's a father doll and this is the doll Vasily Kashirin."

A little longer, it seemed, and he would hear the clicking of the mechanism, the squeaking of unoiled cogs. When his mother burst into tears, for a single instant he again caught a fleeting glimpse of something human in her, but with the very first words she uttered it vanished, and it was curious and terrible to see water running from the doll's eyes.

Later, in his cell, when the terror had become unbearable, Vasily Kashirin tried to pray. Of all that in the guise of religion had surrounded him in the merchant home of his youth, there remained only a loathsome, bitter, irritating taste, and he had no faith. But once, far back in his early childhood perhaps, he had heard five words, and they had filled him with tremulous emotion, remaining full of gentle poetry for the rest of his life. Those words were: "Comfort of all that mourn."

Sometimes, at painful moments, he would whisper to himself without praying or being really aware of what he was saying: "Comfort of all that mourn," and suddenly he would feel better and want to go to someone who was dear to him and complain softly:

"Our life...but is this really life? Oh, my dear one, is this really life?"

Then suddenly he would feel ridiculous, and want to ruffle up his hair, stick out his knee, and bare his chest for someone to hit it: "There you are, hit that!"

He told no one, not even his closest friends, about his "Comfort of all that mourn," and seemed not even to know of it himself, so deeply was it hidden in his soul. And he would recall it rarely and then only with caution.

Now that terror at the clearly apparent, insoluble mystery had covered him from head to foot, as water covers a young willow on the riverbank during the spring floods, he felt a desire to pray. He wanted to kneel but felt embarrassed in front of the soldier, and folding his arms across his chest, whispered softly:

"Comfort of all that mourn!"

And filled with yearning, uttering the words with tender emotion, he said again:

"Comfort of all that mourn, come to me, give strength to Vaska Kashirin."

Long ago, when he was in his first year at the university and still used to go on the spree, before he knew Werner and joined the revolutionary group, he used to call himself "Vaska Kashirin" in a vain and pitiful way. For some reason he felt like calling himself that again now. But the words sounded unresponsive and dead:

"Comfort of all that mourn!"

69

Something stirred within him. It was as if someone's gentle, sorrowful image had floated by in the distance and softly faded away without illumining the darkness before death. The clock on the steeple was striking. The guard in the corridor rattled something, his sword or his rifle perhaps, and gave a long, gasping yawn.

"Comfort of all that mourn! But you are silent! Have you nothing to say to Vaska Kashirin?"

He smiled imploringly and waited. But all was emptiness both in his soul and around him, and the gentle, sorrowful image did not return. Unnecessarily, agonizingly, he recalled the lighted wax candles, the priest in his cassock, the ikon painted on a wall, and his father bending then straightening again, praying as he did so and watching distrustfully to see whether Vaska was praying or getting up to mischief. And Vasily felt even more terrified than before he had begun to pray.

Everything vanished.

Madness was creeping painfully over him. His consciousness was dimming like the dying embers of a scattered campfire, turning cold like the corpse of a man who has just died and whose heart is still warm but whose hands and feet are already stiff with cold. Once more, flaring blood-red, his failing senses told him that he, Vaska Kashirin, might go out of his mind, might experience torments for which there was no name and reach a degree of pain and suffering never known by a single living creature before; that he could beat his head against the wall, put out his eyes with his finger, say and shout whatever he liked, assure them with tears that he could not bear any more—and nothing would happen. Nothing would happen.

And nothing did happen. His legs, which had their own consciousness, their own life, went on walking and supporting his trembling, wet body. His hands, which had their own consciousness too, tried in vain to close the smock that hung open on his chest and to warm his trembling, wet body. His body was shaking and cold. His eyes were open. And he felt almost at peace.

But there was another moment of wild terror. It was when some people came into his cell. He did not even think what this meant—that it was time to go for execution, but simply saw the people and took fright, almost like a child.

"I won't go! I won't go!" he whispered inaudibly with numbed lips, and moved quietly away to the back of his cell like he used to as a child, when his father raised his hand.

"It's time to go."

They were talking, walking around him, giving him something.

He closed his eyes, swayed, and in anguish began to get ready. His consciousness must have begun to return, because he suddenly asked an official for a cigarette. And the man obligingly opened his silver cigarette-case that had a smutty picture on its lid.

X
The Walls Crumble

The anonymous prisoner nicknamed Werner was a man weary of life and the revolutionary struggle. There was a time when he had been passionately fond of life, enjoying the theater, literature and contact with others. Gifted with a splendid memory and strong will, he had studied several European languages to perfection and could easily pass as a German, Frenchman, or Englishman. He usually spoke German with a Bavarian accent, but could, if he wished, speak like a native Berliner. He liked to dress well, had beautiful manners, and alone of all his comrades could appear at fashionable balls without running the risk of being recognized.

But for a long time now, without his comrades noticing it, a somber contempt for mankind had been ripening in his soul. In it there was both despair and painful, almost mortal fatigue. A mathematician rather than a poet by temperament, he had so far never known inspiration or ecstasy, and at times felt like a madman trying to square the circle in pools of human blood. The enemy against which he struggled daily inspired no respect in him, for it was a close network of stupidity, treachery, falsehood, filthy defilement and vile deceit. The final thing that had destroyed forever, it seemed, his desire to live, was the murder of an agent provocateur that he had carried out on the instructions of the organization. He had killed the man quite calmly, but when he saw the deceitful, dead face that was now so peaceful and so pitifully human, he suddenly ceased to have any respect for either himself or his cause. It was not that he felt repentance but that he simply lost his self-esteem, becoming uninteresting, insignificant and tiresomely trivial in his own eyes. But being a man of single, undivided will, he did not leave the organization, and remained outwardly unchanged, except that something chill and terrifying now lay deep in his eyes. And he said nothing to anyone.

He possessed another rare quality too: just as there are people who have never had a headache, so he had never known fear. When others were afraid, he looked upon it without censure but also without any particular sympathy, as if fear were a rather widespread disease that he himself had never suffered from. He pitied his friends, especially Vasya Kashirin, but it was a cold, almost formal pity that even some of the judges were probably not devoid of.

Werner realized that execution meant not just death but something else too. Nevertheless, he decided to face it calmly, as if it were something incidental, and to live to the end as if nothing had happened or would happen. Only in this way could he express his supreme contempt for the execution and preserve his essential, inalienable freedom of spirit. At the trial—and even his friends who were well acquainted with his cool fearlessness and superciliousness would perhaps not have believed it—he thought neither of life nor of death. Instead, calmly, intently and deep in thought, he tried to work out a difficult game of chess. An excellent chess player, he had begun the imaginary

71

game on his first day in prison and went on playing it all the time. The verdict that sentenced him to execution by hanging did not move a single chessman from its place on the invisible board.

Even the fact that he would probably not be able to finish the game did not stop him, and he began the morning of his last day on earth by correcting a move of the day before that had not been entirely successful. Pressing his hands between his knees, he sat for a long time without moving, then got up and, deep in thought, began to walk about the cell. He had a peculiar gait: bending the upper part of his body forward a little, he struck the ground firmly and precisely with his heels, so that even on dry ground his feet left a deep, visible imprint. Softly, under his breath, he whistled a simple little Italian aria, and this helped him to think.

But for some reason things were going badly this time. With the unpleasant feeling that he had made some serious, even gross, error, he went back over his game several times and checked it almost from the beginning. There was no error, but the feeling that he had still made one not only failed to disappear but grew more and more strong and annoying. Suddenly the unexpected, offensive thought occurred to him: did his mistake not lie in the fact that by playing chess he wanted to divert his attention from the execution and shield himself from the fear of death that was apparently inevitable in the condemned man?

"No, why?" he replied coolly, and calmly folded the invisible chessboard in his mind. With the same profound concentration with which he played, as if he were answering questions in a difficult examination, he tried to take stock of the horror and hopelessness of his position: looking around the cell and trying not to miss anything, he counted the hours left until the execution and conjured up an approximate but fairly accurate picture of the hanging itself, then shrugged his shoulders.

"Well?" he replied to someone in a half-questioning tone. "That's all. So where's the fear, then?"

There really was no fear. Not only was there no fear but something that seemed to be the opposite of it was growing within him—a feeling of ill-defined yet immense, courageous joy. And the mistake, still undiscovered, no longer provoked either annoyance or irritation, but spoke loudly of something fine and unexpected, as if he had thought a dear, close friend was dead, then the friend turned out to be alive and well and was even laughing.

Werner shrugged his shoulders again and felt his pulse: his heart was beating fast but strongly and evenly, with particularly audible force. Again, as attentively as a man who is in prison for the first time, he examined the walls, the bolts, and the chair screwed to the floor, and thought:

"Why do I feel so good, so happy, so free? Yes, free! I think about the execution tomorrow, and it seems not to exist. I look at the walls, and they seem not to exist either. And I feel so free that it's just as if I weren't behind bars at all but had just come out of some prison where I'd spent my whole

72

life. What is it?"

His hands were beginning to shake—something he had never known before. His thoughts raced in more and more frenzied confusion. It was as if tongues of fire were flaring up in his head, as if the fire were trying to break out and illumine with a great light the expanse around that was still shrouded in the darkness of night. And then it did break out, and the illumined expanse of distance shone far and wide.

The dull lassitude that had wearied him for the last two years had vanished, and the heavy, cold, dead snake with its closed eyes and ghastly closed mouth had fallen from his heart. In the face of death his beautiful youth was returning in all its gaiety. But there was more than just his beautiful youth. With the amazing lucidity of mind that comes to man at rare moments and raises him to the heights of contemplation, Werner suddenly saw both life and death, and was astounded by the magnificence of this unprecedented spectacle. It was as if he were walking along a very high mountain ridge, narrow as the edge of a knife-blade; on one side he could see life, and on the other, death, like two deep, beautiful, glittering seas that merged on the horizon into a single, infinitely wide expanse.

"What is this? What a wondrous sight!" he said slowly, automatically rising and drawing himself up as if in the presence of a superior being. And destroying walls, space and time with his swift, all-penetrating look, he cast a sweeping glance somewhere far into the depths of the life he was leaving behind him.

That life appeared in a new light now. He no longer tried, as before, to translate what he had seen into words, and anyway there were no such words in the still meager, scant language of men. The paltry, filthy, evil thing that had aroused contempt in him for his fellow men, and at times had even caused him revulsion at the sight of a human face—that had vanished completely. So it is for the man who ascends in a balloon: the litter and dirt in the crowded streets of the small town he has left behind him disappear from sight, and ugliness turns into beauty.

With an involuntary movement, Werner walked to the table and leaned on it with his right hand. Though proud and commanding by nature, never before had he adopted such a proud, free, masterful pose, never had he turned his head like that, never had he looked in that way—for never had he been so free and commanding as here in prison, only a few hours away from execution and death.

His fellow men appeared in a new light too, seeming unexpectedly charming and good to his lucid eye. Soaring above time, he saw clearly how young mankind really was, mankind that only yesterday had howled like a wild beast in the forests. What had once seemed unforgivable, terrible and vile in people now suddenly became touchingly endearing, as endearing as a child's inability to walk like an adult, as his incoherent prattle shining with flashes of peculiar genius, as his funny slips, blunders and painful bruises.

"You are my dear ones!" said Werner suddenly with an unexpected smile, and immediately lost all the impressive quality of his pose, becoming once more the prisoner who feels cramped and uncomfortable under lock and key and is rather tired of the annoying, inquisitive eye peering at him from the flat surface of the door. It was strange: he forgot almost immediately what he had just seen so vividly and distinctly. What was stranger still, he did not even try to recall it. He simply settled himself a little more comfortably, avoiding his usually stiff position, and with a faint, gentle smile that was quite unlike his normal one, examined the walls and the bars on the window. Then something else happened that had never happened to him before: he suddenly began to weep.

"My dear friends!" he whispered, weeping bitterly. "My dear friends!"

By what mysterious paths had he come from a feeling of proud, boundless freedom to this tender, impassioned pity? He did not know and did not even think about it. And did he really pity them, his dear friends, or did his tears hide something else that was more lofty and passionate still? His heart that had suddenly risen from the dead and broken into emerald leaf could not tell him this either. He wept and whispered:

"My dear friends! You are my dear friends!"

In this man who wept so bitterly and yet smiled through his tears, no one would have recognized the cool, haughty, audacious, world-weary Werner —neither the judges, his friends, nor he himself.

XI
They Are Taken

Before being seated in the carriages, all five condemned were assembled in a large, cold room with an arched ceiling that resembled an empty waiting room or an office which was no longer used. They were permitted to talk to each other.

But only Tanya Kovalchuk took advantage of this permission straightaway. Without a word, the others shook hands firmly—hands that were as cold as ice and hot as fire—and trying to avoid each other's eyes, huddled awkwardly and distractedly together. Now that they were all together, they seemed to be ashamed of what each had felt while alone; and they were afraid to look at one another, so as not to see or show the peculiar, new, rather shameful thing that each felt or suspected lay behind him in his recent past.

But they glanced at each other once or twice, smiled, then immediately felt relaxed and at ease as before: no change had taken place, and if something had happened, then it had affected them all so equally that for each of them individually it was imperceptible. They all talked and moved in a strange way, jerkily and in fits and starts, either too quickly or too slowly.

74

Sometimes they choked on their words and repeated them many times; sometimes they did not finish a sentence they had begun or thought they had already finished it, but did not notice. They all screwed up their eyes, inquisitively examining familiar things without recognizing them, like people who normally wear glasses and suddenly take them off. They all kept turning around sharply again and again, as if someone behind them was calling to them all the time and showing them something. But they did not notice this either. Musya's and Tanya's ears and cheeks were burning hot; Sergei was rather pale at first, but he soon picked up and became his old self.

Only Vasily attracted their attention. Even here, amongst the others, he looked extraordinary and terrible. Werner roused himself and said quietly to Musya with tender concern:

"What's wrong with him, Musya? Is he really afraid, eh? What do you think? We'd better go to him."

From somewhere a long way off Vasily looked at Werner as if not recognizing him, and lowered his eyes.

"Vasya, what have you done to your hair, eh? But what's wrong? It's all right, old fellow, it's all right, it'll soon be over. You must keep a grip on yourself, you must, you must."

Vasily said nothing. When it had already begun to look as if he would not say anything at all, there came a belated, toneless, terribly distant reply— as the grave might respond to long appeals:

"But I'm all right. I've got a grip on myself."

And he said again:

"I've got a grip on myself."

Werner was glad.

"That's it, that's it. There's a good fellow. Right, right."

But he met Vasily's somber, leaden gaze that was fixed on him from far away in the distance, and thought with momentary anguish: "Where is he looking at me from? Where is he speaking from?" And with profound tenderness, as people speak only to the dead, he said:

"Can you hear me, Vasya? I love you very much."

"And I love you very much too," replied Vasily, his tongue moving with difficulty.

Suddenly Musya took Werner by the hand, and expressing her amazement in an earnest way like an actress on stage, said:

"Werner, what's wrong with you? Did you say 'I love you'? You've never said 'I love you' to anyone before! And why are you so...happy and gentle? Why is it?"

"Why's what?"

And, like an actor, expressing what he felt in an earnest way too, Werner squeezed Musya's hand hard and said:

"Yes, I love people very much now. But you mustn't tell the others. I feel ashamed of it, but I love people very much."

75

Their eyes met and shone with brilliant light, and everything around them grew dim. So all other lights grow dim in the momentary flash of lightning, and even the heavy, yellow flame of a candle casts a shadow on the ground.

"Yes," said Musya. "Yes, Werner."

"Yes," he replied. "Yes, Musya, yes!"

They had understood something and confirmed it forever. His eyes shining, Werner roused himself again and stepped quickly towards Sergei.

"Sergei!"

But it was Tanya Kovalchuk who answered. Delighted and almost weeping with maternal pride, she tugged furiously at Sergei's sleeve.

"Just listen, Werner! Here I am weeping for him and grieving over him, while he does gymnastics!"

"The Müller system?" asked Werner with a smile.

Embarrassed, Sergei frowned.

"You shouldn't laugh, Werner. I've finally convinced myself that..."

They all burst out laughing. Finding strength and fortitude in each other's company, they were gradually becoming their old selves, but they did not notice this either, thinking they were all still the same as before. Suddenly Werner stopped laughing and said with extreme seriousness:

"You're right, Sergei. You're perfectly right."

"No, you see," said Sergei gladly. "Of course, we..."

But just then they asked them to get into the carriages. They were so obliging that they let them take their seats in pairs as they wished. And in general they were very obliging, even inordinately so, trying either to display their humane consideration for the condemned, or to show that they were not in the least responsible for what was taking place and that it was all happening of its own accord. But they were pale.

"Musya, you go with him," said Werner, pointing to Vasily, who stood motionless.

"All right," Musya nodded. "But what about you?"

"Me? Tanya can go with Sergei and you can go with Vasya... I'll go by myself. It doesn't matter, I'll be all right, you know."

When they went out into the courtyard, the damp, warm darkness blew softly but strongly into their faces and eyes, and took their breath away, gently pervading their trembling bodies and swiftly cleansing them. It was hard to believe that this amazing thing was simply the spring wind, a damp, warm wind. This astonishing, real spring night smelt of melting snow as the sound of dripping water rang out in the boundless expanse of air. Briskly and busily, hard on each other's heels, the little drops fell rapidly and in concert, tapping out a ringing song; but suddenly one would get out of tune and all the rest would be caught in merry plashing and hurried confusion. Then a big drop would sound its firm, stern note, and the hasty spring song would ring out its melody once more. And over the city, above the roofs of the prison, hung a pale glow from the electric lights.

"Oh-ah!" Sergei Golovin heaved a deep sigh then held his breath, as if reluctant to let such fresh, beautiful air out of his lungs.

"Has the weather been like this long?" Werner asked. "It's very spring-like."

"Only since yesterday," came the obliging, courteous reply. "There's still a lot of frost about, though."

One after the other the dark carriages drove softly up, took two passengers each, and rolled away into the darkness to where a lantern swung beneath the gates. The gray shapes of the escort surrounded each carriage, and the shoes of their horses clinked on the stones and slipped on the wet snow.

As Werner was bending and about to get into the carriage, a guard said to him vaguely:

"There's somebody else in here who's going with you."

Werner was astonished.

"Going where? Where's he going? Oh, I see! Somebody else? But who is it?"

The guard said nothing. And indeed, in a corner of the carriage, in the darkness, crouched something small and motionless but alive—its open eye flashed in the slanting ray of light from the lantern. As he sat down, Werner nudged the man's knee with his leg.

"Sorry, friend."

The other did not reply. Only when the carriage began to move did he suddenly ask haltingly in broken Russian:

"Who are you?"

"My name is Werner, sentenced to be hanged for an attempt on the life of X. And you?"

"I'm Yanson. You mustn't hang me."

In two hours this journey would bring them face to face with that great, unsolved mystery, the passage from life to death—and still they were becoming acquainted. Life and death were moving in two different planes at the same time, yet to the very end, down to the most absurd and ludicrous trivialities, life was still life.

"What did you do, Yanson?"

"I killed my boss with a knife. And stole his money."

From the sound of his voice it seemed as if Yanson was falling asleep. Werner found his limp hand in the darkness and squeezed it. Just as limply Yanson took his hand away.

"Are you afraid?" asked Werner.

"I don't want to be hanged."

They fell silent. Werner found the Estonian's hand again and pressed it tightly between his own hot, dry palms. It lay there motionless, like a little piece of planking, but Yanson no longer tried to take it away.

It was cramped and stuffy in the carriage, and there was a smell of soldiers' greatcoats, mustiness, manure and wet leather boots. The young policeman sitting opposite Werner breathed hotly on him, his breath smelling of onions and cheap tobacco. But the keen, fresh air outside forced its way through chinks here and there in the sides of the carriage, and because of this, spring made itself felt even more strongly inside the stifling moving box than outside. The carriage kept turning first to the right, then to the left, and then seemed to go backwards; sometimes it felt as if they had been circling round and round for hours on the same spot. At first, bluish electric light penetrated the thick curtains drawn over the windows, then suddenly, after one turning, it grew dark, and from this alone they guessed that they had turned off down remote streets on the outskirts of the city and were nearing the S—sky station. Sometimes, when they turned sharply, Werner's bent knee bumped in a friendly way against the policeman's, and it was hard to believe that execution was imminent.

"Where are we going?" asked Yanson suddenly.

He was rather dizzy from the prolonged swinging motion of the dark, box-like carriage and felt slightly sick.

Werner told him, and gripped the Estonian's hand more tightly still. He felt like saying something particularly friendly and affectionate to this sleepy little man whom he already loved more than anyone else in the world.

"Dear friend! You seem uncomfortable sitting like that. Move up here close to me."

Yanson was silent for a moment then answered:

"No thanks. I'm all right. Will they hang you too?"

"Yes!" replied Werner with sudden gaiety, almost laughing, and waved his hand in a particularly free-and-easy, simple gesture. It was as if they were talking about an absurd, foolish trick that some dear but awfully silly people were wanting to play on them.

"Have you a wife?" asked Yanson.

"No, nothing of the kind! I'm single."

"So am I," said Yanson. "So am we," he said, correcting himself after thinking for a moment.

Werner was beginning to feel dizzy too. At times he felt as if they were on their way to some festive occasion. It was strange, but nearly all the others felt the same, and together with their anguish and terror they were filled with a vague sense of gladness at the extraordinary thing that was about to happen. Reality was intoxicated by madness, and coupling with life, death gave birth to apparitions. It was quite possible that flags were flying on the buildings.

"Here we are at last!" said Werner gaily when the carriage stopped, and he jumped lightly down. But with Yanson things took rather longer: silently and very limply somehow he resisted, not wanting to get out. He seized the door handle, and a policeman loosened his feeble fingers and pulled his hand away. Then he grabbed hold of a corner of the carriage, of the door or the high wheel, but with a slight effort on the policeman's part immediately let go. Without a word, he clung sleepily to things rather than clutched at them, and allowed himself to be pulled away easily and without effort. In the end he stood up.

There were no flags flying. As usual during the night, the station was dark, deserted and lifeless. Passenger trains were no longer running, and the train that was silently waiting on the track for these passengers needed neither bright lights nor noisy bustle. Suddenly Werner felt bored. Not afraid or depressed, but bored—an immense, slow, deadly boredom that makes one want to go away somewhere, lie down, and shut one's eyes tightly. He stretched and gave a long yawn. Yanson stretched too and yawned quickly several times in succession.

"If only they'd hurry up!" said Werner wearily.

Yanson said nothing and shivered.

As the condemned walked down the deserted platform cordoned off by soldiers and went towards the dimly lit carriages, Werner found himself next to Sergei Golovin. Pointing to something, Sergei began to speak, but only the word "lantern" was clearly audible, while the rest of the sentence was lost in a long, tired yawn.

"What did you say?" asked Werner, he too answering with a yawn.

"That lantern. Its lamp's smoking," said Sergei.

Werner looked around: it was true, the lamp was smoking badly, and the glass at the top was already black with soot.

"Yes, it's smoking."

And suddenly he thought: "But what does it matter to me if that lamp's smoking, when..." The same thought evidently occurred to Sergei too: he shot Werner a swift glance and turned away. But they both stopped yawning.

They all walked to the carriages of their own accord, except Yanson who had to be taken by the arm. At first he dug his heels in and it seemed as if the soles of his shoes were stuck to the planks of the platform. Then he bent his knees and hung on the policemen's arms, his feet dragging along the ground like those of a drunk and his toes scraping the platform. It took them a long time to push him through the carriage door, but they did it without saying a word.

Vasily Kashirin walked unaided, vaguely imitating the movements of his friends and doing everything as they did. But as he climbed the steps to the carriage platform he fell back and a policeman took him by the elbow to steady him. Vasily began to shake, and jerking his arm away, uttered a piercing cry:

"A-ah!"

"Vasya, what's the matter?" shouted Werner, rushing towards him.

Shaking violently, Vasily made no reply. Embarrassed and even upset, the policeman explained:

"I tried to hold him up, but he..."

"Come on, Vasya, I'll help you," said Werner, and tried to take him by the arm. But Vasily jerked his arm away again and shouted more loudly still:
"A-ah!"

"Vasya, it's me, Werner!"

"I know. Don't touch me. I'll go by myself."

And still shaking, he climbed into the carriage unaided and sat down in a corner. Bending forward and indicating Vasily with his eyes, Werner asked Musya softly:

"Well, how is he, do you think?"

"Bad," replied Musya just as softly. "He's dead already. Tell me, Werner, does death really exist?"

"I don't know, Musya, but I think not," replied Werner gravely and thoughtfully.

"That's what I thought. But what about him? I was so worried about him in the carriage, it was just like riding with a corpse."

"I don't know, Musya. Perhaps death does exist for some people. For the time being, that is, but later it won't exist at all. It used to exist for me, for instance, but now it doesn't."

Musya's rather pale cheeks flushed scarlet.

"Used to, Werner? Used to?"

"Yes. But now it doesn't. Just as it doesn't exist for you either."

There was a noise in the doorway of the carriage. Stamping his feet, breathing loudly and spitting, Mishka the Gypsy came in. He flung a glance around him and stopped short, acting in a deliberately obstinate way.

"There's no room here, mister policeman!" he shouted at the weary officer who was looking at him angrily. "You make it so there's space in here for me, or I'll not go, and you can hang me right here from that lamp. They gave me a carriage too, the sons of bitches, but d'you call that a carriage? The devil's guts, yes, but not a carriage!"

But then he suddenly bent his head, stretched out his neck, and walked forward towards the others. Framed by his dishevelled hair and beard, his black eyes were wild and piercing with a slightly mad look in them.

"Ah! Ladies and gentlemen!" he drawled. "So here we are! How do you do, sir?"

He thrust out his hand at Werner and sat down facing him. Leaning forward close to him, he winked and quickly ran his hand across his neck.

"You as well, eh?"

"Yes!" smiled Werner.

"But not all of you, surely?"

"Yes."

"Oho!" said the Gypsy, baring his teeth in a grin, and his eyes probed them all, his glance pausing for a moment on Musya and Yanson. And again he winked at Werner and said:

"Because of that Minister?"

"Yes. And what about you?"

"I'm here, sir, for something different. What do we want with a Minister, eh? I'm a thief, sir, that's what I am. A killer. It's all right, sir, you can make room for me, it's not my fault they've shoved me in here with you folks. There's plenty of room for everybody in the next world."

Looking out wildly from under his tousled hair, he swept them all with a single swift, mistrustful glance. Without saying a word they all looked at him seriously and even with apparent concern. The Gypsy grinned and quickly slapped Werner several times on the knee.

"So that's how it is, sir! Just like the song goes: 'Rustle not, mother forest, with your green oak leaves.'"

"Why do you call me 'sir,' when we're all..."

"True," agreed the Gypsy with satisfaction. "What kind of sir can you be if you'll be hanging next to me? Now him, there's a sir," he said, pointing to the silent policeman. "But that one of yours over yonder, he's no better than us," he added, indicating Vasily with his eyes. "Sir, hey sir! Are you afraid, eh?"

"I'm all right," replied Vasily, his tongue moving only with difficulty.

"What do you mean, 'all right'? You're nothing of the kind! Don't be ashamed, there's nothing to be ashamed of! It's only a dog that wags its tail and grins when it's being taken off to be hanged, but you're a man, aren't you? And who's that there, the lop-eared one? He's not one of your lot, is he?"

His eyes skipped quickly over them all, and with a hissing sound he kept spitting out the sweet saliva that filled his mouth. Crouching motionless in the corner like a small bundle, Yanson moved the flaps of his shabby fur cap slightly but made no reply. Werner answered for him:

"He killed his boss."

"Good Lord!" said the Gypsy in surprise. "How can they let folks like him go around killing people?"

For a long time now, out of the corner of his eye, the Gypsy had been scrutinizing Musya. Turning quickly, he suddenly stared straight at her.

"Miss, hey, miss! What are you doing here, eh? She's got little pink cheeks and she's laughing! Look, can't you see her laughing?" he said, grasping Werner by the knee with strong fingers that seemed made of iron. "Look, look!"

Blushing and smiling with slight embarrassment, Musya returned the Gypsy's direct gaze, looking into his piercing, rather mad eyes that were so full of wild, grave inquiry.

No one said a word.

The wheels clattered with their staccato, businesslike rhythm as the little carriages jolted along the narrow track and ran diligently onwards. On a curve or near a level crossing the little engine gave a thin, painstaking whistle, as if the driver was afraid of knocking someone down. It was ridiculous to think that so much ordinary human conscientiousness, so much effort and care was being applied in taking people to be hanged, and that the most senseless act on earth was being carried out in such a simple, reasonable way. The carriages ran onwards, and in them people sat as they usually sit, traveling as people usually travel. Later there would be a stop as usual—"the train stops for five minutes here."

Then would come death, eternity, the great mystery.

XII
They Are Brought

The little carriages ran diligently onwards.

For several years Sergei Golovin had lived with his parents in the country near this same railway line. He had often traveled this way both in the daytime and at night, and knew the line well. If he closed his eyes, he could imagine he was going home this time too—he had stayed late with friends in town and was coming back by the last train.

"It won't be long now," he said, opening his eyes and glancing out of the dark, barred window that revealed nothing.

No one moved, no one replied, and only the Gypsy quickly spat out his sweet saliva over and over again. His eyes began to wander over the carriage, probing the windows, the doors, and the guards themselves.

"It's cold," said Vasily Kashirin with stiff lips that seemed and really were almost frozen, and the word "cold" sounded like "co-a-d."

Tanya Kovalchuk began to fuss about.

"Here, take this shawl and tie it around your neck. It's very warm."

"Round my neck?" asked Sergei suddenly and took fright at his own question.

But as all the others were thinking the same, no one heard what he said. It was as if no one had said a thing or as if they had all said the same thing together.

"Never mind, Vasya, put it on, put it on, and you'll feel warmer," Werner advised him, then turned to Yanson and asked affectionately:

"Dear friend, aren't you cold?"

"Werner, perhaps he'd like a smoke. Would you like a smoke, my friend?" asked Musya. "We've got some cigarettes."

"Yes!"

"Give him a cigarette, Sergei," said Werner, overjoyed.

But Sergei was already taking out a cigarette, and they all watched lovingly as Yanson's fingers took it. They went on watching as the match burned and a puff of blue smoke rose from Yanson's mouth.

"Thanks," said Yanson. "That's good."

"How strange!" said Sergei.

"What's strange?" asked Werner, turning around. "What's strange?"

"Well this—a cigarette."

He held the cigarette, an ordinary cigarette, in his ordinary, living fingers, and with a pale face looked at it in amazement and even, it seemed, in horror. They all stared at the slender little tube with the smoke rising from its tip in a curling blue ribbon that was swept aside by their breath, while the ash grew dark as it lengthened. The cigarette went out.

"It's gone out," said Tanya.

"Yes, it's gone out."

"Oh, what a nuisance!" said Werner, frowning and looking anxiously at Yanson, whose hand with the cigarette in it hung down like a dead man's. Suddenly the Gypsy turned quickly, and bending his face close to Werner's and showing the whites of his eyes like a horse, whispered:

"Sir, what if we...the escort...eh? Shall we have a go?"

"You mustn't," replied Werner, his voice a whisper too. "Drain your cup to the dregs."

"What for? It's a lot more fun dying in a scrap, isn't it? I give him one, then he gives me one, and you don't even notice they've finished you off. Just like you've not croaked at all!"

"No, you mustn't," said Werner, and turning to Yanson, asked: "Dear friend, why aren't you smoking?"

All of a sudden Yanson's flabby face crumpled pitifully: it was as if someone had suddenly jerked a string that set the wrinkles on his face in motion, and they had all become distorted. As if in his sleep he began to whisper in a dry, tearless, almost affected voice:

"I don't want to smoke. Ah-ha! Ah-ha! Ah-ha! You mustn't hang me. Ah-ha, ah-ha, ah-ha, ah-ha!"

They began to fuss around him. Weeping copiously, Tanya Kovalchuk stroked his sleeve and straightened the dangling flaps on his shabby cap:

"My little one! Don't cry, my dear one! My poor little one!"

Musya looked away. The Gypsy caught her eye and grinned.

"His Honor's a queer fish! He drinks hot tea but his belly stays cold," he said with a short laugh. But his own face had turned bluish-black, the color of cast iron, and his big, yellow teeth were chattering.

Suddenly the carriages gave a jolt and slackened speed noticeably. Everyone except Yanson and Kashirin stood up, then just as quickly sat down again.

"It's the station!" said Sergei.

It became so hard to breathe that it seemed as if all the air had been suddenly pumped out of the carriage. Their swollen hearts burst from their breasts, rising into their throats and pounding madly, crying out in terror as they choked with blood. Their eyes looked down at the quivering floor, while their ears listened as the wheels turned more and more slowly, slipped, turned again, then suddenly stopped.

The train had come to a halt.

What followed was a dream. It was not that it was very frightening: it was illusory, delirious and alien somehow, for the dreamer himself remained elsewhere, and only his ghost moved immaterially, spoke soundlessly, and suffered without pain. In the dream they got out of the carriage, divided into pairs, and smelled the unusually fresh spring air of the forest. In the dream Yanson put up a feeble, pointless resistance and was dragged from the carriage without a word.

They came down the steps.

"Do we really have to go on foot?" asked someone almost gaily.

"It's not far," replied someone else just as gaily.

Then in a big, dark, silent crowd they walked through the forest along a rough spring track that was soft and wet. From the forest and snow came waves of cool, pungent air; their feet slipped, sometimes sinking into the snow, and their hands clutched involuntarily at their friends; breathing loudly, the escort walked beside them, struggling over the fresh snow. Someone's voice said angrily:

"They might have cleared the path! You could go head over heels in the snow here!"

Someone else explained apologetically:

"They have cleared it, your Honor. It's just the thaw that's the trouble, it can't be helped."

Consciousness was returning, but only incompletely, in snatches and strange fragments. First, in a businesslike way, the mind suddenly acknowledged the fact:

"No, it's true, they couldn't really clear the path."

Then everything went dim once more and only the sense of smell was left, bringing them the unbearably strong odor of air, forest and melting snow; and then everything became extraordinarily clear—the forest, the night, the track, and the fact that very soon, in just a moment, they would be hanged. Snatches of restrained, whispered conversation could be heard:

"It's nearly four."

"I told you we set off too early."

"It gets light at five."

"Yes, that's right. We should have..."

They stopped in the darkness in a small clearing. Some distance away, through the thin trees with their bare winter branches, two small lanterns were silently moving. That was where the gallows were.

"I've lost one of my galoshes," said Sergei Golovin.

"What?" asked Werner, not understanding what Sergei had said.

"I've lost one of my galoshes. I'm cold."

"Where's Vasily?"

"I don't know. Oh, there he is, standing over there."

Vasily stood somber and motionless.

84

"Where's Musya?"

"I'm here. Is that you, Werner?"

They began to look around, trying not to look towards where the small lanterns went on silently moving with terrible meaning. To the left the bare trees seemed to thin out, and something big, white and flat showed through them. From the same direction there came a damp wind.

"It's the sea," said Sergei Golovin, sniffing and filling his mouth with air. "That's the sea."

Musya replied in a sonorous voice:

" 'My love, wide as the sea!' "

"What did you say, Musya?"

" 'The shores of life cannot contain my love, wide as the sea.' "

" 'My love, wide as the sea,' " repeated Sergei pensively, surrendering to the sound of her voice and the words of the song.

" 'My love, wide as the sea,' " echoed Werner, and suddenly said in gay surprise: "Little Musya! How young you still are!"

All of a sudden, close by his ear, Werner heard the Gypsy's hot, breathless whisper:

"Sir, hey, sir! Is this a forest, then? My God, what is all this? And what's that over yonder where those lanterns are? Is it a gallows, then? What is all this, eh? What is it then, eh?"

Werner looked at him: the Gypsy was filled with mortal agony.

"We must say goodbye..." said Tanya Kovalchuk.

"Wait a moment, they've still got to read out the sentence," replied Werner. "But where's Yanson?"

Yanson was lying in the snow and people were busy with something beside him. Suddenly there came the acrid smell of liquid ammonia.

"What's going on there, doctor? Will you be long?" asked someone impatiently.

"It's all right, he's only fainted. Rub his ears with snow. He's already coming around, so you can read the sentence."

The light of a shaded lantern fell on a sheet of paper and white, ungloved hands. Both paper and hands were trembling slightly, and so was the voice:

"Ladies and gentlemen, do I need to read out the sentence? You all know what it is, don't you? What do you think?"

"There's no need to read it," said Werner, answering for them all, and the lantern quickly went out.

They all declined the services of the priest too. The broad, dark silhouette moved swiftly and silently away into the depths of the forest and disappeared. Dawn was evidently approaching: the snow had turned white, the shapes of people had grown dark, and the forest had become thinner, sadder and more ordinary.

"Ladies and gentlemen, you must go forward in twos. You may choose

85

your own partners, but do please hurry."

Werner pointed to Yanson, who was already on his feet, supported by two policemen.

"I'll go with him. Sergei, you take Vasily and go first."

"All right."

"Shall we go together, Musya?" asked Tanya Kovalchuk. "Well, let's kiss then."

They all quickly kissed one another. The Gypsy kissed so hard that they could feel his teeth; Yanson kissed softly and limply with his mouth half open, but he seemed not even to understand what he was doing. When Golovin and Kashirin had already moved a few steps away, Kashirin suddenly stopped and said loudly and clearly but in a voice that was completely unfamiliar and quite unlike his normal one:

"Goodbye, friends!"

"Goodbye, friend!" they shouted to him.

They went away. It grew quiet. The lanterns beyond the trees became still. Those waiting expected to hear a shriek, the sound of a voice, a noise of some kind—but it was as quiet beyond the trees as it was in the clearing, and the lanterns shone yellow and motionless.

"Oh, my God!" cried someone in a strange, hoarse voice. They looked around: it was the Gypsy suffering in his mortal agony. "They're hanging 'em!"

They turned away, and it grew quiet once more. The Gypsy clutched at the air and cried:

"What's all this, ladies and gentlemen, eh? Have I got to go by myself, then? It's more fun with a bit of company! Ladies and gentlemen! What's all this?"

He seized Werner by the arm with fingers that tightened then relaxed their grip almost playfully, and asked:

"Sir, dear friend, won't you go with me, eh? Do us a favor, don't say no!"

Filled with pain, Werner replied:

"I can't, my friend, I'm going with him."

"Oh, my God! So I've got to go by myself, then! How can that be? My God!"

Musya stepped forward and said softly:

"Come with me!"

The Gypsy started back, and rolling the whites of his eyes wildly at her, said:

"With you?"

"Yes."

"Just look at you! You're so little! Aren't you afraid? No, it'd be better if I went by myself. What a thought!"

"No, I'm not afraid."

86

The Gypsy bared his teeth in a grin.

"Just look at you! But I'm a thief, you know! Don't you mind? No, it'd be better if you didn't. I won't be angry with you."

Musya was silent, and in the faint light of dawn her face looked pale and mysterious. Then she suddenly went quickly up to the Gypsy and flinging her arms around his neck, kissed him firmly on the lips. He took her by the shoulders, held her away from him, shook her, and then with a loud, smacking sound kissed her on the lips, nose and eyes.

"Let's go!"

All of a sudden the soldier nearest them swayed and unclasped his hands, letting go of his gun. But he did not bend down to pick it up. Instead he stood motionless for a moment, then turned sharply and like a blind man walked away into the forest over the untrodden snow.

"Where are you off to?" whispered his companion in alarm. "Stop!"

But the other went on struggling through the deep snow just as silently as before. He must have stumbled against something, because he threw up his arms and fell flat on his face. And he remained lying on the ground.

"Pick up your gun, you miserable devil! Or I'll pick it up for you!" said the Gypsy threateningly. "You don't know your job!"

The lanterns began to move about busily again. It was Werner's and Yanson's turn.

"Goodbye, sir!" said the Gypsy loudly. "We'll meet again in the next world, so if you see me, don't turn away. And bring me a drop of vodka sometime—it'll be a bit hot for me there!"

"Goodbye."

"I don't want to be hanged," said Yanson limply.

But Werner took him by the arm, and the Estonian walked a few steps by himself. Then they saw him stop and fall into the snow. People bent over him, lifted him up, and carried him along, while he struggled feebly in their arms. Why did he not cry out? He had probably forgotten he had a voice.

Again the yellow lanterns became still.

"I'll go by myself, then, Musya," said Tanya Kovalchuk sadly. "We've lived together, and now..."

"Little Tanya, my dear one..."

But the Gypsy intervened passionately. Holding Musya by the hand as if afraid she might still be taken away, he said in a rapid, businesslike way:

"Oh, miss! You can go by yourself, you're a pure soul, you can go wherever you like by yourself! Don't you see? But I can't. A thief like me...do you understand? I can't go by myself. Where are you off to, they'd say, you murderer? I used to steal horses too, you know, I swear it! But with her it'll be like ...like being with a little child, you see. D'you understand?"

"Yes. All right then, off you go. Let me kiss you once more, Musya."

"Kiss, kiss," said the Gypsy encouragingly. "With this business you've got to say goodbye properly."

Musya and the Gypsy went forward. The woman trod carefully, slipping occasionally and holding up her skirts out of habit. Supporting her firmly by the arm, telling her to take care, and feeling for the path with his feet, the man led her to her death.

The lanterns became still. Around Tanya Kovalchuk all was quiet and empty. Gray in the pale, soft light of the new day, the soldiers were silent.

"There's only me left," said Tanya suddenly and sighed. "Sergei's dead, Werner and Vasya too. There's only me left. Soldiers, dear soldiers, there's only me left. Only me..."

The sun was rising over the sea.

They laid the corpses in boxes. Then they took them away. With necks stretched out, eyes staring wildly, and swollen blue tongues protruding like terrible, strange flowers from lips flecked with bloody foam, the bodies were carried back down the same track along which they had come when alive. The spring snow was just as soft and fragrant, and the spring air just as fresh and keen as before. And the wet, worn galosh that Sergei had lost showed up black against the snow.

So it was that men greeted the rising sun.

1908

Ivan Bunin in the early 1900s.

IVAN BUNIN (1870-1953)

Bunin was born into an impoverished noble family in the Central Russian town of Voronezh. His childhood and youth were spent on the family estate in Oryol Province and in the district town of Yelets, where he had four years' schooling—the sum total of his formal education. Leaving home in 1889, he took a succession of jobs, among them that of assistant editor for a paper in Oryol, then traveled widely in southern and western Russia. After visiting Moscow and Petersburg for the first time in 1895, he took up writing as his career, rapidly becoming one of the foremost authors of the day.

In 1900 Bunin visited Austria, Germany and Switzerland. In 1903 he was awarded the Pushkin Prize for literature by the Russian Academy, a distinction that was to be followed six years later by his election to honorary membership of the same body. In 1906 he met his second wife (his first marriage, in 1898, had ended in separation) and the following year they left together for Palestine. For the next decade Bunin traveled widely—to the Near and Far East, North Africa, Turkey, Greece, France and Italy, where he visited Gorky on Capri.

The outbreak of World War I found him back in Russia, and in 1917 he adopted a resolutely anti-Bolshevik position. In 1918 he left Moscow for the south, where he worked briefly for a local paper in Odessa, before sailing for Constantinople in January 1920. After spending time in Sofia, Belgrade and Prague, he finally settled in Grasse, near Cannes, where he became one of the principal figures in the Russian literary emigration. In 1933 he was awarded the Nobel Prize for literature—the first Russian ever to win that honor. During World War II Bunin remained in Grasse and endured considerable hardship under the Nazi occupation. In the late 1940s his health began to deteriorate, and from 1951 onwards he was virtually bedridden, though he went on writing until shortly before his death.

Bunin first won recognition as a lyric poet (his first poem was published in 1887) and as an excellent translator, notably of Longfellow's "The Song of Hiawatha" (1896). Later he was also to translate Musset, Leconte de Lisle, Mickiewicz and Shevchenko. 1894 saw the publication of his first tale, and 1897 the appearance of his first collection of stories, *To the World's End*, in which he wrote of the ruin of small landowners and the suffering of peasants. The longer prose works which followed brought him fame: *The Village* (1910) and *Dry Valley* (1911), both of which show the barbarity and poverty of Russian rural life. The next five years saw a succession of brilliant short stories, among them "The Brethren" (1914), "A Grammar of Love" and "The Gentleman from San Francisco" (1915), "Light Breathing" and "The Dreams of Chang" (1916).

Contrary to the general rule, the quality of Bunin's work did not deteriorate once he was in voluntary exile. His thirty years in France saw the publication of prose works perhaps even finer than those of his prerevolutionary period, among them "The Consuming Fire" (1923), "The Rose of Jericho" (1924), "Mitya's Love" (1925), "Sunstroke" (1927), and the short, largely autobiographical novel *The Life of Arsenev* (1938). Many of Bunin's later works are tinged with nostalgia for the past and sadness at the onset of old age—"Dark Avenues" (1938), "Mistral" (1944), and his last story, "Bernard" (1952), in which he looks back on his achievement as a writer.

I

...I remember a fine, early autumn. August was a month of warm showers that seemed to fall specially for the sowing—showers just at the right
time, in the middle of the month, around St. Lawrence's Day. The saying is
that "autumn and winter are kind if the water's calm and there's rain on St.
Lawrence's Day." Then came an Indian summer when gossamer settled abundantly on the fields. That's a good sign too: "A lot of webs in late summer
means a good autumn," they say... I remember a cool, still, early morning... I
remember a big, golden orchard with dry, thinning trees, I remember avenues
lined with maples, the delicate fragrance of fallen leaves and—the smell of
Antonov apples, the scent of honey, the odor of a cool autumn. The air is so
pure it hardly seems to be there at all, and the whole orchard rings with the
sound of voices and the squeaking of carts. It is the traveling peddlers, the
market gardeners, who with the help of hired peasants are piling the apples in
heaps before sending them off to town that same night—at night it has to be,
when it is so glorious to lie in the cart gazing up into the starry sky, smell the
odor of tar in the cool air, and listen to the long line of carts squeaking cautiously along the high road in the darkness. A peasant loading apples eats
them one after another with a succulent crunch, but such is the custom here
that the master does not stop him, saying instead:

"Go on, eat your fill! What can I do? Everybody drinks mead on barrel-
ling day!"

And all that disturbs the cool stillness of morning is the replete chirp-
ing of thrushes in the coral-red rowan trees in the thicket, the sound of
voices, and the hollow thudding of apples being poured into measures and
tubs. In the distance, through the thinning trees, can be seen the straw-strewn
track leading to a large hut, and the hut itself around which the traders have
set up house for the summer. The smell of apples is strong everywhere, but
particularly here. Inside the hut are beds, a single-barrelled gun, a samovar
green with age, and some crockery in the corner. Scattered around outside
lie bast mats, boxes, and all kinds of tattered belongings, while nearby a pit
has been dug in the ground for the fire. At midday a magnificent bacon stew
is cooked there, while in the evening the samovar is heated, and a long stream
of bluish smoke spreads through the orchard among the trees. But on feast-
days there is a regular fair around the hut, and red Sunday finery can be seen
continually flitting through the trees. There is a crowd of peasant girls, bold
wenches wearing sarafans that smell strongly of paint; the gentry's servants
come in their rough, strangely beautiful clothes; and the village elder's wife is

there too, young and pregnant with a broad, sleepy face and the sedate look of a Kholmogory cow. She wears a headdress called "antlers"—her hair is parted down the middle and plaited at each side, and the plaits are covered with several kerchiefs, making her head look enormous. Her feet in their calf-length, hobnailed boots are planted firmly and stolidly on the ground. Her sleeveless jacket is of velveteen and her apron very long, while her homespun skirt is a deep violet with brick-red stripes and wide gold braid along the hem...

"A fine girl!" says one of the traders, shaking his head. "There's not many like her about these days..."

Little boys in white twill shirts and short trousers, their hair bleached white by the sun, keep coming up to the hut. They come in twos and threes, tripping along on their little bare feet and looking askance at the shaggy sheepdog tied to an apple tree. One of them buys something, of course, because the things for sale only cost an egg or a kopek, but there are plenty of other customers too so business is brisk, and the consumptive trader in the long frockcoat and russet boots is in good spirits. Together with his brother, a merry halfwit with a guttural voice whom he keeps out of charity, he deals in little jokes and humorous sayings, and sometimes even picks out a tune on his Tula accordion. And till late in the evening there is a crowd of people in the orchard. Near the hut can be heard the sound of voices and laughter, and sometimes the thud of dancing feet too...

In fine weather it gets very cold towards nightfall and there is a heavy dew. After breathing your fill of the rye-like scent of fresh straw and chaff on the threshing-floor, you walk briskly home to supper past the earthen wall surrounding the orchard. The sound of voices in the village or the creaking of a gate are extraordinarily clear in the chill sunset. It grows dark. And then there is another smell: a campfire has been lit in the orchard and the fragrant smoke of burning cherry branches comes drifting towards you. In the darkness, in the depths of the orchard, you see something resembling a scene from a fairy tale: as though in a corner of hell, a crimson flame ringed with gloom blazes near the hut, and dark silhouettes that seem carved of ebony flit around the fire, while their giant shadows walk among the apple trees. First a black arm several feet long falls across the whole of a tree, then two legs are clearly seen that look like black pillars. Then suddenly, all this slips down from the tree, and one long shadow falls on the whole avenue, from the hut as far as the wicket-gate itself...

Late at night, when the lights go out in the village and the brilliant stars of the Great Bear already glitter high in the sky, you run into the orchard once more. With the dry leaves rustling underfoot, you grope your way blindly to the hut. There in the clearing it is a little brighter, and the Milky Way shines white above your head.

"Is that you, young master?" someone calls softly from the darkness.

"Yes. Aren't you asleep yet, Nikolai?"

94

"We can't sleep, sir. It's late, isn't it? Sounds like the train's coming over yonder..."

We listen carefully for a long time, then feel the ground trembling slightly. The trembling becomes a noise, grows louder, and then, just beyond the orchard wall, it seems, the wheels beat out their rapid rhythm. Rattling and rumbling, the train comes rushing on...closer and closer, growing more and more loud and angry... And then suddenly the sound begins to die away, becoming muffled as though disappearing into the earth...

"Where's your gun, Nikolai?"

"Over there, beside that box, sir."

You shoulder the single-barrelled gun that is as heavy as a crowbar, and fire at random. With a deafening crash a crimson spurt of flame flashes into the sky, dazzling you for a moment and extinguishing the stars, while the cheerful echo roars out and rolls away to the horizon, dying away in the pure, keen air in the far, far distance.

"Uh! Well done!" says the trader. "Give 'em a scare, young master, give 'em a scare! What trouble they're givin' us! They've shook down all the pears by the wall again..."

Shooting stars streak the black sky with their fiery trails. You gaze so long into the sky's dark blue depths brimming with constellations that the earth begins to spin beneath your feet. Then you rouse yourself, and thrusting your hands into the sleeves of your jacket, run quickly down the avenue towards the house... How cold it is, how heavy the dew is, and how good it is to be alive on this earth!

II

"Juicy apples mean a good year to come," they say. All's well in the village if there's a good crop of Antonov apples, because it means there'll be a good crop of wheat too... I remember a year when the harvest was very good.

At the crack of dawn, when the cocks are still crowing and black smoke rises from the peasants' huts, you throw open the window onto the cool orchard cloaked in lilac mist with the morning sun shining brightly through it, and cannot resist the temptation: you order your horse to be saddled while you run down to wash in the pond. The willows on the bank have lost nearly all their small leaves, and the turquoise sky shows through their bare branches. The water beneath them has become limpid, icy and heavy somehow, and it dispels your drowsiness in the twinkling of an eye. Having washed then eaten breakfast with the farmhands in the servants' room—a breakfast of hot potatoes and black bread sprinkled with damp, coarse salt—you delight in the feel of the smooth leather saddle beneath you as you ride through the village of Vyselki on your way out hunting. Autumn is the season of patron saints' days, and at this time of year the people are smart and contented, and the village itself looks altogether different. If there has been a good harvest and castles of golden wheat tower above the threshing floors, if the geese cackle shrilly and clearly on the river in the mornings, then life in the village is not bad at all. Besides, Vyselki has been renowned as a prosperous village as long as anyone can remember, ever since grandfather's day. Vyselki people always lived to a ripe old age—the first sign that a village is prosperous—and they were all tall with large frames and hair as white as snow. You were always hearing someone say: "Yes, Agafya there's eighty-three if she's a day!" Or conversations like this:

"And when are you going to die, Pankraty? You must be nearly a hundred by now, aren't you?"

"What's that you say, sir?"

"I'm asking how old you are!"

"But I don't know, sir."

"Well, d'you remember Platon Apollonich?"

"Of course I do, sir, I remember him clearly."

"You see now! That means you can't possibly be less than a hundred."

Standing erect before his master, the old man smiles a meek, guilty smile. Well what can he do, he says, he's sorry, he's lived too long. And he would probably have lived longer still had he not eaten too many onions on St. Peter's Day.

I remember his wife too. The old woman would always be sitting on a bench on her porch with her back bent and her head shaking, panting breathlessly and clutching the seat—and thinking about something the whole time. "About her wealth, most likely," the village women used to say, because she had, it was true, a great deal of wealth in her trunks. But she seemed not to hear them. With feeble eyes she gazed sadly into the distance from under her raised eyebrows, shook her head, and tried to remember something. She was a big woman, and everything about her was somber somehow. Her homespun skirt looked as if it was a hundred years old and her rope shoes were the kind they put on the dead, while her neck was yellow and withered, and her blouse with its dimity lapels was always as white as snow—"good enough to bury her in," people said. Near the porch lay a large stone slab: she had bought it herself for a gravestone, as she had bought her shroud too—a splendid shroud with angels and crosses on it and a prayer printed round the edges.

The houses in Vyselki were in keeping with the old folk too: they were of brick and had been built by their forefathers. But the rich peasants—Savely, Ignat and Dron—had big cottages built of double or triple lengths of timber, because in those days in Vyselki it was not yet fashionable to divide property up. Families like these kept bees, prided themselves on their iron-gray carthorses, and maintained their farmsteads in good order. Beyond their threshing floors stretched dark fields of thick, lush hemp, while the drying

96

and threshing barns nearby were all neatly thatched. The small granaries and lofts had iron doors on them guarding rolls of canvas, spinning wheels, new sheepskins, decorative harness, and grain measures bound with copper hoops. Their gates and sledges had crosses burned into the wood. And I remember there were times when I thought it must be extraordinarily fascinating to be a peasant. As I rode through the village on a sunny morning, I kept thinking how good it must be to mow, thresh, sleep on the threshing floor among the stacks of straw, and on holidays rise with the sun to the deep, melodious sound of church bells pealing from the village, wash at the water barrel, and put on a clean, twill shirt and trousers and a pair of indestructible hobnailed boots. And if, I imagined, on top of all this you had a robust, beautiful wife dressed in festive clothes, and a drive to church for mass followed by dinner at your bearded father-in-law's—a dinner of hot mutton served on wooden platters with fine white loaves, honey on the comb, and home-brewed beer—then you could not wish for more!

Until very recently—and even I can remember this—the kind of life led by most of the rural gentry had much in common with that of wealthy peasants in its thriftiness and old-world, rustic prosperity. Such was the estate of aunt Anna Gerasimovna, for example, which was about twelve versts from Vyselki. By the time you got there, it would be completely light. With the dogs on the leash you had to ride at a walking pace, but you did not feel like hurrying anyway, as it was so grand to be out in the open fields on such a cool, sunny morning. The terrain is flat and you can see far into the distance, while the sky is so light, so boundlessly wide and deep! The brilliant sun casts its slanting rays on the fields, and the road, rolled smooth by carts after the rains, is greasy and shines like steel rails. Around you fresh, luxuriantly green winter crops spread their broad carpet far and wide. A young hawk soars in the clear air and hangs poised high above, its little, pointed wings fluttering. Clearly visible, the telegraph poles go running away into the bright distance, and their wires glide like silver strings over the curve of the clear sky. Merlins sit perched on them, looking just like black notes on a sheet of music.

I have neither known nor seen serfdom, but I remember sensing it at aunt Anna Gerasimovna's. The moment you rode into her yard you felt that here it was still completely in force. The estate was not large but it was all old and strongly built, surrounded by hundred year-old birches and willows. Though low-roofed, the many outbuildings were designed in a convenient way, and they all seemed cast in the same mold, with dark oak logs and thatched roofs. Only the smoke-blackened servants' hall stood out because of its size or rather its length, and from it peered those last Mohicans of the house serfs—some decrepit old men and women and a senile, retired cook who looked like Don Quixote. As you ride into the yard, they all draw themselves up and make a very low bow. The gray-haired coachman on his way from the coach house to take your horse, doffs his cap even at the coach house door and walks right across the yard with his head bared.

He used to be aunt Anna's postilion, but now he drives her to church—in a closed sleigh in winter, and a little cart in summer, a sturdy, iron-bound cart of the kind priests use. Aunt Anna's garden was famous for its neglected state, its nightingales, its turtle-doves, and its apples, while her house was renowned for its roof. It stood at the head of the courtyard right beside the garden with the branches of the lime trees surrounding it. Though it was small and squat, it seemed as if it would last forever, so solid did it look beneath its unusually steep, thick thatch blackened and hardened by time. Its facade always seemed to be alive to me: it was as if an old face beneath a huge hat were peering out with deepset eyes—those windows with panes iridescent like mother-of-pearl in sun and rain. And on each side of those eyes were porches, two big old porches with columns. Replete pigeons were always sitting on their pediment, while thousands of sparrows poured like rain from one roof to the next... And how comfortable the guest felt in this nest under the turquoise autumn sky!

You go into the house and first of all you notice the smell of apples, but then you catch other smells too, of old mahogany furniture and dried lime blossom that has been lying on the windowsills since June... All the rooms—the hall, drawing room, and footmen's quarters—are cool and twilit, because the house is surrounded by trees and the upper windowpanes are of colored glass—dark blue and lilac. All is quiet and clean, though I do not believe that the armchairs, inlaid tables, or mirrors in their fluted, narrow gilt frames have ever been moved from their places. Then you hear a slight cough and aunt Anna comes in. She is not a big woman, but like everything around her, she is sturdy. A large Persian shawl is draped over her shoulders. She enters the room in an imposing but welcoming way, and immediately, while she talks endlessly of inheritances and the good old days, the little delicacies begin to appear: first pears and apples of four kinds—Antonov, Belle Dame, Borovinka winter apples, and the Abundant variety—to be followed by a wonderful dinner of pink boiled ham with peas, stuffed chicken, turkey, pickles, and red kvass that is strong and very, very sweet... The windows are open on to the garden, and through them comes the cool, bracing breath of autumn...

III

In recent years the only thing that has sustained the failing spirits of the gentry has been hunting.

In the old days estates like aunt Anna Gerasimovna's were no rarity. There were also those that were going to rack and ruin but whose owners still lived in style, maintaining vast properties and fifty-acre orchards. Some of these estates have survived to the present day, it's true, but all the life has gone out of them... There are no troikas, no Kirghiz horses, no hounds, no borzois, no servants, not even any owners left now—hunting landowners like my late brother-in-law, Arseny Semyonich.

From the end of September our orchards and threshing floors were deserted and the weather usually showed a sudden change. For days on end the wind blustered and tore at the trees, and the rain drenched them from morning till night. Towards evening sometimes the tremulous, golden light of the setting sun broke through the gloomy, low clouds in the west. The air grew pure and clear and the sunlight flashed blindingly through the leaves and branches as they stirred in the wind, moving like living tracery against the sky. The watery, blue sky gleamed bright and cold above the heavy, leaden clouds to the north, while behind them other clouds like snow-capped mountain ranges rose slowly into view. You would stand by the window and think: "Perhaps it'll clear up." But the wind would not die down. It worried the orchard, tore incessantly at the stream of smoke rising from the chimney above the servants' hall, and heaped up ominous, tangled masses of ash-gray clouds once more. Racing by close to the earth, they soon enveloped the sun, obscuring it like smoke. Its brilliance faded and died, and the little patch of blue sky was gone, while the orchard became bleak and desolate and the rain began to shower the earth once more...softly and cautiously at first, then more and more heavily, finally becoming a downpour with stormy winds and darkness. Night would fall, long and troubled...

After a drubbing like this the orchard emerged almost completely bare, hushed, submissive, and strewn with wet leaves. But then how beautiful it looked when fine weather set in again with the cold, clear days of early October—autumn's crowning glory! The leaves left on the trees will stay there now till the first frosts. The black orchard will show up against the cold turquoise sky and wait obediently for winter, warming itself in the brilliant sunshine. But the fields are already dark black where they are freshly ploughed and bright green where the winter crops are sprouting... It's time to go hunting!

And now I see myself on Arseny Semyonich's estate, in a room in the big house filled with sunlight and smoke from pipes and cigarettes. There are many people there, all of them sunburnt with weatherbeaten faces and wearing tight-fitting coats and long boots. They have just eaten a hearty dinner and are flushed and excited by all the noisy talk about the forthcoming hunt, and even though the meal is over they do not forget to finish off their vodka. Outside in the yard a hunting horn blares and the dogs begin to howl in their various voices. A black borzoi, Arseny Semyonich's favorite, climbs on the table, and starts gobbling up from the dish the remains of the hare in gravy. But coming out of his study with his hunting crop and revolver, Arseny Semyonich suddenly fires an ear-splitting shot, and with a terrible yelp the dog leaps off the table, knocking over plates and wineglasses. The room becomes fuller still of smoke, but Arseny Semyonich just stands there laughing.

"A pity I missed!" he says, his eyes flashing.

He is tall and lean but broad-shouldered and well built, with the face of a handsome gypsy. There is a wild gleam in his eyes, and he looks very dashing in his crimson silk shirt, wide velvet trousers, and long boots. Having alarmed both dog and guests with his shot, he declaims with comic solemnity in a baritone:

'Tis time, 'tis time, to saddle my mettlesome Cossack steed
And sling the clear-voiced horn over my shoulder!

Then he says loudly:
"Well, there's no point in wasting precious time!"
I remember to this day how avidly and deeply my young lungs drank in the cold air of a damp, clear afternoon, when as evening drew on I rode with Arseny Semyonich's noisy band, thrilling to the melodious hubbub of the dogs in the deciduous woods somewhere near Red Knoll or Thundering Island, whose names alone are enough to excite the huntsman. I used to ride a vicious, stocky, powerful Kirghiz horse, and as I reined him in hard I almost felt that he and I were one. Eager to break into a gallop, he snorted, his hooves rustling loudly through the light, deep carpet of dark, fallen leaves, while every sound echoed hollowly in the emptiness of the damp, cool forest. Somewhere in the distance a dog bayed and another answered it with a passionate, plaintive cry, then a third gave tongue—and suddenly the whole forest was filled with the thunderous noise of furious barking and shouting, resounding as if it were all made of glass. A loud shot rang out amidst the uproar—and the chase was on, and everything went whirling away into the distance.
"Tally-ho!" yelled someone in a frantic voice that echoed through the forest.
"Ah, tally-ho!" the intoxicating thought flashes through your mind. You whoop at your horse and as though breaking loose from a chain, tear through the forest, no longer seeing a thing as you hurtle along. Only the trees go streaking by as mud flies up from under your horse's hooves and sticks to your face. You come racing out of the forest to see the variegated pack strung out across the green fields and you spur your horse on harder still to head the quarry off—over green fields, ploughland and stubble, till at last you reach another wood and the furiously barking, howling pack disappears from view. Then, wet through and trembling with exertion, you rein in your foaming, breathless horse and greedily drink in the icy dampness of the wooded hollow. The shouts of the huntsmen and the barking of the dogs die away in the distance, while all around you is perfect silence. Their trunks almost bare, the tall pines stand motionless, and it seems you are in some forbidden kingdom. From the ravines comes the dank smell of mushrooms, rotten leaves and wet bark. The dampness becomes more and more noticeable and the forest grows cold and dark... It's time to find somewhere to

spend the night. But it is hard to gather the pack again after the hunt. For a long time the despairing, melancholy sound of the horns rings through the forest, and for a long time the shouting and swearing of men and the yelping of dogs can be heard... Finally, when it is already quite dark, the whole band of huntsmen bursts in upon some bachelor landowner whom they hardly know, and fills the yard of his farmstead with noise, as lanterns, candles and lamps are brought out of the house to welcome the guests...

Sometimes the hunting party would stay for several days at some hospitable neighbor's. At the crack of dawn, in the icy wind and first wet snow, they would ride off into the woods and fields and return towards dusk, flushed and covered with mud, their clothes smelling of pungent horse sweat and the hair of the beast they had brought to bay—and then the carousing would begin. The crowded, brightly-lit house feels very warm after a whole day out in the icy fields. With their jackets unbuttoned, everyone wanders from room to room, eating and drinking in a disorderly fashion and noisily discussing the day's hunting over the body of the big wolf lying in the middle of the room. Baring its teeth and showing the whites of its eyes, it lies with its bushy tail flung out, while its pale, cold blood stains the floor. After the vodka and the food you feel so blissfully tired, so sweetly drowsy, that the conversation going on around you seems to be muffled by water. Your chapped face burns, and if you close your eyes, the ground seems to float beneath your feet. And when you get into bed and sink into your soft feather mattress in some old corner room with a little ikon stand and a sanctuary lamp before it, visions of fiery-colored dogs go flashing before your eyes. Your whole body begins to ache with the sensation of galloping, and before you know it you are sinking with all these images and sensations into a sound, sweet sleep, forgetting even that this room was once the chapel of an old man whose name is surrounded by somber legends from the age of serfdom, and that he died in this very room and probably in this very bed.

If you happened to oversleep next morning and miss the hunting party's departure, your rest was particularly enjoyable. You wake up and lie in bed for a long time. The whole house is still. You can hear the gardener going quietly from room to room lighting the stoves, and then you hear the fire-- wood crackling and spitting. Ahead of you lies a whole day of peace in a house that is already sunk in wintry silence. You dress in a leisurely way, wander about the orchard, and find by chance a cold apple lying among the wet leaves. For some reason it seems unusually delicious and quite unlike any other apple you have eaten. Then you settle down to the books—books of grandfather's time bound in thick leather with little gold stars on their morocco spines. How glorious they smell, these volumes that look like church prayerbooks with their thick, rough, yellowed pages! They have a pleasant, sourish, musty smell like old perfume... The notes in their margins are splendid too, made with a goose-quill in a large, gentle, rounded hand. You open a book and read: "A thought worthy of philosophers both ancient and modern, the flower of intellect and sincere feeling..." And you cannot help being carried away by the book itself. It is *The Gentleman Philosopher*, an allegory published about a hundred years ago at his own expense by a "knight of many decorations" and printed by the charity board press. It is the story of how a "gentleman philosopher, possessing both the time and the aptitude for discourse—something to which the mind of man is sometimes elevated—one day conceived the idea of creating a model of the world in the spacious domain of his own estate..." Then you come across *The Satirical and Philosophical Writings of Monsieur Voltaire*, and for a long time you revel in the charmingly precious style of the translation: "My dear sirs! In the sixteenth century Erasmus composed a work in praise of folly" (an affected pause—a semicolon); "but you now command me to extoll reason for you..." Then, from the distant days of Catherine, you pass on to the romantic age, with its almanacs and sentimentally pompous, prolix novels... The cuckoo springs from its clock above your head and its sadly mocking call echoes through the empty house. And little by little a strange, sweet melancholy steals into your heart...

Then you open *The Secrets of Alexis* or *Victor, A Child in the Forest*, and read: "The clock strikes midnight! Solemn silence replaces the day's hubbub and the merry songs of the villagers. Sleep spreads its somber wings over the surface of our hemisphere, and they scatter darkness and dreams upon men... Dreams... How often they simply prolong the suffering of the wretched!..." And before your eyes there flit beloved, old words: steep cliffs and leafy groves, the pale moon and sad solitude, apparitions and phantoms, Cupid's arrows, lilies and roses, "the playful pranks of mischievous children," lily-white hands, Lyudmilas and Alinas... And here are journals with the names of Zhukovsky, Batyushkov and the Lyceum pupil Pushkin in them. And sadly you recall grandmother, with her polonaises on the clavichord and her languorous rendering of verses from *Eugene Onegin*. And the old, dreamy life rises before you... How lovely were the girls and women who once used to live on the nobles' estates! Their portraits gaze down at me from the wall with their beautiful, little aristocratic heads and old-fashioned coiffures, and lower their long eyelashes meekly and gracefully over wistful, tender eyes...

IV

The smell of Antonov apples is disappearing from the landowners' estates. Those days were such a short time ago and yet it seems to me that almost a whole century has passed since then. All the old people in Vyselki are dead, Anna Gerasimovna is dead too, and Arseny Semyonich has shot himself... The era of the small landowners, people impoverished to the point of beggary, has come. But even this beggarly existence is a good one!

I see myself in the country again, in late autumn. The days are bluish and dull. In the mornings I mount my horse and with a gun, a horn and just one dog ride off into the open fields. The wind sings and drones in the muzzle of my gun and blows hard into my face, sometimes bringing dry snow with it. All day long I roam the desolate plains... Famished and chilled to the marrow, I return to the estate towards dusk, and feel warmth and joy in my soul when I see the lights of Vyselki glimmering ahead and catch the smell of smoke and human habitation drifting towards me. I remember that at home they liked to sit in the twilight, talking softly in the semidarkness without any lights on. When I go into the house I find that the double windows have already been replaced for the cold weather, and this puts me in even more of a peaceful winter mood. In the footmen's room a servant is lighting the stove, and just as I did when I was a child I squat beside the heap of straw that already smells strongly of wintry cold, and gaze into the blazing stove or at the windows where the twilight is turning dark blue and sadly fading. Then I go into the servants' hall that is brightly lit and crowded. The kitchen maids are chopping cabbage, and I listen to the rhythmic, staccato tapping of their flashing knives and their harmonious country songs that are both sad and gay... Sometimes one of the neighboring small landowners calls and takes me away for a long stay with him... The life of a small landowner is good too!

He rises early. After a good stretch he gets out of bed and rolls himself a fat cigarette of cheap black tobacco or simply of shag. The pale light of an early November morning reveals a plain study with bare walls, a few dry, yellow fox pelts above the bed, and the stocky figure of a man in wide trousers and a loose, unbelted shirt, while the mirror shows a sleepy face with Tatar features. In the warm, twilit house there is dead silence. Outside the door, in the corridor, the old cook snores softly. She has worked in the manor house since she was a little girl, but that does not stop the master from shouting hoarsely so all the house can hear:

"Lukeria! Samovar!"

Then, putting on his boots, flinging a coat over his shoulders, and not bothering to button his shirt-collar, he goes out on to the porch. The hall that has been locked all night smells of dogs. Stretching lazily, yawning with little yelps and grinning, the hounds surround him.

"Get back!" he says in a slow, indulgent bass, and walks through the orchard to the threshing floor. He breathes in deeply, filling his lungs with the keen air of dawn and the smell of the bare garden chilled by the night. Curled and blackened by frost, the leaves rustle under his feet in the avenue of birches where half the trees have already been felled. Silhouetted against the gloomy, low sky, jackdaws sleep on the ridge of the threshing barn roof, their feathers ruffled up against the cold... "A marvelous day for hunting!" thinks the master, and pausing in the middle of the avenue gazes for a long time into the distance, looking at the deserted fields of green winter crops with calves wandering over them. His two bitches whine at his feet, while Zalivai is already beyond the orchard and bounding across the prickly stubble, calling to his master, it seems, and begging to be let out into the open fields. But what can you do with hounds at this time of year? The quarry is out in the open now, on the freshly ploughed fields and new tracks, and is afraid to stay in the woods because the leaves rustle in the wind... Oh, if only I had some borzois!

In the threshing barn work is beginning. Slowly gathering speed, the threshing drum begins to hum. Pulling lazily on the traces, sinking their hooves into the circle of dung on the floor and swaying as they move, the horses walk around and around, driving the machine. The driver sits in the middle of the driving gear, revolving on his little bench. He keeps shouting at the horses in a monotone and using his whip only on the brown gelding— it is lazier than the rest and goes to sleep on its feet because it is blindfolded.

"Come on, girls, get moving!" shouts the staid corn-feeder sternly as he puts on his loose, linen shirt.

Running about with barrows and brooms, the peasant girls hastily sweep the threshing floor.

"Good luck!" says the corn-feeder, and the first trial sheaf of rye flies through the drum with a droning screech and is tossed up from beneath like a tattered fan. The droning of the drum grows more and more insistent as the work goes on apace, and soon all the different noises merge into one— the agreeable sound of threshing. The master stands at the barn door and watches the red and yellow kerchiefs, the arms, the rakes and the straw flickering in the darkness within, all of it moving rhythmically and busily to the humming of the drum, the monotonous shouting of the driver, and the cracking of his whip. Clouds of chaff fly towards the door, and the master stands there covered in gray dust from head to foot. He keeps glancing out into the fields... Soon, very soon now, they will begin to turn white and be covered by the first frost...

The first frost, the first snow! He has no borzois to go hunting with in November, but winter is coming and he can put his hounds to work. And once again, as in the old days, the small landowners go visiting each other, drinking away the last of their money and disappearing for days on end in the snow-covered fields. And in the evening at some remote farmstead the windows of one wing of the house shine far into the winter darkness. There, in that small building, clouds of tobacco smoke drift through the air and tallow candles burn dimly as a guitar is tuned...

At dusk a wind tempestuous blew,
It threw my gates wide open...

someone begins in a chesty tenor. And pretending it is all nothing but fun, the others join in discordantly with desperate, sad bravado:

It threw my gates wide open,
And buried roads in snowdrifts too...

1900

Ivan Bunin / THE GENTLEMAN FROM SAN FRANCISCO

Alas, alas, that great city Babylon, that mighty city!
For in one hour is thy judgement come!

Revelation

The gentleman from San Francisco—no one in either Naples or Capri could remember his name—was on his way to the Old World with his wife and daughter to spend two whole years there devoted entirely to pleasure.

He was firmly convinced that he was fully entitled to a rest, to some enjoyment, and to a trip that was excellent in every way. He had his own reasons for thinking as he did: firstly, he was rich, and secondly, he had only just begun to live, though he was already fifty-eight. Until then he had not really lived but only existed, not at all badly, it's true, but nevertheless placing all his hopes on the future. He had worked indefatigably—the Chinese whom he shipped in by the thousand for his factories knew very well what that meant!—and had finally seen that he had accomplished a great deal and had done almost as well as those on whom he had once modeled himself. And so he decided to take a short rest. The class of people to which he belonged was accustomed to start enjoying life by taking a trip to Europe, India and Egypt. So he decided to do the same. Above all, of course, he wanted to reward himself for his years of toil, but he was glad to give his wife and daughter pleasure too. His wife had never been noted for her impressionability, but all middle-aged American women are mad about traveling anyway. As for his daughter, a rather sickly girl who was not getting any younger, the trip was absolutely essential: to say nothing of the good it would do her health, what about those lucky encounters that often take place on board ship? You sometimes find yourself sitting next to a multimillionaire at dinner and examining the frescoes on the saloon walls with him.

The itinerary drawn up by the gentleman from San Francisco was extensive. In December and January he hoped to bask in the sun of southern Italy, enjoy the ancient monuments, the tarantella, the serenades given by wandering singers, and something else that men of his age feel with particular poignancy—the love of young Neapolitan girls, even though it is not always entirely disinterested. He proposed to spend carnival week in Nice and Monte Carlo, where the most select people gather at this time of year, and where some indulge excitedly in motorcar and yacht races and others in roulette; some in what is customarily called flirtation and others in shooting pigeons, which rise most beautifully from their lofts to soar over emerald lawns against a backdrop of forget-me-not blue sea, then suddenly fall to the ground with a thud in little white bundles. He wanted to devote the beginning of March to Florence and arrive in Rome by Easter to hear the *Miserere* sung

105

there. His plans also included Venice and Paris, a bullfight in Seville, bathing on the English beaches, Athens, Constantinople, Palestine, Egypt, and even Japan—on the way home, of course... And to begin with everything went splendidly.

It was late November, and icy fogs and squalls of wet snow accompanied them all the way to Gibraltar; but they sailed on quite safely. There were many passengers on board. The famous *Atlantis* was like a huge hotel with every imaginable convenience—an all-night bar, Turkish baths and her own newspaper—and life on board went very smoothly. They rose early, woken by blasts on the funnel echoing harshly down the corridors at that twilight hour when day was breaking so slowly and cheerlessly over the gray-green expanse of ocean rolling heavily in the fog. Putting on their flannel pyjamas, they drank coffee, chocolate or cocoa. Then they took their baths, did their exercises to give themselves a feeling of well-being and work up a good appetite, dressed, and went to breakfast. Till eleven they were supposed to walk briskly up and down the decks breathing in the cool freshness of the ocean, or to play shuffleboard and other games so as to work up an appetite again. At eleven they fortified themselves with sandwiches and beef tea. Thus fortified, they read the ship's newspaper with interest and waited quietly for lunch, a meal that was even more nourishing and varied than breakfast. The next two hours were devoted to rest. The decks were lined with long wicker armchairs and the passengers lay in them wrapped in rugs, gazing at the cloudy sky and the foaming waves racing by beyond the rail, or sinking into a sweet doze. Between four and five, refreshed now and bright, they were served strong, fragrant tea with biscuits. At seven more blasts on the funnel heralded the approach of what constituted the supreme purpose of all this shipboard existence, its crowning glory... And then the gentleman from San Francisco hurried to his sumptuous cabin to dress for dinner.

At night the decks of the *Atlantis* blazed in the darkness with their countless fiery eyes, and a great multitude of servants toiled in the kitchens, sculleries and wine stores below. The ocean heaving beyond the ship's side was terrifying, but no one thought about it, believing firmly in the power exercised over it by the captain, a red-haired man of monstrous bulk and weight who always looked sleepy. In his uniform with its broad, gold stripes he resembled an enormous idol who rarely emerged from his mysterious quarters to mix with the passengers. On the foredeck the siren wailed constantly with demonic gloom or howled in frenzied fury, but few of those at dinner could hear it, for it was drowned by the fine string orchestra that tirelessly played its exquisite music in the two-tiered dining saloon. Flooded with festive light and crowded with ladies in décolleté and gentlemen in dinner jackets and tailcoats, the saloon was patrolled by slim waiters and deferential *maîtres d'hôtel*, one of whom, the wine waiter, even wore a chain around his neck like a Lord Mayor. The gentleman from San Francisco looked very much younger in his dinner jacket and starched shirt. Lean and

106

rather short, ungainly but well-built, he sat in the pearly-gold radiance of the great saloon at a table decked with bottles of wine, glasses of the finest crystal, and a vase of curly hyacinths. His yellowish face with its neatly trimmed, silver moustache had a Mongolian look about it, while his big teeth gleamed with their gold fillings and his powerful bald head shone like old ivory. His wife, a large, broad, placid woman, was dressed expensively but suitably for her age. His daughter wore a gown that was elaborate but light, transparent and innocently revealing. She was a tall, slender girl with magnificent hair arranged in a charming way and breath that was fragrant with little violet pastilles. Near her lips and between her shoulderblades were the most delicate of little pink pimples lightly dusted with powder... Dinner lasted over an hour, and afterwards dancing began in the ballroom, during which some of the men—including, of course, the gentleman from San Francisco—sat with their feet up smoking Havana cigars until they were purple in the face, getting drunk on liqueurs from the bar, where they were served by Negroes in red jackets with eyeballs like shelled hard-boiled eggs. Beyond the ship's side the mountains of black water heaved and boomed, while the storm whistled loudly in the sodden, heavy rigging, and the whole ship shuddered as she fought her way through both the storm and the mountainous waves, ploughing through their shifting masses as time and again they flung their foaming crests high in the air. Smothered by the fog, the siren moaned in mortal anguish while the men on watch on the bridge froze in the bitter cold, their heads spinning with the unbearable strain of prolonged, intense concentration. But the ship's belly below the water line resembled the dark, fiery depths of the inferno, its last, ninth circle—that belly where the giant furnaces blazed with a muffled roar as their red hot maws devoured the coal flung into them by men stripped to the waist and streaming with pungent, grimy sweat, their bodies purple in the heat of the flames. And meanwhile, up in the bar, with their legs flung carelessly over the arms of their chairs, people sat sipping brandy and liqueurs amid clouds of fragrant smoke, while in the ballroom everything shone with brilliant light, warmth and joy as the couples first whirled in a waltz then swayed in a tango. And all the time, with shamelessly voluptuous sadness, the music kept on insistently pleading for one thing, always one and the same thing... In this glittering crowd there was a great millionaire, a clean-shaven, lanky man in an old-fashioned tailcoat; there was a celebrated Spanish writer, a world-famous beauty, and an elegant pair of lovers whom everyone watched with curiosity and who made no secret of their happiness, for they danced only with each other. Everything they did looked so exquisite and charming that only the captain knew they had been hired by Lloyds to play at love for good money and had been sailing on various ships for a long time now.

In Gibraltar the sun gladdened them all and it felt like early spring. A new passenger appeared on board and aroused general interest. He was the Crown Prince of some Asian kingdom who was traveling incognito. A small, perfectly expressionless man with a broad face and narrow eyes behind gold-rimmed spectacles, he looked slightly unpleasant because his large moustache was translucent like that of a corpse, but he was unaffected, modest and likeable on the whole. In the Mediterranean there was a heavy swell running, its waves as variegated as the tail of a peacock and driven on by the tramontane wind that flew merrily and madly towards the ship in brilliant sunshine under a perfectly clear sky... And then, on the second day, the sky began to turn pale and the horizon was shrouded in mist: land was approaching, Ischia and Capri appeared, and through binoculars Naples was already visible, gleaming like lumps of sugar scattered at the foot of something blue-gray... Many of the ladies and gentlemen had already put on their light fur coats. The ship's boys, meek Chinese who never spoke above a whisper—bandy-legged youths with thick, maidenly eyelashes and jet-black pigtails down to their heels—were quietly carrying rugs, walking sticks, trunks and toiletcases towards the companionways... The gentleman from San Francisco's daughter stood on deck beside the prince whom she had been introduced to by a lucky chance the previous evening. She pretended to be looking intently into the distance as he pointed something out, explaining something to her in a soft, rapid voice. He was so short that he looked like a little boy beside the other passengers, and was not in the least prepossessing. Instead, he looked distinctly odd in his spectacles, bowler hat, and English overcoat, while the whiskers of his thin moustache were coarse like horsehair and the delicate, dark skin on his flat face seemed as if it had been stretched taut and lightly varnished. But the girl stood listening to him and was so excited that she could not understand a word he was saying. Her heart beat swiftly with strange rapture, for everything, absolutely everything, about him was different from other people—his slender hands, his clear skin with the blood of ancient kings coursing beneath it, even his clothes which were quite plain and European but particularly neat somehow—all held an indescribable fascination for her. And meanwhile, the gentleman from San Francisco himself, wearing gray gaiters over his boots, kept glancing at the famous beauty standing beside him, a tall blonde with a marvelous figure and eyes made up in the latest Paris fashion. Holding a close-cropped, cringing little dog on a silver chain, she talked to it the whole time. And feeling vaguely uncomfortable, the daughter tried not to notice what her father was doing.

He was quite generous when traveling and so had complete faith in the solicitude of all those who brought him food and drink and served him from morning till night, anticipating his every wish, safeguarding his cleanliness and repose, carrying his things, summoning his porters, and delivering his trunks to hotels. So it was everywhere, so it had been on board ship, and so it should be in Naples too. Drawing nearer, the city grew larger. The ship's band was already crowded on deck, its brass instruments flashing in the sun. Suddenly it burst into a deafening, triumphant march, while the giant captain appeared on his bridge in full dress uniform and waved to the passengers in greeting

108

like a gracious pagan god. When at last the *Atlantis* entered harbor, bringing her massive, many-storied bulk dotted with faces alongside, and dropping her clattering gangways onto the quay, countless people—hotel porters and their assistants in gold-braided caps, commissionaires of every kind, whistling urchins and strapping ragamuffins with packets of colored postcards in their hands—all rushed towards the gentleman from San Francisco, offering their services. And he grinned at the ragamuffins as he walked towards the courtesy car belonging to the same hotel where the prince was probably staying, and said quietly through his teeth first in English then in Italian:

"Go away! Via!"

Life in Naples immediately began to follow an established pattern: early in the morning there was breakfast in the twilit dining room, a cloudy sky that held little promise, and a crowd of guides at the doors into the lobby. Then came the first smile of the warm, pinkish sun, a view from the high hanging balcony of Vesuvius completely shrouded in shimmering morning mist, a glimpse of the rippling, silver-pearl waters of the bay with the faint outline of Capri on the horizon, and the sight of tiny little donkeys pulling two-wheeled carts along the embankment below, while detachments of little, toy-like soldiers went marching by to the sound of bright, defiant music. After that came the waiting car and a slow drive through the damp, crowded streets that were narrow as corridors and led between tall buildings with many windows; then visits to funereally stark museums lit pleasantly and evenly but with a tiresome, snow-like brilliance, or to cold churches smelling of wax, where the same thing was repeated over and over again: a majestic entrance screened by a heavy, leather curtain, and inside, vast emptiness, silence, the still lights of a seven-branched candelabra glowing red far back on the lace-draped altar, a solitary old woman amid the dark, wooden pews, slippery gravestones underfoot, and on the wall someone's "Descent from the Cross"—a painting that was sure to be famous. At one there was lunch on San Martino hill, where a good many people of the most select kind would meet towards midday and where the gentleman from San Francisco's daughter once nearly fainted: she thought she saw the prince sitting in the room though she already knew from the papers that he was in Rome. At five tea was served in the hotel's elegant drawing room that was so beautifully warm with its rugs and blazing fires. And then once again came preparations for dinner—once again the mighty gong boomed commandingly on every floor, once again the lines of ladies in décolleté rustled down the stairs in their silks and glittered in the mirrors on the walls, once again the palatial dining room flung its wide doors hospitably open to show the red jackets of the musicians on their platform and the black crowd of waiters around the *maître d'hôtel* as he ladled out the thick, pink soup with consummate skill... And again the dinners were so lavish with all their various dishes, their mineral waters and wines, their many rich sweets and fruit, that by eleven in the evening the maids had to take hot water bottles to all the rooms for the guests to warm their stomachs with.

December, however, turned out to be a poor month that year. When visitors talked to the hotel porters about the weather, they just shrugged their shoulders guiltily and muttered that they could not remember a winter like it, though this was not the first year they had been obliged to mutter exactly the same thing and blame it on the fact that terrible things were happening all over the world: there were cloudbursts and storms on the Riviera of a kind never known before, there was snow in Athens, Etna was all covered in snow too and glowing at night, and the tourists were leaving Palermo in droves to escape from the cold... Every day the morning sun would deceive them: after midday the sky invariably turned gray and fine rain began to fall, growing heavier and colder as the day wore on. Then the palms by the hotel entrance gleamed dully like tin-plate and the city looked particularly dirty and crowded. The museums seemed too monotonously alike; the cigar-butts thrown down by the fat cabbies whose wing-like rubber capes flapped in the wind smelt intolerably acrid; the vigorous cracking of their whips over the heads of their scrawny-necked nags sounded patently artificial; the boots of the men sweeping the tram-lines looked revolting; and the women splashing through the mud in the rain with their black heads uncovered seemed hideously short-legged. As for the dampness and the stench of rotten fish that came from the sea where it frothed along the embankment—the least said the better. The lady and gentleman from San Francisco began to quarrel in the mornings. Their daughter either had a headache and went about looking pale or suddenly came to life and took delight in everything, becoming both charming and beautiful. Beautiful, too, were the complex, tender feelings aroused in her by the uncomely man with rare blood in his veins, for after all it does not matter exactly what awakens a girl's heart—whether it is wealth, fame, or noble lineage... Everyone assured them that it would be quite different in Sorrento and on Capri—it was warmer and sunnier there, the lemon trees were in bloom, the people more honest, and the wine more wholesome. And so the family from San Francisco decided to set off with all their trunks for Capri, intending to look around the island, tread the stones where the palaces of Tiberius once stood, visit the fabulous caverns of the Blue Grotto, and listen to the Abruzzi pipers who roam the island for a month before Christmas singing praises to the Virgin Mary. And then they would go to stay in Sorrento.

On the day of their departure—a most memorable day for the family from San Francisco!—even the usual early morning sun was absent. A heavy mist shrouded the whole of Vesuvius and hung in a low, gray cloud over the leaden sea. The island of Capri was not visible at all, as if it had never existed on the face of the earth. And the little steamer making towards it rolled so heavily from side to side that the family from San Francisco had to lie on their backs on the sofas in the vessel's wretched lounge, their feet wrapped in rugs and their eyes closed with nausea. The lady was suffering most of all, or

110

so she thought. She was overcome several times by nausea and thought she was dying, but the stewardess who came running up with a little basin only laughed, for she had pitched and rolled day in, day out for many years now, making the crossing in intense heat and bitter cold, yet was still indefatigable. The daughter was dreadfully pale and held a slice of lemon between her teeth. The father, who lay on his back dressed in a loose overcoat and big cap, never unclenched his jaws once during the whole crossing. His face had grown dark, his moustache looked white, and his head ached badly: what with the bad weather in Naples he had been drinking too much in the evenings during the last few days and had spent too long admiring risqué "tableaux vivants" in various haunts. Meanwhile the rain lashed against the rattling windowpanes and ran down onto the sofas, the wind tore at the masts with a howl, and now and then, accompanied by a wave that fell upon the ship, a gust laid the little steamer completely on her side, and something could be heard rumbling and crashing down below. When they called at Castellammare and Sorrento things were a little better, but even there the ship still rolled dreadfully, while the shore with all its cliffs, orchards, pines, pink and white hotels, and smoky, curly-green hills flew up and down outside the windows as though they were all on swings. Small boats kept bumping against the ship's side and a damp wind blew in through the door, while from a wooden barge flying the flag of the "Royal" hotel, an urchin yelled incessantly in a shrill, grating voice in an attempt to entice the travelers. And feeling very old—which is what he should have felt—the gentleman from San Francisco now thought with anger and dejection of all those greedy, miserable little wretches that stank of garlic and were called Italians. Once, during a stop, he opened his eyes and sitting up on the sofa, caught sight of a huddle of decayed stone hovels perched on top of each other under a rocky cliff right by the water's edge. With a few boats, odd heaps of rags, tin cans and brown fishing nets beside them, they looked so wretched that he was filled with despair, remembering that this was the real Italy he had come to enjoy... At last, when it was already dusk, the dark bulk of the island began to draw near with its little red lights glowing along the shore like bright holes pierced in the blackness. The wind dropped, becoming warmer and more fragrant, and snakes of golden light from the lanterns on the jetty rippled over the gentle waves that gleamed like iridescent black oil. Then suddenly the anchor began to rumble on its chain and splashed into the water, and from all sides came the furious cries of boatmen vying with each other for custom. Immediately the lights in the lounge seemed to shine more brightly, while the passengers felt their spirits lifting, and wanted to eat, drink, smoke, and move about... Ten minutes later the family from San Francisco were boarding a large, wooden barge; a quarter of an hour after that they were stepping onto the stone jetty; and then they climbed into an airy little carriage and with a humming sound were pulled up a steep hillside, past vineyards full of vine-props, half-ruined stone walls, and gnarled, wet orange trees covered here and

111

there with straw matting, their gleaming fruit and thick, glossy leaves slipping away and down the hill past the open windows of the carriage... Sweet is the smell of the earth in Italy after rain, and each of her islands has its own particular fragrance!

The island of Capri was damp and dark that night. But now it came to life again for a moment and lights went on here and there. On the funicular platform at the top of the hill there already stood a crowd of those people whose duty it was to give the gentleman from San Francisco a fitting welcome. There were other new arrivals too, but they deserved no attention—a few Russians who had settled on Capri, absentminded, slovenly fellows with spectacles and beards and the collars of their threadbare, old overcoats turned up; and a group of long-legged, round-skulled German youths in Tyrolean costume with canvas rucksacks on their backs, who had no need of anyone's services and were not in the least lavish with their money. Quietly avoiding both the Russians and the Germans, the gentleman from San Francisco was noticed straightaway. He and his ladies were quickly helped out of the carriage and people went running on ahead to show him the way. Once again he was surrounded by urchins, and this time by those sturdy women of Capri too, who carry the cases and trunks of respectable tourists on their heads. Their little wooden clogs began to clack across the small square that looked like an opera set with its round electric light swinging in the damp breeze above their heads, while the horde of little boys began to whistle and turn somersaults all around them. And as if walking across a stage, the gentleman from San Francisco made his way through them all towards a medieval archway between the houses, beyond which an echoing little street sloped down towards the brightly-lit hotel entrance. The tufts of a palm tree rose above the flat roofs to the left and dark blue stars twinkled in the black sky above and ahead. And it all seemed as if it was in honor of the guests from San Francisco that this damp, little stone town on a rocky island in the Mediterranean had come to life, as if it was they who had made the hotel owner so hospitable and happy, and as if the Chinese gong summoning all the guests to dinner just as they entered the lobby was waiting to boom only for them.

The owner, an extremely elegant young man who greeted them with a courteous, dignified bow, gave the gentleman from San Francisco a momentary start. He suddenly remembered that amidst all the other confused dreams which had plagued his sleep the previous night, he had seen the spitting image of this man wearing the same morning coat and with the same hair brushed till it shone like a mirror. Astonished, he almost stopped in his tracks. But since for many years now his soul had not contained one iota of what might be called mystical feelings, his amazement immediately faded away. Jokingly he mentioned this strange coincidence of dream and reality to his wife and daughter as they walked down the hotel corridor. But his daughter glanced at him in alarm when she heard his words; her heart was filled with melancholy and she suddenly felt a terrible sense of loneliness on this

112

dark, alien island...

A person of illustrious rank—Rais XVII—who had been visiting Capri, had only just left, and the guests from San Francisco were given the suite he had occupied. They were assigned the hotel's most beautiful and efficient maid, a Belgian girl whose waist was slender and firm in its corsets and whose starched cap was shaped like a little toothed coronet. They were given the most distinguished-looking valet too, a black-haired, fiery-eyed Sicilian, and the hotel's smartest boots, the small, stout Luigi, who had held many similar jobs in his time. A minute later the French headwaiter knocked softly on the gentleman from San Francisco's door. He had come to inquire whether the new guests would be dining, and in the event of an answer in the affirmative—of which, however, there was no doubt—to inform them that there was lobster, roast beef, asparagus, pheasant, and so forth on the menu that day. The gentleman from San Francisco could still feel the floor moving beneath his feet—that lousy little Italian steamer had made him feel so sick—but without hurrying and doing it rather awkwardly as he was not used to it, he went and closed the window that had banged when the headwaiter came in, filling the room with the smell of distant kitchens and wet flowers in the garden below. With unhurried precision he replied that they would indeed be dining, that their table should be placed well back in the room, a good way from the door, and that they would be drinking the local wine. Every word he uttered was echoed by the headwaiter in the most varied tones, all of which, however, meant only one thing: that there was and could be no doubt as to the correctness of the gentleman from San Francisco's wishes, and that all his instructions would be carried out to the letter. Finally the headwaiter bowed and asked tactfully:

"Will that be all, sir?"

And receiving a drawling "yes" in reply, he added that there would be a tarantella in the lobby that evening, danced by Carmella and Giuseppe, who were well known all over Italy and "the tourist world," as he put it.

"I've seen her on postcards," said the gentleman from San Francisco in a tone that expressed nothing. "And that Giuseppe—is he her husband?"

"Her cousin, sir," the headwaiter replied.

And after a moment's pause, thinking something but saying nothing, the gentleman from San Francisco dismissed the man with a nod.

Then once again he began to dress for dinner with as much care as if he were preparing for his wedding. He switched on all the lights, flooding every mirror in the room with brilliant reflections of furniture and open trunks. He began to wash and shave, ringing continually for service, while the sound of other impatient bells coming from his wife's and daughter's rooms resounded down the corridor and clashed with his own. And Luigi, in his red apron, pulling grimaces of horror that had the maids weeping with laughter as they went running by with tiled buckets in their hands, kept bounding along the corridor to answer the gentleman's bell with the agility characteristic of many fat

113

men. Rapping on the door with his knuckles, he asked with feigned timidity and deference exaggerated to the point of idiocy:

"Ha sonato, signore?"

And from behind the door came the slow, rasping, offensively courteous voice:

"Yes, come in..."

What did the gentleman from San Francisco feel, what did he think on that night that was so momentous for him? Like anyone else who has been tossed about in a boat and felt sick, he was just very hungry, dreaming with relish of his first spoonful of soup and his first sip of wine, and he even performed the customary ritual of dressing for dinner with a certain excitement that left him no time for thoughts or feelings.

When he had washed, shaved and put his false teeth nicely back in place, he stood in front of the mirrors and with his silver-mounted brushes damped and tidied what was left of his pearly-white hair, smoothing it over his dark yellow skull. Then he pulled his cream silk underwear onto his sturdy, old body, its waistline thickened by excessively rich food, and drew his black silk socks and dancing shoes onto his thin, flat feet. Next, squatting down, he adjusted the silk braces that held up his black trousers, tucked in his snow-white shirt with its bulging front, put a pair of links into his brilliant white cuffs, and began struggling to fix his stiff collar onto the stud beneath it. He could still feel the floor heaving beneath his feet and his fingertips were hurting badly, while the collar stud kept nipping the flabby skin in the hollow under his Adam's apple. But he persevered and finally managed it. His eyes shining with the effort and his face blue-gray because the collar was throttling him, he sank down utterly exhausted in front of the dressing-table mirror and looked at his full-length reflection that was repeated in all the other mirrors in the room.

"Oh, it's awful!" he muttered, hanging his powerful, bald head and not even trying to think or understand just what it was he found so awful. Then, as he always did, he carefully examined his short fingers with their joints hardened by gout, and their large, curved, almond-colored nails, and said again with conviction: "It's awful..."

But just then the dinner gong boomed for the second time, echoing through the hotel as if it were a pagan temple. And getting up hurriedly, the gentleman from San Francisco tightened his collar still more by fastening his bow tie, drew in his belly by buttoning his waistcoat, put on his dinner jacket, straightened his cuffs, and looked at himself in the mirror once more... That Carmella, he thought to himself, looking like a mulatto girl with her dark skin and fetching eyes, that Carmella in her flowery orange dress must be a very good dancer. And coming briskly out into the corridor, he crossed the carpet to his wife's room next door and asked in a loud voice whether they would be long.

"Five minutes!" answered his daughter from behind the door, her voice

114

ringing and gay.

"Fine," said the gentleman from San Francisco.

And taking his time, he set off down the corridors and red-carpeted stairs in search of the reading room. The hotel staff he met on the way pressed close to the wall as he passed, but he walked on as though not noticing them. There was an old woman who was late for dinner hurrying along in front of him as fast as she could go, an old woman with milk-white hair and a stoop but wearing a low-cut dress of light gray silk. She ran in a comical fashion, like a hen, and he easily caught up with her and left her behind. At the glass doors leading into the dining room where all the guests had already sat down and begun to eat, he stopped in front of a small table piled high with boxes of Egyptian cigarettes and cigars, and taking a fat Manila, threw three lira down on the table. As he walked through the winter garden on the verandah he glanced out of the open window. A gentle breeze came wafting towards him from the darkness and he caught a faint glimpse of the top of an old palm tree spreading out its huge branches against the stars, while in the distance he heard the steady murmur of the sea... In the quiet, comfortable reading room lit only by the lamps above its tables, a gray-haired German was standing rustling the papers as he read. With his astonished, mad eyes darting behind round, silver-rimmed spectacles, he looked like Ibsen. Surveying him coldly, the gentleman from San Francisco sat down in a corner in a deep leather armchair that stood under a lamp with a green shade, put on his pince-nez and, jerking his head because his collar was choking him, disappeared completely behind his newspaper. He glanced quickly through a few headlines, read a couple of sentences about the never-ending war in the Balkans, turned the page with an habitual gesture—and suddenly the lines of print flashed before his eyes with glassy brilliance, his neck went taut, his eyes bulged, and his pince-nez slipped from his nose... He lunged forward, tried to gulp down some air—and began to wheeze wildly. His lower jaw dropped, filling his mouth with the gleam of gold fillings, his head sagged onto his shoulder and began to shake, the front of his shirt bulged like the bottom of a basket, and his whole body slid to the floor, writhing, kicking up the carpet with its heels and struggling desperately with someone.

Had the German not been in the reading room, they would have managed to hush up this terrible incident in a swift, skillful manner, instantly whisking the gentleman from San Francisco away by his head and feet and taking him out by some back way that led as far from the hotel as possible— and not one of the guests would have heard what he had got up to. But the German tore out of the reading room, alarming not only the whole dining room but the entire hotel too. Many of the guests leapt up from the table, turned pale, and ran to the reading room, shouting, "What is it? What's happened?" in all their different languages. But nobody could give them a sensible answer or make out what was wrong, because to this day people still find death the most amazing thing in the world and flatly refuse to believe in it. The hotel owner rushed from one guest to the next in an effort to stop them running about and calm them with hasty assurances that it was nothing at all, a mere trifle, a little fainting fit that had come over the gentleman from San Francisco... But no one would listen to him, for many of them could see the waiters and valets tearing off the gentleman's tie, waistcoat and crumpled dinner jacket, and even for some reason pulling his dancing shoes off his flat, silk-stockinged feet. But he was still writhing. He struggled obstinately with death, absolutely refusing to give in to this thing that had come so unexpectedly and rudely upon him. He tossed his head from side to side, wheezing hoarsely like a man with his throat cut and rolling his eyes like a drunk... When they had carried him hastily into room number forty-three and laid him on the bed—it was the smallest, dampest, coldest, worst room in the hotel, at the end of the ground floor corridor—his daughter came running in with her hair dishevelled and her bosom showing, lifted high by its corsets. After her came his wife, imposingly large and all dressed for dinner, her mouth agape and round with horror... But by then his head had already stopped shaking.

A quarter of an hour later everything had more or less returned to normal in the hotel. But the evening was irreparably spoiled. Some of the guests went back to the dining room and finished their meal, but they ate in silence with offended expressions on their faces, while the hotel owner went from table to table, shrugging his shoulders in helpless, seemly annoyance, feeling he was the innocent victim, assuring everyone that he understood perfectly well "how unpleasant it all was," and promising to do "everything in his power" to remove this unpleasantness. But the tarantella had to be cancelled nevertheless and all unnecessary lights switched off, with the result that most of the guests went off to have a drink in town. Everything became so quiet that the clock could clearly be heard ticking in the lobby, deserted now except for the parrot which muttered something in an expressionless voice, fussing about in its cage before going to sleep and finally managing to nod off with one claw resting on the top perch in a ridiculous fashion... The gentleman from San Francisco lay on a cheap iron bed, covered with coarse, woollen blankets, in the dim light of a single bulb that shone from the ceiling. An icebag hung down on his chill, wet forehead. His blue-gray, already dead face was gradually growing cold, and the hoarse gurgling that broke from his open mouth illumined by its gold was becoming weaker. It was no longer the gentleman from San Francisco who was hoarsely wheezing—he no longer existed—but someone else. His wife, his daughter, the doctor and the servants stood and looked at him. Suddenly the thing they had been expecting and fearing finally happened—the wheezing stopped. And slowly, very slowly, as they all stood watching, a pallor crept over the dead man's face and his features began to grow finer and clearer...

The hotel owner came in. "Gia è morto," said the doctor to him in a whisper. His face impassive, the owner shrugged his shoulders. With tears quietly streaming down her cheeks, the lady went up to him and said timidly

116

that the dead man should now be carried to his own room.

"Oh no, madam," replied the owner hastily and civilly but completely without his former amiable courtesy, speaking not in English but in French as he was not in the least interested now in the trifling sum that the visitors from San Francisco might leave in his till. "That's quite impossible, madam," he said, adding by way of explanation that he set much store by their suite and that if he agreed to her request, then the whole of Capri would hear about it and the tourists would begin to avoid those rooms.

The daughter, who had been looking at him strangely all this time, sank into a chair, and covering her mouth with her handkerchief, burst out sobbing. But her mother immediately stopped crying and her face flushed an angry red. She raised her voice and began to demand what she wanted, speaking in her native tongue and still not believing that all respect for her family was gone for good. With polite dignity the owner put her in her place: if madam disapproved of the procedure in his hotel, then he would not dream of detaining her; and he declared firmly that the body was to be removed the next morning at dawn, adding that the police had already been informed and that their representative would arrive shortly to carry out the necessary formalities... Was it possible, madam asked, to get a coffin on Capri, even if it was only a plain, ready-made one? No, he was sorry, but it was quite impossible, and there was no time to have one made. They would have to arrange things in some other way... His English soda water, for instance, came in big, long boxes...the partitions could be taken out of one of them...

That night all the hotel was asleep. They opened the window in room forty-three—it looked out on a corner of the garden where a stunted banana tree grew under the high stone wall that had broken glass set along its top—switched off the light, locked the door, and went away. The dead man was left in the darkness with the blue stars gazing down at him from the sky and a cricket singing its carefree but melancholy song on the wall... Two maids were sitting on the windowsill in the dimly lit corridor and darning something. Luigi came up, wearing slippers and carrying a pile of clothes over his arm.

"Pronto?" ("Ready?"), he asked anxiously in a loud whisper, indicating the dreadful door at the end of the corridor with his eyes, and waving his free hand lightly in that direction. "Partenza!" he said softly, using the word people usually shout in Italy when a train pulls out of the station, and the maids fell on each other's necks bent double with soundless laughter.

Then, bounding softly down the corridor, he ran right up to the door, tapped on it very gently, and cocking his head on one side, asked most deferentially in a low voice:

"Ha sonato, signore?"

And squeezing his throat and thrusting his lower jaw forward, he drawled in a rasping, sad voice that seemed to come from the other side of the door:

"Yes, come in..."

At dawn—when it grew light outside the window of room forty-three and a damp breeze rustled the ragged leaves of the banana tree, when the morning sky rose and spread its light blue cloak over the island of Capri and when the sharply-etched, clear peak of Monte Solaro was gilded by the sun rising over the distant blue mountains of Italy, when the stonemasons who repaired the island's paths for the tourists set off to work—a long soda water box was brought to room forty-three. Shortly afterwards it became very heavy and pressed painfully against the knees of the junior porter who was taking it quickly in a one-horse cab along the white road that wound to and fro past stone walls and vineyards, down the slopes of Capri, dropping lower and lower till it reached the sea. The cabby, a sickly-looking man with red-rimmed eyes wearing a shabby old jacket whose sleeves were too short and boots that were worn out, had a hangover—he had been playing dice in the trattoria all night. He kept on whipping his sturdy little horse that was decked out in Sicilian style, with all kinds of bells jingling briskly on its high brass saddle and its bridle adorned with colored woollen pompoms, while the plume two feet long sticking up from its trimmed forelock swayed as it walked. The cabby was silent, depressed by his dissipation and his vices, and by the fact that the night before he had lost all his money down to the last penny. But the morning was fresh, and in air like this, close to the sea under a blue sky, a man soon loses his hangover and becomes carefree once more. And besides, the cabby was consoled by the unexpected sum given him by a gentleman from San Francisco whose dead head was shaking about in the box behind him... Looking no bigger than a beetle as it lay far below on the bright, soft blueness that fills the Bay of Naples with such rich abundance, the little steamer was already sounding the final blasts on its funnel, and they echoed cheerfully all over the island, its every outcrop, ridge and stone so clearly visible that the air hardly seemed to be there at all. Near the jetty the junior porter was overtaken by his senior colleague who came racing up in a car with the mother and daughter in it, both of them pale-faced with dark shadows under their eyes from weeping and lack of sleep. And ten minutes later the little steamer churned up the water again and set off once more on its run to Sorrento and Castellammare, carrying the family from San Francisco away from Capri forever... And peace and quiet descended upon the island once more.

On that island two thousand years ago there lived a man who was unspeakably vile in the gratification of his lust and who for some reason wielded power over millions of people and committed atrocities beyond all measure. Mankind has never forgotten him, and many, very many people come from all over the world to look at the ruins of the stone house on one of the island's steepest cliffs where he used to live. On that beautiful morning all those who had come to Capri precisely for this reason were still asleep in their hotels, though the little, mouse-gray donkeys with their red saddles were already being led up to the hotel entrances for the tourists to ride on. After

118

waking and eating their fill, Americans and Germans—men and women, young and old—would again clamber on these donkeys, to be followed at a run up the steep, stony paths all the way to the top of Monte Tiberio by the old beggarwomen of Capri, who goad the animals on with sticks in their sinewy hands. Reassured by the thought that the old man from San Francisco—who had been going to ride with them but had instead just scared them by reminding them of death—had already been shipped off to Naples, the visitors to Capri slept soundly, while all was still quiet on the island and the shops in the town were still shut. Only the market in the small square was open, selling its fish and vegetables, and only simple folk were there. Among them, doing absolutely nothing as usual, stood the tall old boatman, Lorenzo, a carefree idler who was so handsome that he was renowned throughout Italy and had often sat for painters. He had brought two lobsters with him that he had caught during the night, and he had already sold them for next to nothing; now they were rustling in the apron of the cook from the hotel where the family from San Francisco had spent the night. Lorenzo could stand there quite happily now till evening if he wished, glancing around him in his customary regal fashion and looking picturesque in his tattered clothes with his clay pipe in his mouth and his red woollen beret pulled down over one ear. Meanwhile, down the steep slopes of Monte Solaro, along the ancient Phoenician path with its steps cut out of the rock, two Abruzzi mountain-dwellers were coming down from Anacapri. Under his leather cloak one of them had a set of bagpipes—a large goatskin bag with two pipes attached to it—while the other carried something that looked like a wooden flute. Down they came, and the whole of Capri, joyous, beautiful, and sunlit, was spread out at their feet. Everything lay before them: the rocky outcrops of the island and the fabulous dark blue sea in which it floated, the morning mist shining over the water to the east where the brilliant sun was already burning hot as it rose higher in the sky, and the hazy, azure bulk of Italy, her mountains both near and far still shimmering in the morning light, mountains whose beauty no words can express. Halfway down, the men slackened their pace. There, above the path, in a niche in the rocky face of Monte Solaro, stood the Mother of God, the whole of her bathed in the warm brilliance of the sun. Clad in snow-white, plaster raiments and wearing a royal crown turned rusty-gold by rain, the meek, gracious Virgin Mary stood with eyes uplifted to the sky, that eternal, blissful abode of Her thrice-blessed Son. The men bared their heads and poured forth naive and humbly joyous words of praise to the sun, the morning, the Virgin Mary—the immaculate protectress of all who suffer in this wicked yet beautiful world—and to the One born of Her womb in a poor shepherd's shelter in Bethlehem, far away in the land of Judea...

And meanwhile, the body of the old man from San Francisco was returning home, home to the shores of the New World and its grave. After suffering many indignities and much lack of consideration at the hands of men, and after wandering from one harbor warehouse to another for about a week,

119

it found itself at last aboard the same famous ship that such a short while ago had brought it so respectfully to the Old World. But now the gentleman from San Francisco was hidden from the living, and was lowered in his tarred coffin deep into the dark hold. And again, once more, the ship set forth on her long voyage. It was night when she sailed past Capri, and as they slowly disappeared over the dark sea, her lights seemed sad and dismal to those watching from the island. But there, on board, in rooms flooded with the light of brilliant chandeliers, a great ball was being held as usual.

There was a ball on the second night out as well, and one on the third too. Again a furious storm raged over the ocean, while the wind howled like a dirge and the mountainous waves raced by, black like a huge funeral pall edged with silver foam. To the Devil watching from the rock of Gibraltar—that stony gateway between two worlds—the countless, fiery eyes of the ship were scarcely visible behind the curtain of snow as the vessel sailed away into the blizzard and the night. The Devil was vast, like the rock itself, but the ship was vast too, a thing with many decks and many funnels created by the arrogance of the New Man with an old heart. The storm tore at her rigging and her wide-mouthed funnels that were white with snow, but she was steadfast, majestic and awesome. High on her very top deck, lost amid the flurries of snow, stood the comfortable, dimly-lit quarters where like a pagan idol her corpulent master presided solemnly over the ship in a light, fitful doze. He heard the frenzied howling and bass wailing of the siren smothered by the storm, but was reassured by the proximity of something in the next room that for him was really the most incomprehensible thing of all: that large, almost armored cabin filled incessantly with the mysterious humming, flickering and dry crackling of dark blue lights that flared and burst around the pale-faced radio operator as he sat with a semi-circular, metal hoop over his head. At the very bottom of the *Atlantis,* in her underbelly far below the water line, her massive twelve-ton boiler and countless other machines shone with dull steel, hissing steam, dripping boiling water and exuding oil. There, in that kitchen where the ship's motion was cooked over hellish fires burning red-hot from below, seethed power that was terrifying in its enormity, power that was transmitted down the endlessly long, round vault dimly lit by electric light, down into the vessel's very keel. There, stretched out like a living monster in this tunnel that resembled the muzzle of a giant gun, the colossal propeller shaft slowly rotated in its oily bed, turning on and on with a relentless rhythm that crushed the soul. But the center of the *Atlantis,* her dining saloons and ballrooms, were filled with light and joy, buzzing with the sound of elegant passengers' voices, ringing with the music of the orchestra, and fragrant with the scent of fresh flowers. And once again, the slender, lissom couple of hired lovers writhed agonizingly to the music, occasionally clinging convulsively to each other amid the dazzling throng of lights, silks, diamonds, and women's bare shoulders: the sinfully modest girl with her downcast eyes and innocent-looking coiffure, and the tall young man with

120

black hair that seemed glued to his head above a face pale with powder. In his narrow dress coat with its long tails and his elegant patent-leather shoes, the handsome fellow looked like an enormous leech. And no one knew that this couple had long ago grown sick and tired of writhing in bogus bliss to the shamelessly melancholy music, or that far, far below—in the depths of the dark hold close to the sultry bowels of the ship as she fought her way through darkness, ocean, and blizzard—there stood a coffin...

October 1915

N. D. Teleshov (seated) with Ivan Bunin, Moscow 1910.

What does it matter of whom one speaks? Every creature on this earth is worthy of it.

One day Chang came to know the world and the captain, his master, with whom his earthly existence was joined. And since then six whole years have passed and run out like the sand in a ship's hourglass.

And now again it was night—was it a dream or reality?—and again morning was coming—was it reality or a dream? Chang is old, Chang is a drunkard, and he dozes all the time.

Outside in the city of Odessa it is winter. The weather is foul and gloomy, much worse even than the weather in China when Chang and the captain first met. Fine, raw snow is falling, driving slantwise over the frozen, slippery asphalt of the deserted boulevard along the shore, and whipping painfully in the face of every Jew who runs awkwardly to the right or left, with his back bent and his hands thrust in his pockets. Beyond the harbor, it too deserted, beyond the bay clouded with snow, the naked shores of the steppe are faintly visible. All the harbor mole is shrouded in thick, gray mist; from morning till night the sea leaps over it with foaming, bellying waves. The wind whistles loudly in the telephone wires...

On days like this life in the city does not begin early. Nor do Chang and the captain wake early either. Six years—is that a lot or a little? In six years Chang and the captain have grown old, though the captain is not yet forty, and their fortunes have taken a sharp turn for the worse. They no longer sail the seas but live "ashore," as sailors say, and not where they once used to live but in a narrow, rather gloomy street, in the attic of a five-story house that smells of coal and is inhabited by Jews of the kind who come home to their families only towards evening and eat supper with their hats perched on the back of their heads. The ceiling in Chang and the captain's room is low, and the room is big and cold. What is more, it is always gloomy: the two windows in the sloping wall-cum-roof are small and round and look like portholes. Between the windows stands something like a chest of drawers, while by the wall to the left is an old iron bedstead; this is all the furniture in their dismal abode, not counting the fireplace from which a cool wind always blows into the room.

Chang sleeps in the corner by the fireplace. The captain sleeps on the bed. Anyone who has lived in an attic will easily imagine what this bed sagging almost to the floor and what its mattress are like, while its dirty pillow is so thin that the captain has to put his jacket under it. And yet even on this bed the captain sleeps very soundly, lying on his back with a gray face and his eyes closed, motionless as a corpse. What a marvelous bed he used to have before! Smooth and high, with drawers under it and a deep, comfortable mattress, fine, smooth sheets and cooling, snow-white pillows! But even then, even when his ship was rolling, the captain did not sleep as soundly as he does now: he gets very tired during the day now, and anyway what has he to worry about nowadays, what could he miss by oversleeping, and how could the new day bring him joy? Once there were two truths on earth which constantly alternated with each other: the first was that life is ineffably beautiful, while the second was that life is meaningful only for the insane. Now the captain maintains that there is, was, and forever shall be only one truth, the second of the two, the truth of the Jew Job and of that sage from an unknown tribe, Ecclesiastes. As he sits in the alehouse, the captain often says now: " 'Remember, man, in the days of thy youth those days and years of which thou shalt say: I have no pleasure in them!' " But all the same, days and nights exist as before, and now once again morning was coming. And Chang and the captain were waking up.

But once awake, the captain does not open his eyes. Not even Chang knows what the captain is thinking at this moment, as he lies on the floor near the unlit fire from which the sea's coolness has gusted all night. Chang knows only one thing: that the captain will go on lying there like that for at least an hour. Shooting him a sidelong glance, Chang closes his eyes again and dozes off once more. Chang is a drunkard too, he too is dulled and feeble in the mornings, and feels for the world that languid revulsion so familiar to all who sail in ships and suffer from seasickness. And so, nodding off at this morning hour, Chang has an agonizing, tedious dream...

He dreams:

The old, sour-eyed Chinaman came up onto the steamer's deck, squatted on his haunches and began to whine, begging all who passed to buy the bundle of rotten little fish he had brought. It was a cold, dusty day on the wide Chinese river. Under the reed sail of the man's boat rocking on the silty water sat a puppy—a little ginger dog with a ruff of thick, coarse fur and something foxlike and wolflike about him. With his ears pricked up, he gravely scanned the high iron wall of the ship's side with his intelligent black eyes.

"Sell your dog instead!" shouted the ship's young captain gaily from his bridge where he stood idly watching, his cry loud enough for a deaf man to hear.

The Chinaman, Chang's first master, suddenly looked up, struck dumb both by the captain's shout and his own joy, and began to bow and click with his tongue: "Ve'y good dog, ve'y good!" And so the puppy was bought —all for a silver ruble—and called Chang, and that very day he sailed away with his new master to Russia. To begin with, for three whole weeks, he suffered so badly from seasickness and was so stupefied that he did not see a thing: neither the ocean, nor Singapore, nor Colombo...

In China autumn was beginning and the weather was bad. And Chang began to feel sick before they had barely sailed out into the estuary. Rain and gloom drove towards them, whitecaps gleamed over the flat expanse of water, and the rolling, gray-green swell ran and splashed, its waves sharp-edged and confused, while the flat coast melted away and was lost in the mist—and more and more water appeared all around. Chang in his little fur coat silvered with rain, and the captain in his waterproof with the hood up, stood on the bridge, its height even more apparent now than before. The captain gave orders while Chang shivered and turned his muzzle from the wind. The water spread wider, enveloping the inclement horizon and merging with the murky sky. Driving at them from every quarter, the wind tore spray from the rushing, heavy swell, whistling in the yards and making the canvas awnings below boom and slap, while the sailors in their wet capes and hob-nailed boots untied the canvas, caught it and rolled it up. The wind sought a way to blow more strongly, and as soon as the ship leaned to the wind and veered sharply to starboard, it lifted her on such a great, seething wave that unable to check herself she crashed down the slope of the roller, buried in foam, while in the chart house a coffee cup left on the table by a cabin-boy flew to the floor with a ringing crash... And from that moment it all began!

After that there were all kinds of days: first the sun burned like fire in the shining azure sky, then stormclouds banked up like mountains and rolled away with terrifying thunder, then violent downpours fell upon both ship and sea like a deluge; but the ship rolled and rolled all the time, even when she lay at anchor. Completely worn out, not once in those three weeks did Chang leave his corner in the hot, twilit corridor among the empty second-class cabins on the quarterdeck. He lay by the high threshold of the door leading on deck that opened only once every twenty-four hours when the captain's orderly brought him food. And of all the voyage to the Red Sea Chang remembered only the heavy creaking of the bulkheads, his nausea, and the sinking feeling in his heart as one minute the quivering stern plunged into the abyss and the next reared high into the sky. And he remembered his acute, mortal terror when against this towering stern that suddenly lurched sideways with its screw crashing in the air, a whole mountain of water smashed with the crack of a cannon shot and extinguished the daylight from the port-holes, streaming down their thick glass in cloudy torrents. The sick Chang could hear distant shouts of command, the resounding whistle of the bosun, and the tramp of sailors' feet somewhere above his head. He heard the roar and splash of the water, made out with half-open eyes the twilit corridor stacked with tea in matting bales—and went crazy, drunk with nausea, the heat and the strong smell of tea...

But at this point Chang's dream suddenly stops short.

He shudders and opens his eyes: now it was not a wave striking the stern but a door banging somewhere down below as someone slammed it with all his might. And then the captain noisily clears his throat and slowly rises from his sagging bed. He pulls on his battered shoes and laces them up, takes his black jacket with its gold buttons from under his pillow and puts it

on, and goes to the chest of drawers, while Chang in his threadbare, ginger
fur coat gets up from the floor and gives a yelp-like yawn of displeasure. On
the chest stands an open bottle of vodka. The captain drinks straight from it,
then gasping a little and puffing into his moustache, makes for the fireplace
and pours some vodka for Chang into the dish standing near it. Chang begins to
lap greedily. But the captain lights a cigarette and lies down again—to wait till
the day has properly begun. Already the distant rumble of trams can be
heard, and from far below on the street comes the continuous sound of
hooves clopping on the roadway, but it is still too early to go out. And the
captain lies there and smokes. Having finished lapping, Chang lies down too.
He leaps up on the bed, rolls into a ball at the captain's feet, and drifts slowly into the blissful state that vodka always produces. As his half-closed eyes
grow misty, he looks feebly at his master, and feeling a growing affection towards him, thinks what a human being might express thus: "Oh, foolish man,
foolish man! There is only one truth on earth, and if only you knew what a
wonderful truth it is!" And again, half in dream, half in reality, Chang sees
that distant morning, when after crossing the agonizing, restless ocean the
steamer carrying the captain and him from China sailed into the Red Sea...
    He dreams:
    Passing Perim and moving more and more slowly as if lulling him to
sleep, the ship swung to and fro, and Chang fell into a deep, sweet sleep. And
suddenly he woke. And once awake, he was amazed beyond all measure: all
was quiet, the stern quivered evenly and did not fall away, the water splashed
regularly as it ran beyond the ship's side, and the warm smell of cooking drifting under the door leading on deck was fascinating... Chang stood up and
looked into the empty passengers' saloon: there in the gloom something gol-
den-lilac shone softly, something barely perceptible to the eye yet unusually
joyous—there, looking out into the blue, sun-filled emptiness, into the expanse of air, the rear portholes were open, and over the low ceiling sinuous,
mirror-like rivulets of light streamed and flowed but did not run away. And
the same thing happened to Chang as happened time and again in those days
to his master, the captain: he suddenly realized that there are not one but
two truths in the world—one, that to live on earth and sail the seas is terrible,
and the other... But Chang did not have time to think about the other:
through the door that was suddenly flung open, he caught sight of the ladder
leading to the spar-deck, the shining, black bulk of the steamer's funnel, the
clear sky of a summer's morning, and the captain coming quickly from under
the engine-room ladder, washed and shaved and fragrant with eau-de-Cologne.
With his light brown whiskers turned up in the German fashion and a radiant
look in his sharp, bright eyes, the whole of him was spruce and white as snow.
And at the sight of all this, Chang rushed forward so joyfully that the captain
caught him in midair, gave him a smacking kiss on the head, and turning back,
in three leaps sprang with Chang in his arms first onto the spar-deck, then onto the upper deck, and from there higher still, to the very bridge where Chang

126

had been so terrified in the mouth of the great Chinese river.

On the bridge the captain went into the chart house, while Chang, put down on the floor, sat for a while with his fox's tail spread like a trumpet over the smooth planking. Behind him it was very bright and hot in the low sun. It must have been hot in Arabia too as she passed by close to starboard with her golden coast, her brown-black hills and her peaks that resembled the mountains of a dead planet, they too strewn deep with dry gold—Arabia, with all her wilderness of mountain and sand, visible with such unusual clarity that she seemed only a leap away. But up above, on the bridge, the morning still made itself felt in the slight coolness of the air, and the mate walked briskly to and fro—the same man who later so often drove Chang into a fury by blowing up his nose. He was dressed in white, with a white cap and terrifying dark glasses, and he kept glancing at the sharp point of the foremast in the sky with the finest wisp of cloud curling like a white ostrich feather above it... Then the captain shouted from the chart house: "Chang! Coffee!" and Chang immediately leapt up, ran around the chart house and sprang nimbly over its brass threshold. And beyond the threshold it turned out to be even better than on the bridge: there was a wide leather couch fixed to the wall with some things like round wall clocks hanging above it that shone with glass and needles, while on the floor stood a slop basin filled with a mish-mash of sweet bread and milk. Chang began to lap greedily, while the captain got on with his work: on the wide shelf under the window facing the couch he unfolded a large chart, and laying a ruler on it he firmly drew a long line in scarlet ink. Having finished lapping, with milk on his whiskers Chang leapt up and sat on the shelf right by the window. Through it a sailor's loose shirt with its turndown collar showed blue as the man stood with his back to the window before a wheel with horns on it. And now the captain, who as it turned out later, was very fond of a chat when he was alone with Chang, said to him:

"You see, old fellow, this here's the Red Sea. You and me have to sail through it as cleverly as we can—look how full of little islands and reefs it is—and I've got to get you to Odessa all in one piece, because they already know about you there. I've already let the cat out of the bag by telling a very capricious little girl about you, and I've bragged to her about how nice you are, you see, down that long cable that's laid by clever folk on the beds of all the seas and oceans... Still, Chang, I'm an awfully happy man, so happy you can't even imagine, and that's why I'm very anxious not to run onto one of those reefs and cover myself with everlasting shame on my first long voyage..."

And as he spoke the captain suddenly glanced at Chang and gave him a box on the ear.

"Paws off the chart!" he shouted imperiously. "Don't dare touch official property!"

And with his head reeling, Chang growled and narrowed his eyes. It was the first slap he had ever received and he felt hurt, and again it seemed to him that to live on earth and sail the seas was loathsome. He turned away, dimming and screwing up his transparently bright eyes, and with a soft growl bared his wolf's teeth. But the captain attached no importance to his resentment. He lit a cigarette and went back to the couch, taking a gold watch from the side pocket of his piqué jacket. With his strong nail he prized open its cover, and looking at something shiny and unusually alive that ran busily with a ringing sound inside it, he began to talk in a friendly way once more. Again he began to tell Chang he would take him to Odessa, to Elizabeth Street, that on Elizabeth Street he, the captain, had first of all an apartment, second a beauty of a wife, and third a wonderful little daughter, and that he, the captain, was still a very happy man.

"Still happy, Chang!" said the captain, then added:

"This daughter of mine, Chang, is a playful little girl, inquisitive and persistent—it'll be hard for you sometimes, especially for your tail! But if only you knew, Chang, what a delightful creature she is! I love her so much, old fellow, that I'm even afraid of my love: she means the whole world to me —well, let's say almost—but should it really be like that? And generally speaking, should one love someone so much?" he asked. "Were all those Buddhas of yours really more stupid than you and me? Just you listen to what they say about love for the world and everything physical in general—from sunlight, waves and air, to a woman, a child and the scent of white acacia! Or do you know what Tao is, thought up by you Chinese yourselves? I know very little about it myself, old fellow, and anyway no one knows much about it, but as far as anyone can make out, what is it? The Infinite Mother gives birth and consumes, and in consuming she gives birth anew to all that exists on earth, or in other words—the Way of all that exists which nothing that exists must resist. And yet every minute we constantly resist it and constantly wish to change not only, let's say, the soul of our beloved but the whole world too in our own fashion! It's terrifying to live on this earth, Chang," said the captain, "it's very fine but terrifying, especially for a man like me! I'm so very greedy for happiness and so very often go astray: is the Way of Tao dark and evil, or is it completely the opposite?"

And after a silence he added:

"Where does the essence of it all lie? *When you love someone, no one can possibly make you believe that the person you love might not love you.* And that's the crux of it, Chang. But how magnificent life is, my God, how magnificent!"

Incandescent in the sun that already rode high in the sky, and quivering slightly as she moved, the ship tirelessly clove the Red Sea as it lay becalmed in the boundless expanse of fiery air. The bright emptiness of the tropical sky looked in at the chart house door. Noon drew near, and the brass threshold burned in the sun. The glassy waves rolled by more and more sluggishly, flashing with blinding brilliance and flooding the chart house with light.

Chang sat on the couch listening to the captain. After stroking Chang's head for a while, the captain pushed him to the floor—"no, old fellow, it's too hot!" he said, but this time Chang did not take offense: it was too good living on earth at noon on this joyous day. And then...

But here again Chang's dream stops short.

"Let's go, Chang!" says the captain, throwing his legs off the bed. And again Chang sees with astonishment that he is not on a ship in the Red Sea but in an attic in Odessa, and that outside it really is noon, only not a joyous noon but a dark, tedious, hostile one. And he growls softly at the captain for disturbing him. But paying no attention to him, the captain puts on his old uniform coat and cap and with his hands thrust in his pockets and his back bent goes to the door. Willy-nilly Chang is obliged to jump off the bed. The captain goes downstairs heavily and reluctantly, as if out of some tiresome necessity. Chang goes down quite quickly: he feels invigorated by the still unabated irritation with which the blissful state produced by vodka always ends...

Yes, for two years now, day in, day out, Chang and the captain have spent their time visiting restaurants. There they have a drink and a snack as they watch the other drunks eating and drinking beside them amid noise, tobacco smoke and every kind of stench. Chang lies on the floor at the captain's feet. And the captain sits and smokes with his elbows planted firmly on the table in his seafaring way and waits till some rule of his own devising says he must move on to another restaurant or coffeehouse: so Chang and the captain have breakfast in one place, drink coffee in a second, have lunch in a third, and eat supper in a fourth. Usually the captain is silent. But sometimes he happens to meet one of his old friends, and then he talks incessantly all day long about the insignificance of life, constantly treating first himself then his companion to wine, and then Chang too, who always has some small dish on the floor in front of him. They will spend today just like that: today they have arranged to have breakfast with an old friend of the captain's, an artist in a top hat. This means that to begin with they will sit in a fetid alehouse amid red-faced Germans—obtuse, busy people who work from morning till night in order, of course, to eat, drink, work again and beget children like themselves. Then they will go to a coffeehouse crammed with Greeks and Jews whose whole life, though equally senseless, is very uneasy, wholly taken up with the continual expectation of rumors from the stock exchange. From the coffeehouse they will set off for a restaurant where all manner of human riffraff gather—and they will sit there till late into the night...

The winter day is short, and over a bottle of wine and a chat with a friend it is shorter still. And now Chang, the captain and the artist have already visited both the tavern and the coffeehouse, and sit endlessly drinking in the restaurant. And again, planting his elbows on the table, the captain passionately assures the artist that there is only one truth on earth—one that is evil and base. "Just you look around," he says, "just you remember all those people you and I see every day in the tavern, the coffeehouse and on the street! I've seen the whole globe, my friend, and life's the same everywhere! It's all falsehood and nonsense that men pretend to live by: they have neither God, conscience nor rational purpose in life, neither love, friendship, integrity—nor even simple pity. Life's a boring winter's day in a dirty tavern, no more..."

And lying under the table, Chang listens to it all through a haze of intoxication in which there is no longer any excitement. Does he agree or not agree with the captain? It is impossible to say for sure, but since it is impossible, things must be bad. Chang does not know or understand whether the captain is right; and anyway we all say "I don't know, I don't understand" only in sorrow; in joy every living thing is sure it knows and understands everything. But suddenly it's as if a ray of sunlight pierces that haze: there comes the sudden tap of the conductor's baton against the music stand on the restaurant platform—and a violin begins to play, and after it a second, then a third... More and more passionately, more and more clearly they play—and after a minute Chang's soul overflows with a completely different yearning, a completely different sorrow. It quivers with incomprehensible delight, with sweet torment, with craving for something—and Chang can no longer make out whether he is dreaming or awake. With all his being he surrenders himself to the music, following submissively behind it into a different world—and once more he sees himself on the threshold of that beautiful world as a foolish, trusting puppy on a steamer in the Red Sea...

"And did this really happen?" he half dreams, half thinks. "Yes, I remember: it was good to be alive in the heat of noon in the Red Sea!" Chang and the captain sat in the chart house then stood on the bridge... Oh, how much light, brilliance, blueness and azure there was! How amazingly multicolored against the sky were all those white, red and yellow sailors' shirts hung out on the bow with their sleeves spread wide! And then Chang, the captain, the sailors with brick-red faces, eyes the color of dark oil, and foreheads white and damp with perspiration, had breakfast in the hot first class saloon to the humming and gusting of an electric fan in the corner. After breakfast Chang had a nap, after morning tea had lunch, and after lunch sat up on deck again in front of the chart house, where a cabin boy had put a deck chair for the captain. He gazed far out to sea, at the sunset turning softly green among the multicolored clouds, big and small, and at the wine-red sun, devoid now of rays, that after brushing the cloudy horizon suddenly lengthened to resemble a dark, fiery mitre... The ship ran on quickly after it, while alongside flashed smooth, humped waves shot with the color of violet-blue shagreen leather. But the sun hastened to set—it was as if the sea were drawing it down—and it grew smaller and smaller, to become a long, fiery ember that flickered and died. And as soon as it died the shadow of some great sorrow immediately fell upon all the earth, and the wind that had stiffened towards nightfall blew more strongly still. With his head bared and his hair stirring in the wind, the captain sat gazing at the dark flame of the sunset, and his face was pensive, proud and sad. But one felt that he was *still* happy and that not only this whole ship running on at his bidding but all the world too was in his power, because all the world was in his soul at that moment—and because, furthermore, even then he already smelled of wine...

Night came, magnificent and terrifying. It was dark and troubled, with fitful wind and such brilliance from the waves flailing noisily round the ship that now and then, as he ran after the captain who paced the deck with rapid, incessant stride, Chang leapt back from the rail with a yelp. And again the captain lifted Chang in his arms and putting his cheek to the dog's pounding heart—after all, it was beating just like his own!—walked with him to the very end of the deck, to the quarterdeck, and stood there for a long time in the darkness, bewitching Chang with a wondrous, awesome spectacle: from under the enormous, high stern, from under the propeller raging with a muffled roar, myriads of fiery white needles poured forth with a dry, rustling sound, breaking loose and immediately whirling away down the snowy trail of sparks left by the ship. One moment that trail was filled with huge, pale blue stars and the next with dense, dark blue clouds that exploded with brilliant light, and as they faded the seething mounds of water smoked mysteriously with pale green phosphorus. From different quarters the wind drove strongly but softly from the darkness onto Chang's muzzle, fanning and cooling the thick fur on his chest. Pressing affectionately close to the captain, he caught the smell of what seemed like cold sulphur and breathed in the odor of the ocean ploughed up to its very depths, while the quivering stern rose and fell in the power of some great, ineffably free force. And Chang rocked to and fro, excitedly contemplating this blind and dark yet immeasurably alive and obscurely rebellious Abyss. And now and then some especially wild and weighty wave rushed past the stern and illumined the captain's hands and silver clothing with an eerie light...

That night the captain took Chang into his cabin. It was large and comfortable, and softly lit by a lamp with a red silk shade. On the desk close by the captain's bed two photographs stood in light and shadow near the lamp: a pretty, cross-looking little girl with curls sitting willfully at ease in a deep armchair, and a young lady shown almost full-length, in a big lace hat and smart spring dress with a white lace parasol over her shoulder—as graceful, slim, charming and wistful as a Georgian princess. And to the sound of the black waves racing by outside the porthole, the captain said:

"That woman will not love us, Chang! *Some women's souls, my friend, are eternally parched with a sad thirst for love and for that reason never love anyone.* There are such women—but how can one condemn them for all their heartlessness, their falsity, their dreams of the stage, of having their own car, of picnics on yachts, of some sportsman who pulls out his oiled hair to keep a straight parting? Who can make them out? To each his own, Chang, for do they not obey the most secret commands of Tao just as some denizen of the deep does as it moves at will in these black waters armored with fire?"

"O-oh!" said the captain, sitting down on a chair, shaking his head and untying the laces of one white shoe. "What didn't I feel, Chang, when I first sensed she was no longer completely mine—that night she went to the yacht club ball alone for the first time and came home in the small hours looking like a faded rose, pale with fatigue and excitement that had still not subsided, her eyes all wide, dark and with such a faraway look in them! If only you knew how in her inimitable way she tried to make a fool of me, and with what simple surprise she asked: 'But aren't you asleep yet, poor darling?' At that I couldn't say a word, and she immediately understood and fell silent— she just shot me a swift glance—then quietly began to undress. I felt like killing her, but she said coolly and calmly: 'Help me undo my dress at the back, will you?'—and I went up to her obediently and began undoing those hooks and fasteners with shaking hands. And as soon as I saw her body in the open dress, the space between her shoulderblades, and the chemise let down off her shoulders and tucked into her corset, as soon as I caught the scent of her black hair and glanced at the illumined cheval-glass that reflected her breasts lifted high by the corset..."

And without finishing, the captain waved his hand in a gesture of hopelessness.

He undressed, lay down and put out the light. Turning over and settling down in the morocco armchair beside the desk, Chang saw how the black shroud of the sea was furrowed by streaks of white flame that flared then died, how lights glimmered ominously over the black horizon, and how sometimes from that direction a terrible live wave came running at the ship and, rising above the rail with a menacing roar, glanced into the cabin—like some fantastic serpent shining through and through with eyes of semiprecious stones, translucent emeralds and sapphires. And he saw how the ship thrust it aside and ran steadily on amid the ponderous, shifting masses of this primeval, alien and hostile substance called the ocean...

That night the captain suddenly shouted something in his sleep, and scared by his own cry that rang with mournful despair, immediately awoke. After lying for a moment in silence, he gave a sigh and said with a wry smile:

"Yes, yes! 'As a jewel of gold in a swine's snout—so is a fair woman!' Thrice right art thou, Solomon the Most Wise!"

He found his cigarette case in the darkness and lit a cigarette, but after inhaling twice, dropped his arm and fell asleep with the cigarette glowing red in his hand. And again it grew quiet—only the waves glittered, rolled and ·went rushing by. From behind black stormclouds the Southern Cross...

But then Chang is suddenly deafened by a thunderous crash and leaps up in terror. What has happened? Has the ship struck submerged rocks again through her drunken captain's fault like she did three years ago? Has the captain fired his pistol again at his charming, sad wife? No, it is not night all around, there is no sea and it is not a winter's noon on Elizabeth Street, but a very bright restaurant full of noise and smoke; the drunken captain has banged his fist on the table and is shouting at the artist:

"Rubbish, rubbish! A jewel of gold in a swine's snout, that's woman for you! 'I have decked my bed with coverings of tapestry, with fine linen of Egypt: come, let us take our fill of love, for the goodman is not at home...' O-oh, woman! 'Her house inclineth unto death, and her paths unto the dead...' But enough, enough, my friend. It's time and they're locking up, so let's go!"

And a minute later the captain, Chang and the artist are already outside on the dark street, where the snow-laden wind is blowing out the lamps. The captain kisses the artist farewell and they go their separate ways. Sullen and half asleep, Chang runs sideways along the pavement behind the captain as he reels quickly along... Once more the world is full of darkness, weariness and cold...

So, monotonously, Chang's days and nights go by. Then suddenly, like the ship, the world runs headlong onto a submerged reef hidden from inattentive eyes. Waking up one winter's morning, Chang is struck by the immense silence that reigns in the room. He leaps from his place and rushes to the captain's bed—and sees that the captain is lying with his head flung back, his face stiff and pale, his eyelids half-open and motionless. And seeing those eyelids, Chang gives a desperate howl as if a car hurtling along the avenue had knocked him down and torn him in two...

Later, as the door of the room swings to and fro and people come and go and come again, people of different kinds all talking loudly janitors, policemen, the artist in the top hat, and all sorts of other folk whom the captain used to sit with in restaurants—Chang seems to turn to stone... Oh, how terrible it was when the captain used to say: " 'That day the keepers of the house shall tremble and those that look out of the windows shall be darkened; and they shall be afraid of that which is high, and fears shall be in the way: because man goeth to his long home, and the weeping women make ready to surround him; for the pitcher is broken at the fountain and the wheel is fallen above the well...' " But now Chang no longer feels terror. He lies on the floor with his muzzle towards the corner and his eyes tightly closed so as not to see the world and to forget about it. And the world moves above him with a distant, muffled roar, like the sea above him who sinks ever deeper into its abyss.

He comes to once more on the church porch, by the church door. Stunned and only half alive, he sits beside it hanging his head, the whole of him trembling slightly. And suddenly the church door is flung open and Chang's eyes and heart are struck by a wondrous picture filled with resonant singing: before him is a twilit, Gothic hall, lights like red stars, a whole forest of tropical plants, an oak coffin raised high on a black dais, a crowd of people in black, two women wondrous in their deep mourning and marmoreal

133

beauty—like two sisters of different ages—and above it all a great booming and thundering, exultation, emotion, grandeur, a choir of angels wailing in ringing voices of mournful gladness, and celestial singing that drowns everything else. And all Chang's hair stands on end with pain and rapture at this vision filled with sound. And leaving the church at that moment, his eyes red with weeping, the artist stops in amazement.

"Chang!" he says anxiously, bending over him. "Chang, what is it?"

And touching Chang's head with a trembling hand, he bends lower still, and their tear-filled eyes meet brimful of such love for one another that Chang's whole being cries soundlessly to all the world: oh, no, no—there is yet another truth on earth, a third truth that is unknown to me!

That day, returning from the cemetery, Chang moves into the home of his third master—once more up into the heights, to an attic, but one that is warm and fragrant with the scent of cigars, spread with rugs, set with antique furniture, and hung with huge pictures and brocade tapestries... It is growing dark, the fire is full of burning hot, dusky scarlet embers, and Chang's new master sits in his armchair. When he came home, he did not even take off his coat and top hat, but sat down with a cigar in the deep armchair, smoking and gazing into his twilit studio. And Chang lies still on the rug by the fire with his eyes closed and his muzzle resting on his paws.

Someone else now lies still too—there, beyond the darkling city, beyond the cemetery wall, in what is called a vault, a grave. But that someone is not the captain, no. If Chang loves and senses the captain and sees him in his mind's eye with that divine power which none can comprehend, then the captain is still with him, in that world without beginning and without end where Death cannot reach. In that world there can be only one truth—the third, but what it is remains known only to that last Master, to whom Chang too must soon now return.

Vasilevskoe, 1916

Alexander Kuprin in the early 1900s.

ALEXANDER KUPRIN (1870-1938)

Descended on his mother's side from princely Tatar stock, Kuprin was born in the remote south Russian town of Narovchat in Penza Province. Left fatherless at the age of one, he spent his youth in charitable institutions in Moscow. After training at the Alexander Military Academy, in 1890 he left Moscow to serve in the Tsarist army in southwest Russia. Appalled by the philistinism and brutality of provincial army life, he resigned after only four years' service and became a journalist in Kiev. His time spent working for various Kiev papers (1894-1901) laid the foundations for his literary career. After extensive traveling in southern Russia and an amazing series of casual jobs—among them dental technician, pig-breeder and lavatory pan salesman— in 1901 he moved to Petersburg to devote himself seriously to literature.

The early 1900s saw editorial work for the periodicals *Journal for All* and *God's World*, close friendships with Chekhov, Gorky and Bunin, and marriage. When World War I broke out, Kuprin opened a military hospital in his house near Petersburg and then spent seven months on active service in Finland. In late 1919, accompanied by his second wife and a daughter, he left Russia first for Helsinki and then Paris, where he spent almost twenty years beset by financial difficulties, psychological problems and declining health. In 1937 he returned to the Soviet Union but died the following year.

Though the tale "Moloch" (1896) first made Kuprin known, it was his novel *The Duel* (1905) which brought him fame. Highly critical of conditions and attitudes prevailing in the Russian army, the work appeared just when the disastrous war with Japan was drawing to its ignominious close. The decade that followed brought the publication of many of Kuprin's best tales: "The River of Life" and "Gambrinus" (1906), "Sulamith" (1908), "The Bracelet of Garnets" and "The Lestrigons" (1911), and "Anathema" (1913). 1915 saw the appearance of the third and final part of *The Pit*, his long, semi-documentary study of prostitution.

Kuprin's work written in emigration—his novel *The Junkers* (1928-32), and the tales "The Wheel of Time" (1929) and "Jeannette" (1933), for example—is generally inferior in quality and is pervaded both by nostalgia for the Russia of his youth and by sadness at the long separation from his native land.

Alexander Kuprin / AT THE CIRCUS

I

Doctor Lukhovitsyn, who was regarded as the attending circus physician, asked Arbuzov to undress. Despite the fact that he was hunchbacked, or perhaps precisely because of this disability, the doctor was an avid devotee of the circus, displaying an enthusiasm that was rather amusing in a man of his age. Actually, the performers very rarely resorted to his help, because circus people know how to deal with bruises, dislocations and faints by using their own remedies that have been handed down unchanged from generation to generation, probably since the time of the first Olympic games. All the same, that did not prevent the doctor from seeing every evening performance, being on close terms with all the leading riders, acrobats and jugglers, or showing off a little by using in conversation odd words from the jargon of the ring and stables.

But of all those connected with the circus, it was the weightlifters and professional wrestlers that aroused his particular admiration, one which assumed the proportions of a real passion. So when Arbuzov had taken off his starched shirt and the knitted jersey that all circus performers wear, and stood there stripped to the waist, the little doctor rubbed his hands with pleasure as he walked all around him and admired his huge, sleek body with its firm muscles jutting out as hard as wood beneath the shining, pale pink skin.

"My goodness, what magnificent strength!" he said, squeezing Arbuzov's shoulders as hard as he could with his strong, slender fingers. "This isn't like a man's body at all, it's more like that of a horse, it really is! You could give an anatomy lecture right now, using your body as a model, and you wouldn't need a chart. Now then, my friend, just bend your arm at the elbow, will you?"

The wrestler sighed, and glancing sleepily at his left arm, bent it upwards, so that a large, firm sphere the size of a child's head rose above the elbow, inflating and stretching the delicate skin as it rolled up towards the shoulder. At the same time, at the touch of the doctor's cold fingers, the whole of Arbuzov's naked torso was suddenly covered with small, hard goosepimples.

"Yes, old fellow, God's been good to you all right!" said the doctor, still in raptures. "Do you see these mounds here? In anatomy they're called biceps, that means with two heads. And these are called supinators and pronators. Turn your hand as though you're turning a key in a lock. Right, right, that's fine. Do you see how they move? And these—can you feel me touching your shoulders? These are the deltoid muscles. Yours are just like a colonel's

138

epaulettes. My goodness, you really are a powerful specimen! What if you just hit someone, like that...accidentally, eh? Or what if somebody tried to attack you in the dark somewhere? Eh? God preserve him, I say! Heh-heh-heh! Well now, so we're complaining of sleeping badly and of slight, general weakness, are we?"

The wrestler had been smiling a shy yet condescending smile all this time. Though he had long ago grown used to appearing half-naked in front of others who were fully clothed, he still felt self-conscious, almost ashamed of his big, strong, muscular body as he stood in front of the puny doctor.

"I'm afraid I might have caught cold, doctor," he said in a thin, feeble, rather hoarse voice that did not match his massive frame at all. "The thing is, our dressing rooms are disgraceful—there are drafts everywhere. During the performance, as you know, you break out in a sweat, and then you've got to change in a draft. So you catch a chill."

"Does your head ache? Have you got a cough?"

"No, I don't cough at all, but my head," and Arbuzov rubbed the back of his close-cropped head with his palm, "well, it's true, it's not quite right somehow. It doesn't ache, but it feels...sort of heavy somehow... And I'm sleeping badly too, especially when I first go to bed. I start falling asleep, you know, then suddenly something seems to jerk me up, just as if I've had a fright, you see. And my heart even starts pounding with fear. And that happens three or four times, and I keep waking up. And in the morning my head feels bad and...I'm just generally off color somehow."

"Does your nose bleed?"

"Sometimes, doctor."

"Mm-yes. I see..." drawled Lukhovitsyn meaningfully, and raising his eyebrows, he immediately lowered them again. "I suppose you've been doing a lot of training recently, have you? Do you get very tired?"

"Yes, I have been doing a lot, doctor. It's carnival time now, you see, so I have to do weightlifting every day. And sometimes, when there's a morning performance too, it's twice a day. And then every other day, besides my usual appearance, I have to wrestle... So of course I do get a bit tired sometimes..."

"Right, right," agreed the doctor, breathing in and shaking his head. "Now we'll listen to your chest. Spread your arms out wide. That's splendid. Now breathe in. Steady, steady. Breathe in...deeper...more evenly..."

Barely tall enough to reach Arbuzov's chest, the little doctor put his stethoscope to it and began to listen. Looking with concern at the back of the doctor's head, Arbuzov noisily breathed in then out again, pursing his lips like a little trumpet so as not to blow on the parting in the doctor's smooth, glossy hair.

Having sounded and tapped his patient, the doctor sat down on a corner of his desk, and crossing his legs, clasped his bony knees in his hands. His jutting, birdlike face that was broad across the cheekbones and narrow towards the chin, was serious, almost stern. After thinking for a moment, he began to speak, looking over Arbuzov's shoulder at the bookcase:

"I can't find anything seriously wrong with you, my friend, though these palpitations and nosebleeds should perhaps be taken as gentle warnings from the next world. You see, you have a tendency towards hypertrophy of the heart. Now this—how shall I put it—is a condition to which all who engage in strenuous muscular activity are susceptible—people like blacksmiths, sailors, gymnasts, and so on. As a result of constant, excessive exertion, the walls of their hearts become unusually thick, and the result is what we call *cor bovinum*, or ox heart. One fine day a heart like this just refuses to work any longer, becomes paralyzed, and then—that's it, the show's over. Don't worry though, you're still a very long way off that unpleasant moment, but to be on the safe side I advise you not to drink coffee, strong tea, spirits, or other stimulants. Do you understand?" asked Lukhovitsyn, drumming his fingers softly on the desk and glancing at Arbuzov from under his brows.

"Yes, doctor."

"And in other things too the same restraint is advisable. You understand, of course, what I mean, don't you?"

The wrestler, who at that moment was fastening his collar buttons, blushed and smiled in embarrassment.

"Yes...but you know, doctor, don't you, that in our profession we have to be moderate anyway. And to tell you the truth, there's hardly time even to think about things like that."

"Well that's splendid, my friend. So you go and have a couple of days' rest, or more if you can. You're wrestling against Reber tonight, aren't you? Well try to get the bout put off to another time. You can't? Well say you're feeling ill, that's all. Anyway, I simply forbid you to fight, d'you hear? Show me your tongue. There you are, you see, your tongue's bad too! You feel weak, don't you? Hey! Come on, tell me the truth! I won't tell anybody anyway, so what the hell are you worrying about? That's what doctors and priests get paid for, keeping other people's secrets. You feel really bad, don't you? Aren't I right?"

Arbuzov confessed that he did not feel well at all. From time to time he felt very weak and a kind of lassitude came over him. He had no appetite and felt feverish in the evenings. Couldn't the doctor prescribe some drops or something for him?

"No, my friend, do as you wish, but you shouldn't fight tonight," said the doctor flatly, jumping off his desk. "As you know, I'm not new to this game, and I've always told the wrestlers I've known just one thing: before a bout observe four rules: one, have a good sleep the night before; two, eat a nourishing, tasty meal a few hours before the match, but three, fight on an empty stomach; and lastly, four—and this is more of a psychological point— never for one moment lose confidence in the belief that you will win. Now the question is, how on earth will you fight tonight when you've been feeling ill all day? Forgive the indiscreet question... I know how to keep my mouth shut, you know...but is this bout on the level? Or has it been fixed? I mean, has it been agreed in advance who will beat whom and in which bout of the contest?"

"Oh no, doctor, what do you mean? Reber and I have been chasing each other all over Europe for a long time now. Even the caution money is real, and not just for publicity. We've both paid a deposit of a hundred rubles to a third party."

"All the same, I don't see any reason why you can't put the bout off to another time."

"On the contrary, doctor, there are very good reasons why that's impossible. Just judge for yourself. Our contest consists of three bouts. Now Reber won the first and I took the second, so that means the third is the deciding bout. But we've got to know each other's style of wrestling so well that we can say almost without any doubt who'll win the third bout. Now suppose I'm not sure of my strength—what prevents me from going sick or lame or something, and asking for my money back? So what will Reber have fought the first two bouts for if I do that? Just for fun? That's why, doctor, we agreed that the one who turns out to be sick on the day of the deciding bout is considered the loser anyway and forfeits his money."

"Yes, it's a nasty business," said the doctor, and again raised then lowered his eyebrows in a meaningful way. "Well then, my friend, why not say to hell with your hundred rubles and forfeit them?"

"Two hundred, doctor," Arbuzov corrected him. "According to my contract with the circus manager, I must pay a forfeit of a hundred rubles if I withdraw on the day of the bout, even if I'm ill."

"Well, to hell with it...so you lose two hundred!" said the doctor, growing angry now. "If I were you, I'd still refuse to fight... To hell with the money, forget it, your health's more important. And anyway, my friend, you're still running the risk of losing your caution money if you fight when you're sick against a dangerous opponent like that American."

Arbuzov shook his head self-confidently and his thick lips curved into a scornful grin.

"Oh, rubbish!" he said disdainfully. "Reber only weighs two hundred pounds and he hardly comes up to my chin. You wait and see, I'll have him flat on his back inside three minutes. I'd have thrown him in the second bout too if he hadn't got me up against the ropes. As a matter of fact it was a swinish trick on the referee's part to allow dirty wrestling like that. Even the audience protested about it."

The doctor smiled a barely perceptible, crafty smile. Coming into constant contact with circus life as he did, he had long ago become familiar with the unshakeable, boastful self-assurance of all professional wrestlers, weightlifters and boxers, and with their tendency to blame their defeats on chance factors. He prescribed bromide, to be taken an hour before the bout,

141

gave Arbuzov a friendly slap on his broad back, and wished him luck.

II

Arbuzov came out onto the street. It was the last day of Shrovetide week, which was late that year. It was still cold, but the soft, gentle breath of spring that tickles the chest so joyfully was already in the air. Over the well-trodden, dirty snow two lines of carriages and sleighs went racing silently by in opposite directions, and the warning shouts of their drivers rang out particularly softly and clearly in the cool air. At the crossroads they were selling toffee apples from new, white tubs, halva the color of the snow on the street, and colored balloons. The balloons could be seen from far away. They rose in bright, multicolored clusters and floated over the heads of the passersby who filled the pavements to overflowing with a seething, black torrent. In the balloons' swaying movements, first swift then lazy, there was something freshly vernal and joyously childlike.

At the doctor's Arbuzov had hardly felt ill at all, but outside in the fresh air he was overcome by the familiar, wearisome feeling of sickness once more. His head felt big, heavy and empty somehow, and every step he took echoed inside it with an unpleasant rumbling sound. There was a taste of burning in his dry mouth, and a dull ache in his eyes as if someone was pressing them with their fingers, and when he shifted his gaze from one object to another, two big, yellow spots danced over the snow, the houses and the sky.

On a round pillar at the crossroads his eye was caught by his own name, printed in big letters. Mechanically, he went up to the pillar. Among the multicolored posters announcing entertainments offered during the holidays, he saw a special green notice pasted up below the usual red circus poster. Filled with indifference, he read it through from beginning to end as though in a dream:

DUVERNOIS BROS. CIRCUS
To take place today—the third and deciding wrestling bout
According to Franco-Roman rules
Between the famous American champion
Mr. John Reber
And the great Russian wrestler and weightlifter
Mr. Arbuzov
For a prize of 100 rubles   Details on posters

Two workmen—metalworkers judging by their soot-streaked faces—had stopped by the pillar, and one of them began to read the notice about the wrestling match aloud, mangling the words as he did so. Arbuzov heard his own name, and it sounded ragged, alien and pale, drained of all meaning as

142

sometimes happens if one repeats the same word over and over again for a long time. The workmen had recognized him. One of them nudged his companion and stepped respectfully aside. Annoyed, Arbuzov turned away, and thrusting his hands in his coat pockets, went on his way.

At the circus the matinee performance was already over. As daylight reached the ring only through a snow-covered window in the dome of the roof, the circus looked like a huge, cold, empty barn in the semi-darkness.

Coming in from the street, Arbuzov had difficulty making out the first row of seats, the plush-covered barriers and ropes down the aisles, the boxes with their gilded sides, and the white columns with shields nailed to them decorated with horses' heads, clowns' masks and monograms of various kinds. The circle and gallery were lost in darkness. High above, hauled up on its pulleys under the dome, the gymnasts' apparatus gleamed with its cold nickel and steel—ladders, rings, horizontal bars and trapezes.

In the ring itself two men were rolling about on the floor. Screwing up his eyes, Arbuzov peered at them for a long time before recognizing his American opponent, who was training as he did every morning with one of his assistants, Harvan, also an American. In professional wrestlers' jargon these assistants are called "wolves" or "dogs." Accompanying a famous wrestler all over the world, they help him in his daily training, see to his wardrobe if his wife is not traveling with him, rub his muscles down with special rough mittens after his morning bath and cold shower, and generally render him a multitude of small services directly connected with his profession. As these "wolves" are either young wrestlers—men who are still unsure of themselves, have yet to learn all the secrets of their profession and to master all the holds—or old, mediocre wrestlers, they rarely win any prizes in contests. But before a bout with a wrestler in his own class, the professional invariably sets his own "dogs" on him first, so that by watching the sparring he can detect the weaknesses and common mistakes of his future opponent, and assess the man's strong points that he must watch out for. Reber had already set one of his assistants on Arbuzov—an Englishman called Simpson, a second-rate wrestler who though pudgy and sluggish was renowned for his monstrously powerful grip. The bout had been arranged at the circus director's request with no prize reserved for the winner, and Arbuzov had thrown the Englishman twice, almost nonchalantly, using rare and spectacular throws that he would never have risked against an opponent who was in the least bit dangerous. At the time Reber had made a mental note of Arbuzov's main strengths and weaknesses—his great height and weight together with terrible power in his arm and leg muscles, and audacity and determination in his holds combined with a plastic grace of movement that always won the audience's hearts. But at the same time Reber had noted the comparative weakness of Arbuzov's wrists and neck, his shortness of breath, and his excessive impulsiveness. And there and then he had decided that with an opponent like Arbuzov he must fight defensively, irritating and weakening him until he was played out. He planned to avoid the front and back holds from which it would be hard to extricate himself, and above all, resolved to withstand his opponent's first onslaughts in which this Russian savage displayed truly enormous strength and energy. Reber had used these defensive tactics in the first two bouts as well, one of which had gone to Arbuzov and the other to himself.

Growing accustomed to the half-light, Arbuzov now clearly made out both wrestlers. They wore gray singlets that left their arms bare, broad leather belts, and trousers fastened with straps at the ankle. Reber was in one of the most important and difficult positions in wrestling—the one called the "bridge." Lying face upwards with the back of his head and the tips of his heels touching the ground, arching his back and keeping his balance with his hands buried deep in the sand and sawdust of the ring, his body formed a resilient, live curve. Meanwhile, bringing all his weight to bear on Reber's protruding belly and chest, Harvan strained every nerve in an attempt to straighten this arched mass of muscles, topple it over and pin it to the ground.

Every time Harvan gave another jolt, both wrestlers grunted with the strain, and gasping painfully with the effort took huge, deep breaths. Big and heavy, with the muscles on their bare arms bulging terribly, they seemed frozen on the floor of the ring in their fantastic poses. In the dim half-light of the empty circus they looked like two monstrous crabs entangled in each other's claws.

Since there exists among wrestlers a peculiar code of ethics by which it is considered reprehensible to watch one's opponent while he is training, Arbuzov pretended not to notice them, and skirting the barrier, walked towards the exit leading to the dressing rooms. Just as he moved aside the heavy red curtain that separated the ring from the performers' passageway, someone pulled it from the other side, and under a shiny top hat set at a rakish angle Arbuzov saw before him the black mustache and laughing dark eyes of his good friend, the acrobat Antonio Batisto.

"Buon giorno, mon cher monsieur Arbousoff!" he cried in a singsong voice, flashing his fine, white teeth and opening his arms wide as though wanting to embrace the wrestler. I have jus' finished my répétition. Allons donc prendre quelque chose. Let's go and have a drop of something, shall we? One little glass of brandy? But don't break my arm, will you? Let's go to the canteen."

Everyone in the circus liked Antonio, from the manager down to the stableboys. He was an exceptionally fine, all-around performer: equally good either juggling or performing on the trapeze and horizontal bar, he could train dancing horses or stage pantomimes, and, most important of all, was indefatigable in devising new acts—a talent that is particularly prized in the circus world where art, by its very nature, hardly develops at all, remaining even today very nearly the same as it was under the Roman Emperors.

Arbuzov liked everything about Antonio: his gaiety, his generosity and his exquisite tact that was exceptional even among circus performers, who outside the ring—which traditionally allows a certain roughness of manner—are usually noted for their gentlemanly courtesy. Despite his youth, he had already performed in all the big cities of Europe, and in every troupe to which he had belonged he was considered the most desirable and popular colleague of all. He had an equally poor command of all the European languages, and in conversation mixed them all up the whole time, mangling the words in a rather deliberate way, because in every acrobat there is always a little of the clown.

"Do you know where the manager is?" asked Arbuzov.

"Il est à l'écurie. He went to the stables to look at a sick horse. Mais allons donc. Let's go then. I'm very pleased to see you. My dear fellow?" Antonio suddenly added in a tone of inquiry, laughing at his own pronunciation and putting a hand under Arbuzov's elbow. "Fine, good luck, samovar, cabby," he added in his usual patter, seeing that the wrestler was smiling.

In the canteen they each had a glass of brandy and chewed slices of lemon dipped in sugar. After the liquor Arbuzov's stomach felt cold at first, then it grew pleasantly warm. But his head started to spin immediately and a kind of drowsy weakness spread through his whole body.

"Oh, sans doute, you will have une victoire—a victory," said Antonio, swiftly twirling his little stick in his left hand and flashing his big, white, even teeth under his black moustache. "You're such a brave homme, such a fine, strong wrestler. I used to know a remarkable wrestler—he was called Karl Abs...yes, Karl Abs. But now he ist gestorben...he is dead. Oh, even though he was a German, he was a great fighter! He once said to me: 'French wrestling is nothing, it's just child's play. And a good wrestler, ein guter Kämpfer, needs very, very little,' he used to say: 'just a powerful neck like a buffalo's, a very strong back like a porter's, long arms with firm muscles und ein gewaltiger Griff...' How do you say that in Russian?" (Antonio clenched and unclenched his right fist several times in front of his face.) " 'Oh, and very strong fingers too! Et puis, he must have legs as steady as a statue's, and of course the most important'...how do you say it?..'the most important thing is a heavy torso. And if besides this he has a strong heart, les poumons'...what is that in Russian?..'lungs like those of a horse, then a bit of sang-froid and a bit of courage, and if he can also savoir les règles de la lutte a little, know all the rules of wrestling, then those are all the small things a good wrestler needs.' Ha-ha!"

Laughing at his own joke, Antonio grasped Arbuzov under the arms with an affectionate gesture, as if about to tickle him, and at that moment his face suddenly became serious. His dark, handsome, mobile features had the amazing trick of being able to change from gay laughter to a stern, gloomy, almost tragic expression so rapidly and unexpectedly that he seemed to have two separate faces—one laughing and the other serious—which in some incomprehensible way he could switch at will.

"Of course, Reber is a dangerous opponent... In America they wrestle comme les bouchers, like butchers. I've seen wrestling in Chicago and New York... Pah, what filth!"

Emphasizing his words with rapid, Italian gestures, Antonio began to talk entertainingly and in detail about American wrestlers. They are allowed to use all the brutal and dangerous holds that are absolutely forbidden in European rings. In America wrestlers squeeze each other's throats, put their hands over their opponent's nose and mouth while holding his head in a terrible grip called the iron collar, the collier de fer, and make him lose consciousness by skillful pressure on the carotid artery. Dreadful holds are passed down from teachers to pupils as impenetrable professional secrets, holds whose effect is not always clear even to doctors. With a knowledge of such holds, it is possible, for example, to cause momentary paralysis of one's opponent's arm by a gentle and apparently accidental blow on the triceps, or by an imperceptible movement to cause him such intolerable pain that he throws all caution to the winds. Reber himself had recently been taken to court in Lodz, because during a bout with the famous Polish wrestler Wladislawski he had grasped his opponent's arm over his shoulder in a tour de bras hold and, ignoring the protests of the audience and of Wladislawski himself, had started to bend it in the opposite direction to the natural one, and had kept on bending it till he tore the Pole's shoulder tendons. American wrestlers, Antonio explained, took no artistic pride in their skill and wrestled only for the money. The cherished ambition of every one of them was to make fifty thousand dollars, then immediately put on weight and let himself go, and open a little bar somewhere in San Francisco, where rat-fighting and the most brutal forms of American boxing could flourish on the sly with the police knowing nothing about it.

Arbuzov had known all about this, including the Lodz scandal, for a long time, and he was less interested in what Antonio was telling him than in the strange feelings of sickness that he was now noting with some surprise. Sometimes Antonio's face seemed to move up very close to his own, and the acrobat's every word rang out so loudly and harshly that it reverberated inside his head with a dull, rumbling sound. Then a moment later Antonio's face began to recede, moving further and further away till it became dim and ludicrously small, and then his voice sounded soft and muffled as if he were talking to Arbuzov on the telephone or from several rooms away. And the most amazing thing of all was that the way these impressions changed depended on Arbuzov himself and on whether he gave way to the pleasantly lazy feeling of drowsy languor that had taken possession of him, or whether with an effort of will he shook it off.

"Oh, I have no doubt that you will throw him, mon cher Arbousoff, my dear fellow, my good friend," said Antonio, laughing and mangling the affectionate Russian nouns. "Reber, c'est un animal, un accapareur. He's just a tradesman, like one man's a water-carrier, another's a cobbler, and another's

146

...un tailleur who sews trousers. He's got nothing here...dans le coeur...nothing at all, no feeling, no tempérament. He's just a big, rough butcher, while you're a real expert. You're an artist, and it always gives me pleasure to watch you."

Just then the manager came quickly into the canteen. He was a small, fat, thin-legged man with hunched shoulders and no neck, wearing a top hat and open fur coat. His round, bulldog's face, thick moustache and severe eyes under sternly frowning brows made him look very much like Bismarck. Antonio and Arbuzov touched their hats. The manager did likewise and then, as if he had been restraining himself for a long time and had only been waiting for a suitable opportunity, immediately began cursing a stableboy who had annoyed him.

"The oaf, the Russian swine...he went and watered a sweating horse, damn him!.. I'll go to a Justice of the Peace and he'll award me three hundred rubles' damages against him, the bastard. I'll...to hell with him!.. I'll go and smash his face in, I'll flog him with my riding crop!"

And as though seizing on this thought, he turned abruptly and, mincing along on his feeble, thin legs, set off at a run for the stables. Arbuzov caught up with him near the door.

"Mr. Manager, sir..."

The manager suddenly stopped, and with the same displeased expression on his face thrust his hands into his coat pockets and waited to hear what Arbuzov had to say.

The wrestler asked him to postpone that day's bout for a day or two. If the manager liked, he would give in return two or even three evening weight-lifting performances over and above what had been agreed between them. In addition would the manager kindly undertake to discuss with Reber the question of changing the date of the bout?

The manager listened, turning only halfway towards Arbuzov and looking beyond him and out of the window. When he was satisfied that the wrestler had finished, he brought his severe eyes hung with their sallow bags to bear on him and snapped sternly:

"Hundred rubles' forfeit."

"Mr. Manager, sir..."

"I don't need you, damn it, to tell me I'm the manager," he interrupted, beginning to seethe with anger. "You arrange things with Reber yourself, it's none of my business. My business is the contract and yours is the forfeit."

He turned his back abruptly on Arbuzov and walked to the door, his mincing feet moving rapidly. But when he reached the door he suddenly stopped and turned, shaking with fury. His flabby cheeks quivering, his face purple with rage, his neck red and swollen, and his eyes bulging wildly, he shouted breathlessly:

"To hell with you! I've got Fatinitsa, my best riding horse, on her last legs!.. That Russian groom, the swine, the scum, that stupid ape, goes and gives my very best horse too much to drink, then you come along with all this nonsense about postponement. Go to hell! Today's the last day of this idiotic Russian carnival and I haven't a single spare seat left. The public will create ein grosser Skandal if I cancel the wrestling. To hell with you! They'll ask for their money back and tear the place apart! Schwamm drüber! I won't listen to any nonsense from you, so I haven't heard a thing and I don't know anything about it!"

And he rushed out of the canteen, slamming the heavy door so hard behind him that the glasses on the counter responded with a faint, tinkling sound.

III

Saying goodbye to Antonio, Arbuzov set off home. Before the bout he wanted to have some dinner and get some sleep so as to clear his head a little. But when he went outside he felt ill again. The noise and bustle of the street seemed somewhere far, far away, and they were as alien and unreal as if he were watching a multicolored, moving picture. Crossing the streets, he felt acutely afraid of being run into from behind by horses and knocked off his feet.

He lived in furnished rooms not far from the circus. Even on the stairs he caught the smell that always filled the corridors—the smell of cooking, kerosene fumes and mice. Feeling his way down the dark corridor towards his door, Arbuzov kept expecting to stumble against some obstacle in the darkness, and to this feeling of tense expectation was added an involuntary, agonizing sense of melancholy anxiety, bewilderment, fear and the awareness of his own solitude.

He was not hungry, but when his dinner was brought from the "Eureka" restaurant downstairs, he forced himself to eat a few spoonfuls of red borshch that smelled like a dirty dishcloth, and half a pale, stringy chop in carrot sauce. After his meal he felt thirsty, so he sent the serving boy for some kvass then lay down on his bed.

Immediately the bed began to rock gently beneath him, floating like a boat, while the walls and ceiling slowly drifted away in the opposite direction. But there was nothing unpleasant or frightening about this sensation; on the contrary, together with it his body was filled with an increasingly strong feeling of warm, weary languor. Covered with soot and furrowed with thin, sinuous cracks that looked like veins, the ceiling first rose high above him, then came down very close, and in its constant vacillation there was an enervating, somnolent smoothness of movement.

Somewhere on the other side of the wall cups were rattling; the constant sound of hurried footsteps could be heard in the corridor, muffled by the matting on the floor; and the rumbling sound of the street came in at the window, sweeping and indistinct. For a long time all these sounds clashed with one another, overlapping and intermingling, then suddenly, merging for a few moments, they arranged themselves into a wonderful melody which was so unexpected and richly beautiful that it caused a tickling in his chest and made him feel like laughing.

Raising himself a little on the bed to have a drink, Arbuzov looked around his room. In the thick, violet twilight of a winter's evening all the pieces of furniture looked quite different from the way they usually looked: they had the strange, mysterious expression of things that were alive. The low, squat, grave-looking chest of drawers, the tall, narrow wardrobe with its business-like but callous, derisive air, the goodnatured, round table, and the elegant, coquettish mirror—through his languorous, lazy drowsiness they were all watching Arbuzov vigilantly, expectantly and menacingly.

"I must be feverish," he thought and repeated aloud:

"I'm feverish," and his voice echoed in his ears with a faint, hollow, indifferent sound that came from somewhere far away in the distance.

Rocking on his swaying bed and feeling a pleasantly drowsy, burning sensation in his eyes, Arbuzov sank into a fitful, feverish sleep. But in his delirium he continued to experience the same constantly changing succession of sensations that he had felt while awake. First he seemed to be making a terrible effort to move and pile up one on top of the other huge blocks of granite with polished sides that were smooth and hard to the touch but at the same time soft as cotton wool, so that they gave beneath his hands. Then all the blocks collapsed and slid to the ground, and in their place was left something flat, unsteady and ominously still. It had no name, but it resembled both the smooth surface of a lake and a length of thin wire that stretched to infinity and hummed with a monotonously wearisome, soporific sound. But then the wire disappeared and he was piling up the huge blocks once more. Again they collapsed with a thunderous crash and again only the ominous, melancholy wire was left in all the world. And all the time he could still see the ceiling with its cracks and hear all the strangely intermingling sounds coming from outside his room, yet all this belonged to some alien, hostile, ever-watchful world that was pitifully dull in comparison with the visions in which he was truly alive.

It was already quite dark when Arbuzov suddenly sprang up and sat on the bed, seized by a feeling of wild terror and excruciating physical anguish. It began in his heart that had suddenly stopped beating, and filled his whole chest, rising into his throat and gripping it tightly. The air could not reach his lungs because something inside was preventing it from entering them. He kept opening his mouth convulsively, gasping for air and trying to breathe, but he could not manage it and began to suffocate. These terrible sensations only lasted three or four seconds, but to Arbuzov it seemed that the attack had begun many years ago and that while it lasted he had turned into an old man. "It's death!" the thought suddenly flashed through his mind, but just then someone's invisible hand touched his silent heart as one touches a motionless pendulum, and with a frenzied jolt that was enough to burst open his chest, it began to beat once more—timorously and confusedly yet avidly too. At the same time hot waves of blood rushed to his face, sweeping into his arms and legs and covering his whole body with sweat.

Through the open door appeared a big, close-cropped head with thin, protruding ears like the wings of a bat. It was little Grisha, the serving boy who helped the valet, asking whether Arbuzov wanted some tea. From behind the boy's back the light from the lamp in the corridor slipped gaily and reassuringly into the room.

"Do you want me to put the samovar on, Nikita Ionych?"

Arbuzov heard these words perfectly well and they left a clear imprint in his mind, but he could in no way bring himself to understand what they meant. Just then his mind was working desperately hard trying to recall some unusual, rare and highly significant word that he had heard in his sleep just before the attack had made him leap up.

"Nikita Ionych, shall I put the samovar on, then? It's after six."

"Wait a moment, Grisha, just a minute," replied Arbuzov, hearing the boy as before but not understanding what he said. Then suddenly he remembered the word he had been searching for: "Boomerang." A boomerang was that funny bit of curved wood he had seen tossed around in the circus at Montmartre by some naked black savages—agile, little muscular fellows they were. And immediately, as though freed from its shackles, Arbuzov's attention shifted to the boy's words that were still echoing in his memory.

"After six, d'you say? Well then, fetch the samovar quickly, Grisha."

The boy went out. For a long time Arbuzov sat on his bed with his feet on the floor, and peering into the dark corners of the room listened to his heart that was still beating unevenly and anxiously. His lips moved softly, clearly repeating the supple, sonorous word that had struck him so forcibly:

"Boo-me-rang!"

IV

At about nine o'clock Arbuzov left for the circus. Grisha, a passionate admirer of circus performers, walked behind him carrying a straw bag with the wrestler's costume in it. At the brightly-lit circus entrance there was a gay, noisy crowd. Cabs kept driving up one after the other and at a wave of the statuesque policeman's hand they described a semicircle and drove off into the darkness past the carriages and sleighs that lined the street. Red circus posters and the special green notices about the wrestling match could be seen everywhere—on both sides of the entrance, near the booking office, in the vestibule and along the corridors—and Arbuzov saw his own name printed in enormous letters everywhere. The corridors smelled of the stables, of gas from the lights, of the sand and sawdust scattered in the ring, and of the usual odor of auditoriums—a mixture of new kid gloves and powder. These smells always used to disturb and excite Arbuzov a little on evenings before a bout, but now they grated on his nerves in an unpleasantly painful way.

Behind the scenes, near the passage by which the performers reached the ring, there hung behind wire netting and lit by a gas lamp a handwritten schedule of the evening's acts under printed headings like "Arbeit. Pferd. Klown." Arbuzov glanced at the list in the vague and naive hope that he would not find his own name on it. But in the second part of the program, under the familiar word "Kampf," he saw the two names Arbusow und Roeber written in a large, slanting, semi-literate hand.

In the ring the clowns were shouting in their expressionless, guttural voices and guffawing idiotically. Antonio Batisto and his wife Henrietta were standing in the passage waiting for the act to finish. They wore identical leotards of soft mauve embroidered with gold sequins and shot at the elbows and knees with a silky luster, while on their feet they had white satin slippers.

Henrietta wore no skirt. Instead, around her waist there hung a long, thick, gold fringe that glittered when she moved. The mauve satin blouse that she wore next to the skin without a corset was loose and did not hamper the movements of her supple torso in the slightest. On top of her leotard she had flung a long, white, Arabian burnous that gently set off her pretty little dark head.

"Eh bien, monsieur Arbousoff?" she said, smiling affectionately and stretching out from under the burnous a slender, bare arm that was strong and beautiful. "How do you like our new costumes? They're Antonio's idea. Will you come to the ring and watch our act? Please do. You've got a good eye and you always bring me luck."

Coming up, Antonio gave Arbuzov a friendly slap on the back.

"Well, how's things, my dear fellow? All right? I'm betting Vincenzo a bottle of brandy that you'll win. So mind you do!"

A roar of laughter echoed through the circus and a storm of applause broke from the audience. The two clowns, their white faces streaked with black and crimson paint, came running out of the ring into the corridor. They seemed to have forgotten the broad, inane grins on their faces, while their chests heaved rapidly after the exhausting somersaults they had performed. The audience called them back and made them do something else, then called them again and once more after that. Only when the orchestra began to play a waltz and the audience grew quiet did the clowns leave for their dressing room, both covered in sweat and suddenly gone to pieces somehow, utterly crushed by fatigue.

The artistes who were not performing that evening, wearing tailcoats and trousers with gold stripes down them, quickly and dexterously lowered the big net from the roof and tied it with ropes to the pillars. Then they lined

151

up along both sides of the passage and someone drew back the curtain. With her eyes sparkling coquettishly and tenderly under her fine, bold eyebrows, Henrietta flung her burnous over Arbuzov's arm, quickly tidied her hair with an habitual feminine gesture, and taking her husband by the hand, ran gracefully out into the ring. Passing the burnous to one of the grooms, Arbuzov followed close behind them.

All the circus people loved to watch this couple perform. The other artistes were amazed not only by their beauty and ease of movement but also by their sense of timing that was developed to an incredible degree of precision—a kind of special sixth sense that is hardly known outside ballet and the circus, but one that is essential for all complex, coordinated movements performed to music. Without wasting a single second and moving in perfect time to the flowing sounds of the waltz, Antonio and Henrietta climbed nimbly up into the dome, to a height level with the upper rows of the gallery. From opposite sides of the circus they blew kisses to the audience—he sitting on the trapeze and she standing on a small platform covered with the same mauve silk that her blouse was made of, with a gold fringe round its edges and the initials A and B in the middle.

Everything they did was perfectly coordinated and timed, and looked so simple and easy that even the artistes watching them completely forgot how difficult and dangerous their act really was. Flinging his whole body backwards as if about to fall into the net, Antonio suddenly hung upside down by his feet from a steel bar and began to sway to and fro. Standing on her mauve platform and grasping her trapeze in outstretched hands, Henrietta watched her husband's every movement with tense expectation. Then suddenly, picking up the rhythm of the music, she pushed off from the platform with both feet and flew towards him, arching her whole body and stretching her shapely legs out behind her. The ropes of her trapeze were twice as long as Antonio's and it swung twice as far as his too, so their trapezes first swayed in parallel, then met, then swung apart...

And then, at some imperceptible signal, she let go of her trapeze, plunged through the air, and suddenly, sliding her hands down Antonio's arms, she locked her fingers tightly with his. For several seconds, knit closely together into a single strong, lissom body, they swayed through the air in a wide, sweeping curve, and Henrietta's little silk shoes skimmed the raised edge of the net. Then Antonio turned her over and flung her into space again just when her trapeze that was still swinging to and fro went flying by above her head. She caught at it quickly and with a single swing flew across to her mauve platform again on the other side of the circus.

The last number in their act was the "flight from the heights." With Henrietta sitting on it, the ring hands hauled the trapeze up by its pulleys right into the dome itself. There, at a height of fifty feet, with her head almost touching the panes of the dormer window in the roof, the artiste moved cautiously across to a fixed horizontal bar. Lifting his head with an effort,

152

Arbuzov watched her, thinking that Antonio must look quite small to her now from up there, and the thought made him feel giddy.

Satisfied that his wife was firmly established on her horizontal bar, Antonio again hung upside down and began to swing to and fro. The orchestra, which until then had been playing a melancholy waltz, suddenly stopped and fell silent. Only the monotonous, plaintive hissing of the filaments in the electric lights could be heard. There was an awesome tension in the silence that suddenly descended upon the audience of thousands who were watching the acrobats' every movement with fearful, avid attention...

"Pronto!" shouted Antonio abruptly in a confident, gay voice, and flung down into the net the white handkerchief he had been wiping his hands with as he swung constantly to and fro. Arbuzov saw how at her husband's cry Henrietta, who stood under the dome holding onto the trapeze wires with both hands, quickly swung her whole body forward with a nervously expectant movement.

"Attenti!" shouted Antonio again.

The filaments in the lamps went on singing their monotonous, plaintive song, while the silence in the circus became painfully ominous.

"Allez!" cried Antonio in an abrupt, commanding voice.

His peremptory cry seemed to thrust Henrietta from her perch. Arbuzov saw how something large, mauve and flashing with golden sparks plunged headlong through the air, spinning as it fell. With a chill in his heart and a sudden feeling of irritating weakness in his legs, the wrestler closed his eyes, and only opened them when, echoing Henrietta's high-pitched, joyful, throaty cry, the whole circus heaved a deep, noisy sigh like a giant casting a heavy burden off his back. The orchestra began to play a furious gallop, and swaying to and fro in time to it as she hung from Antonio's hands, Henrietta gaily moved her legs back and forth and knocked them one against the other. When her husband let go of her, she sank softly deep into the net, but flung upwards again by its resilient mesh, she immediately sprang to her feet. Balancing on the quivering net, she bowed to the cheering audience, radiant with a sincerely joyful smile, flushed and charming... As he threw the burnous over her shoulders in the passage, Arbuzov noticed how rapidly her breast rose and fell, and how hard the delicate blue veins on her temples were throbbing...

V

The bell rang for the interval and Arbuzov went to his dressing room to change. Reber was in the room next door. Through the wide chinks in the hastily-assembled partition Arbuzov could see every movement his opponent made. While he was dressing, the American first hummed some tune in his little bass voice that was out of key, then began to whistle, occasionally exchanging with his trainer a few abrupt, brief words which sounded so strange and muffled that they seemed to come from the very depths of his stomach. Arbuzov knew no English, but every time Reber laughed or sounded cross, it seemed to him that they were talking about him and today's bout, and at the sound of the American's self-assured, croaking voice he was filled increasingly with a feeling of weakness and fear.

When he had taken off his outer garments, he felt cold and suddenly began to shiver, filled with the violent trembling of a feverish chill that made his belly, legs and shoulders shake and his teeth chatter loudly. To warm himself, he sent Grisha to the canteen for some brandy. The liquor calmed and warmed him a little, but after he had drunk it a soft, sleepy weariness spread through his whole body just as it had that morning.

People kept knocking on his door and coming into the room the whole time. There were cavalry officers with their legs sheathed in tight riding breeches like leotards, strapping high school boys in funny little caps, and foppish students all wearing pince-nez for some reason and smoking cigarettes, talking very loudly and addressing each other familiarly the whole time. They all kept touching Arbuzov's arms, chest and neck, and going into raptures at the sight of his bulging muscles. Some of them slapped him affectionately and approvingly on the back as if he were a prize horse, and gave him advice on how to fight the bout. At first their voices sounded to Arbuzov as if they were coming from a long way away, from under the ground somewhere, but then they suddenly bore down on him and beat him excruciatingly about the head. Meanwhile he dressed with habitual, mechanical movements, carefully smoothing then pulling on the thin singlet and fastening the wide leather belt tightly around his waist.

The orchestra began to play and one after another the annoying visitors went out of the dressing room. Only Doctor Lukhovitsyn was left. He took Arbuzov's arm, felt his pulse and shook his head.

"It's sheer madness for you to fight now. Your pulse is going like a hammer and your hands are as cold as ice. Look in the mirror and see how dilated your pupils are."

Arbuzov glanced into the little mirror that stood on the table propped up against the wall, and saw in it a large, pale, expressionless face that seemed unfamiliar to him.

"Well, it's all the same to me, doctor," he said lazily, and putting his foot up on an empty chair, began carefully wrapping around his calf the thin straps attached to his shoes.

Someone went running quickly down the corridor and shouted at the door of each dressing room in turn:

"Monsieur Reber, Monsieur Arbuzov, into the ring please!"

Arbuzov was suddenly filled with an insurmountable lassitude that made him want to stretch his arms and back long and sweetly as if about to fall asleep. In one corner of the dressing room was a large, untidy pile of Circassian costumes for the pantomime in the third part of the program. Looking at this heap of clothes, Arbuzov thought there could be nothing better in the whole world than to climb up on it, lie down comfortably, and bury his head in the soft, warm costumes.

"I must go," he said, getting up with a sigh. "Doctor, do you know what a boomerang is?"

"A boomerang?" asked the doctor in surprise. "I think it's a special kind of weapon the Australians kill parrots with. Or perhaps it's not parrots at all... But what on earth do you want to know that for?"

"I just remembered the word, that's all... Well, come on, doctor, let's go."

By the curtain in the wide, boarded passageway the circus staff were crowding—performers, officials and grooms. When Arbuzov appeared, they began to whisper among themselves and quickly cleared a space for him just behind the curtain. Close behind him came Reber. Trying not to look at one another, the wrestlers stood side by side, and at that moment Arbuzov saw with blinding clarity just how absurd, brutal and senseless the thing was that he was about to do. But he also felt and knew that some merciless, nameless power was keeping him there and forcing him to behave in precisely this way. And he stood motionless, gazing at the heavy folds of the curtain in dumb, sad resignation.

"Ready?" asked a voice from above where the orchestra platform was.

"Ready, let's go!" came the reply from below.

They heard the urgent tapping of the conductor's baton, and then the first bars of a march swept over the circus in gaily rousing waves of brassy sound. Someone flung back the curtain while someone else clapped Arbuzov on the shoulder and gave him the terse command: "Allez!" Shoulder to shoulder, stepping with ponderous, self-assured grace, and still not looking at each other, the wrestlers walked past the performers lining the passage. Reaching the middle of the ring, they separated in different directions.

One of the ringmasters came out into the ring too, and standing between the wrestlers began to read an announcement about the contest from a piece of paper. He had a strong foreign accent and made a lot of mistakes as he read:

"Ladies and gentlemen! You are about to see a wrestling bout according to Franco-Roman rules, between the famous wrestlers Mr. John Reber and Mr. Arbuzov. The rules allow them to use any hold they wish from the head to the waist. The contestant whose shoulderblades touch the ground first is the loser. Scratching, pulling the hair or the legs, and strangling are forbidden. This bout is the third and decisive one. The winner will receive a prize of one hundred rubles... Before the match begins the contestants will shake hands as a solemn promise that they will fight fairly and observe all the rules."

The audience listened to him with such rapt, silent attention that they all seemed to be holding their breath. This was the climax of the whole evening—a moment of impatient, tense expectation. Their faces were pale, their

155

mouths half open, their heads thrust forward, and their eyes riveted with avid curiosity on the two wrestlers who stood motionless on the canvas covering the sand of the ring.

Both men wore tight, black singlets that made their trunks and legs look slimmer and more slender than they really were, but made their bare arms and necks seem more powerful and massive still. Reber stood with one leg slightly in front of the other and one hand resting on his hip in a casual, self-assured pose. With his head flung back he surveyed the upper rows of the gallery. He knew by experience that the sympathies of the gallery would lie with his opponent because Arbuzov was younger and more handsome and graceful, but above all because he had a Russian name. With his calm, care-free look Reber seemed to be throwing down a challenge to the audience scrutinizing him. He was of medium height, broad in the shoulders and broader still in the hips, with short, stocky legs bowed like the roots of a mighty tree, and with the long arms and hunched back of a big, strong ape. He had a small, bald head with a bull neck that, beginning from the crown of his head, ran down smoothly and evenly without any folds of skin, widening towards the base where it merged directly with his shoulders. Seen from the back, this terrible neck aroused in the audience a vaguely fearful notion of brutal, superhuman strength.

Arbuzov stood in the pose that professional wrestlers customarily adopt when they are being photographed, that is with their arms crossed on their chest and their chin pulled down. His skin was lighter than Reber's and his build almost flawless: his neck emerged from the low singlet like a round, smooth, powerful pillar, and it carried the head freely and easily—a handsome head with close-cropped auburn hair, a low forehead, and regular features that at this moment wore an expression of indifference. Pressed together by his folded arms, his pectoral muscles rose beneath his singlet like two bulging spheres, while the round tops of his shoulders shone like pink satin in the blue light of the electric lamps.

Arbuzov looked fixedly at the ringmaster while he read. Only once did he take his eyes off him and turn to look at the audience. Filled with people from top to bottom, the whole circus seemed flooded by a continuous black wave. On it, piled one on top of the other, the round, white spots of faces stood out in regular, straight lines. Gazing at this dark, faceless mass, Arbuzov felt the chill breath of merciless fate. He realized with his whole being that he could not now escape the brightly-lit, bewitched circle of the ring, that some-one else's vast, alien will had brought him here, and that no power on earth could turn him back. And at this thought he suddenly felt helpless, bewildered and weak, like a child who has lost his way, and in his soul stirred an agonizingly real, animal fear, the somber, instinctive terror that fills the young ox as it is led over the bloodstained asphalt into the slaughterhouse.

The ringmaster finished reading and walked away towards the exit. The orchestra began to play once more, its notes cautious but clear and gay, and in the shrill sound of the trumpets there was a sly note of cruel, hidden triumph. There was a terrible moment when Arbuzov thought that the insinuating sounds of the march, the sorrowful hissing of the lamps, and the awesome silence of the audience were all a continuation of his delirium that afternoon when he had seen the long, monotonously humming wire stretching out before him. And once again a voice inside his head uttered the bizarre name of the Australian weapon.

Until then, though, he had been hoping that at the very last moment before the bout anger would suddenly blaze up in him as it always did, bringing with it a swift surge of physical strength and the sureness of victory. But now, when the wrestlers turned to face each other and Arbuzov for the first time met the cold, piercing gaze of the American's small blue eyes, he realized that the outcome of the bout was already decided.

The men came forward towards each other. Reber drew swiftly closer with soft, catlike steps, his terrible neck thrust forward and his knees slightly bent, looking like a beast of prey about to leap upon its quarry. Meeting in the middle of the ring, they exchanged a brief, firm handshake, drew back, then immediately leapt around to face one another. And in the rapid, hot touch of Reber's strong, calloused hand, Arbuzov sensed the same sureness of victory as in his piercing eyes.

At first they tried to grab each other by the wrists, the elbows and the shoulders, twisting away and dodging each other's lunges at the same time. Their movements were economical and cautious, soft and slow like those of two big cats beginning to play. Leaning forward with their heads close together and breathing hotly on each other's necks, they changed their positions constantly and circled the whole ring. Once, taking advantage of his superior height, Arbuzov grasped the back of Reber's neck in his palm and tried to force it down, but the American's head quickly sank between his shoulders like that of a tortoise and his neck became hard as iron, while with his legs planted wide apart he dug his heels hard into the ground. At the same time Arbuzov felt Reber's fingers squeezing his biceps with all their might, trying to cause them pain and weaken them more quickly.

So they circled the ring, hardly moving their feet at all, never letting each other get out of reach, and making slow, lazy, apparently hesitant movements to catch each other off guard. Then Reber suddenly seized his opponent's arm with both hands and jerked it violently towards him. Arbuzov had not anticipated this hold and took two steps forward, but at the same instant felt himself being girdled from behind and lifted off the ground by powerful arms that were crossed on his chest. Instinctively, so as to increase his weight, he leaned the upper part of his body forward, and to avoid a fall spread his arms and legs wide apart. Reber made several attempts to pull Arbuzov's back against his own chest, but realizing he could not lift such a heavy man, he forced him down on his hands and knees with a quick jolt, then knelt beside him and clasped him by the neck and back.

157

For a few moments Reber seemed to be thinking, planning what to do next. Suddenly, with a skillful movement he thrust his hand under Arbuzov's arm from behind and bent it upwards, then grasped his neck in his strong, hard palm and began to force it downwards. At the same time his other arm encircled Arbuzov's belly from below and tried to topple him over. Arbuzov resisted, tensing the muscles of his neck, spreading his arms wider, and bending closer to the ground. The wrestlers remained motionless, as though frozen in one position, and an onlooker might have thought they were simply sparring or resting, had he not noticed their faces and necks gradually filling with blood and their straining muscles bulging more and more sharply under their singlets. Their breathing was loud and raucous, and the pungent odor of their sweat reached the front rows of the stalls.

Suddenly Arbuzov felt the now familiar physical anguish welling up near his heart, filling his whole chest and clutching him convulsively by the throat. Immediately everything became wearisome, futile and desperately dull: the brassy sounds of the orchestra, the sad humming of the lights, the circus, Reber, and the wrestling bout itself. Something like longstanding habit still made him resist, but Reber's hoarse panting on the nape of his neck already sounded like the triumphant roaring of some wild beast. Now one of his hands, torn from the ground, was searching in vain for support in the air. Then his whole body lost its balance, and suddenly pinned down on his back on the cold canvas, he saw above him Reber's sweating, red face with its disheveled, tangled mustache, its teeth clenched in hate, and its eyes crazed by fury...

Getting to his feet, Arbuzov saw Reber as if through a haze, bowing in all directions to the audience. Leaping from their seats, the people were shouting frenziedly, gesturing and waving their handkerchiefs, but to Arbuzov it all seemed like a long familiar dream—a dream that was fantastic and absurd yet at the same time tedious and petty in comparison with the anguish now rending his chest. Reeling, he made his way to his dressing room. The heap of costumes piled in the corner reminded him vaguely of something he had been thinking about recently, and he sank down on it, clutching at his heart with both hands and gasping for air.

Suddenly, together with his feeling of anguish and breathlessness, he was overcome by weakness and nausea. Everything went green before his eyes, then began to grow dark and sink into a deep, black abyss. Inside his head someone shouted distinctly in a harsh, shrill voice—it sounded like the snapping of a thin string—the word "Boo-me-rang!" Then everything vanished: thought, consciousness, pain and anguish. And it was just as simple and quick as if someone had blown on a candle burning in a dark room and put it out...

1901

158

Alexander Kuprin / EMERALD

I dedicate this tale to the memory of that incomparable piebald trotter, Kholstomer*

I

The four year-old stallion Emerald—a sturdy racehorse of American stock with a smooth, gray coat the color of silvery steel—woke in his stall at about midnight as usual. Beside him to left and right, and facing him across the corridor, the other horses munched their hay in steady rhythm, as if all in time with each other, crunching the fragrant fodder and snorting occasionally at the dust. In the corner on a pile of straw snored the groom on duty. By the sequence of days and the particular sound of the man's snoring, Emerald knew it was Vasily, a young fellow the horses didn't like because he smoked stinking tobacco in the stables, often came drunk into their stalls, jabbed them in the belly with his knee, brandished his fist before their eyes, pulled roughly at their halters, and always shouted menacingly at them in an unnaturally raucous, bass voice.

Emerald went up to the grill in the door. Straight opposite him in her stall stood the little black mare, Dandy Lady, who was still not fully grown. Emerald could not make out her body in the darkness, but every time she left her hay for a moment and turned her head, her big eye gleamed for a few seconds with a beautiful violet light. Flaring his soft nostrils, Emerald drew a long, deep breath, and catching the barely perceptible but strong, exciting scent of her hide, neighed briefly. Turning quickly, the mare replied playfully with a thin, tremulous, affectionate neigh.

Immediately beside him to his right Emerald heard a jealous, angry breathing. It was Onegin, a restive, old red stallion who still raced for prizes occasionally in individual city events. The horses were separated by a light partition of planks and could not see one another, but putting his head with a snort to the right-hand edge of the grill, Emerald clearly smelled the warm odor of well-chewed hay issuing from Onegin's rapidly breathing nostrils... So the stallions sniffed at each other for a while in the darkness, flattening their ears, arching their necks, and growing more and more angry. Then suddenly, both gave a spiteful whinny, neighed loudly and stamped their hooves.

"Stop fooling around, you devils!" shouted the groom sleepily in his familiar, threatening voice.

The horses started back from their grills and pricked up their ears. For a long time now they had not been able to stand one another, but since the graceful black mare had been put into the same stable three days ago—something that is not done as a rule and that had come about only because space was short during the hasty race preparations—not a day passed without several serious quarrels between them. Here in the stables, on the race course,

++++++++++++++++++++
**"Strider," the horse in Leo Tolstoy's story of that title (1885).

159

and at the water trough they constantly tried to provoke each other to a fight. But in his heart Emerald felt rather afraid of this lanky, self-confident stallion with his pungent, vicious horse's smell, his Adam's apple that jutted out like a camel's, his somber, sunken eyes, and especially his strong backbone hard as stone, tempered by the years, and toughened by racing and many previous fights.

Pretending that he was not in the least afraid and that nothing had happened a moment ago, Emerald turned, dropped his head into the manger, and began to stir the hay with his supple, softly firm lips. At first he only bit playfully at odd stems, but soon the taste carried him away and he sank his muzzle deep into the fodder. And at the same time slow, idle thoughts ran through his head, merging with memories of images, smells and sounds, then vanishing forever in the black abyss that surrounded the present instant.

"Hay," he thought, and remembered the head groom, Nazar, who gave the horses their hay in the evening.

Nazar was a nice old man; there was always such a comfortable smell of black bread and a hint of wine about him; his movements were leisurely and gentle, and when he was in charge the oats and hay seemed more tasty. It was pleasant to listen to him cleaning out a stall and talking to the horse under his breath, reproaching it affectionately and wheezing all the time. But he lacked something essential—that basic feeling for a horse—and during exercise you could sense through the reins that his hands were imprecise and unsure.

Vaska lacked it too, and though he shouted at them and hit them, all the horses knew he was a coward and weren't afraid of him. And he didn't know how to ride either, but kept tugging on the reins and fussing all the time. The third groom, the squint-eyed one, was better than either of them, but he wasn't fond of horses. He was cruel and impatient, and his hands weren't supple but seemed made of wood. And the fourth one, Andryashka, was still just a little boy; he played with the horses like a suckling foal and kissed them furtively on the top lip between the nostrils, which wasn't particularly pleasant or funny.

But that tall, lean, hunched fellow with a clean-shaven face and gold-rimmed spectacles—oh, now he was altogether different! He was just like some unusual horse—wise, strong and fearless. He never got angry, never used the whip, and never even threatened you with it, but when he sat in the two-wheeled buggy how glad, proud, and pleasantly fearful it made you feel to obey every touch of his strong, intelligent fingers that understood everything. Only he knew how to bring Emerald to that happy, harmonious state when every nerve in the body is strained to the utmost in swift flight, and when he did it all felt so enjoyable and easy.

And immediately Emerald saw in his imagination the short road leading to the race course and almost every house and post along it. He saw the sand of the race track, the stand, horses running by, green grass and the yellow finishing tape. He suddenly remembered the dark bay three year-old that had sprained his ankle during exercise the other day and gone lame. And as he thought about him, Emerald tried mentally to limp a little.

One wisp of hay that reached his mouth was remarkable for its peculiar, unusually delicate taste. He went on chewing it for a long time, and when he swallowed it he could still detect for a while the subtle, perfumed scent of withered flowers and fragrant, dry grass. A dim, completely vague, distant recollection slipped through his mind. It was like what sometimes happens to smokers, when a chance whiff of cigarette smoke on the street suddenly resurrects for an irrepressible instant a twilit corridor with old-fashioned wall-paper and a solitary candle on the dresser, or a long journey by night, the rhythmical jingling of harness bells, and languorous drowsiness, or a blue forest not far off, blinding snow, the noise of moving beaters, and the fever-ish impatience that makes the knees shake—and for an instant, touching it with obscurely wistful tenderness, there flit through one's soul forgotten feelings of bygone days that are deeply moving and yet now so elusive.

Meanwhile, the little dark window above the manger, invisible until now, began to turn gray and show up faintly in the darkness. The horses munched more lazily and one after the other heaved a deep, soft sigh. Outside the cock crowed its familiar cry, as clear, shrill and cheerful as a trumpet. And for a long time in various places far around, the cries of other cocks went on echoing ceaselessly in their turn.

Sinking his head into the trough, Emerald kept on trying to retain in his mouth, revive and intensify the strange taste that had awakened in him this subtle, almost physical echo of incomprehensible recollection. But he failed to revive it, and without noticing it, dozed off.

II

His body and legs were perfectly shaped and flawless, so he always slept standing up, swaying backwards and forwards very slightly. Sometimes he quivered, and then for a few seconds his sound sleep gave way to a light, easy doze, but his brief moments of sleep were so deep that during them all his muscles, nerves and skin rested and were refreshed.

Just before dawn he dreamed of an early spring morning, a red sunrise over the earth, and a low, fragrant meadow. The grass was thick and lush, brilliantly, magically and delightfully green, glowing gently pink in the dawn as man and beast see it only in their earliest years, and all over it the dew spar-kled with quivering fire. In the light, thin air every possible smell drifts to-wards him with astonishing distinctness. Through the cool of morning he catches the smell of smoke curling blue and limpid above a chimney in the village, and every flower in the meadow has a different scent, while on the damp, rutted road beyond the hedge a multitude of smells are mingled: there

161

is the smell of people and tar, horse dung and dust, steamy cow's milk from the passing herd and fragrant resin from the pine stakes of the fence.

Emerald, a seven-month foal, races aimlessly about the field, his head bent low and his back legs kicking in the air. He feels as if the whole of him is made of air and his body is weightless. Fragrant white flowers of camomile stream away beneath his feet as he hurtles straight into the sun, while the wet grass whips against his pasterns and his knees, cooling and darkening them. Blue sky, green grass, golden sun, miraculous air, the heady ecstasy of youth, strength and swift flight!

But then he hears a brief, anxious, affectionate neigh which is so familiar to him that he always recognizes it from afar, even amidst a thousand other voices. Running full tilt, he stops and listens for a second with his head raised high, then twitching his delicate ears and flicking his short, fluffy tail like a little broom, he answers with a long, tremulous cry that makes his lean, graceful, long-legged body shudder, and races to his mother.

The quiet, bony old mare lifts her wet muzzle from the grass, sniffs the foal quickly and attentively, then immediately begins to feed again as though in a hurry to perform some pressing task. Bending his supple neck beneath her belly and tilting his muzzle upwards, the foal thrusts his lips between her back legs in his usual way, and finding the warm, resilient teat filled with copious, sweet, faintly sourish milk that spurts into his mouth in hot, fine streams, he drinks on and on, unable to tear himself away. His mother moves her hindquarters aside and pretends to bite her foal in the flank.

In the stables it had grown quite light. The bearded, stinking old billygoat that lived among the horses went up to the door barred on the inside with a beam, and began to bleat, looking back at the groom. Barefoot and scratching his tousled head, Vaska went to open the door for him. It was a crisp, blue, chilly autumn morning. The rectangle of the open door was immediately clouded with warm steam drifting from the stables, and the odor of hoarfrost and fallen leaves floated through the stalls.

The horses knew very well that in a moment oats would be poured into their troughs, and they grunted softly with impatience at their grills. The greedy, capricious Onegin beat his hooves against the wooden planking, and biting in his nasty way with his top teeth at the scored, ironbound rim of his trough, stretched out his neck, gulped and belched. Emerald scratched his muzzle against the grill.

The other grooms arrived—there were four altogether—and began to take the oats around the stalls in iron measures. While Nazar was pouring the rustling, heavy grain into Emerald's manger, the stallion butted busily towards the fodder, first over the old man's shoulder, then under his arm, his warm nostrils quivering. Fond of the gentle horse's impatience, the groom deliberately did not hurry but screened the trough with his elbows and growled with goodnatured roughness:

"Now then, you greedy beast... A-all right, you'll have time enough...

Damn you... Poke me once more with that snout of yours, and I'll poke you! Just you wait!"

From the little window above the manger a merry, rectangular shaft of sunlight came slanting down, and in it swirled millions of specks of golden dust, separated by the long shadows cast by the window frame.

III

Emerald had only just finished his oats when they came to take him out into the yard. It had grown warmer and the ground had softened slightly, but the stable walls were still white with rime. Thick steam rose from the heaps of manure that had just been raked from the stalls, and the sparrows clustering on them chirruped excitedly as if quarreling among themselves. Bending his neck in the doorway and stepping carefully over the threshold, Emerald joyfully drank in the heady air, then tossing his head and shaking his whole body, gave a sonorous snort. "Bless you!" said Nazar gravely. Emerald could not stand still. He longed for powerful movement, the tickling sensation of the air as it streamed into his eyes and nostrils, the delight of deep breathing, and the hot pounding of his heart. Tied to the tethering post he neighed and danced on his back legs, and bending his head to one side, squinted behind him at the black mare with his big, dark, staring eye, its red veins showing on the white.

Panting with the effort, Nazar lifted a bucket of water above his head and poured it over the stallion's back from his withers to his tail. It was a sensation Emerald knew well—invigorating and pleasant yet frightening in its customary unexpectedness. Nazar brought more water and splashed his flanks, chest, legs and crupper. And each time he pressed his calloused palm down close over the hair, squeezing out the water. Glancing behind him, Emerald saw his high, slightly curving rump that had suddenly grown dark and was shining glossily in the sun.

It was a racing day. Emerald knew it by the peculiar, nervous haste with which the grooms bustled around the horses; because their trunks were short, some of them tended to overreach themselves, so they had leather guards put on their pasterns, while others had their legs bandaged with linen strips from the ankle to the knee, or had broad, protective bands trimmed with fur tied around their chests behind their front legs. Light, two-wheeled buggies with high seats were brought out of the coach-house; their metal spokes glittered gaily as they turned and their red rims and wide, red, curved shafts shone with fresh varnish.

Emerald had already been thoroughly dried, brushed and rubbed down with a woollen mitten when the head jockey, the Englishman, arrived. This tall, lean, long-armed, slightly stooping man was respected and feared by both horses and men alike. He had a clean-shaven, sunburned face and firm, thin lips that curved mockingly. He wore gold-rimmed spectacles and his clear, blue eyes gazed through them with steady, unflinching calm. With his long legs in their high boots planted wide apart and his hands thrust deep in his trouser pockets, he watched the grooms at work, chewing a cigar first in one and then the other corner of his mouth. He wore a gray jacket with a fur collar and a black cap with a narrow brim and a long, straight, rectangular peak. From time to time he made brief remarks in an abrupt, offhand tone, and all the grooms and stableboys immediately turned to look at him, while the horses pricked up their ears in his direction.

He watched with particular care as Emerald was harnessed, inspecting the horse's whole body from his forelock to his hooves. Feeling the precise, attentive eyes upon him, Emerald lifted his head with pride, half turned his supple neck and pricked up his delicate, translucent ears. The man tested the tightness of the saddle-girth himself, pushing a finger between it and the horse's belly. Then the horses were covered with gray linen horsecloths decorated with red edging, red circles for the eyes and red monograms down by the back legs. Two grooms, Nazar and the squint-eyed one, took Emerald by the bridle and led him to the race course along the familiar road that ran between the two rows of big, widely-spaced, stone buildings. To the race course it was less than a quarter of a mile.

In the paddock many horses were already being led around in a ring, all in the same direction—the same way they would run around the track, that is to say counterclockwise. Shaft-bow horses were being led around too, small animals with strong legs and short, cropped tails. Emerald immediately recognized the little white stallion who always galloped beside him to pace him during a race, and both horses neighed softly in affectionate greeting.

IV

On the race course the bell had begun to ring. The grooms took off Emerald's horsecloth. Screwing up his eyes against the sun and showing his long, yellow, horse's teeth, the Englishman came up with his whip under his arm, buttoning his gloves as he walked. One of the grooms lifted Emerald's luxuriant tail that fell right to his pasterns and carefully laid it on the seat of the buggy so that its light-colored tip hung down. The pliant shafts swayed resiliently with the horse's weight. Emerald glanced back and saw his driver sitting almost up against his crupper with his legs stretched out and spread wide along the shafts. Without hurrying he picked up the reins, shouted a monosyllabic word of command to the grooms, and they both let go of the horse's bridle at the same time. Rejoicing at the forthcoming race, Emerald was about to rush forward, but checked by the strong hands he only reared a little, tossed his head, and at a long, striding trot ran through the gates onto the course.

Along by the wooden fence that formed an oval a mile long ran a wide racetrack of yellow sand that was slightly damp and firm and gave pleasantly beneath Emerald's feet as it answered the pressure of his hooves. Distinct hoofprints and the straight, even tracks left by gutta-percha tires furrowed the ribbon of sand.

Alongside it stretched the stand, a tall, wooden building two hundred horselengths long, where, supported by slender pillars, a black crowd that rose like a mountain from the ground to the roof buzzed and seethed. From the slight, barely perceptible stirring of the reins Emerald understood he could increase speed and gave a grateful snort.

He moved at a steady, swinging trot, his back hardly swaying at all, his neck stretched out and bent slightly towards the left shaft, and his muzzle lifted straight in the air. Because of his far-reaching, unusually long stride, his movement did not produce the impression of speed from a distance; it seemed as though the trotting horse were unhurriedly measuring out the track with his front legs that were as straight as a pair of dividers, barely touching the ground with the tips of his hooves as he ran. It was a real American gait, one in which everything is designed to facilitate the horse's breathing and reduce wind resistance to a minimum, where all movement superfluous to the action of running and wasteful of energy is eliminated, and where external beauty of form is sacrificed to ease, economy of movement, deep respiration, stamina and vigorous running, so turning the horse into an impeccable, live machine.

Now, in the interval between two races, the horses were being limbered up, something that is always done to put trotters in good wind. There were a lot of them running around the outer track in the same direction as Emerald and around the inner one towards him. He was overtaken by a sturdy, gray trotter with dark, dappled markings and a white muzzle, an animal of pure Orlov stock with a tightly reined neck and a tail that stuck straight up like those of horses at fairs. His damp flanks and his broad, fat chest that was already dark with sweat shook as he ran, while his front legs kicked out sideways at the knee and his belly slapped loudly at every stride.

Then up from behind came a graceful, long-bodied, halfbreed mare with a thin, dark mane. She had been beautifully trained according to the same American system as Emerald. Her short, sleek coat shone just like his, iridescent with the muscles moving under her skin. While their drivers talked about something, the two horses moved side by side for a while. Emerald sniffed at the mare and tried to frisk as they went, but the Englishman would not allow it so he desisted.

Towards them at a round trot raced a huge, black stallion all covered with bandages, knee guards and protectors. The left-hand shaft of his buggy stuck a good foot further forward than the right, and through the ring fastened above his head passed a steel check-rein that held the highly-strung horse's head in a cruel grip from above and both sides. Emerald and the mare

165

both glanced at him at the same time and instantly saw that he was a trotter of unusual strength, speed and stamina, but one who was terribly stubborn, vicious, conceited and quick to take offense. Close behind the black came a ludicrously small, light gray, smart little stallion. From a distance one might have thought he was racing along at an incredible speed: he stamped his feet so rapidly, flung his legs up so high at the knee, and looked so earnest and businesslike with his uplifted neck and pretty little head. Emerald only shot him a contemptuous, sidelong glance and pointed an ear in his direction.

The other driver brought the conversation to a close, and giving a brief, neighing laugh, put his mare into an easy trot. Calmly, without any effort whatsoever, as if her speed did not depend on her at all, she pulled away from Emerald and ran on, her smooth, shining back with its faint dark marking down the spine swaying evenly.

But immediately both she and Emerald were rapidly overtaken by a fiery-chestnut trotter with a big white patch on his forehead. He galloped with frequent, long leaps, first stretching out and bending close to the ground, then almost bringing his front and back feet together in the air. With his whole body flung back, his driver lay rather than sat on his seat, hanging on to the taut reins. Emerald became agitated and lunged impetuously to one side, but the Englishman pulled imperceptibly on the reins, and his hands that were so supple and sensitive to the horse's every movement suddenly became hard as iron. Near the stand the chestnut stallion overtook Emerald again after already making another circuit of the track. He was still galloping but was covered in lather now, his eyes bloodshot and his breathing raucous. Bent forward, his driver was lashing him on the back with all his might. Finally the grooms managed to block the horse's path near the gates and catch him by the reins and bridle. He was led off the course, covered in sweat, gasping for breath, shaking and worn to a shadow in a single moment.

Emerald made one more half-circuit at a round trot, then turning off onto the track that cut across the race course, went through the gates into the paddock.

V

On the race course the bell had rung several times. Now and again racing trotters whirled like lightning past the open gates, and the people in the stands suddenly started shouting and clapping. Emerald walked quickly beside Nazar in the line of other trotters, tossing his bent head and twitching his ears in their linen covers. After the limbering-up the blood coursed hot and gay in his veins, and his breathing grew deeper and easier as his body rested and cooled, while in every muscle he felt an impatient desire to run some more.

Half an hour passed. On the race course the bell rang again. Now

Emerald's driver got into the buggy without gloves on. He had broad, white, magic hands that filled the horse with fear and devotion.

The Englishman drove slowly out onto the course while the horses that had just limbered up left it one after the other to enter the paddock. Only Emerald and the enormous black stallion he had met on the way from the stables were left on the course. The stands were black from top to bottom with a dense crowd, and in this dark mass of people countless light-colored faces and hands showed in gay confusion beside multicolored hats, sunshades and white programs that fluttered in the air. Gradually increasing speed as he passed the stand, Emerald felt a thousand eyes intently watching him. He understood clearly that they expected swift movement of him, together with the utmost effort and a mightily pounding heart, and the realization lent his muscles a glad feeling of ease and a self-conscious firmness. The familiar little white stallion with the small boy on his back galloped beside him to his right with its short stride.

At an even, measured trot, his body leaning slightly to the left, Emerald made a sharp turn and began to approach the post with the red circle on it. From the racetrack came a brief ring of the bell. Almost imperceptibly the Englishman adjusted his position on the seat and his hands suddenly became firm. "Off you go now, but save your strength. It's early yet," Emerald understood from them, and as a sign that he had done so, he looked back for a second, then set his sensitive, delicate ears straight again. The white stallion galloped steadily to one side and a little behind him, and Emerald could hear his cool, regular breathing near his withers.

The red post is left behind. One more sharp turn and the track straightens out, then drawing near, the second stand with its buzzing crowd shows dark and motley in the distance, growing swiftly larger with every step. "More!" the driver allows, "more, more!" Emerald becomes a little excited and wants to strain every nerve all at once in the effort of running. "Can I?" he thinks. "No, it's still too early, don't get agitated," reply the reassuring, magic hands. "Later."

Both Emerald and the black stallion pass the first distance post at the very same second but on opposite sides of the diameter joining the stands. The slight resistance of the taut ribbon and its rapid snapping make Emerald flatten his ears for an instant, but he immediately forgets about it, for the whole of him is engrossed by the miraculous hands. "A bit more! Don't get excited! Go steady!" commands his driver. The swaying black stand floats by. A few more yards, and all four of them—Emerald, the little white stallion, the Englishman and the boy standing in his short stirrups and pressing against his horse's mane—merge happily into a single dense, whirling mass inspired by a common will, the common beauty of powerful motion, a common rhythm that sounds like music. Ta-ta-ta-ta! beat out Emerald's hooves rhythmically and evenly. Tra-ta, tra-ta! echoes the shaft-horse with its abrupt rapping. One more turn, and the second stand comes racing towards them.

"Shall I increase speed?" asks Emerald. "Yes," reply the hands, "but take it easy."

The second stand goes whirling by and is left behind. The people are shouting something. It distracts Emerald and he becomes excited. Losing the feel of the reins and missing the overall, regular rhythm, he takes four uneven steps with his right foot. But the reins immediately draw taut, and tearing his mouth they twist his neck downwards and pull his head to the right. Now it's awkward running on the right foot. Emerald grows angry and doesn't want to change step, but seizing the opportunity his driver calmly and masterfully puts him into a fast trot. The stand is left far behind, Emerald gets into step again, and the hands become amiable and gentle once more. Emerald senses his guilt and tries to trot twice as fast. "No, no, it's still too early," says the driver kindly. "We've plenty of time to put it right. It doesn't matter."

And so, in perfect harmony and without getting out of step, they run another circuit and a half. But the black horse is in splendid form today too. When Emerald got out of step he managed to put six lengths between them, but now Emerald is making up the ground he has lost and by the next-to-last post finds himself three and a quarter seconds in front. "Now you can go! Go on!" commands his driver. Emerald lays back his ears and flings a single swift glance behind him. The Englishman's whole face is aflame with a keenly intent, resolute expression, and his clean-shaven lips are pursed in an impatient grimace that reveals his big, yellow, tightly clenched teeth. "Give it all you've got!" command the reins in the hands now lifted high. "More, more!" And suddenly the Englishman cries in a loud, ringing voice that soars like the wail of a siren:

"O-a-a-a-a-ay!"

"That's it, that's it, that's it, that's it!.." shouts the boy in a shrill, clear voice in time to his horse's galloping.

Now the rhythm reaches its very highest pitch and hangs by a slender thread that threatens to snap at any moment. Ta-ta-ta-ta! beat out Emerald's hooves evenly on the ground. Trra-trra-trra! echoes the little white stallion galloping in front and drawing Emerald on after him. The pliant shafts sway in time to Emerald's step, and almost lying on his stallion's neck the boy rises and falls in the saddle in time to the horse's galloping.

The air streaming towards him whistles in Emerald's ears and tickles his nostrils, as steam spurts from them in big, gusting clouds. It grows harder to breathe and his skin feels hot. He rounds the last turn, his whole body leaning into the curve. The stand rises up like a live thing before him and from it comes whirling the roar of a thousand voices that frightens, excites and gladdens him. Trotting is no longer enough for him and he wants to gallop, but those amazing hands behind implore and command and reassure him: "Don't gallop, dear fellow!.. Just don't gallop!.. That's it, that's it, that's it!" And hurtling headlong past the post, Emerald breaks the finishing tape without even noticing it. Shouts, laughter and applause flood down from the stand in a torrent. The white leaves of programs, sunshades, canes and hats whirl and flutter amidst stirring hands and faces. The Englishman gently lets go of the reins. "It's over. Thanks, old fellow!" his movement tells Emerald, and checking his momentum with difficulty the horse changes to a walking pace. At that moment the black stallion is only just coming up to his finishing post on the opposite side of the course, seven seconds behind.

Lifting his numbed legs with difficulty, the Englishman jumps heavily down from the buggy, and removing the velvet seat, takes it to the scales. Running up, the grooms cover Emerald's hot back with a horsecloth and lead him away into the paddock. After them rolls the roar of the crowd and a long ring on the bell from the members' pavilion. A light, yellowish lather falls from the horse's muzzle onto the grooms' hands and the ground.

After a few minutes, Emerald, already unharnessed, is led to the stand again. A tall man in a shiny new hat and long coat whom Emerald often sees in the stables, pats him on the neck and pushes a sugar lump into his mouth with his palm. The Englishman is standing there in the crowd too and smiling, screwing up his face and showing his long teeth. They take the horse-cloth off Emerald's back and stand him in front of a box on three legs covered with a black cloth, under which a gentleman in gray is hiding and doing something.

But now the people are pouring from the stands in a spilling black mass. They press close around the horse on every side, shouting, waving their arms and bending their flushed faces and shining eyes close to one another. They are displeased about something, prod Emerald's legs, head and flanks with their fingers, ruffle up the hair on the left side of his crupper where the brand is, and then all start shouting again. "Fake horse, sham trotter, swindle, cheat, money back!" hears Emerald, and not understanding the words, twitches his ears uneasily. "What are they arguing about?" he thinks in surprise. "I ran very well, didn't I?" And for an instant he is struck by the Englishman's face. Always so calm, controlled and faintly mocking, now it is blazing with anger. And suddenly the Englishman shouts something in a high-pitched, choking voice and quickly swings his arm, and the dry crack of a slap halts the general uproar.

VI

Emerald was taken home and after three hours given some oats. And in the evening, when he was being watered at the well, he saw the great yellow moon rising above the fence, and it filled him with unaccountable terror.

And then tedious days followed.

He was not taken to be weighed, exercised or raced any more. Instead, every day strange people, many people, came to see him, and he was led out into the yard where they examined and felt him in every way, looking in his

169

mouth, scraping his hair with pumice and continually shouting at one another.

Then he remembered how late one evening he was taken from the stables and slowly led down long, stony, deserted streets past houses with lighted windows. Then came the station, a dark, jolting goods truck, fatigue and trembling in his legs from the long journey, the whistling of engines, the rattling of rails, the suffocating smell of smoke, and the tiresome light from a swinging lantern. At one station he was taken from the truck and led for a long time down a strange road past barren, desolate, autumn fields and villages until he was brought to an unfamiliar stable and locked up in a separate stall far from the other horses.

At first he kept remembering the races, his Englishman, Vaska, Nazar and Onegin, and often dreamed of them, but in time he forgot everything. They were hiding him away from someone, and all his beautiful young body languished, pined and disintegrated from inactivity. From time to time more strangers came and jostled around him again, pulling and prodding him and quarreling angrily among themselves.

Sometimes through the open door Emerald would see other horses walking and running at liberty and he would cry out to them, complaining and indignant. But his door was immediately closed again and time dragged on in tedious solitude once more.

In charge of this stable was a sleepy man with a large head, little dark eyes, and a thin, black mustache on his fat face. He seemed quite indifferent to Emerald, but he filled the horse with incomprehensible terror.

And then, early one morning, when all the grooms were asleep, softly and without the slightest noise this man came into Emerald's stall on tiptoe, poured some oats into his manger and went out again. Emerald was rather surprised at this, but obediently began to eat. The oats were sweet, yet slightly bitter and sharp to the taste. "Strange," he thought, "I've never tasted oats like this before."

Then suddenly he felt a slight griping pain in his belly. It came, went away, then came again more strongly than before, increasing every minute. Eventually the pain became unbearable and Emerald gave a dull moan. Rings of fire whirled before his eyes and his whole body grew damp and flaccid with sudden weakness. Then his legs shook and gave way beneath him, and the stallion crashed to the floor. He tried to get up, but could only stand on his front feet and collapsed on his side once more. A whirlwind began to roar in his head; in it the Englishman went floating by, showing his long horse's teeth, and Onegin ran past, thrusting out his camel's Adam's apple and neighing loudly. Some relentless force bore Emerald headlong downwards, deep into a cold, dark pit. He could no longer move.

Spasms suddenly convulsed his legs and neck, and arched his back. All his hide began to quiver rapidly and was covered with acrid lather.

For an instant the dancing yellow light of a lantern seared his eyes and then was extinguished with his failing sight. His ear still caught the sound of

170

a man's harsh cry, but he no longer felt the heel that dug him in the flank. Then everything vanished—forever.

1907

Alexander Kuprin / THE BRACELET OF GARNETS

L. van Beethoven. 2 Son. (op. 2, No. 2).
Largo Appassionato

I

In the middle of August, before the new moon, a spell of abominable weather suddenly set in of the kind that is so peculiar to the northern coast of the Black Sea. First a thick, heavy mist hung over both land and sea for days on end, and the huge siren on the lighthouse roared day and night like a mad bull. Then all day long an incessant drizzle fell that was as fine as spray, turning the clay roads and tracks into a mass of thick mud in which carriages and carts became thoroughly bogged down. Then, from the northwest, off the steppes, a fierce hurricane began to blow. It made the treetops sway, and they bent low then straightened again, lashing like waves in a storm, while at night the tin roofs of the dachas rattled as if someone was running over them in hobnailed boots. The window frames shook, doors banged, and there was a wild howling in the chimneys. Several fishing boats were blown off course and two failed to return altogether. Not till a week later were the men's bodies washed up at various places along the coast.

The inhabitants of the seaside resort—Greeks and Jews for the most part, people who were fond of life but rather nervous like all southerners—hurriedly moved into town. Along the muddy road stretched an endless line of drays, piled high with all kinds of household belongings: mattresses, sofas, trunks, chairs, washstands and samovars. It was pitiful, dreary and sad to peer through the cloudy, muslin-like curtains of rain and see all these shabby goods and chattels that looked so grubby and wretched; to see the cooks and maids sitting on the wet tarpaulins that covered the carts, holding flatirons, tin cans and baskets in their hands; to see the sweating, exhausted horses that kept on coming to a halt, their knees trembling and their flanks heaving rapidly and steaming; and to see the draymen all wrapped in bast matting, cursing the rain in their hoarse voices. It was sadder still to see the deserted dachas with their sudden abundance of space, their emptiness and bareness, their ravaged flower beds, their broken windows, their abandoned goods and their endless holiday rubbish—cigarette ends, scraps of paper, bits of broken crockery, cardboard boxes and empty medicine bottles.

But towards the beginning of September there was an unexpected change in the weather. Quiet, cloudless days suddenly set in that were sunnier, clearer and warmer than they had been even in July. On the prickly yellow stubble that covered the dry, reaped fields the autumn gossamer gleamed like mica. Grown still now, the trees shed their yellow leaves in submissive silence.

Princess Vera Nikolaevna Sheina, the wife of a Marshal of the Nobility, had been unable to leave her dacha because the repairs being done to her town house were not yet finished. And now she was overjoyed at the delightful days that had set in, with their stillness, their feeling of solitude, their pure air, the twittering of swallows on the telephone wires as they gathered before migrating, and the caressing, salty breeze that blew gently off the sea.

II

Besides, today—September seventeenth—was her nameday. Associating it with cherished, distant memories of childhood, she had always been fond of this day, and always expected it to bring something miraculously happy. As he left for town that morning on urgent business, her husband had put on her bedside table a box containing a pair of beautiful earrings made of pear-shaped pearls, and this gift had gladdened her even more.

She was alone in the house. Her bachelor brother Nikolai, the assistant public prosecutor who usually lived with them, had gone off to town too, for a court hearing. Her husband had promised to bring a few of their very closest acquaintances home to dinner. It was lucky her nameday had come while they were still at the dacha. In town they would have had to spend a good deal of money on a grand gala dinner or perhaps even a ball, while here in the country they could manage with very little expense. Despite his distinguished position in society, or perhaps precisely because of it, Prince Shein could barely make ends meet. His huge family estate had been almost completely ruined by his forebears, while his position obliged him to live above his means: to give receptions, make donations to charities, dress well, keep horses, and so on. Princess Vera, whose once passionate love for her husband had long ago turned into a genuine feeling of firm, loyal friendship, spared no effort to help him avoid total ruin. Without his noticing it, she denied herself many things, and ran the house as economically as she could.

Now she was walking about the garden and carefully cutting flowers for the dining table with her scissors. The flowerbeds were empty and looked untidy. The variegated, double carnations were past their best, and so were the stocks—half in bloom and half laden with slender green pods that smelt of cabbage—while for the third time that summer the roses had buds and blooms on them, though they were small and sparse now as if the bushes had gone wild. On the other hand, the dahlias, peonies and asters were flowering magnificently, displaying their chill, haughty beauty and filling the keen autumn air with a sad, grassy fragrance. The other flowers, their season of luxuriant love and abundantly fruitful motherhood now over, quietly scattered the innumerable seeds of future life on the ground.

On the road only a short distance away Princess Vera caught the familiar sound of a triple-tone car horn. It was her sister, Anna Nikolaevna

Friesse, who had promised that morning on the telephone to come and help her get the house ready for the evening and receive the guests when they arrived.

Vera's sharp ears had not deceived her, and she went to meet her sister. A few moments later an elegant limousine pulled up sharply outside the dacha gates, and jumping smartly from his seat, the chauffeur flung open the door.

The sisters kissed joyfully. Since early childhood they had felt a warm, solicitous friendship for each other. In appearance they were strangely dissimilar. Vera, the elder, looked like her mother—an English beauty—with her tall, supple figure, her delicate but proud, cold face, her beautiful though rather large hands, and those charmingly sloping shoulders that one sees on old-fashioned miniatures. Anna, on the other hand, had inherited the Mongol blood of their father, a Tatar prince whose grandfather had not been baptized until the early nineteenth century and whose ancient line went back to Tamerlane himself, or Lang-Temir as their father proudly used to call that great murderer in Tatar. Half a head shorter than her sister, Anna was rather broad-shouldered, vivacious and frivolous, and very fond of teasing people. Her face—it was of a markedly Mongol cast with rather prominent cheekbones, narrow little eyes which she screwed up still more because she was nearsighted, and a small, sensual mouth whose slightly pouting, full lower lip gave it a haughty expression—her face held an elusive, unaccountable fascination that lay, perhaps, in its smile, in the intense femininity of all its features, or perhaps in its capacity for provocatively coquettish, piquant mimicry. Her graceful plainness attracted men's attention much more often and excited them far more forcefully than her sister's aristocratic beauty.

She was married to a very wealthy and very stupid man who did absolutely nothing, though he was on the board of some charitable institution and bore the title of Gentleman of the Emperor's Bedchamber. She could not stand him, but had borne him two children nevertheless—a boy and a girl; then she had made up her mind not to have any more and had not done so. As for Vera, she had longed for children, feeling that the more she had the better it would be, but for some reason she had failed to have any. In an unhealthy, passionate way she adored her sister's pretty little anemic offspring, with their pallid, flour-colored faces, flaxen, doll-like curls, and perpetual exemplary behavior.

Anna was a gaily disordered creature, full of charming, though sometimes strange, capriciousness. She readily indulged in the most risqué flirtation in all the capitals and spas of Europe, but was never unfaithful to her husband, though she ridiculed him both to his face and behind his back. She was extravagant and terribly fond of gambling and dancing, had a passion for powerful impressions and striking spectacles, and would frequent dubious cafes when she was abroad. But at the same time she was well known for her generous kindness and her profound, sincere piety—something that had even

175

made her <u>secretly become a Catholic</u>. Her back, bosom and shoulders were extraordinarily beautiful. When she attended grand balls she would uncover herself far beyond the limits that decorum and fashion allowed, but people said that under her low-cut dress she always wore a hair shirt.

<u>Vera, on the other hand, was without any affectation whatsoever.</u> Coldly and rather haughtily polite to everyone, <u>she was as aloof and serene as a queen.</u>

III

"My goodness, how nice it is here! How very nice!" said Anna, walking with rapid little steps down the path beside her sister. "Let's sit on the bench by the cliff edge for a while, shall we? I haven't seen the sea for such a long time. And how marvelous the air is here! It gladdens your heart just to breathe it! Last summer, in Miskhor in the Crimea, I made an amazing discovery. Do you know what seawater smells of when the surf's coming in? Just imagine—it smells of mignonette."

"You're always imagining things," said Vera with an affectionate smile.

"No, no, it does. I remember once how everybody laughed at me when I said there was a kind of pink tint in moonlight. But the other day the artist Boritsky—the one who's painting my portrait—said that I was right and that artists have known about it for a long time."

"Is this artist your latest flame?"

"What strange ideas you get into your head!" said Anna with a laugh, and went quickly up to the cliff edge that fell like a sheer wall to the sea far below. Looking down, she cried out in terror and started back, her face grown suddenly pale.

"Oh, what a long way down!" she said in a faint, trembling voice. "When I look down from a height like this, I always get a nasty kind of sweet, tickling feeling in my chest...and my toes ache... And yet I feel drawn to it, drawn to that edge..."

She was about to bend over the cliff edge again, but her sister stopped her.

"For heaven's sake, Anna dear! You make me feel giddy too when you do that. Sit down, please!"

"All right then, all right, there, I've sat down... But just look how beautiful it all is, how glorious—you just can't look at it enough. If only you knew how thankful I am to God for all the wonderful things he has made for us!"

They both became thoughtful for a moment. Far, far below them lay the sea. They could not see the shore from where they were sitting, and so the expanse of water seemed more boundless and majestic still. <u>The sea was softly calm and gaily blue</u>, showing lighter only where smooth, slanting

176

streaks revealed the presence of currents, while on the horizon it was a rich, dark blue.

Fishing boats, so tiny that they were hardly visible, lay motionless on the smooth water not far from the shore. And further away, as if hanging in the air without moving forward, was a three-masted vessel rigged overall with identical, graceful, white sails bellying in the wind.

"I see what you mean," said the elder sister thoughtfully, "but somehow I don't feel the same as you do about it. When I see the sea again after a long interval, it excites and gladdens and astonishes me all at the same time. It's as if I'm seeing some vast, solemn miracle for the first time in my life. But later, when I've gotten used to it, it begins to oppress me with its flat emptiness... Looking at it bores me, so I try not to look any more. I get tired of it."

Anna smiled.

"What is it?" asked her sister.

"Last summer," said Anna archly, "a large party of us rode from Yalta to Uch-Kosh. It's over there, beyond that stretch of forest, above the waterfall. To begin with we found ourselves in cloud and it was very damp. You could hardly see a thing, but we kept climbing upwards, following a steep path among the pines. Then all of a sudden somehow the forest came to an end and we rode out of the mist. Just imagine: there was a narrow little platform on a rock, and at our feet—a precipice. The villages down below were no bigger than matchboxes, and the woods and orchards looked like little patches of thin grass. The whole region fell away below us, just like a map. And further away lay the sea, stretching in front of us for fifty or sixty miles! I felt as if I was hanging in the air and was just about to fly. Everything was so beautiful, so light and airy! Filled with delight, I turned and said to our guide: 'Well, Seid-ogly, isn't it marvelous?' But he just clicked his tongue and said: 'Oh, lady, I'm sick and tired of it all! I see it every day.'"

"Thanks for the comparison," said Vera with a laugh. "No, I just think we northerners can never understand the fascination of the sea. It's the forest I love. Do you remember our forest in Yegorovskoe?.. Could you really ever get tired of that? The pines!.. And those beautiful mosses!.. And the deathcap mushrooms! They looked just as if they were made of red satin embroidered with white beads. And everything was so still...and cool."

"It makes no difference to me, because I love everything," replied Anna. "But most of all I love my little sister, my sensible little Vera. There's only the two of us in all the world, you know."

She put her arms round her sister and pressed close to her, cheek to cheek. Then suddenly she remembered something.

"But how silly of me! Here we are, sitting talking about mother nature like people in some novel, and I've completely forgotten about the present I've brought you. Here, have a look at it. I'm only afraid you mightn't like it."

She took from her handbag a little notebook in a wonderful binding: on its dark blue velvet cover that was faded and worn with age there wound a dull gold, filigree pattern of rare intricacy, delicacy and beauty—obviously the devoted work of a highly skilled, patient craftsman. The notebook was attached to a little gold chain that was as slender as a thread, and the leaves inside the cover had been replaced by wafers of ivory.

"What a beautiful thing! How lovely!" said Vera, and gave her sister a kiss. "Thank you. But where did you find a treasure like this?"

"In an antique shop. You know my passion for rummaging about in old junk, don't you? Well, that's how I came across this prayer book. Look, can you see how the pattern makes the shape of a cross here? It's true I only found the binding and had to think all the rest up myself—the pages, the clasps, and the pencil. But Mollinet just couldn't understand what I wanted, however hard I tried to explain it to him. The clasps should have been made in the same style as the rest of the pattern—in dull, old gold with delicate fretting—but he's gone and done goodness knows what to it instead. The chain's a real Venetian one though, and it's very old."

Vera stroked the beautiful binding fondly.

"What great antiquity there is here!.. How old might this notebook be?" she asked.

"I wouldn't like to say exactly, but it must date from about the end of the seventeenth or the middle of the eighteenth century..."

"How strange," said Vera with a pensive smile. "Here I am holding in my hands something that may have been touched by the Marquise de Pompadour or even by Marie Antoinette herself... But you know, Anna, only you could have the crazy idea of turning a prayer book into a lady's *carnet!* Anyway, let's go and see what's happening inside."

They went into the house across a large, stone terrace enclosed on every side by trellises of dense Isabella vines. Smelling faintly of strawberries, the abundant clusters of black grapes hung heavily amid the dark green foliage that here and there shone gold in the sunlight. The whole terrace was flooded with a green twilight that immediately made the women's faces look pale.

"Do you want dinner served here?" asked Anna.

"Well, I did to begin with... But the evenings are so chilly now that it'd be better in the dining room. The men can come out here to smoke, though."

"Is anyone interesting coming?"

"I don't know yet. All I know is that grandfather's coming."

"Oh, dear grandfather! How lovely!" exclaimed Anna, clasping her hands. "I don't seem to have seen him for ages."

"Vasya's sister's coming and Professor Speshnikov too, I think. I was simply at my wits' end yesterday, Anna. You know how fond they both are of good food—grandfather and the professor, I mean. Well, the trouble is, you can't get anything decent either out here or in town, however much you pay. Luka found some quail somewhere—he ordered them from a hunter he knows—and he's doing something with them. We managed to find some beef that's reasonable—alas!—the inevitable roast beef! And we've got some very good crayfish."

"Well, that doesn't sound too bad at all. Don't you worry about it. Between ourselves though, Vera, I know you're fond of good food yourself."

"But there'll be something unusual too. This morning a fisherman brought a gurnard. I saw it myself and it really is a monster. It's frightening even to look at it."

Anna, who was avidly inquisitive about everything whether it concerned her or not, immediately asked for the gurnard to be brought in so she could see it.

Luka, the tall, sallow, cleanshaven cook, came in carrying a big, white, oblong washtub which he held carefully but with difficulty by the handles, trying not to spill water on the parquet floor.

"Twelve and a half pounds, ma'am," he said with the peculiar pride of a cook. "We weighed it a short while ago."

The fish was too big for the basin and lay on the bottom with its tail curled up. Its scales were shot with gold and its fins were a bright red color, while from each side of its huge, rapacious snout protruded two long, delicate blue wings that folded like fans. It was still alive and its gills were working vigorously.

The younger sister touched the fish's head cautiously with her little finger. But the gurnard suddenly lashed its tail and with a shriek Anna jerked her hand away.

"Don't worry, ma'am, we'll arrange everything very nicely," said the cook, evidently aware of Anna's alarm. "A Bulgarian fruit-grower's just brought two melons—pineapple ones. They look like cantaloupes, but they smell much more fragrant. And may I ask what sauce ma'am wishes served with the gurnard: tartare, polonaise, or perhaps just rusks in butter?"

"Do as you think best. And now you may go," said the Princess.

IV

After five o'clock the guests began to arrive. Prince Vasily Lvovich brought several people with him: his widowed sister, Lyudmila Lvovna Durasova, a stout, goodnatured but unusually taciturn woman; a rich young idler and rake, Vasyuchok, who was known to the whole town by that familiar name and who was very good company because he could sing and recite poetry, as well as arrange *tableaux vivants*, plays and charity bazaars; the famous pianist Jenny Reiter, a friend of Princess Vera's from their time together at the Smolny Institute; and Prince Vasily's brother-in-law, Nikolai Nikolaevich. Then Anna's husband arrived by car, bringing with him the cleanshaven and outrageously fat Professor Speshnikov and the local vice-governor, von Seck. The last to arrive was General Anosov, who came in a fine, hired landau accompanied by two officers: Colonel Ponamaryov of the General Staff, a thin, peevish, prematurely aged man who was worn out by excessive clerical work, and Guards Lieutenant Bakhtinsky of the Hussars, who was reputed to be the best dancer and master of ceremonies in Petersburg. ~~Grandfather~~

General Anosov, a tall, corpulent, silver-haired old man, climbed heavily down from the running-board of his landau, holding on to the rail of the box with one hand and to the back of the carriage with the other. In his left hand he carried an ear-trumpet, and in his right a rubber-tipped cane. He had a large, coarse, ruddy face with a fleshy nose, and his narrowed eyes with the spreading, slightly puffy bags under them had the genially dignified but faintly contemptuous expression characteristic of courageous, simple people who have frequently come face to face with danger and death. Recognizing him from a distance, both sisters went running up to the landau just in time to help him down half jokingly by the arms.

"Anyone would think I was...a bishop!" he said in an affectionate, rather husky bass.

"Grandad, dear, darling grandad!" said Vera in a tone of faint reproach. "Every day we've been expecting to see you, but you won't even let us catch a glimpse of you!"

"Our grandad's lost all shame here in the south," said Anna with a laugh. "I think you might have remembered your god-daughter, grandad. But instead you're behaving just like Don Juan, you shameless man, and you've quite forgotten we exist..."

Baring his majestic head, the General kissed both the sisters' hands in turn, then kissed them on the cheek before kissing their hands again.

"Girls...wait...don't scold me," he said, pausing for breath after each word because of his shortness of wind, something he had suffered from for a long time now. "Upon my honor...those miserable doctors...have been treating my rheumatism all summer...by making me bathe...in some kind of dirty ...jelly...ugh! it smells awful... And they just wouldn't let me go... You're the first people...I've visited...I'm so glad...to see you... How are you getting on? You look quite the lady...little Vera...you're very like...your late mother these days... When will you be asking me to be a godfather?"

"Oh, never, I'm afraid, grandad..."

"Don't give up hope...you've still got your whole life ahead of you... Pray to God... And as for you, Anna, you've not changed a bit... Even at sixty...you'll still be the same merry little fidget you are now. But just a moment, let me introduce these gentlemen to you."

"I had that honor a long time ago!" said Colonel Ponamaryov with a bow.

"I was introduced to the Princess in Petersburg," echoed the Hussar.

"Well then, Anna, may I introduce Lieutenant Bakhtinsky? He's a dancer and a ruffian, but a splendid cavalryman. Bakhtinsky, my dear chap, get that thing from the carriage, would you?.. Come along then, girls... What are you going to give us to eat, Vera my dear? After that strict diet they kept me on... I've got an appetite...like an ensign who's just passed out of the Academy."

General Anosov had been an army comrade and devoted friend of the late Prince Mirza-Bulat-Tuganovsky. After the Prince's death he had transferred all his affectionate friendship and love to Tuganovsky's daughters. He had known them when they were very small and had even been godfather to Anna, the younger of them. Then, as now, he was Commandant of the large but almost defunct fortress in the town of K., and used to visit the Tuganovskys every day. The children simply adored him, not only because he spoiled them, gave them presents and took boxes for them at the circus and theater, but also because no one played with them as fascinatingly as he did. But what captivated them most of all, what was imprinted more firmly than anything else in their memories, were his stories of military campaigns, battles and bivouacs, victories and retreats, cruel frosts, wounds and death—unhurried, simple tales told with epic calm between evening tea and that tiresome hour when children are sent to bed.

By present standards this fragment of olden days was a colossal and extraordinarily picturesque figure. In him were combined those simple but profound and moving traits that even in his own time were much more often seen among rank and file soldiers than officers—those purely Russian, peasant characteristics which, when taken together, produce an exalted character that has sometimes made our ordinary soldier not only an invincible warrior but also a great martyr, almost a saint. These traits comprise simple, ingenuous faith, a lucid, cheerfully goodnatured outlook on life, cool, businesslike courage, submissiveness in the face of death, compassion for the vanquished, infinite patience, and amazing moral and physical stamina.

Beginning with the Polish War, Anosov had taken part in every campaign except the Japanese one. He would not have hesitated to go to that war either, but he had not been called up, and so had obeyed his own immensely modest maxim: "Don't go looking for death until you're called." In all his years of service he had never once struck any of his men, let alone had them flogged. During the Polish revolt he once refused to shoot some prisoners, despite his regimental commander's personal order to do so. "If a man's a spy," he said, "I'll not only have him shot but will kill him with my own hands if you order me to do so. But these men are prisoners, and I can't kill them." And he said this so respectfully and simply, without a trace of defiance or bravado, looking his superior straight in the eye with such a clear, unflinching gaze, that instead of shooting him for insubordination, they let him be.

During the 1877-79 war he rose very quickly to the rank of colonel, despite the fact that he was a man of little education or, as he himself put it, had only graduated from the "backwoods academy." He took part in the crossing of the Danube, marched through the Balkans, sat out the siege of Shipka, and was present at the final attack at Plevna; he was wounded five times, once seriously, and in addition got a severe concussion from a shell splinter. Radetsky and Skobelev knew him personally and treated him with exceptional respect. It was of him that Skobelev once said: "I know one officer who's far braver than I am, and that's Major Anosov."

He returned from the war almost deaf from the shell splinter; he had had to have three toes amputated after getting frostbite during the Balkan campaign; and he had contracted extremely severe rheumatism at Shipka. After two years of peacetime service they had tried to pack him off into retirement, but Anosov had stubbornly refused to go. At this point the commander of the local military district, who had himself witnessed Anosov's cool courage during the crossing of the Danube, used his influence to help him just at the right moment. The authorities in Petersburg decided not to hurt the distinguished colonel's feelings, and gave him the post of Commandant in the town of K. for life—a position that was honorary rather than vital for the purposes of national security.

Everyone in town knew him, both young and old alike, and they laughed goodnaturedly at his foibles, his strange habits, and his peculiar clothes. He never carried arms, and went about in an oldfashioned frock coat and a forage cap with a wide brim and an enormous, straight peak, carrying a cane in his right hand and an ear-trumpet in his left; he was always accompanied by two fat, lazy, wheezing pugs whose tongues stuck out between their tightly clenched teeth. If he happened to meet anyone he knew during his customary morning stroll, the passersby could hear him shouting and the pugs barking in unison from several blocks away.

Like many deaf people, he was passionately fond of opera, and sometimes, during a languorous duet, his commanding bass would boom through the theater: "Now that was a splendid C, damn him! Good enough to crack a nut!" Restrained laughter would ripple across the auditorium, but the General never even suspected that he was the cause of it: naively, he thought he had merely whispered a comment in his neighbor's ear.

In accordance with his duties as Commandant he frequently visited— together with his wheezing pugs—the main guardhouse where officers under arrest would find respite from the burden of military service in conditions of immense comfort, enjoying tea, cards and anecdotes. He would question each of them carefully: "What is your name? Who put you under arrest? For how long? What for?" Sometimes he would unexpectedly commend an officer for a gallant though unlawful act, or sometimes start taking him to task for it, shouting so loudly that he could be heard outside on the street. But having berated the man to his heart's content, the General would then immediately go on to inquire where the officer's dinner was brought from and how much he paid for it. It occasionally happened that some second lieutenant—who had gone astray and been sent for a long period of detention from a Godforsaken place with no guardhouse of its own—would confess that he had to be content with the common soldiers' cooking pot because he had no money. Anosov would then immediately give orders that the poor fellow's dinner should be brought from his own home, which was no more than two hundred yards from the guardhouse.

It was in the town of K. that Anosov had become good friends with the Tuganovsky family and had grown so attached to the children that he felt a genuine need to see them every evening. If it so happened that the young ladies went out somewhere or his official duties detained him, he felt genuinely miserable and did not know what to do with himself in the big rooms of his Commandant's residence. He would take his leave every summer and spend a whole month on the Tuganovskys' estate of Yegorovskoe which was about forty miles from K.

He had transferred all his hidden tenderness of soul, all his need for heartfelt love, to the Tuganovsky children, and especially to the girls. He had been married once himself, but it was so long ago that he could hardly remember it. Even before the war his wife had run off with a traveling actor who had captivated her with his velvet jacket and lace cuffs. The General had paid her an allowance right up to her death, but never allowed her in his house, despite all her tearful letters and protestations of repentance. They had had no children.

V

Contrary to Vera's expectations, the evening was so warm and still that the candles on the terrace and in the dining room burned with a steady flame. Over dinner Prince Vasily Lvovich amused them all. He had an extraordinary and highly original gift for telling stories. He would take as the basis of his tale a real episode in which the chief character was either one of those present or someone they all knew. But he would exaggerate so much, wearing such a serious expression and using such a businesslike tone the whole time, that his listeners would split their sides laughing. That evening he was telling the story of Nikolai Nikolaevich's unsuccessful attempt to marry a certain rich and beautiful lady. The only element of truth in it was that the lady's husband had refused to give her a divorce. But in the Prince's story fact and fiction were skillfully interwoven. He had the grave, always rather prim Nikolai running down the street at night wearing only his socks and carrying his shoes under his arm. At a corner the young man was stopped by a policeman, and it was only after a lengthy and stormy explanation that Nikolai managed to prove that he was the assistant public prosecutor and not a burglar. According to the storyteller, the wedding very nearly took place, but at the most crucial moment the desperate band of false witnesses who had a hand in the affair suddenly went on strike, demanding an increase in their

183

fee. Out of stinginess (and he was rather stingy), but also because he was opposed to strikes on principle, Nikolai flatly refused to pay them any more, citing a specific article of the law that had been upheld by a ruling in the Court of Appeals. Then, in answer to the familiar question: "Does any man present know any just cause why these two persons may not lawfully be joined together in matrimony?" the infuriated false witnesses all cried in chorus: "Yes, we do! Everything we testified under oath in court is a complete and utter falsehood that the prosecutor forced us to testify by his intimidation and coercion. As for this lady's husband, being acquainted with him we can only say that he is the most respectable man on earth, as chaste as Joseph and as kind as an angel."

Having embarked on the subject of stories about marriage, Prince Vasily did not spare Anna's husband, Gustav Ivanovich Friesse, either. He told how on the day after his wedding Gustav had called the police to help him evict his bride from her parental home because she possessed no separate passport, and to install her in her lawful husband's place of abode. The only part of this anecdote that was true was the fact that for the first few days of her marriage Anna had been obliged to remain continually with her sick mother since Vera had returned to the south, while for his part poor Gustav Ivanovich had given way to gloom and despair.

Everyone was laughing. Anna was smiling too with her narrowed eyes. Gustav Ivanovich guffawed in delight, and his lean face tightly covered with its smooth, shining skin, his thin but sleek, fair hair, and his sunken eyes in their hollow sockets, all made his head look like a skull baring its appallingly bad teeth in a terrible grin. He still adored Anna just as much now as he had on the first day of their life together; he was always trying to sit beside her and touch her inconspicuously, and he paid court to her with such patent self-satisfaction and love that one often felt both embarrassment and pity for him.

Before getting up from the table, Vera Nikolaevna mechanically counted the guests. There were thirteen of them. She was superstitious and thought to herself: "Now that's bad! Why didn't I think of counting them before? It's Vasya's fault too—he didn't say anything on the phone about how many there'd be."

When friends met at the Sheins' or the Friesses' they usually played poker after dinner because both sisters were terribly fond of gambling. In this connection certain rules had even been drawn up in both houses: all the players were given an equal number of little ivory tokens of a specific value, and the game would go on until all the tokens had passed to one of the players; then the game would end for that evening, however much the players insisted on continuing it. Taking new tokens from the kitty was strictly forbidden. Such rigorous rules had been devised as a result of experience, so as to hold in check the princesses Vera and Anna, who knew no restraint when gambling. The total losses in a game like this seldom exceeded one or two hundred rubles.

They sat down to poker on this occasion too. Vera, who was not playing, was about to go out onto the terrace where the table was being laid for tea, when the maid suddenly called her from the drawing room with a rather mysterious look.

"What is it, Dasha?" she asked in annoyance, walking through into the little study next to her bedroom. "Why have you got such a silly look on your face? And what's that you're holding?"

Dasha put a small, square object on the table. It was neatly wrapped in white paper and carefully tied with a pink ribbon.

"It's not my fault, ma'am, I swear it," she began to babble, blushing at the Princess' sharp words. "He came in and said..."

"Who's 'he'?"

"A redcap, ma'am, ... a messenger."

"Well?"

"He came into the kitchen and put this on the table. 'Give it to your mistress,' he says, 'only make sure you give it to her personally.' I asked him who it was from, and he says: 'It's all written down in here.' And then off he went."

"Go and catch up with him."

"But I can't, ma'am. He came when you were in the middle of dinner, and I didn't dare disturb you. It was about half an hour ago."

"Very well then, you may go."

She cut the ribbon with her scissors and threw it into the wastepaper basket together with the paper that had her address on it. Inside the wrapping she found a small jewel case of red plush that was evidently brand new. She lifted the lid which was lined with pale blue silk, and saw an oval gold bracelet pressed into the black velvet. It had a note inside it carefully folded into a beautiful octagon. She unfolded it quickly. The handwriting seemed familiar, but like the true woman she was, she immediately put the note aside to have a look at the bracelet.

It was of low-grade gold, very thick but hollow, and covered on the outside with small, old, poorly-polished garnets. But in the center of the bracelet, surrounding a strange little green stone, there rose five beautiful cabochon garnets, each about the size of a pea. When with a chance movement Vera happened to turn the bracelet in front of the electric lamp, five beautiful, deep red, living fires suddenly blazed deep beneath the smooth, egg-shaped surface of the stones.

"It's just like blood!" she thought with a sudden feeling of alarm.

Then she remembered the letter and unfolded it once more. She read the following lines, written in a small, magnificently copperplate hand:

Your Excellency,
Deeply Respected Princess

Vera Nikolaevna!

Respectfully congratulating you on the bright and joyous day of Your Angel,* I make bold to dispatch to you my humble, loyal gift.

"Oh, it's him again!" thought Vera with annoyance. But she still read the letter to the end...

I would never have allowed myself to present you with anything that I had chosen: I have neither the right, the taste, nor—I confess—the money to do so. Moreover, I believe there is no treasure on earth worthy of adorning you.

But this bracelet belonged to my great-grandmother, and my late mother was the last person to wear it. In the middle, among the big stones, you will see a green one. This is a very rare kind of garnet—a green garnet. According to an old tradition that lives on in our family, this stone imparts the gift of prescience to the women who wear it and guards them from painful thoughts, while it protects men from violent death.

All the stones have been carefully transferred from the old silver bracelet to this one, and you may rest assured that no one has ever worn this bracelet before.

You may throw this absurd trinket away immediately or give it to someone else, but I shall be happy simply to know that your hands have touched it.

I beseech you not to be angry with me. I blush at the recollection of my impertinence seven years ago, when I dared to write preposterous, stupid letters to you—you were just a young lady then—and even to expect a reply to them. But now I feel for you nothing but reverence, everlasting admiration, and the humble devotion of a slave. Now I can only wish you happiness every moment of my life and rejoice if you are happy. In my mind I pay homage to the chair on which you sit, the parquet floor across which you walk, the trees which you touch in passing, and the servants to whom you speak. But I feel no envy for either the people or the things around you.

Once again I ask your forgiveness for having troubled you with this long and unnecessary letter.

Your obedient servant until death and after.

G. S. Z.

"Shall I show it to Vasya or not? And if I do—then when? Now or after the guests have gone? No, it'd be better to wait until they've gone—if I do it now, we'll both look ridiculous—this poor man and me too."

So it was that Princess Vera considered what to do, unable all the while to take her eyes off the scarlet, blood-red fires flickering deep inside the five garnets.

++++++++++++++++
*Princess Vera's nameday (September 17), the day of the saint after whom she is named. The day is important since it commemorates the martyrdom not only of St. Vera (*vera* is the Russian for "faith"), but also of her sisters Nadezhda ("hope") and Lyubov ("charity"), and their mother Sofia (known in the West as "wisdom"). All four were martyred in about 137 AD during the reign of the Roman Emperor Hadrian.

VI

It was only with the greatest difficulty that Colonel Ponamaryov was prevailed upon to sit down and play poker. He said that he knew nothing about the game, that in general he did not approve of gambling even for fun, and that he was only fond of and fairly good at vint.* But he could not resist the general persuasion to play and in the end gave in.

To begin with they had to teach him and correct his mistakes, but he mastered the rules of the game quite quickly, and before even half an hour had passed he had all the chips piled in front of him.

"That's not fair!" said Anna, pretending to be offended. "You might have let us have a bit of fun!"

Three of the guests—Speshnikov, the colonel and the vice-governor, a rather dull, correct, boring German—were the kind of people that Vera simply did not know how to occupy or amuse. She arranged a game of vint for them and invited Gustav Ivanovich to be the fourth player. Anna thanked her from a distance by lowering her eyelids, and Vera understood her immediately. Everyone knew that unless Gustav Ivanovich were made to sit down and play cards, he would hover around his wife all evening as if tied to her apron strings, showing his bad teeth in a skull-like grin and putting Anna in a bad mood.

Now things began to go smoothly, without any feeling of constraint, and the atmosphere was lively. Accompanied by Jenny Reiter, Vasyuchok softly sang a few Italian folk canzonets and Oriental songs by Rubinstein. His voice lacked power but it was responsive and sure with an agreeable timbre. Jenny Reiter, a very exacting musician, was always willing to accompany him. But then people said he was paying court to her.

Sitting on a couch in the corner, Anna was flirting with the Hussar in the most brazen fashion. Smiling, Vera went up to them and listened.

"No, no, please don't laugh," said Anna gaily, narrowing her passionate, lovely Tatar eyes at the officer. "Of course, you think it's hard work galloping at breakneck speed at the head of your squadron or clearing the hurdles at the races, don't you? But just look at the work we do. We've just finished organizing a lottery. Now do you think that was easy? Pah! A great crowd of people, the room full of smoke, janitors, cabbies or whatever they're called...all badgering you with their complaints, grievances and what have you... And you're on your feet all day long! And that's not all either, because there's a concert to arrange next in aid of needy working women from the intelligentsia. Then after that there's a grand charity ball..."

"At which you will not refuse me the mazurka, I make bold to hope?" interrupted Bakhtinsky, and with a slight bow clicked his heels under his chair.

"Thank you... But what I feel saddest of all about is our children's home. You know, our home for depraved children..."

++++++++++++++++
*A Russian card game resembling auction bridge.

"Oh yes, I quite understand. That must be very amusing, isn't it?"

"Stop it! You should be ashamed of yourself, laughing at things like that! But do you know what the trouble is? We want to give shelter to these unfortunate children whose souls are full of hereditary vices and bad example, we want to give them warmth and affection..."

"Hm!.."

"...to improve their morals and awaken a sense of duty in their souls... Do you understand what I mean? And every day scores and scores of children are brought to us, but there's not a single one who's depraved among them! If you ask the parents whether their child is depraved, they take offense—as you can imagine! And so the home's open and consecrated, and everything's ready—but it hasn't got a single inmate, neither girl nor boy! Perhaps we ought to offer a prize for every depraved child that's brought to us."

"Anna Nikolaevna," interrupted the Hussar in an ingratiating, earnest tone. "Why offer a prize? Take me free. On my honor, you'll not find a more depraved child anywhere."

"Stop it! It's impossible to have a serious conversation with you," she said, bursting out laughing and leaning back against the couch with eyes that sparkled with merriment.

Sitting at the large, round table, Prince Vasily Lvovich was showing his sister, Anosov and his brother-in-law a comic family album of cartoons drawn by himself. All four of them were laughing heartily, and little by little the other guests who were not playing cards gathered around them.

The album was a sort of supplement or series of illustrations to Prince Vasily's satirical stories. With his customary imperturbable calm he showed, for example, "The Story of the Amorous Adventures of the Brave General Anosov in Turkey, Bulgaria and Elsewhere"; "The Adventures of Prince Nikolai Bulat-Tuganovsky the Coxcomb in Monte Carlo," and so on.

"Now, ladies and gentlemen, here you see a brief biography of our beloved sister, Lyudmila Lvovna," he said, shooting his sister a swift, amused glance. "Part One—Childhood. 'The child grew and her name was Lima.'"

The page of the album showed the beautiful figure of a little girl drawn in a deliberately childlike way, with her face in profile but with both eyes visible. She had dotted lines instead of legs sticking out from under her skirt, while the fingers of her outstretched hands were spread wide.

"Nobody ever called me Lima," said Lyudmila Lvovna with a laugh.

"Part Two. First Love. A cavalry cadet kneels before the maid Lima and presents her with a poem of his own composing. It contains these lines of truly pearl-like beauty:

> *Your beautiful foot, I do opine,*
> *Is a thing of passion divine!*

"And here's a true likeness of that foot.

"Here the cadet is persuading the innocent Lima to elope from her parental home. Here is the elopement itself. And here is a critical situation: the enraged father catches up with the fugitives. The faint-hearted cadet heaps all the blame on the meek Lima:

You took so much time powdering your face,
That now we're pursued in a terrible chase...
You sort things out howsoever you wish,
But it's into the bushes I swiftly dismiss.

The story of the maid Lima was followed by a new tale entitled "Princess Vera and the Amorous Telegraphist."

"This moving poem is only illustrated in ink and crayon so far," explained Vasily Lvovich with a serious air. "The text is still being composed."

"This is something new," remarked Anosov, "I've not seen it before."

"It's the very latest issue. Something quite new on the bookstalls."

Vera touched his shoulder gently.

"I'd rather you didn't," she said.

But Vasily Lvovich either did not catch what she said or attached no real importance to it.

"The beginning dates from long, long ago. One fine day in May a girl called Vera receives in the post a letter with a pair of little doves billing on the first page. Here's the letter, and here are the doves.

"The letter contains a passionate declaration of love, written without any regard for the rules of orthography. It begins thus: 'O Beautiful Golden-Haired One, you who...are a stormy sea of flame raging in my breast. Like a venomous serpent your glance has bitten deep into my tormented soul,' and so on. It ends with the humble words: 'My means are only those of a poor telegraphist, but my feelings are worthy of St. George. I dare not reveal my full name—it is too unbecoming. I sign myself only with my initials: P. P. Z. Please reply to the main post office, poste restante.' And here, ladies and gentlemen, you see a portrait of the telegraphist himself, drawn very skillfully in crayon.

"Vera's heart is pierced (here's the heart and here's the arrow). But as befits a well-behaved and well-brought up young lady, she shows the letter to her honorable parents and also to her childhood friend and betrothed, the handsome young Vasya Shein. And here's the illustration. Given time, of course, the drawings will have explanations in verse added to them.

"Sobbing, Vasya Shein returns their engagement ring to Vera. 'I dare not stand in the way of your happiness,' he says, 'but I implore you not to make any hasty decisions. Think it over, reflect a little, and examine both your own feelings and his. You know nothing about life, my child, and you fly like a moth to a brilliant flame. But I—alas!—I know the cold and hypocritical

189

world. Remember that telegraphists are fascinating but perfidious creatures. It gives them indescribable pleasure to deceive an innocent victim with their proud beauty and false feelings, and then mock her cruelly.'

"Six months pass. Spinning in the whirl of life's waltz, Vera forgets her admirer and marries the handsome young Vasya, but the telegraphist does not forget her. One day he dresses up as a chimneysweep and after smearing himself with soot, makes his way into Princess Vera's boudoir. As you can see, he leaves the marks of his five fingers and two lips everywhere: on the rugs, the pillows, the wallpaper, and even on the parquet floor.

"Then, disguised as a peasant woman, he comes to work as an ordinary scullery maid in our kitchen. But the excessive favors bestowed on him by Luka the cook oblige him to flee.

"Here he is in the lunatic asylum. And here you see he's taken monastic vows. But every day without fail he sends passionate letters to Vera. And where his tears fall on the paper, the ink runs and becomes smudged.

"In the end he dies, but before his death he bequeaths to Vera two buttons off his telegraphist's uniform and a perfume bottle filled with his tears..."

"Ladies and gentlemen, who would like some tea?" asked Vera Nikolaevna.

VII

The long autumn sunset was fading. After glowing like a narrow slit on the very edge of the horizon, burning out between the dove-gray clouds and the earth, the last crimson strip of sky had died. Now neither the earth, the trees, nor the sky were visible. Only the big stars glimmered high overhead as their eyelashes flickered in the darkness of night, while the pale blue beam from the lighthouse rose upwards like a slender pillar and seemed to spill over the vault of heaven in a hazy pool of liquid light. Moths fluttered against the bell-glasses over the candles. The star-shaped flowers of the white tobacco plants in the front garden gave off a stronger fragrance in the cool darkness.

Speshnikov, the vice-governor and Colonel Ponamaryov had left long ago, promising to send the horses back from the tram terminus to pick up the General. The remaining guests were sitting on the terrace. Despite his protests, the sisters had made Anosov put his coat on and had wrapped his legs in a warm rug. He sat between Vera and Anna with a bottle of Pommard, his favorite red wine, in front of him. The sisters looked after him with great care, filling his slender glass with the thick, heavy wine, passing him the matches and cutting him some cheese. The old General wrinkled up his eyes in bliss.

"Yes...it's autumn...autumn," he said, gazing at the candle flame and shaking his head pensively. "Autumn, and it's already time for me to leave. Oh, what a pity! And the fine weather's only just begun. How I'd like to live down here by the sea in peace and quiet..."

"You could stay with us, grandad," said Vera.

"I can't, my dear, I can't. Duty calls... My leave's over now... But I must say, it would be very nice! Just smell those roses... I can smell them from here. And during the summer when it was very hot you couldn't smell a single flower except the white acacia...and even that smelt of sweets."

Vera took two small roses, one pink and the other carmine, out of a small vase and stuck them into the buttonhole of the General's coat.

"Thank you, Vera my dear." Anosov bent his head towards his lapel, sniffed the flowers, and suddenly smiled the splendid smile of a kind old man.

"I remember the time we came into Bucharest and took up our quarters. One day I was walking down the street when I suddenly caught the strong smell of roses. I stopped and saw two soldiers standing with a beautiful crystal bottle of attar of roses beside them. They had already oiled their rifle-bolts and greased their boots with it. 'What have you got there?' I asked. 'It's some kind of oil, your Honor. We tried putting it in the kasha but it's no good because it burns your mouth. It smells all right, though.' I offered them a ruble and they gave me the bottle with pleasure. There was less than half the oil left, but considering how expensive it was, there must still have been at least two hundred rubles' worth. The soldiers were quite happy with the transaction and said: 'And here's something else, your Honor—Turkish peas of some sort. However long we cook them they still won't go soft, the damned things!' I could see they were coffee beans, so I said to the men: 'They're all right for Turks but they're no good for soldiers.' Fortunately though, they'd not stuffed themselves with opium—I saw cakes of it trampled into the mud in several places."

"Grandad, tell us frankly," asked Anna, "did you ever feel afraid in battle? Were you ever frightened?"

"What a strange thing to ask, Anna dear! Yes, of course I was afraid. Don't you believe people who tell you they weren't afraid and who say the whistling of bullets is the sweetest music on earth to them. Only cranks or braggarts talk like that. Everybody's afraid. It's just that some go all to pieces when they're frightened, while others keep a grip on themselves. And you see, the fear always stays the same, but the ability to control yourself keeps on improving with practice. That's why you get men who are courageous soldiers and heroes. So that's how it is, you see. But I was once very nearly frightened to death."

"Tell us about it, grandad," begged both the sisters at once.

They still listened to Anosov's stories with the same rapture as when they were small children. Anna even involuntarily spread her elbows on the table just like a child and propped her chin on her palms. There was a comfortable charm in his unhurried, simple way of talking, and the very turns of phrase with which he spoke of his memories of war acquired in the telling an

191

unwittingly odd, clumsy, rather bookish flavor. It was as if he were following some old, stock narrative pattern that he was very fond of.

"The story's a very short one," he replied. "It was at Shipka, during the winter, after I'd been shellshocked. There were four of us in our dugout and it was there that this terrible thing happened to me. One morning, when I got up, I imagined my name wasn't Yakov but Nikolai, and I just couldn't convince myself otherwise, however hard I tried. Realizing I was going out of my mind, I shouted for some water, doused my head with it, and came to my senses."

"I can imagine what success you had with women on your campaigns, Yakov Mikhailovich," said Jenny Reiter, the pianist. "You must have been very handsome in your younger days."

"Oh, but our grandad's still handsome even now!" exclaimed Anna.

"I wasn't handsome," said Anosov with a serene smile, "but I didn't miss out all the same. Something very touching happened in Bucharest too. When we entered the city, the people welcomed us in the main square with a cannonade that broke a lot of windows; but the windows with glasses of water standing in them remained intact. And do you know how I found that out? Well, I'll tell you. When I arrived at the billet assigned to me, I saw a squat, little bird cage standing on the windowsill. On top of the cage was a big cut-glass bottle full of clear water with goldfish swimming in it, while among them was a canary sitting on its perch. Just imagine—a canary in water! I was amazed, but when I looked more closely, I saw that the bottom of the bottle had a wide, deep hollow in the middle, so that the canary could easily fly in and sit on its perch there. After that I realized I was very slow on the uptake indeed.

"Going into the house, I saw a very pretty Bulgarian girl. I showed her the document authorizing me to be billeted there, and took the opportunity to ask her why the windowpanes were still intact after the cannonade. She told me it was because of the water. She explained about the canary too: how slow I'd been!.. Then while we were talking, our eyes met, something like an electric current suddenly flowed between us, and I knew I had fallen in love with her at first sight—passionately and forever."

The old man fell silent and carefully sipped the dark wine.

"But you did declare yourself to her later, didn't you?" asked the pianist.

"Hm...yes, of course... Only I did it without words. It was like this..."

"Grandad, I hope you're not going to embarrass us!" said Anna with a roguish laugh.

"No, no—our romance was most proper. You see, everywhere we were billeted the townsfolk had their own misconceptions and reservations about us, but in Bucharest the people were so friendly that one day when I began to play the violin, all the girls immediately put their best clothes on and came out to dance, and from then on this used to happen every day.

192

"One evening, while people were dancing in the moonlight, my Bulgarian girl disappeared down the hall and I followed her. On seeing me, she pretended to be sorting dry rose petals—something, incidentally, that the local inhabitants gather by the sackful. But I put my arms around her, held her close, and kissed her several times.

"From then on, as soon as the moon rose and the stars shone in the sky, I would hurry to my beloved and for a while forget all my daily cares with her. And when our campaign took us away from those parts, we swore an oath of everlasting love and said farewell forever."

"And is that all?" asked Lyudmila Lvovna with disappointment.

"But what more do you want?" replied the general.

"No, Yakov Mikhailovich, forgive me for saying so, but that's not love ——it's just an army officer's bivouac adventure."

"I don't know, my dear, really, I just don't know whether it was love or some other feeling..."

"But...tell me...have you really never known genuine love? You know, the kind of love that...well...in a word...is sacred, pure, and everlasting...one that is not of this earth... Have you really never known a love like that?"

"I honestly can't say," said the old man falteringly, rising from his armchair. "Probably not. To begin with, when I was young, there was never any time, what with going out, playing cards and fighting wars... It seemed as if good health, youth and life itself would last forever. Then suddenly I looked around and saw I was already an old wreck... Well now, Vera my dear, you mustn't keep me any longer. I'll say goodbye... Hussar," he said to Bakhtinsky, "it's a warm night, so let's walk down and meet our carriage."

"I'll come with you, grandad," said Vera.

"So will I," echoed Anna.

Before leaving, Vera went up to her husband and said to him softly:

"If you look in my desk drawer...you'll find a red box with a letter in it. Read it."

VIII

Anna and Bakhtinsky went on ahead, while the general followed about twenty yards behind, walking arm in arm with Vera. The night was so dark that for the first few minutes, till their eyes became accustomed to the gloom, they had to feel for the way with their feet. Anosov, who despite his age still possessed amazingly keen eyesight, had to help his companion, and from time to time his large, cool hand fondly stroked Vera's as it rested lightly in the crook of his arm.

"That Lyudmila Lvovna's a funny person," he said suddenly, as if continuing his train of thought aloud. "I've seen it happen so many times in my life: as soon as a woman's getting on for fifty, particularly if she's a widow or spinster, she feels an urge to meddle in other people's love affairs. She either spies, gloats and gossips, or interferes and tries to arrange other people's happiness, or starts talking a lot of sickly-sweet nonsense about exalted love. But I'd say that people nowadays have forgotten how to love each other. I just can't see any real love these days, and I didn't see any in my time either!"

"Now how on earth can that be, grandad?" objected Vera mildly, squeezing his arm gently. "Why do you say such bad things about people? After all, you were married yourself once. Doesn't that mean you loved your wife sincerely, despite everything?"

"It means absolutely nothing at all, my dear Vera. Do you know how I came to be married? One day I saw a fresh-looking little girl sitting near me. As she breathed, her bosom stirred under her blouse, then she lowered her long, long eyelashes and suddenly blushed all over. The skin on her cheeks was so soft, her little neck was so white and innocent, and her hands were so warm and gentle. Oh, to hell with it all! And then her mama and papa were always hovering about, eavesdropping at doors and gazing at me with such sad eyes full of dog-like devotion. And as I was leaving, what quick little kisses there'd be behind the door... At tea a little foot would touch mine under the table as if by accident... Well, and that was that! 'Dear Nikita Antonych, I've come to ask for your daughter's hand. Believe me, this sacred being...' But papa was already starting to cry and coming forward eagerly to kiss me... 'My dear boy! I suspected it long ago... Well, may God grant you... Just mind you take care of the little treasure...' And then three months later the little treasure was going about in a shabby housecoat with slippers on her bare feet, her hair all straggly, unkempt and done up in curling-papers, running around with army orderlies like a cook and putting on airs with young officers, lisping, giggling and making eyes at them the whole time. For some reason she started calling me Jacques in company, pronouncing it down her nose in a languorous drawl, like this: 'Ja-a-acques.' She was extravagant, devious, sluttish and greedy. And her eyes always looked so deceitful... But it's all over now, finished and done with. Deep down I'm even grateful to that miserable little actor she ran off with... Thank God we had no children..."

"Have you forgiven them, grandad?"

"Forgiven isn't the word, Vera dear. To begin with I was like a madman. If I'd seen them then I'd certainly have killed both of them. But gradually I felt better and better about it, and eventually had nothing but contempt for them. And that was a good thing—God saved me from causing unnecessary bloodshed. Besides, I was spared the fate of most husbands. What would have happened to me if it hadn't been for that vile episode? I'd have become a beast of burden, a despicable conniver and abettor, a milch cow, a front, some sort of necessary household utensil... No! It's all turned out for the best, Vera dear."

"No, no, grandad, forgive me, but the old feeling of resentment still rankles in you... And you apply your own unfortunate experience to the whole of mankind. Just take Vasya and me, for example. Now you couldn't say our marriage was unhappy, could you?"

Anosov did not speak for quite a long time. Then he said slowly and reluctantly:

"Well, all right...let's say yours is an exception... But in the majority of cases why is it that people get married? Let's take the woman. She's ashamed to stay single, particularly when all her friends are married. It's hard being an extra mouth to feed in the family. She wants to be a housewife, mistress in her own home, an independent lady... And what's more, there's the need, the purely physical need, to be a mother and start building her own nest. But men have different reasons for getting married. First of all, they get tired of bachelor life, of having untidy rooms, of eating in restaurants, of dirt, cigarette-ends, torn linen that doesn't match, debts, friends who are over-familiar, and so on and so forth. Secondly, they feel family life is more advantageous, more wholesome and economical. Thirdly, they think some little ones will come along, and though they themselves will die, they feel a part of them will still be left on earth...something like the illusion of immortality. Fourthly, there's the temptation of innocence, as happened in my case. Besides that, there are sometimes thoughts of the dowry too. But where does love come in all this? Disinterested, selfless love that expects no reward? The love which is said to be 'stronger than death?' You know, the kind of love for which performing any feat, going through any torture, or even giving your own life isn't a terrible trial but pure joy. Wait, Vera, wait, you're wanting to tell me about Vasya again, aren't you? I really am very fond of him, you know. He's a fine fellow, and who knows, perhaps the future will show his love for you in a very beautiful light. But you know the kind of love I mean. Love should be a tragedy, the greatest mystery on earth! No creature comforts, no calculations, no compromises should affect it."

"Have you ever known of a love like that, grandad?" asked Vera quietly.

"No," replied the old man emphatically, "though I do know of two instances that came close to it. But one was the result of stupidity, while the other...well...that was a kind of bitterness...and nothing but pity...I'll tell you about them if you like. It won't take long."

"Please do, grandad."

"All right. A regimental commander in our division (but not in our regiment) had a wife. I assure you, Vera dear, she had the plainest face imaginable. She was ginger-haired, bony, long and scraggy with a great big mouth... Her makeup used to peel off her face just like plaster off an old house in Moscow. But you know, she was a real regimental Messalina—full of spirit, very masterful and contemptuous of others, and with a tremendous passion for variety. And she was a morphine addict into the bargain.

"Then one autumn a new ensign joined our regiment, a green young fellow straight from the Academy. In a month that old nag had him completely under her thumb. He was her page, her servant, her slave and her perpetual dancing partner, carrying her handkerchief and fan for her and rushing out into the frost and snow to call her horses without a coat on. It's terrible when a fresh, innocent young fellow lays his first love at the feet of an experienced, ambitious, old libertine. Even if he manages to get away unscathed, you can still consider him done for. He'll be marked for life.

"By Christmas she was already tired of him and went back to one of her well-tried former flames. But the ensign couldn't do without her and followed her about like a ghost. He became completely exhausted and went all thin and dark. Putting it in high-flown language, 'death had already laid its hand on his lofty brow.' He was terribly jealous of her, and they say he used to stand under her window for nights on end.

Then one day in spring they arranged some kind of outing or picnic for officers in the regiment. I knew both him and her personally, but I wasn't there that day. As usual on occasions like that, everybody had a lot to drink. They walked back to town at night along the railway track. Suddenly they saw a goods train coming towards them, climbing very slowly up a rather steep incline and whistling as it went. And then, just as the lights of the engine drew level with the party, she suddenly whispered in the ensign's ear: 'You keep telling me you love me, but if I told you to throw yourself under that train, I bet you wouldn't!' Without a word, he ran and flung himself on the track. They say he'd probably judged it so he'd fall right between the engine's front and rear wheels—that way he'd have been cut clean in two. But some idiot took it into his head to try to hold him back and push him away, only he didn't manage it. The ensign grabbed hold of the rails and got both his hands cut off."

"Oh, how dreadful!" exclaimed Vera.

"He had to resign from the army. His friends collected a little money for him when he left. It would have been awkward for him to stay in town anyway: he would have been a living reproach both to her and the whole regiment. And so he was done for...he'd been destroyed in the vilest way imaginable... He became a beggar...and froze to death on a wharf somewhere in Petersburg.

"The second case was quite pathetic. The woman involved here was just like the first, except that she was young and beautiful. She behaved very, very badly. Even we were shocked, and we all tended to regard love affairs like that in a rather free and easy way. But her husband didn't mind. He knew all about it and saw what was going on, but didn't say a thing. His friends kept dropping hints, but he just brushed them aside—'Stop it, stop it... It's nothing to do with me, nothing to do with me... As long as Lenochka's happy!..' What a fool he was!

"In the end she took up once and for all with Lieutenant Vishnyakov, a subaltern from their company. And the three of them lived together in a *ménage à trois* just as if it were the most lawful kind of arrangement imaginable. But then our regiment was ordered to the front. When the ladies saw us

196

all off, she was there too, and really you felt ashamed just to look at her: she might have glanced at her husband just once, if only for decency's sake, but oh no! She hung on her lieutenant's neck for all she was worth and wouldn't let go. And when we'd taken our seats in the carriages and the train started to move, the shameless creature shouted to her husband in parting: 'Mind you take care of Volodya! If anything happens to him, I'll leave you and never come back! And I'll take the children with me too!'

"Perhaps you think the captain was a spineless kind of fellow, a pansy or a ninny? Not a bit of it—he was a very brave soldier. At the battle of Zelyonie Gori he led his company against a Turkish redoubt six times, and out of two hundred men he had only fourteen left. He was wounded twice but refused to go to the dressing station. That's the kind of man he was, and the soldiers simply worshipped him.

"But it was *she*...his Lenochka, who told him what to do!

"And he ran around after that idler and coward Vishnyakov, that lousy drone, as if he were his nanny or his mother. When we camped at night in mud and rain he'd wrap him in his own greatcoat, or go and supervise the men digging trenches for him, while Vishnyakov lounged around in his dugout or played cards. Then at night he'd inspect the sentry posts for him. And this, mark you, Vera, was when the Bashi-Bazouks were cutting down our pickets as easily as an old woman in Yaroslavl cuts the heads off the cabbages in her kitchen garden. It's a sin to say so, but really, everyone was glad to hear Vishnyakov had died in a hospital of typhus..."

"Well, and what about women, grandad? Have you ever met any women who love sincerely?"

"Oh, of course I have, Vera my dear. I'll go even further: I'm sure almost every woman is capable of supreme heroism if she's in love. You see, she kisses you, embraces you, gives herself to you—and *already* she's a mother. If she loves someone, then for her love comprises the whole meaning of life—the whole universe! But it's not in the least her fault that love has taken on such vulgar characteristics among mankind and degenerated into nothing more than an everyday convenience, a minor entertainment. It's men who are to blame for that, with their chickens' bodies and rabbits' souls, men who are sated at twenty and incapable of strong feelings, heroic actions, tenderness, or adoration of those they profess to love. People say all those things used to exist once. But even if they didn't, weren't they what the best minds and souls of mankind dreamed of and longed for—minds like those of poets, novelists, musicians and artists? The other day I was reading the story of Manon Lescaut and the Chevalier des Grieux... Can you believe it?—it brought tears to my eyes... Now tell me, my dear, in all honesty, doesn't every woman in her heart of hearts dream of such a love—a love that's entire, all-forgiving, prepared for anything, humble and selfless?"

"Oh, of course, grandad, of course..."

"But because such love no longer exists, women take vengeance on men for its absence. Another thirty years or so will pass... I'll not see it, Vera my dear, but you might. Mark my words, in about thirty years from now women will acquire unprecedented power in the world. They will dress like Indian gods and trample us men underfoot like despicable, groveling slaves. Their extravagant whims and caprices will become agonizing laws for us. And all because for generation after generation we've been unable to worship or revere love. This will be their revenge. You know the principle: to every action there is an equal and opposite reaction."

He was silent for a while, then suddenly asked:

"Tell me, Vera dear, if it's not too difficult for you, what's this story about a telegraphist that Prince Vasily was telling us this evening? How much of it is fact and how much is his usual fiction?"

"Do you really want to know, grandad?"

"As you wish, Vera, as you wish. But if for some reason it's unpleasant for you..."

"Not at all. I'll tell you with pleasure."

And she told the General in detail about the crank who had started to pursue her with his love as long ago as two years before she was married.

She had never seen him and did not know his name. He had only ever written to her, and he signed himself G. S. Z. Once he had mentioned that he worked as a minor clerk in some official establishment—but he never said a word about any telegraph office. Apparently, he watched her movements constantly, because in his letters he would indicate very precisely what soirées she had attended and with whom, and what she had been wearing. At first his letters were curiously passionate and vulgar in tone, though they were quite proper. But one day Vera had written to him ("By the way, grandad," she said, "don't tell the family that: none of them knows about it") asking him not to pester her any more with his protestations of love. Since then he had spoken no more of his love and had written only occasionally: at Easter, New Year, and on her nameday. Princess Vera also told the general about the parcel she had received that evening and even told him almost word for word what was said in the strange letter from her secret admirer...

"Ye-es," said Anosov slowly when she had finished. "Perhaps he's just an abnormal chap, a crank, but—who knows?—perhaps your life's road has been crossed, my dear Vera, by the very kind of love that women dream of but that men are no longer capable of. Just a moment. Can you see lights moving ahead? It must be my carriage."

Just then they heard the loud roaring of a car behind them, and the rutted road shone white in the brilliant light from the vehicle's acetylene lamps. Gustav Ivanovich came driving up.

"Anna, I've got your things with me. Get in," he said. "Your Excellency, may I give you a lift?"

"No, it's all right, thank you, my dear fellow," replied the general. "I'm not fond of that car of yours. It does nothing but shake and smell, and

I don't enjoy riding in it. Well, goodbye, Vera my dear. I'll come and see you more often now," he said, kissing her hands and forehead.

Everybody said goodbye. Friesse drove Vera Nikolaevna to the gate of her dacha, and then, turning in a swift circle, vanished into the darkness in his roaring, breathless machine.

IX

With an unpleasant feeling Princess Vera walked up the steps on to the terrace and went into the house. Even from a distance she could hear her brother Nikolai's loud voice and see his tall, lean figure pacing the room rapidly. Vasily Lvovich was sitting at the card table and with his big, fair, close-cropped head bent low, was drawing on the green cloth with a piece of chalk.

"I insisted on this a long time ago!" Nikolai was saying in annoyance, gesturing with his right hand as though flinging some invisible weight to the ground. "I insisted long ago that these idiotic letters should stop. Even before you and Vera were married, I tried to convince you that you were both amusing yourselves with them like children, seeing only the funny side of them... Here comes Vera herself, by the way... Vera my dear, Vasily Lvovich and I were just talking about this madman of yours, this P. P. Z. I think this correspondence is impertinent and vulgar."

"There wasn't any correspondence at all," Shein interrupted him coolly. "He was the only one who wrote..."

Vera blushed at these words and sat down on the sofa in the shadow of a large house plant.

"I'm sorry," said Nikolai Nikolaevich, and tearing it from his breast, flung the invisible, heavy object down again.

"I don't see why you call him mine," put in Vera, gladdened by her husband's support. "He's as much yours as mine..."

"All right, I apologize again. All I mean is that we must put an end to his foolishness. In my opinion this business is getting beyond the stage where we can just laugh about it and draw funny little pictures... Believe me, the only thing I'm concerned about is Vera's and your good name, Vasily Lvovich."

"Well, but I think you're making rather too much of it, Kolya," replied Shein.

"Perhaps, perhaps... But if you're not careful, you'll find yourself in a ridiculous position."

"I don't see how," said the Prince.

"Just suppose..." Nikolai said, picking up the red box from the table and immediately flinging it down again in disgust, "suppose we keep this idiotic bracelet, this monstrous, priestly trinket, or suppose we throw it out or give it to Dasha. Then, firstly, P. P. Z. will be able to boast to his friends and acquaintances that Princess Vera Nikolaevna Sheina accepts gifts from him, and secondly, this first success will encourage him to attempt further exploits. Tomorrow he'll be sending her a diamond ring, the day after that a string of pearls, and then—before you can say Jack Robinson—he'll be in the dock for embezzlement or fraud, and you'll both be called as witnesses... A fine state of affairs that'll be!"

"No, no, the bracelet must be sent back without fail!" cried Vasily Lvovich.

"I think so too," agreed Vera, "and as soon as possible. But how can we do it? After all, we don't know either the man's name or address."

"Oh, that's no problem at all!" replied Nikolai Nikolaevich scornfully. "We know the initials of this P. P. Z.... What do you call him, Vera?"

"G. S. Z."

"That's splendid. What's more, we know he works as an official somewhere. That's quite enough. Tomorrow I'll get hold of the municipal directory and look for a clerk or civil servant with those initials. If for some reason or other I can't find him, then I'll just call a detective and tell him to track him down. If there's any difficulty, I'll have this piece of paper with his handwriting on it. In short, by two o'clock tomorrow afternoon I'll know the exact name and address of this fellow and even the times when he's at home. And once I've discovered that, then tomorrow we'll not only send his treasure back to him but also take measures to ensure he never reminds us of his existence again."

"What have you in mind?" asked Prince Vasily.

"What have I in mind? I'll go and see the governor and ask him to..."

"No, not the governor—please. You know what terms we're on with him... There's a real danger we'll make ourselves look ridiculous."

"All right. I'll go and see the chief of police then—he's a friend of mine at the club. He'll send for this Romeo and shake his finger under his nose. Do you know how he does it? He brings his finger right up to the man's nose and doesn't move his hand at all, but just waggles his finger and shouts: 'I, sir, will not tolera-a-ate it!' "

"Ugh! Fancy doing it through the police!" said Vera, pulling a wry face.

"You're right, Vera," agreed the Prince. "It'd be better not to drag any outsiders into this business. There'll be rumors and gossip... We all know what this town of ours is like—it's just like living in a glass jar... It'd be better if I went to see this...young man myself...though who knows, he may be sixty... I'll give the bracelet back to him and give him a jolly good talking to."

"In that case I'll come with you," Nikolai Nikolaevich interrupted him quickly. "You're too soft, so let me do the talking... And now, my friends," he said, taking out his pocket watch and glancing at it, "you'll excuse me if I go to my room for a while. I'm so tired I can hardly keep on my feet, and

I've got two cases to look through before I go to bed."

"Somehow I feel sorry for this unfortunate man," said Vera hesitantly.

"There's no need to feel sorry for him!" replied Nikolai sharply, turning in the doorway. "If anyone of our acquaintance had dared to play that trick with the bracelet and letter, Prince Vasily would have challenged him to a duel. And if he hadn't, then I would. In the old days I'd have just ordered this fellow to be taken to the stables and flogged. Wait to hear from me tomorrow, Vasily Lvovich—I'll ring you at the office."

X

The dirty stairs smelled of cats, mice, kerosene and washing. Before they reached the fifth floor Prince Vasily Lvovich stopped.

"Wait a moment," he said to his brother-in-law. "Let me get my breath back. Oh, Kolya, we shouldn't have come..."

They went up another two flights. It was so dark on the landing that Nikolai Nikolaevich had to strike two matches before he could make out the number of the flat.

When he rang the bell the door was opened by a stout woman in spectacles with gray hair and gray eyes. She stooped a little, apparently because of some illness.

"Is Mr. Zheltkov in?" asked Nikolai Nikolaevich.

The woman's eyes flitted anxiously from one visitor to the other and then back again. Their respectable appearance seemed to reassure her.

"Yes, please come in," she said, opening the door. "It's the first on the left."

Bulat-Tuganovsky knocked three times, briefly but firmly. There was a rustling sound inside. He knocked again.

"Come in," answered a faint voice.

The room was extremely low but very long and wide, and almost square in shape. Its two round windows that looked rather like portholes hardly let in sufficient light. In fact, it was very like the messroom on board a cargo vessel. Against one wall stood a narrow little bed, and against another was a large, wide sofa covered with a beautiful though frayed Turkoman rug, while in the middle of the room stood a table spread with a colored Ukrainian cloth.

To begin with the occupant's face was not visible: he stood with his back to the light, rubbing his hands in embarrassment. He was tall and lean with long, silky hair.

"Mr. Zhelt-kov, if I'm not mistaken?" asked Nikolai Nikolaevich haughtily.

"Yes. Very pleased to meet you."

Holding out his hand, he took two steps towards Tuganovsky, but at the same moment, as though not noticing his gesture of welcome, Nikolai Nikolaevich turned away to face Shein.

"I told you we weren't mistaken."

Zheltkov's thin, nervous fingers began to run up and down the lapels of his short, brown jacket, fastening then unfastening the buttons. Finally, pointing to the sofa and bowing awkwardly, he said with an effort:

"Please, do sit down."

Now the whole of him was visible: he was very pale, with a delicate, girlish face, light blue eyes and the chin of a willful child with a dimple in it; he must have been about thirty or thirty-five.

"Thank you," said Prince Shein simply, examining him very carefully.

"Merci," replied Nikolai Nikolaevich briefly. And both visitors remained standing. "We've only called for a few minutes. This is Prince Vasily Lvovich Shein, Marshal of the Nobility for the province. My name's Mirza-Bulat-Tuganovsky and I'm the assistant public prosecutor. The matter which we would be grateful to discuss with you is of equal concern to both the Prince and myself, or rather the Prince's wife, who is my sister."

Completely taken aback, Zheltkov suddenly sank down on the sofa and mumbled with stiff lips: "Please sit down, gentlemen." But evidently remembering that he had suggested the same thing earlier, though without success, he leapt up, and pulling at his hair, ran to the window before coming back to the sofa. And once again his trembling hands began to run up and down, pulling at the buttons on his jacket, tugging at his light, reddish mustache, and fingering his face.

"I'm at your service, Your Excellency," he said in a toneless voice, looking at Vasily Lvovich with eyes full of entreaty.

But Shein said nothing. It was Nikolai Nikolaevich who began to speak.

"First of all, allow me to return your gift," he said, and taking the red box from his pocket, laid it carefully on the table. "It certainly does credit to your taste, but we earnestly request that you send no more presents of this kind."

"Forgive me... I know I'm very much to blame," whispered Zheltkov, looking down at the floor and blushing. "Would you like a glass of tea?"

"You see, Mr. Zheltkov," Nikolai Nikolaevich went on, as though he had not heard Zheltkov's last words, "I'm very glad to find you're a respectable man, a gentleman who understands things perfectly, and I think we can come to an agreement straightaway. Now, unless I'm mistaken, you've been pursuing Princess Vera Nikolaevna for about seven or eight years, haven't you?"

"Yes," answered Zheltkov softly, and lowered his eyelashes reverently.

"And till now we've not taken any action against you, though you'll agree that we could have and indeed *should* have done so. Isn't that true?"

"Yes."

"Yes. But by your latest act, namely sending this garnet bracelet, you have overstepped the limits of our patience. Do you understand? Its limits. I'll not conceal from you the fact that our first thought was to go to the authorities for help, but we didn't do so, and I'm very glad we didn't, because—I repeat—I can see straightaway that you're an honorable man."

"I beg your pardon. What did you say?" asked Zheltkov suddenly, and he gave a laugh. "You were thinking of going to the authorities?.. Is that what you said?"

He put his hands in his pockets, and settling himself comfortably in a corner of the sofa, took out his cigarette case and matches, and lit a cigarette.

"Did you say you were thinking of going to the authorities?.. You'll forgive me, Prince, if I sit down, won't you?" he said, turning to Shein. "Well, go on."

The Prince drew a chair up to the table and sat down. Without taking his eyes off him, he gazed with avid curiosity and profound bewilderment into this strange man's face.

"You see, my dear fellow, we can take that step any time we wish," went on Nikolai Nikolaevich in a faintly insolent tone. "To come intruding into someone else's family..."

"I'm sorry, but I must interrupt you..."

"No, I'm sorry, but now it's my turn to interrupt you..." the prosecutor almost shouted.

"As you wish. Go on, I'm listening. But I've a few words to say to Prince Vasily Lvovich."

And no longer paying any attention to Tuganovsky, he said:

"This is the most difficult moment of my life, Prince. And I must speak without regard for convention... Will you listen to me?"

"Yes," said Shein. "Oh, Kolya, please be quiet," he said impatiently, noticing Tuganovsky's angry gesture. "Go on."

For a few moments Zheltkov gasped as if he were out of breath, then suddenly launched into a swift torrent of words as though plunging headlong from a cliff. Only his jaws moved; his lips were as white and motionless as those of a corpse.

"It's hard for me to say...these words...to say I love your wife. But seven years of hopeless, perfectly proper love give me the right to say them. I admit that at first, before Vera Nikolaevna was married, I wrote foolish letters to her and even expected her to reply. I admit that the last thing I did—sending her the bracelet—was even more foolish. But... I look you straight in the eye and feel you'll understand me. I know it's beyond my power ever to stop loving her... Tell me, Prince...let's assume you find all this most unpleasant...tell me, what would you do to put a stop to my feelings? Deport me to another town, as Nikolai Nikolaevich says? That would make no difference, because I'd still go on loving Vera Nikolaevna just as much there as I do here. Put me in prison? But even there I'd find a way of letting her know of my existence. There's only one way out left, and that's death... If you wish, I'll accept it in any way you please."

"Instead of talking business, we're involved in some kind of poetry recital," said Nikolai Nikolaevich, putting on his hat. "The question's very simple: we are offering you one of two things—either you cease pursuing Vera Nikolaevna completely, or, if you will not agree to do so, we shall take such measures as our standing, acquaintances and so on permit."

Though he heard what Nikolai Nikolaevich said, Zheltkov did not even look at him, but turned to Prince Vasily Lvovich and asked:

"Would you mind if I went out for ten minutes? I'll be quite honest with you: I'm going to speak to Princess Vera Nikolaevna on the telephone. I assure you I'll tell you as much of our conversation as I can."

"All right," said Shein.

When Vasily Lvovich and Tuganovsky were left alone together, Nikolai Nikolaevich immediately set upon his brother-in-law.

"You can't do this!" he shouted, flinging the usual invisible object to the ground with his right hand. "You just can't do it! I told you beforehand I'd deal with all the business part of the conversation, but you've gone all soft and let him go rambling on about his feelings. I'd have said everything there is to say in a couple of words."

"Wait," said Prince Vasily Lvovich, "everything'll be sorted out in a few moments. The main thing is that I've seen his face and I feel this man isn't capable of deliberate falsehood or deception. And just think about it, Kolya, it's true, isn't it, that it's not his fault he's in love, and that you can't really control a feeling like love—a feeling people still can't explain." After thinking for a moment, he added: "I feel sorry for him. And it's not just that I feel sorry for him, but I feel I'm witnessing some immense spiritual tragedy. And I just can't fool about in a situation like this."

"This is sheer decadence," said Nikolai Nikolaevich.

Ten minutes later Zheltkov came back. His eyes were shining and deep, as though filled with unshed tears. It was clear too that he had completely forgotten such things as social decorum or who should sit where, and had stopped behaving like a perfect gentleman. And again, with painfully acute sensitivity, it was Prince Shein who realized it.

"I'm ready," said Zheltkov, "and as from tomorrow you'll never hear from me again. As far as you're concerned, I'll be dead. But there's one condition—and I say this to *you*, Prince Vasily Lvovich—I've embezzled official funds, you see, and I've got to leave this town anyway. Will you let me write one last letter to Princess Vera Nikolaevna?"

"No! Enough is enough! No more letters!" shouted Nikolai Nikolaevich.

"All right, you may write once more," said Shein.

"That's all right then," said Zheltkov with a proud smile. "You won't hear of me again, and of course you'll never see me again either. Princess Vera Nikolaevna didn't want to speak to me at all to begin with. When I asked her whether I could stay in this town so that I could see her from time to time—without her seeing me, of course—she replied: 'Oh, if only you knew how sick and tired I am of all this business! Please finish it as quickly as you can.' And so I will finish it. I think I've done all I can, haven't I?"

When he returned to the dacha that evening, Vasily Lvovich told his wife all about the meeting with Zheltkov. It was as if he felt it his duty to do so.

Vera was disturbed by what he said but not surprised or embarrassed. That night, when her husband came to her bed, she suddenly turned to the wall and said:

"Leave me alone—I know that man's going to kill himself."

XI

Princess Vera Nikolaevna never read the papers, firstly, because they dirtied her hands, and secondly, because she could never understand the kind of language people use nowadays.

But fate willed that she should open exactly the right page and come upon the column which contained the following news:

"A Mysterious Death. At about seven o'clock yesterday evening, G. S. Zheltkov, an official in the Weights and Measures Office, committed suicide. According to information which has come to light during the investigation, his death was the result of his embezzlement of official funds. So, at least, the dead man wrote in his suicide note. Since the testimony of witnesses has established that he died by his own hand, it has been decided not to order a post mortem."

Vera thought to herself:

"Why did I have a feeling this would happen? Precisely this tragic outcome to it all? And what was it: love or madness?"

All day long she wandered around the flower garden and the orchard. Her steadily increasing feeling of unease made her restless. And all her thoughts were directed towards that mysterious man, that ridiculous P. P. Z. whom she had never seen and probably never would see now.

"Who knows, perhaps your life's road has been crossed by a real, selfless, true love," she thought, remembering Anosov's words.

At six o'clock the postman came. This time Vera Nikolaevna recognized Zheltkov's handwriting, and with a tenderness that surprised her she unfolded the letter.

Zheltkov wrote thus:

It is not my fault, Vera Nikolaevna, that God chose to send me, as an immense happiness, the love I feel for you. It so happens that nothing in life interests me—neither politics, learning, philosophy, nor concern for the future happiness of mankind. For me life consists only in you. But now I feel that I have forced my way into your life like some embarrassing intruder. Forgive me for this, if you can. I am leaving today and shall never return, and nothing will ever remind you of me again.

I am infinitely grateful to you merely for the fact that you exist. I have examined myself, and what I feel for you is not a disease or the obsession of a maniac—it is love, a love with which God has chosen to reward me for something.

Perhaps I seemed ridiculous to you and your brother, Nikolai Nikolae-vich. But as I leave you, I say in rapture before you: "And hallowed be Thy name."

Eight years ago I saw you in a box at the circus, and at that very first moment, I said to myself: "*I love her because there is nothing like her and nothing finer on earth—no creature, plant, star, nor human being is more beautiful and more gentle than you.*" *All earth's beauty seemed to be embodied in you...*

Just think, what should I have done? Flee to another town? But my heart would still have been close beside you, at your feet, and every moment of the day would still have been filled with you, with thoughts and dreams of you...like some blissful delirium. I feel very ashamed of that stupid bracelet of mine and blush inwardly at the thought of it—but what of it?—it was just a mistake. I can imagine what effect it had on your guests.

In ten minutes I shall leave. I shall just have time to stick a stamp on this letter and drop it in the mailbox so as not to entrust it to anyone else. Please burn it when you have read it. I have just lit the stove and am now burning all that was most precious to me in life: your handkerchief which, I confess, I stole. You left it on a chair during a ball at the Assembly of the Nobility. Your note—oh, how I used to kiss it!—in which you forbade me to write to you any more. The program of an art exhibition that you once held in your hand then left on a chair on your way out... Now it is finished. I have destroyed everything, but I still believe and even feel certain that you will remember me. And if you do, then... I know you are very musical, because I used to see you most often at performances of the Beethoven quartets—so if you do remember me, then play or ask someone else to play the Sonata in D major, op. 2, No. 2.

I do not know how to finish this letter. From the bottom of my heart I thank you for being the one and only joy of my life, my sole thought and consolation. May God grant you happiness, and may nothing temporal or commonplace trouble your beautiful soul. I kiss your hands.

G. S. Z.

Her lips swollen and her eyes red with weeping, Vera Nikolaevna went to her husband. Showing him the letter, she said:

"I don't want to hide anything from you, but I feel something terrible has come into our lives. You and Nikolai Nikolaevich probably didn't handle things properly."

Prince Shein read the letter carefully then folded it neatly, and after a long silence, said:

"I don't doubt this man's sincerity, and what's more I dare not attempt to understand his feelings for you."

"Is he dead?" asked Vera.

"Yes, he's dead. I believe he loved you and I don't think he was in the least bit mad. I never took my eyes off him and watched his every movement, his every change of expression. For him there was no life without you. I felt I was witnessing some immense suffering from which people die, and I almost realized that this was a dead man standing before me. You see, Vera, I didn't know how to behave or what to do..."

"Look, Vasya," Vera Nikolaevna interrupted him, "would it be hurtful for you if I went into town and had a look at him?"

"No, no, Vera, please do. I'd go myself, but Nikolai's bungled the whole thing and I'm afraid I'd feel awkward about it."

XII

Vera Nikolaevna left her carriage two blocks before it reached Luteranskaya Street. She found Zheltkov's apartment without much difficulty. The door was opened by the same gray-eyed, stout old woman in silver-rimmed spectacles, who asked just as she had the day before:

"Who do you wish to see?"

"Mr. Zheltkov," answered the Princess.

The way she was dressed—in hat and gloves—and her slightly peremptory tone seemed to produce a profound impression on the landlady. She began to talk.

"Certainly, please come in, it's the first door on the left, but...just at the moment there's... He left us so quickly, you see. Well, what if he did embezzle some money? He should have told me about it. We don't make much, you know, letting rooms to bachelors, but if it was only a matter of six or seven hundred rubles, I could have got that together and paid it in for him. If only you knew what a wonderful man he was, madam. Eight years I had him here, and he was more like my own son than a lodger."

There was a chair in the hall and Vera sank down on it.

"I'm a friend of your late tenant," she said, choosing every word carefully. "Tell me something about the last minutes of his life, what he said and did."

"Two gentlemen came to see him, madam, and they had a very long talk with him. Afterwards he told me they'd offered him a job as bailiff on an estate. Then he ran out to telephone and came back again looking all happy. After that the two gentlemen went away and he sat down to write a letter. Then he went out to put the letter in the mailbox, and then we heard something that sounded like a shot from a toy gun, but we didn't pay any attention to it. He always used to have a drink of tea at seven o'clock, you see, and Lukeria—our maid—went and knocked on his door, but he didn't answer, so she knocked again and then again. In the end we had to break the door open, but he was already dead."

"Tell me something about the bracelet," asked Vera Nikolaevna.

"Oh, the bracelet—I completely forgot about that. But how do you know about it? Before he wrote the letter, he came to me and said: 'Are you a Catholic?' 'Yes,' I said. Then he said: 'You people have a nice custom'— that's what he said, 'a nice custom, of hanging rings, necklaces and gifts on pictures of the Virgin Mary. So please fulfill my request: would you hang this bracelet on the ikon for me?' I promised I would."

"Will you let me see him?" asked Vera.

"Of course, madam, of course. That's his door, the first on the left. They were going to take him away to the dissecting room today, but he's got a brother who persuaded them to give him a Christian burial. Please go in."

Vera braced herself and opened the door. There were three wax candles burning in the room and it smelled of incense. Zheltkov was lying on a table that stood slantwise across the room. His head rested on only the very lowest of supports, a small, soft cushion that seemed to have been put there deliberately as though it would make no difference to a corpse. There was an expression of profound dignity in his closed eyes, and his lips were set in a blissfully serene smile, as though before parting with life he had learned some profound, sweet secret that explained the whole meaning of his existence. She recalled having seen the same tranquil expression on the death masks of those two great martyrs, Napoleon and Pushkin.

"Would you like me to go out, madam?" asked the old woman, and there was something extraordinarily intimate in her tone.

"Yes, I'll call you later," said Vera, and immediately took a big red rose from the side pocket of her jacket. Lifting the head of the corpse a little with her left hand, she laid the flower under his neck with her right. At that moment she realized that the love of which every woman dreams had passed her by. She recalled Anosov's words about exceptional, everlasting love—words that were almost prophetic. Parting the hair on the dead man's forehead, she took his temples firmly in her hands and pressed her lips to his cold, moist brow in a long, affectionate kiss.

As she left, the landlady said to her in her soft Polish voice:

"I can see, madam, that you're not like all the others who only came out of curiosity. Just before he died the late Mr. Zheltkov said to me: 'If ever I die and a lady comes to see me, then tell her that Beethoven's best work is...'—he even wrote it down for me, here, have a look..."

"Show me," said Vera Nikolaevna, and suddenly burst into tears. "Please forgive me—his death has made such a painful impression on me that I can't help it."

And written in the familiar hand, she read the words:

"L. van Beethoven. Son. No. 2, op. 2. Largo Appassionato."

XIII

Vera Nikolaevna returned to the dacha late in the evening and was glad to find neither her husband nor her brother at home.

But Jenny Reiter was there waiting for her. Deeply moved by what she had seen and heard, Vera rushed to her, and kissing her large, beautiful hands, cried:

"Jenny, dear, please play something for me, will you?"

Then she immediately went out into the flower garden and sat down on a bench.

Hardly for a moment did she doubt that Jenny would play the passage from Beethoven's Second sonata, the passage that this dead man with the ridiculous name of Zheltkov had asked for.

And so it was. From its very first chords she recognized that exceptional work, one that is unequaled in its profundity. And her soul seemed to break in two. She found herself thinking that a great love, the kind of love that comes only once in a thousand years, had passed her by. She remembered Anosov's words and wondered why the dead man had made her listen to this particular work by Beethoven, and what was more, had made her listen against her will. And words formed in her mind, coinciding with the music in such a way that they seemed like verses all ending with the words: *"And hallowed be Thy name."*

Now I shall show you in notes of soft music a life that joyously and submissively gave itself to suffering, torment and death. I knew neither complaint, reproach, nor the pain of wounded pride. To you I offer only one prayer: "And hallowed be Thy name."

I recall your every step, your every smile, your every glance, and the sound of your footsteps. My last memories of you are pervaded by sweet sadness, beautiful, quiet sadness. But I shall cause you no sorrow. I leave alone and in silence, for such is the will of God and Fate. "And hallowed be Thy name."

In my sorrowing, dying hour I pray only to you. Life might have been beautiful for me too. But complain not, my poor heart, complain not. In my soul I call upon death to take me, but my heart is full of praise for you! "And hallowed be Thy name."

Neither you nor those around you know how beautiful you are. The clock is striking. It is time. And as I die, at the sorrowful hour of my parting with life, I still sing—glory be to Thee.

Here it comes, death that quietens all things, and still I say—glory be to Thee!..

Princess Vera put her arms around the trunk of an acacia, pressed herself against it, and wept. The tree shook gently. A light wind sprang up and rustled the leaves as if in sympathy with her. The scent of the star-shaped tobacco flowers nearby grew stronger... And meanwhile, as though echoing her sorrow, the wonderful music went on:

Be still, my dear one, be still. Do you remember me? Do you? You see, you are my last, my one and only love. Be still, for I am with you. Think of me, and I shall be with you, because you and I loved each other only for an instant and yet forever. Do you remember me? Do you? Now I can feel your tears. Be still. To sleep is so sweet, so sweet, so sweet.

When she had finished playing, Jenny Reiter came out into the garden and saw Princess Vera sitting on the bench weeping.

"What's the matter?" she asked.

With tears shining in her eyes, Vera began to kiss her face, lips and eyes with restless movements, and said:

"Nothing, nothing—he's forgiven me now. Everything's all right."

1910

Mikhail Artsybashev in the early 1900s. In spite of his popularity, very few photographs of Artsybashev have survived, and they are of poor quality; this one is taken from a group photograph.

MIKHAIL ARTSYBASHEV (1878-1927)

Of mixed Tatar descent, Artsybashev was born in the small town of Akhtyrka in Kharkov Province, the son of a retired officer of minor landowning stock. His maternal great-grandfather was the famous Polish statesman Tadeusz Kosciuszko (1746-1817). After attending high school till he was sixteen, he studied art, supporting himself by producing caricatures and essays for minor papers.

His literary career began in 1901 with the publication of his tale "Pasha Tumanov," a macabre story of murder and suicide among high school students. His next notable work, "Horror" (1903), described in detail the rape of an inocent young girl by five drunken civil servants. Tales such as "Blood" (1903) and "The Wife" (1904) that followed it were concerned with similar happenings.

Artsybashev's first long work was his novel *The Death of Ivan Lande* (1904), in which the influence of both Tolstoi and Dostoevsky is apparent. Its pure, selfless hero devotes himself to the love of others only to die a lonely death, abandoned by all. This was followed during 1905 and 1906 by a series of violent and bloody tales about the 1905 Revolution, among them "On the White Snow," "The Bloodstain" and "One Day," works which underline the futility of human existence. "The Human Wave" (1907) reflects the Potemkin mutiny in Odessa and the revolt by sailors in Sevastopol in late 1905.

When Artsybashev's most significant work, the novel *Sanin* was published in 1907, its sensational treatment of sex caused a furor. Rapidly translated into several languages, it occasioned a series of court cases not only in Russia but also in Germany, Austria and Hungary, because of its alleged pornographic content. This *succès de scandale* brought Artsybashev's work very much into vogue during the early 1900s, and for a time it almost eclipsed the great popularity of Andreev's writing.

1912 saw the publication of Artsybashev's story "Millions," a deeply pessimistic tale that reveals the essential loneliness of the rich. His last major work, the novel *At the Brink*, published in the same year, returns to the motif of suicide found in his first tale and asserts that death is the only reality. After this Artsybashev wrote several pieces for the stage which dealt with the same themes, among them *Jealousy* and *Enemies* (1913). In the years that followed he produced several publicistic items such as his *Notes of a Writer* (1917). The same year saw the completion of an edition of his works in ten volumes, published in St. Petersburg.

After the 1917 Revolution Artsybashev became an enemy of the Bolsheviks. Attacked by Soviet critics for his decadence, he was expelled from the USSR in 1923, and *Sanin* and other works were banned. He settled in Warsaw where he edited the emigre journal *For Freedom* until his death.

Mikhail Artsybashev

Mikhail Artsybashev / SANIN *(A Synopsis)*

Vladimir Sanin has spent his formative years away from home and has grown up without guidance or example. When he returns to his family in the provincial town where he was born, both his mother and sister sense his oddness and feel constrained in his presence. Though physically he has hardly changed, something new is apparent in him. He has traveled, known hardship, and engaged in political activity, but has grown tired of the latter and given it up. Now he holds nothing sacred and is determined to take from life all it can offer.

Sexually attracted to his beautiful sister, Lida, Sanin sees that her suitor, the young doctor Novikov, is miserable because he longs to possess her. When Novikov finally brings himself to propose, she gives him no answer, as she is infatuated with Zarudin, a brutish army officer who has determined to seduce her. Aware of Zarudin's baseness, Sanin conceives an intense dislike for him.

After the hero, the novel's most important character is the morbidly introspective Yury Svarozhich, a student of twenty-six banished from Moscow for revolutionary activity on behalf of the Social Democratic Party, to which he is now indifferent. Tormented by the futility of human existence and obsessed by the inevitability of death, he sees himself as a desperate failure and thinks frequently of suicide.

Lida gives herself to Zarudin but then bitterly regrets it. Finding herself pregnant, she asks her lover for his help only to meet with a rebuff. When she tries to drown herself, she is stopped by Sanin, who then tells Novikov of her affair and persuades him to marry her.

Sanin's hostility towards Zarudin provokes the officer to challenge him to a duel. After refusing to fight, Sanin meets Zarudin in the street and hits him in the face in self-defense. Feeling he is disgraced forever, Zarudin shoots himself.

Svarozhich believes himself in love with the attractive young schoolmistress Zina Karsavina, but when they meet in the woods one summer's evening, he fails sexually with her. It is this episode that Karsavina remembers in the section translated below. Secondary characters who appear in the excerpt are: Ivanov, a teacher whose attitude to life resembles Sanin's; Shafrov, a naive, young student who admires Svarozhich; and Pyotr Ilych, a drunken, old chorister.

Excited yet shamed by her sexual experience, Karsavina is visited by Sanin, who thanks her for the joy she has given him and promises her his help if she needs it. Some weeks later, recalling his humiliating failure with Karsavina, and haunted by the premature death of Semyonov, a young consumptive,

Svarozhich shoots himself. His suicide turns Karsavina's ambivalence towards Sanin into hatred. When asked to speak at Yury's funeral, Sanin declares that the world now has one fool less in it. Later he returns with Ivanov to drink at Svarozhich's grave.

Finally, bored by the town and tired of his family, Sanin leaves without saying goodbye. During the journey, filled with disgust for his fellow men, he jumps off the moving train and with a characteristic cry of joy strides away into the steppe towards the rising sun.

XXXVIII

In the wide corridor of the monastery hospice there was a smell of bread, samovars and incense. A well-built monk went hurrying by, carrying a samovar as round and plump as a watermelon.

"Father," said Yury, feeling rather embarrassed at this form of address and expecting the monk to be embarrassed too.

"What can I do for you?" asked the monk courteously as he peered out from behind clouds of steam.

"I believe you have a party of people from town staying here."

"Yes, they're in number seven," replied the monk promptly, as if he had been expecting this question all along. "This way please, they're out on the balcony..."

Yury opened the door of number seven. The big room was dark and seemed full of tobacco smoke, but through the door, out on the balcony, it was light and there was the clink of bottles. People were moving about, laughing and shouting.

"Life's an incurable disease!" Yury heard Shafrov say.

"And you're an incorrigible fool!" retorted Ivanov loudly. "My God!.. You're always saying stupid things like that!"

When Yury came in, he was greeted with drunken exclamations. Shafrov leapt to his feet, nearly pulling off the tablecloth as he did so, and struggled out from behind the table. Grasping Yury's hand in both his own, he mumbled in a voice full of tender affection:

"How good of you to come! Thank you so much! I say! Really, you know..."

Yury sat down between Sanin and Pyotr Ilych and looked around. The balcony was brightly lit by two lamps and a lantern, and it seemed as if the circle of light was surrounded by an impenetrable black wall. But when he turned away from the light, Yury could still make out fairly clearly the strip of sky now greenish in the sunset, the humped silhouette of the hill, the tops of the nearest trees, and far below the faint glimmer of the sleeping river.

Moths and beetles came flying to the lamps out of the forest, whirling and falling, then rising again and quietly crawling over the table, dying a fiery, senseless death.

Yury looked at them and felt sad.

"We're just like they are," he thought, "we fly to the flame too, fly to every brilliantly attractive idea, then flutter around it and die in agony. We think the idea's an expression of the world's will, but it's only our own brain that's burning up!"

"Well, shall we have a drink?" asked Sanin, tilting the bottle towards Yury in a friendly way.

"All right," agreed Yury sadly, and immediately wondered whether drink was not perhaps the only consolation he had left.

Clinking glasses, they drank. The vodka tasted foul to Yury, like bitter, burning poison, and with a shudder of disgust he reached for the *zakuski*.* But for a long time they tasted foul too and he could not swallow them.

"No, whatever happens...even if it means penal servitude or death...I've got to get away from here," he said to himself. "But where can I go? It's all the same wherever you go, because you can't escape from yourself. When a man's above life, it can't satisfy him anywhere or in any form whatsoever... Whether he lives in this miserable little town or in Petersburg...it makes no difference!"

"In my opinion, the individual is nothing!" shouted Shafrov.

Yury looked at his stupid, dull face with its spectacles and small, bleary eyes, and thought to himself that a man like Shafrov really was nothing.

"The individual is nothing! Only those who come from the masses and never lose touch with them, those who don't set themselves against the crowd like bourgeois 'heroes' are so fond of doing—they are the only people who possess real strength..."

"And where does their strength lie?" asked Ivanov aggressively, folding his arms and leaning his elbows heavily on the table. "In struggling against the government of the day? Yes! But how can the masses help them in the struggle for their own happiness?"

"There you go again...you're a superman! You want a special kind of happiness! One that's your very own! But we who belong to the masses believe our happiness lies in struggling for the common good!"

"But what if your idea's wrong?"

"That doesn't matter," said Shafrov, shaking his head categorically. "You've just got to believe in it, that's all..."

"Rubbish," put in Ivanov contemptuously. "Everybody thinks that what he does is the most important and indispensable thing of all... Even a ladies' tailor thinks that... You're well aware of this too, but you've probably forgotten it...and it's a friend's job to remind you of it."

Filled with unaccountable hatred, Yury looked into Ivanov's face. It was pale with the vodka he had drunk and covered in sweat, while his glazed eyes were unnaturally large.

"So what is happiness, in your opinion?" he asked, his lips curling in a sneer.

"Well, certainly not in spending your whole life sniveling and constantly
++++++++++++++++
*Savory snacks or tidbits often served with drinks in Russia.

asking yourself things like 'I've just sneezed...oh, was that the right thing to do? Might it not harm someone? Have I fulfilled my destiny with that sneeze?'"

In Ivanov's cold eyes Yury saw manifest hatred, and he began to tremble all over at the thought that Ivanov apparently considered himself cleverer than he was and was trying to make fun of him.

"All right then, let's see what happens," said Yury to himself.

"That's not a program," he retorted, sneering even more and trying to make every feature of his face express both extreme reluctance to argue and utter contempt.

"So you've got to have a program, have you?" asked Shafrov indignantly, but Yury just shrugged his shoulders scornfully and made no reply.

For a while they drank in silence, then Yury turned to Sanin and without looking at Ivanov but for his benefit all the same, began to say what he considered the most important thing of all in life. He felt that now, if he could say a few words in a logical way and clearly express all his thoughts, then no one would be able to refute them. But to his annoyance, at his very first remarks about how man cannot live without God, and how, having cast down one God, he must then find another to prevent his life becoming meaningless, Ivanov said behind him:

"Do you mean Katerina? Oh, we've heard all that before!"

Yury said nothing and went on expounding his thoughts. Carried away by the argument, he did not notice that he was now energetically defending what was actually a source of doubt for him. Only that morning he had been questioning his faith, but now that he was involved in an argument, he felt that all his ideas were well thought out and that he had firmly established everything.

Shafrov was listening to him with reverence and tender joy, and Sanin was smiling. But Ivanov sat with his back to him, and to every remark that Yury felt was novel and original, he flung out contemptuously:

"And that too—we've heard it all before!"

Yury flared up angrily:

"Well, you know, we've all heard you say that before too! When you can't think of anything else to say, there's nothing easier than to cry 'we've heard it all before' and then keep quiet! If all you can say is you've heard it all before, then I don't think you've really heard anything!"

Ivanov turned pale and his eyes took on a profoundly evil look.

"Perhaps," he said with undisguised mockery, filled with an urge to insult Yury, "perhaps we haven't heard anything yet, either about tragic doubts, the impossibility of living without God, or the empty existence of a naked man on the naked earth..."

Ivanov uttered every phrase in a bombastic tone, then suddenly said spitefully:

"For Christ's sake, why can't you think up something that's a bit more original!"

Yury felt there was some truth in Ivanov's gibe: he suddenly remembered what a mass of books he had read, books about anarchism, Marxism, individualism, the superman, reformed Christianity, mystical anarchism and many other things besides. It was true, they'd heard it all before, yet everything was still just the same as it had always been, and he was already filled with a distressing spiritual lassitude. Nevertheless, not for a single moment did it occur to him to give in and say no more. He began to use a harsh tone, aware that he was offending Ivanov rather than proving his point of view.

Ivanov had turned nasty now and was really terrifying. His face had grown even paler still and his eyes bulged from their sockets, while his voice had become raucous and savage.

Then Sanin intervened with an irritated, bored look on his face.

"Stop it, gentlemen... Don't you find all this terribly boring? After all, you can't hate a man just because he's got his own opinions..."

"These aren't opinions, they're nothing but hypocrisy!" snarled Ivanov. "He's just trying to show us he thinks in a more profound, subtle way than we do, not..."

"But what right have you to say that? Why's it me and not you who's trying to..."

"Listen!" shouted Sanin in a commanding voice, "if you want to fight, then get out, both of you, and fight wherever you like... You've got no right at all to force the rest of us to listen to your stupid quarrel!"

Ivanov and Yury fell silent. They were both flushed and agitated, and tried not to look at one another. For quite a while there was an awkward silence...

"Oh, to hell with it all!" thought Yury, and picking up his glass drained it at one draught.

It was strange, but just then he desperately wanted Ivanov to notice his feat and respect him for it. If Ivanov had done so, then Yury would have felt friendship and even affection for him, but Ivanov paid no attention to him whatsoever. Instantly repressing his humiliating desire, Yury frowned and felt his body being pervaded by the sickening sensation of the vodka that was flooding his insides and even filling his nose.

"I say, Yury Nikolaevich, well done!" cried Shafrov, but Yury felt ashamed it was Shafrov who had congratulated him.

Barely able to withstand the wave of liquor surging into his nose and mouth, and shuddering with revulsion, Yury did not come to for quite some time, and felt about on the table, picking up the *zakuski* then putting them down again. Everything seemed as loathsome to him as poison.

"Yes, I always hesitate to call people like that people," Pyotr Ilych was saying in his imposing, low bass when Yury could finally hear and see once more.

"You hesitate? Good for you, old fellow!" retorted Ivanov maliciously, and though Yury had not heard the beginning of the conversation, he knew by Ivanov's tone that they were talking about him and people like him.

"Yes, I always hesitate... A man should be like...a general!" declared Pyotr Ilych weightily and distinctly.

"That's not always possible... And what about yourself?" retorted Yury with a shudder of malice, not looking at Pyotr Ilych.

"Me? I'm a general at heart."

"Bravo!" yelled Ivanov with such fury that a night bird started up in the nearby thicket and took wing like a flying stone, snapping twigs as it went.

"At heart, perhaps!" remarked Yury, trying to preserve the irony of the words and imagining morbidly that everyone was against him and trying to insult and humiliate him.

Pyotr Ilych looked importantly at him from one side.

"What else can I do? And what does it matter if it is only at heart? A poor, old drunkard like me is only a general at heart, but a man who's young and strong is a general in reality as well... To each his own. But people who are always sniveling, miserable, whining cowards like that... I always hesitate to call them people!"

Yury said something in reply, but somehow, with all the loud talk and laughter nobody seemed to hear him. The venomous insult had stung him to the quick, almost to the point of tears, and he suddenly felt they all despised him.

"But I'm just drunk!" he thought, and just then realized he really was drunk and should not have any more vodka.

His head was swimming in a gentle but loathsome way and the lights of the lamps seemed to be hanging right in front of his eyes, while his field of vision had suddenly become strangely narrow. Everything his gaze rested upon was distinct and bright, but beyond that he was surrounded by darkness. And the voices around him sounded strange somehow: though they were deafeningly loud, he could not catch what they were saying...

Sanin stood up, and though his face was as calm as always, it looked bored now. Yawning, he waved his hand in a gesture of hopelessness, then slowly lit a cigarette and went out of the door.

On the balcony they started making a noise and arguing again, and to the sound of their drunken voices the moths flew silently to the flame as before, crawling over the table and whirling in agonizing, fiery death.

Sanin went out into the hospice courtyard, and the cool, dark blue night softly enveloped his flushed body. Like a little golden egg the moon had risen above the forest, and its fantastic light slipped slowly over the dark earth. Beyond the orchard with its drifting, sweet smell of pears and plums, the other hospice showed dimly white, and one of its windows looked brightly at Sanin through the green foliage.

Suddenly, sounding like the padding of an animal's paws, there was the patter of bare feet in the darkness, and with eyes that were not yet accustomed to the gloom Sanin made out the silhouette of a boy.

"What do you want?" he asked.

"I want to see Miss Karsavina, the teacher," replied the boy in a piping voice.

"What for?" asked Sanin, and at the mention of Zina's name he suddenly remembered her as she had stood on the river bank, her naked body suffused with the glow of youth and the liquid gold of brilliant sunlight.

"I've brought her a note," replied the boy.

"Oh, I see...she's probably in that hospice over there, because she's not in this one... You'd better try there."

Like a little animal the boy pattered away again on his bare feet and vanished into the darkness as swiftly as if he had slipped into the bushes.

Sanin went slowly after him, filling his chest with the sweet, heady air of the orchard. Walking right up to the hospice, he stood under the window, and the shaft of light from it fell on his calm, thoughtful face. Surrounded by dark foliage, big, heavy pears shone clear and white in the light. Standing on tiptoe, he picked one, then saw Zina Karsavina at the window.

Wearing only a night-dress, she was standing sideways to him, and the light falling on her soft, round shoulders gave them the luster of satin. She was looking down intently and thinking about something. Whatever it was seemed to fill her with joy and shame at the same time, because her eyelids were quivering and her lips smiling. Sanin was struck by her smile: something elusively passionate and tender trembled in it, as though she were smiling at someone who was about to kiss her.

He stood there and looked at her, filled with a feeling that was stronger than he was, while she wondered what had happened to her a short time ago and felt agonizingly yet delightfully ashamed.

"Good Lord," she asked herself with the extraordinarily pure feeling that a flower must have when it first comes into bloom, "am I really so depraved?"

And with a feeling of exquisite bliss she recalled for the hundredth time the incomprehensibly alluring sensation she had felt the first time she surrendered to Yury.

"Darling, darling!" she murmured, blushing and mentally reaching out for him, her heart missing a beat as she did so, and again Sanin saw her eyelids quiver and her pink lips smile.

But the girl remembered nothing about the appalling, absurd scene that had followed. A mysterious feeling shielded her from that somber experience in which painful bewilderment and humiliation lay deeply embedded like a thin splinter.

There was a knock at her door.

"Who is it?" she asked, looking up, and Sanin clearly saw her strong yet gentle white neck.

"I've brought you a note," squeaked the boy on the other side of the door.

Zina got up and opened the door. Barefoot and covered with fresh mud up to his knees, the boy came into the room and hurriedly pulled off his cap.

"The young lady sent it," he said.

"Zinochka," wrote Olga Dubova, "if you can, then please come back to town tonight. The School Inspector's arrived and he's going to visit us tomorrow morning. It'll be very awkward if you're not here."

"What is it?" asked Zina's old aunt.

"Olga's asking me to go back to town. The Inspector's come," replied Zina thoughtfully.

The boy rubbed one leg against the other.

"She told me to say you must come back without fail."

"Will you go?" asked the aunt.

"But how can I go by myself?...it's dark."

"The moon's up," said the boy. "It's quite light outside."

"I ought to go," said Zina, hesitating.

"Go on then, or there might be trouble."

"All right, I will!" said the girl, tossing her head decisively. She dressed quickly, then pinned on her hat.

"Goodbye, aunt," she said, going up to the old lady.

"Goodbye, my dear. God be with you."

"Will you come with me?" Zina asked the boy.

He hesitated and rubbed one bare foot against the other again.

"I've come to see my mother... She works in the hospice laundry here."

"But how on earth can I go by myself, Grisha?"

"All right then, let's go," agreed the boy, tossing back his hair with a decisive gesture.

They went out into the orchard. And the dark blue night enveloped the girl just as tenderly and gently as it had Sanin.

"How good everything smells," she said, then suddenly gave a cry as she bumped into Sanin in the darkness.

"It's me," he said with a laugh.

Zina gave him her hand. It was still trembling with fright.

"Oh, how timid you are!" said Grisha condescendingly. The girl laughed in embarrassment.

"I can't see a thing," she said by way of excuse.

"Where are you going?"

"To town. Olga's just sent for me."

"Are you going by yourself?"

"No, the boy's coming with me... He's my knight-errant."

"A knight!" echoed Grisha, stamping his bare feet with pleasure.

"But what are you doing here?" Zina asked.

"Oh, we're on a drinking bout," explained Sanin jokingly.

"Who's 'we'?"

"Shafrov, Svarozhich, Ivanov..."

"So Yury Nikolaevich is with you too, is he?" she asked, blushing in the darkness. She found it as terrifyingly exciting to say that name aloud as to look over the edge of a precipice.

"Why do you ask?"

"Oh, no reason in particular. I just met him here, that's all..." she replied, blushing still more. "Well, goodbye."

Sanin gently kept hold of her outstretched hand.

"Come on, I'll row you over to the other side, or else you'll have to go the long way around."

"Oh no, what on earth for?" said the girl with a shyness she did not quite understand.

"Yes, let him take you across—there's a lot of mud on the dike," said Grisha authoritatively.

"Well, all right... You can go back and see your mother then, Grishka."

"But aren't you afraid to cross the fields by yourself?" asked the boy gravely.

"I'll take you as far as town if you like," said Sanin.

"But what about your friends?"

"Oh, they'll be here until dawn, and anyway I'm pretty sick of them as it is."

"Well, it's very good of you..." said Zina with a laugh. "Off you go then, Grishka."

"Goodbye, Miss..."

Again the little boy seemed to disappear into the bushes, and Zina and Sanin were left alone.

"Take my arm," he suggested, "or you might fall..."

She took hold of his arm, and with a strange feeling of embarrassment and excitement felt the muscles hard as iron moving under his thin shirt. Bumping against one another in the darkness and feeling the firm warmth of each other's body at every step, they set off through the forest on their way down to the river. It was so dark that it felt as if it had been like that since the dawn of time, so dark that there seemed to be no trees in the forest at all, only the thick, silent blackness that breathed its soft warmth upon them.

"Oh, how dark it is!"

"Don't worry," said Sanin softly in her ear, and his voice trembled slightly. "I like the forest best at night... That's when people lose their normal appearance and become more intriguing, mysterious and daring..."

The earth crumbled beneath their feet and they had difficulty stopping themselves from falling.

And because of the darkness, the nearness of this strong man whom she had always liked, and the repeated contact with his firm, hard body, the girl was filled with strange excitement. Her face grew flushed in the darkness and her hand began to burn Sanin's arm. She kept laughing and her laugh was abrupt and shrill.

At the foot of the hill it was lighter, and the moon shone calm and clear above the river. A cool breeze blowing off the water fanned their faces, and the dark forest receded in somber mystery, as though yielding them up to the river.

"But where's your boat?" she asked.

"Here."

The boat was clearly silhouetted in the moonlight, as if etched on the bright, smooth surface of the water. While Sanin was fixing the oars in position, Zina balanced herself with her arms, stepped lightly into the stern, and sat down. Immediately, illumined by the dark blue moon and its shimmering reflection in the water, she became a creature of fantasy. Sanin pushed the boat out and jumped in. With a soft rustling the keel slid over the sand, and cleaving the water with a gentle, bubbling sound, it moved out into the moonlight, leaving long, smoothly spreading ripples in its wake.

"Let me row," said Zina, still filled with urgent excitement. "I love it..."

"All right then, sit down," said Sanin with a smile, standing in the middle of the boat.

Again her lissom body brushed past him as she stepped over the seats and her fingertips touched his outstretched hand. As she passed, Sanin looked up at her, and her breasts slipped past his face, carrying the perfumed scent of her young body with them.

They set off down the river. The dark blue sky with its pensive moon was reflected in the deep water, and the boat seemed to be drifting across an expanse of bright serenity. Zina sat erect and moved the oars gently, bending her curving bosom forward as she stirred the water. Sanin sat in the stern and watched her, gazing at her breast on which it would be so good to lay his hot head, looking at her supple, round arms that could twine themselves so strongly yet so tenderly around his neck, and at her body that was so full of youthful voluptuousness, a body a man could press himself against with furiously passionate abandon. The moon shone on her pale face with its black eyebrows and shining eyes, its light slipping over her white blouse and the skirt that covered her plump knees. Something was happening to Sanin, and he felt as if he were drifting off with her into a fabulous kingdom that was far, far away from human reason and the sober laws of mankind.

"What a beautiful night!" she said, looking around.

"Yes, it is beautiful," he replied softly.

Suddenly she burst out laughing.

"I don't know why, but it makes me feel like throwing my hat in the water and letting my hair down..." she said, giving way to an unaccountable impulse.

"Go on then, do it," said Sanin more softly still.

But she suddenly felt embarrassed and fell silent.

Once again, evoked by the night, the warmth and the open expanse of

225

water, memories of her recent experience with Yury began to flit through Zina's mind, and again she felt both excitement and shame as she looked around her. She felt that Sanin could not possibly know what had happened to her, but this only made her feelings more intense and complex still. She felt an obscure but irresistible desire to make him aware that she was not always so modest and quiet, that she could be and indeed was completely different—a girl who was both brazen and shameless. And this partly conscious desire made her feel hot and gay.

"Have you known Yury Nikolaevich long?" she asked in an unsteady voice, feeling an irresistible urge to slide over the edge of the precipice.

"No," replied Sanin. "Why?"

"I just wondered, that's all... Is it true he's a fine, intelligent man?"

There was a note of almost childlike timidity in her voice, as if she were asking for a present from an older person who might either caress or punish her.

Smiling, Sanin looked at her and replied:

"Yes."

From the tone of his voice Zina realized he was smiling and she blushed almost to the point of tears.

"No, really... Somehow he's... I think he's suffered a lot..." she finished with difficulty.

"He probably has. It's true he's unhappy," agreed Sanin, "but do you feel sorry for him?"

"Of course I do," she said with feigned naiveté.

"Yes, that's understandable... It's just that you've got a strange idea of what the word 'unhappy' means... You think someone who's spiritually discontented and anxiously questions everything he does isn't just unhappy and pitiful but is a special, exclusive, perhaps even splendid person! You think that to be constantly weighing up one's actions is a fine characteristic that entitles a man to consider himself better than others, entitles him not so much to compassion as to respect and love..."

"But why's that?" Zina asked naively.

She had never talked to Sanin so much before, but she had often heard how original he was, and in his presence she now sensed the approach of something intriguing and excitingly new.

Sanin laughed.

"There was a time when man lived the limited life of an animal, unaware of what he was doing or feeling or why. Then came the age of conscious life, and the first stage in it was the reappraisal of all man's feelings, needs and desires. It's to this stage that Yury Svarozhich belongs, the last of the Mohicans in a period of human development that is now sinking into oblivion. Like every terminal thing, he has absorbed all the effusions of his epoch, and they have poisoned him to the very depths of his soul... He has no real life, and everything he does is subject to endless inner questioning: have

I done right or have I done wrong? He takes it to the point of absurdity: when he joins a political party he wonders whether it isn't beneath his dignity to rank himself with others, and when he leaves that party he worries himself sick about whether it isn't degrading to stand aloof from the general movement! But there are lots of people like him, and in fact they make up the majority... Yury Svarozhich is only an exception because he's not as stupid as the rest, and because his inner struggle assumes not ludicrous but occasionally tragic proportions... Some Novikov or other just grows fat on his uncertainty and suffering, like a hog shut up in its pen, but Svarozhich really does carry potential disaster in his breast...''

Suddenly Sanin stopped. His loud voice and his simple, everyday words had banished the fascination of this night, and he regretted it. He said no more, and again began to look only at the girl, at the dark eyebrows on her pale face and at her high breasts.

"I don't understand," she began timidly, "you talk about Yury Nikolaevich as though he himself is to blame for being as he is... But if a man can't be satisfied by life, that means he's above it...''

"A man can't be above life," replied Sanin, "because he himself is only a small part of it... He may be dissatisfied with life, but the reasons for his dissatisfaction lie within himself. It's just that he either cannot or dare not take from life's riches as much as he really needs. Some people spend their whole lives in prison without realizing it, while others are afraid to escape, like a bird that has sat in its cage for a long time... Until he is destroyed, Man is a harmonious combination of body and soul. Only the approach of death destroys that combination naturally, but we ourselves constantly destroy it with our distorted outlook on life... We've branded our physical desires as bestial, we've become ashamed of them, shrouded them in degrading forms and created a onesided existence... Those who are weak by nature fail to notice all this and drag out their lives in chains, but those who are weak only because they are shackled by their own false view of life and of themselves— these people are martyrs. Their pent-up strength craves an outlet, the body longs for joy and is tormented by its own impotence. All their lives these people wander amid inner discord, clutching at every possible straw in the realm of new moral ideals, and in the end they become so melancholy that they are afraid to feel, afraid even to live...''

"Yes, yes..." replied Zina with sudden forcefulness.

A multitude of unexpected, new thoughts were stirring gently within her.

She gazed around her with shining eyes, and the mighty splendor of the force pervading the motionless river, the black forest and the depths of the dark blue sky, flooded her body and soul with its deep, surging waves. Again she was filled by the strange feeling that was already familiar to her—one that she both loved and feared—an obscure yearning for strength, excitement and happiness.

227

"I'm always dreaming of a happy age," began Sanin again after a silence, "when nothing will stand between man and his happiness, and when man will give himself freely and without fear to all the delights available to him."

"But what will happen then? A return to barbarity?"

"No. The age when men lived just like animals was coarsely barbaric and wretched, but our own age, in which the body is dominated by the spirit and constantly pushed into the background, is a senselessly feeble one. But mankind has not lived in vain: it is gradually evolving new conditions of existence in which there will be no place for either bestiality or asceticism..."

"Tell me though, what about love...doesn't it impose heavy obligations on us?" asked Zina suddenly.

"No. The obligations that love imposes on us are only heavy because of jealousy, and jealousy is caused by slavery. Any kind of slavery gives rise to evil... People should enjoy love without fear or constraint... And if they can do so, then even the forms love takes will be extended to become an infinite series of chance meetings, unexpected encounters and coincidences."

"But I wasn't afraid of anything when I was with Yury!" Zina thought proudly, then all of a sudden, as if for the first time, she saw Sanin.

Big and strong, he sat in the stern, his eyes dark with the night and the moon, and his broad shoulders as motionless as if they were made of iron. Full of fascination and awe, Zina looked intently at him. She suddenly realized that before her lay a whole world of novel and unique forces and feelings, and she wanted to enter it.

"But he's so interesting!" the thought flashed through her mind. She laughed bashfully to herself, but a strange excitement filled her with nervous quivering.

Sanin must have sensed the sudden surge of her feminine curiosity, because he began to breathe more rapidly and deeply.

The oars became entangled in the branches lining the narrow creek into which Zina was slowly turning the boat, and they fell limply from her hands. At the same time something seemed to fall deep inside her too.

"I can't manage it here...it's too difficult..." she said guiltily, and her melodious voice rang out softly in the dark creek where invisible ripples streamed quietly by.

Sanin stood up and moved towards her.

"What are you doing?" she asked, filled with unaccountable alarm.

"Let me..."

The girl stood up and tried to move into the stern. The boat began to rock as if it were moving away beneath her feet, and Zina clutched involuntarily at Sanin, nudging him hard with her supple breasts. And at that moment, almost without realizing or even believing it was possible, the girl herself prolonged the contact with an imperceptibly fleeting movement, as though pressing herself against him for an instant as she passed.

228

In a flash, with all his being, he felt the fabulous fascination of this woman's nearness, and with all her being too she understood his feeling, sensing the immense power of his yearning and becoming intoxicated by it before she realized what was happening.

"Ah!.." gasped Sanin in astonished delight, and embraced her with such urgent passion that leaning backwards, she suddenly found herself hanging over the side of the boat and clutching instinctively at her hair and hat.

The boat rocked more violently still, and with a startled, rushing sound the invisible ripples spread out towards the sides of the creek.

"What are you doing?" she cried in a faint voice.

"Let me go!.. For God's sake!.. What are you doing?" she whispered breathlessly after a moment's fiery silence, trying to free herself from his arms of steel. But with a strength that almost crushed her breasts, Sanin pressed the girl to him and she found it hard to breathe. And then all that was a barrier between them ceased to exist. All around them was darkness, the heady smell of water and reeds, a strange coldness, flaring passion, and silence. Suddenly and unaccountably losing all control, she dropped her arms and lay back. Seeing nothing, conscious of nothing around her, she surrendered with burning pain and agonizing delight to the overwhelming strength and will of this alien male.

XXXIX

Not long afterwards she came to and became aware of several things as she half-lay in the boat: the patch of moonlight on the black water, Sanin's face with its strange eyes gazing at her, and the fact that he was holding her in his arms as if she were his own, and that one of the oars was rubbing against her bare knee.

Then, without freeing herself from his embrace, she began to weep softly and uncontrollably.

In her tears there was regret for something that was now irretrievably lost, together with fear, self-pity, and a faint tenderness for him that seemed to come not from her mind or heart, but from the very depths of her young body, a body that for the first time had revealed all its strength and beauty.

The boat drifted gently out into a faintly-lit, wider stretch of the river, and it rocked on the mysterious, dark water where little eddies swirled and went running by with their perpetual soft plashing.

Sanin lifted her up and sat her on his knee. And she sat there as confused and helpless as a little girl.

As if in a dream she could hear him reassuring her, and his voice was full of gentle strength, tenderness, and gratitude.

"I'll drown myself later!" she thought vaguely, listening to his words and feeling as if she were replying to a third person who was about to call her to account: "What have you done? What will you do now?"

"What shall I do now?" she suddenly asked mechanically.

"We'll see," Sanin replied.

She tried to slip off his knee, but he held her back, and she remained submissively where she was. She found it strange that she felt neither anger nor disgust for him.

Later on, when she remembered this night, it all seemed as incomprehensible as a dream. Everything around was silent, dark and solemnly still, as if it were keeping a secret. Fragmented by the black treetops, the moonlight was strangely motionless and ghostly. The darkness under the riverbank and in the depths of the forest gazed at them with its fathomless eyes, and everything seemed rooted to the spot in tense expectation. But she had neither the strength nor the desire to come to her senses, to remember she loved someone else, to become the single girl she had been before, or even to push this man away from her. She did not resist when he began to kiss her again, and accepted almost involuntarily this hot, fresh delight, drifting further and further away with half-closed eyes into a mysteriously alluring world that was still altogether strange to her. At times she felt as if she could neither see, hear nor feel a thing, but every movement he made, every punishment he inflicted upon her submissive body filled her with an extraordinarily acute sensation, a feeling of burning curiosity mingled with humiliation.

Enveloping her heart, the chill of despair prompted despondent, timid thoughts:

"It makes no difference now, no difference at all..." she said to herself, while her body's secret curiosity wanted to know, it seemed, what more this man could do with her, this man who was so remote from her yet so close, so alien yet so tenderly masterful.

Later, when he released her and sat down beside her to row, she closed her eyes as she lay back in the boat, and almost wishing she were dead, quivered at every movement of his firm chest as it moved rhythmically above her breast—a chest that was now so familiar to her.

With a soft crunch the boat beached on the shore. Zina opened her eyes.

All around were fields, water and white mist. The moon shone indistinct and pale, like a phantom that fades at daybreak. It was quite light now, and the sky was limpid. A cool breeze was blowing, heralding the dawn.

"Shall I come with you?" he asked.

"No, I'll go by myself..." she replied mechanically.

Sanin lifted her in his arms, and delighting in the effort, carried her out of the boat, feeling passionate love and grateful tenderness for her as he did so. He pressed her tightly to him, then set her down on the ground. She swayed and could not keep her balance.

"Oh! You're so beautiful!" he said, feeling as if his whole soul was longing for her in an upsurge of tenderness, passion and pity.

230

She smiled with unconscious pride.

He took her by the hand and drew her to him.

"Kiss me!"

"It makes no difference now... But why does he seem so pitiful, so dear to me?.. It makes no difference, so it's better not to think about it!" The incoherent thought flashed through her mind, and she kissed him long and tenderly on the lips.

"Well, goodbye then..." she whispered, getting the sounds of the words mixed up and not realizing what she was saying.

"Darling, don't be angry with me..." he said in a tone of soft entreaty.

Then, as she walked slowly away across the dike, swaying and tripping over the hem of her skirt, he followed her sadly with his eyes, feeling pain at the thought of all the needless suffering she would have to endure—suffering, he believed, that she had not the strength to withstand.

Her shape melted away and was lost in the mist as she walked into the dawn. When he could no longer see her, Sanin sprang back into the boat and lashed the water to seething foam with exultant, mighty strokes of the oars. Reaching a broad stretch of the river where the white mist swirled around him under the dawn sky, he flung down the oars, then leaping to his feet, drew himself up to his full height and gave a joyously resounding cry.

Springing to life, the forest and mist answered him with the same long, joyous cry that died away in the distance...

1907

Maxim Gorky in the early 1900s, St. Petersburg.

MAXIM GORKY (1868-1936)

Alexei Maximovich Peshkov—his pseudonym "Gorky" means bitter or wretched—was born in the town of Nizhny Novgorod (now Gorky) on the Volga. His father was a joiner and his mother the daughter of an owner of several dyeing establishments in Nizhny. After losing his father at three and his mother at eleven, the boy was raised by his grandparents. His upbringing in the provincial lower middle class environment was violent and brutal in the extreme. After five months of primary schooling—the only formal education he ever received—at the age of eleven he was sent out into the world to earn his own living. For the next twelve years he took every conceivable kind of menial job, ranging from bootmaker's apprentice and errand boy to ship's scullion and stevedore. Voracious and haphazard reading was his only consolation during these grim years.

At the age of sixteen he went to Kazan, hoping to enter school or even university. But he could not afford the necessary fees, and so was obliged to take manual jobs instead, among them work in a bakery—the setting for his tale "Twenty-Six Men and a Girl" (1899). While in Kazan, however, he mixed with socialist intellectuals and read underground literature. In December 1887, depressed by the discrepancy between his aspirations and the reality of his situation, he tried to shoot himself, and then spent weeks in a hospital with a perforated lung. Leaving Kazan, he traveled through southern Russia, again taking odd jobs wherever he could.

Returning to Nizhny Novgorod in 1889, Gorky was imprisoned for harboring a revolutionary. Soon after his release later that year, he met the writer Vladimir Korolenko, his first literary mentor. In 1891 he became a hobo again, and set off to tramp the Don, the Ukraine, the Crimea and the Caucasus. When he returned to Nizhny in 1893, Korolenko found him work on a local paper. His five years as a journalist gave Gorky both financial security and immensely valuable experience. 1896 saw his marriage to Catherine Volzhina, a proofreader on a local daily, as well as his first attack of tuberculosis, a disease that was to afflict him for the rest of his life. Two years later he was arrested again because of his connections with the Social Democratic (SD) Party. In 1901—by then a celebrity—he was arrested yet again for his prose poem "The Song of the Stormy Petrel," a symbolic allusion to the gathering revolutionary storm. After his release he went to the Crimea where he met Tolstoi and Chekhov.

In 1902, at the age of thirty-three, he was elected an Honorary Academician, but his election was cancelled on instructions from the Tsar, whereupon both Korolenko and Chekhov resigned from the Academy in protest. Early in 1905 he was imprisoned once more—this time for his political activity after the "Bloody Sunday" massacre on January 9—but he was released a month later because of the pressure brought to bear by public opinion throughout Europe.

In January 1906, Gorky left Russia for the U.S.A., aiming to prevent the Tsarist government from seeking a foreign loan and hoping to raise money for the Bolshevik movement. After a triumphant arrival in New York, it became known that his traveling companion, the actress Maria Andreeva, was not his legal but his common-law wife, and with an outburst of puritanical feeling American opinion suddenly turned against him. Obliged to leave his hotel, Gorky withdrew first to Staten Island and then to the Adirondacks, where he gave vent to his feelings in several angry articles attacking American capitalism in general and New York City in particular. Returning to Europe later that year, he settled on Capri, where he remained until shortly before the First World War and where his villa became the venue for Russian expatriates of many kinds.

During World War I Gorky took up an anti-militarist position, and in 1917 he helped to found *New Life*, an independent, left-wing newspaper. In the same year he criticized both Kerensky's government and what he termed Lenin's "Communist hysteria." Highly critical of measures taken by the Bolsheviks after their *coup d'état*, and shocked by the bloodshed of the Revolution, he openly expressed his fears about the corrupting effect of power on ideological leaders.

During the Civil War, however, Gorky decided to lend his support to the new government, and in 1919 issued an appeal to Russian intellectuals to forget their scruples and join hands with the Bolsheviks. His position after the Revolution was unique. His personal connections with leading Bolsheviks as well as his immense reputation enabled him to save scores of writers, artists and scholars from starvation and death between 1918 and 1921.

In October 1921 he left Russia (officially for health reasons) and after a stay in Germany, settled in Sorrento, where he devoted himself to correspondence and writing. In 1928 he visited Moscow for the celebration of his sixtieth birthday, and in 1931, at the insistent urging of the Kremlin, he returned to Russia for good as the *doyen* of Soviet letters. For the next few years he spent much of his time undertaking public engagements and training younger writers. When he died in June 1936—allegedly poisoned by his political enemies—he was given a hero's funeral in Red Square which was attended by a crowd of three-quarters of a million, together with Stalin and other Kremlin leaders.

Gorky's first published work was the romantic tale "Makar Chudra," printed in September 1892, in a local paper in Tiflis, Georgia, while he was working at the railway yards there. Though he continued to write for the provincial press—the tales "Two Hobos" (1893), "My Fellow Traveler" (1894), and "Old Izergil" (1895), for example—it was his story "Chelkash," written in 1894 and published in 1895 in the influential monthly *Russian Wealth*, that made his name generally known. 1898 saw the publication of a collection of his stories in two volumes which was extremely successful and brought him fame virtually overnight. A series of novels followed, among them *Foma Gordeev* (1899), *The Three of Them* (1901), *Mother* (1907), *A Confession* (1908), *The Small Town of Okurov* (1909), and *The Life of Matthew Kozhemyakin* (1911), all of which show the barbarity of provincial Russian life. The early 1900s saw several plays too: *The Petty Bourgeois* (1901), *The Lower Depths* (1902; an outstanding success), *Children of the Sun* (1905), *Enemies* (1906), and *Vassa Zheleznova* (1910).

After 1910 Gorky devoted himself chiefly to autobiographical and memoir work. His *Childhood* (1913) was followed by its sequels *My Apprenticeship* (1916) and *My Universities* (1923), in which he describes his self-education, while his literary experiences are reflected, for example, in his *Reminiscences of Tolstoi* (1919) and *Notes from My Diary* (1924). Most of his writing after 1925 is retrospective in character and deals with the prerevolutionary past—works such as the novel *The Artamonov Business* (1925) and the drama *Yegor Bulychev and Others* (1932), which show the decline of the Russian bourgeoisie. 1936 saw the publication in revised form of his play *Vassa Zheleznova*, as well as Part Four of his long novel *The Life of Klim Samgin*, begun in 1927 and left unfinished at his death.

K. P. Pyatnitsky and Maxim Gorky in Yalta, February 1902.

One autumn I happened to find myself in a very uncomfortable and awkward position: in the town where I had only just arrived and where I did not know a soul, I found myself without a penny in my pocket and with nowhere to spend the night.

After selling all the clothes I could spare during my first few days there, I left the town for a place called Ustye where there were wharves. When the river was busy with shipping, Ustye was a real hive of activity, but everything was silent and deserted now—this was towards the end of October.

Splashing over the wet sand and scrutinizing it persistently in the hope of finding the remains of something edible, I wandered among the deserted buildings and traders' stalls, thinking how good it must be to have eaten one's fill...

Given the present state of our culture, it is easier to satisfy spiritual hunger than physical hunger. You roam the streets surrounded all the time by buildings that look quite reasonable from the outside and—you can be sure of it—are reasonably furnished inside too; this may give rise to comforting thoughts about architecture, hygiene and many other wise and lofty things; you meet people dressed in comfortable, warm clothes—they are polite and always step aside to let you pass, tactfully trying not to notice the sad fact of your existence. Indeed, the soul of a hungry man always enjoys more wholesome and better nourishment than the soul of a man who is well fed—a situation from which one could doubtless make a very witty deduction apropos of the latter...

Evening was drawing on, it was raining, and a fitful wind blew from the north. It whistled through the empty trading booths and stalls, beat against the boarded-up windows of the inns, and whipped the waves on the river to foam as they roared and broke on the sandy shore, flinging their white crests high in the air, racing away into the murky distance and leaping headlong over one another as they went... It was as though the river sensed that winter was drawing near, and its waves seemed to be fleeing in terror from the icy fetters that the north wind might cast upon them that same night. The sky was lowering and dark, and from it fell an incessant drizzle whose drops were barely visible; nature's mournful elegy being sung around me was made more mournful still by two broken, ugly willows and an upturned boat lying by their roots.

An upturned boat with its bottom knocked out and a pair of wretched, old trees ravaged by the cold wind... Everything around me was blasted, barren and dead, while the sky shed endless tears. All around was desolate and dark—it seemed as if everything was dying, as if soon only I would be left

237

alive, and as if cold death awaited me too.

And I was seventeen at the time—what a splendid age!

On and on I walked over the cold, wet sand, my teeth chattering out a rhythmic hymn to hunger and cold. Then suddenly, going around the back of one of the stalls in my vain search for something to eat, I saw the figure of a woman crouching on the ground in a dress that was soaked with rain and clung tightly to her hunched shoulders. Stopping beside her and looking closely at what she was doing, I saw that she was digging a hole in the sand with her hands and tunneling under one of the stalls.

"What are you doing that for?" I asked, squatting down beside her.

She gave a faint cry and sprang to her feet. Now that she was standing and staring at me with wide-open, gray eyes full of fear, I saw she was a girl of my own age with a very pretty face that was unfortunately marked by three large bruises. This spoiled her face, though the bruises were arranged in a remarkably symmetrical way—one under each eye, both of the same size, and a slightly larger one on her forehead, just above the bridge of her nose. In this symmetry could be seen the handiwork of an artist who was highly skilled in the business of damaging human physiognomies.

The girl looked at me and the fear gradually faded from her eyes... Then she shook the sand off her hands, straightened her cotton scarf, hesitated a moment, and said:

"Are you hungry too? Come on then, you dig for a bit—my arms are tired. There's probably some bread in there..." she said, nodding towards the stall. "This store's still open..."

I began to dig. After waiting and watching me for a while, she squatted down beside me and started to help...

We worked in silence. I cannot say now whether I remembered just then about the Criminal Code, morality, property and such like—things that knowledgeable people say we should bear in mind at every moment of our lives. Wishing to be as truthful as possible, I must confess that I was so absorbed in the business of tunneling under the stall that I completely forgot about everything apart from what might be inside it...

Night was falling. The darkness—damp, raw and cold—was growing thicker and thicker around us. The sound of the waves seemed more muffled than before, but the rain drummed on the planking of the store more and more loudly and heavily... And somewhere we could already hear a night watchman rattling his stick...

"Has it got a floor or not?" asked the girl softly. But I did not understand what she meant so did not answer.

"I said, has this stall got a floor? If it has, then we're wasting our time. We'll get the hole dug, and then there might be thick planks to get through as well... How on earth will we rip them away? It'd be better to break the padlock...it's not a very strong one..."

Women rarely have good ideas, but as you see, they do still have them occasionally... I have always valued good ideas and tried to make use of them as far as possible.

Finding the padlock, I jerked it and pulled it away, bringing its hasps with it... In the twinkling of an eye my accomplice bent down and slid like a snake through the rectangular opening into the store. Her cry of approval rang out from inside:

"Well done!"

One small word of praise from a woman means more to me now than a whole eulogy from a man, even if the man in question is as eloquent as all the ancient orators rolled into one. But in those days I was less kindly disposed than I am now, and paying no attention to the girl's compliment, I asked briefly and fearfully:

"Is there anything there?"

In a monotone she began to enumerate the things she had discovered.

"A basket of old bottles...some empty sacks...an umbrella...an iron bucket."

But all this was inedible and I felt my hopes fading... Then suddenly she cried in a cheerful voice:

"Aha! Here it is..."

"What?"

"Bread...a round loaf... It's wet though... Catch!"

The round loaf rolled out at my feet, and close behind it came my intrepid partner in crime. I had already broken off a piece of bread, stuffed it in my mouth, and begun chewing it...

"Come on, give me a bit... We've got to get away from here now, but where shall we go?" She peered all around, her eyes straining to penetrate the gloom... It was dark, wet and filled with the sounds of wind and water... "There's an upturned boat over there... Shall we go to it?"

"Yes!" I replied, and off we went, breaking off pieces of our booty and stuffing them in our mouths on the way...

The rain was growing heavier and the river roaring more loudly still, while from somewhere or other we caught the sound of a long drawn out, derisive whistle—as though some enormous creature that knew no fear were hissing mockingly at all the established order on earth, at this foul autumn evening and at us, its two heroes... That whistle wrung my heart, but I ate greedily all the same, though no less so than the girl who was walking on my left.

"What's your name?" something prompted me to ask.

"Natasha!" she replied, munching noisily.

I looked at her, and something clutched painfully at my heart. I peered into the darkness ahead, and it seemed to me that the ironic, ugly visage of my destiny was looking at me with a mysterious, chill smile...

The rain drummed relentlessly on the wooden planks of our shelter, its soft sound giving rise to melancholy thoughts, and the wind whistled as it blew into the broken bottom of the boat—driving in through a crack where a loose plank creaked and flapped on and on with a restless, plaintive sound. The waves of the river broke against the shore with a dull booming that was as monotonous and hopeless as if they were telling of something intolerably difficult and tedious, something they were weary of to the point of revulsion, something they would have liked to escape but had to speak of nevertheless. The drumming of the rain merged with their splashing, and above the up-turned boat drifted the prolonged, heavy sigh of the earth that was so aggrieved and exhausted by these everlasting changes from the bright warmth of summer to the damp, misty cold of autumn. The wind whirled over the foaming river and the desolate shore, whirled on and on, singing its doleful song...

Our place under the boat was devoid of comfort: it was cramped and damp, and drops of cold rain kept coming through the broken planks accompanied now and then by gusts of wind... We sat there in silence, shivering with cold. I remember I felt sleepy. Natasha had curled up into a little ball and was leaning with her back against the side of the boat. Clasping her legs and resting her chin on her knees, she stared fixedly at the river with wide-open eyes, and on the white blur of her face her eyes looked huge because of the bruises under them. She did not stir, and I felt her silence and stillness gradually giving rise to fear in me... I wanted to talk to her but did not know how to begin.

It was she who spoke first.

"What a rotten life!" she said clearly and distinctly in a tone of profound conviction.

But this was not a complaint—there was too much indifference in her words for them to be a complaint. This human being had simply thought things over as far as she was able, thought them over and come to a conclusion which she had expressed aloud and which I could not object to without contradicting my own feelings. So I said nothing, and as though unaware of my presence, she went on sitting there motionless.

"If only I could die or something..." she began again, softly and pensively this time. And once again there was not a single note of complaint in what she said. It was evident that, having thought about life in general, she had examined herself and calmly come to the conclusion that to protect herself against life's insults she had no alternative but, as she put it, to die.

I was indescribably sickened by such clarity of thought and felt that if I kept quiet any longer, I would probably burst into tears... And that would have been shameful in front of a woman, the more so as she was not crying herself. I made up my mind to talk to her.

"Who beat you up like this?" I asked, unable to think of anything more intelligent to say.

"Oh, it was Pashka again..." she replied in a loud, steady voice.

"And who's he?"

"My boyfriend... He's a baker..."

"Does he beat you often?"

"When he gets drunk he does..."

Then suddenly, moving up close to me, she began to tell me all about herself, about Pashka and their relationship. She was "one of those girls, who..." as they say, and he was a baker with a ginger moustache who was very good on the accordion. He used to visit her "at Madam's" and she liked him very much because he was a cheerful fellow who was always neat and tidy. He wore a coat that had cost fifteen rubles and boots with a decorative pattern on them... That was why she'd fallen in love with him and he'd become her "special friend." But no sooner had he become her "special friend" than he'd started taking the money other clients gave her for sweets, then getting drunk on it and beating her. That wouldn't have been so bad, only then he'd started "carrying on" with other girls before her very eyes...

"And why shouldn't I feel bad about it? After all, I'm no worse than the others... He's just making fun of me, the swine. The day before yesterday I got permission from Madam to go out, and I went to see him, but when I got there I found Dunka with him—drunk. And he'd had a drop too much as well. I says to him: 'You're a swine, a real swine! And you're a cheat too!' And he beat me black and blue. He kicked me, pulled me around by the hair—the lot... But even that wouldn't have been so bad! Only he tore all my clothes...so what can I do now? How can I face Madam like this? He tore everything: my dress and my blouse that was brand new...and he ripped the scarf off my head as well... Oh God! What'll I do now?" she suddenly howled in a dismal, broken voice.

And the wind howled too, growing more and more strong and cold... My teeth started chattering again. She was shivering with cold as well, pressing so close to me that I could see her eyes shining in the darkness...

"What swine all you men are! I'd trample you all underfoot, I would, and cripple the lot of you! If I saw one of you just going to die... I'd spit in his ugly mug instead of feeling sorry for him! You dirty pigs!.. You go on and on, pestering us and wagging your tails like a lot of filthy dogs, and when some fool of a girl gives in to you, then that's that! You just trample her in the dirt before she knows what's hit her... You lousy swine!.."

She swore in a very colorful way but her oaths lacked power: I could detect neither anger nor hatred in them for those she called "lousy swine." On the whole the tone of what she said was incongruously calm compared with her actual words, and the sound of her voice was sadly monotonous.

Nevertheless, all this had a far more powerful effect on me than the most eloquently persuasive, pessimistic speeches and books, many of which I had heard and read at one time or another, and which I still hear and read to this day. And the reason for this, you see, is that the agony of the dying is always far more natural and striking than the most accurate, artistic descriptions of death.

I felt bad—probably more because of the cold than of what my companion was saying. I groaned softly and gritted my teeth.

Then, almost at the same moment, I felt two cold little hands on me—one touching my neck and the other resting on my face—and at the same time I heard an affectionate, anxious voice ask softly:

"What's the matter?"

For a moment I almost thought it was someone else asking me this question, not Natasha who had only just declared that men were swine and then wished them all to perdition. But she was already speaking quickly and hurriedly to me...

"What's wrong, eh? Are you cold or something? Are you freezing? Oh, what a one you are! You just sit there and say nothing...looking all glum! You should've told me you were cold a long time ago, you see... Come on now...lie down on the ground...stretch out...and I'll lie down too...there! Now put your arms around me...tighter... There now, you should feel warmer now... Then later on we'll lie with our backs to each other... We'll get through the night somehow or other... What happened? Did you start drinking or something? Did you get fired?.. Well never mind!"

She was trying to comfort me...trying to cheer me up...

May I be thrice damned! How terribly ironical all this was! Just think of it: at that time of my life, you see, I was seriously concerned with the fate of mankind, dreaming of political upheaval and the reorganization of society, and reading a variety of devilishly clever books whose profundity was probably beyond even their authors' comprehension—at that time, you see, I was trying my hardest to become a "major active force," Yet here I was being warmed by the body of a streetwalker, a wretched, downtrodden, badly beaten creature who had no place or worth in life—someone whom I hadn't had the sense to help before she helped me, and even if I had, I'd scarcely have known how to set about it.

Oh, for a moment I almost thought it was all a dream, an absurd, painful dream...

But alas! I could not possibly think that, for cold drops of rain were falling on me, the woman was pressing her breast hard against my chest and I could feel her warm breath on my face. And though it smelt faintly of vodka, how invigorating it was!.. The wind howled and moaned, while the rain drummed on the boat and the waves splashed, and even though we clung tightly together, we were both still shivering with cold. It was all completely real, and I am sure no one has ever had such a painful, bad dream as that night of reality.

And Natasha went on and on, talking sympathetically and gently, as only women can. Under the influence of her ingenuous, tender words, a little ember began to glow softly inside me, and its warmth melted something in my heart.

Then the tears began to stream thick and fast from my eyes, cleansing

242

my soul of much of the resentment, stupidity, anguish and filth that had settled on it like scum over the years... And now Natasha was already trying to reassure me:

"There now, that's enough, my love, don't cry! That's enough! With God's help you'll be all right, you'll get your job back...and then everything'll be all right..."

And she kept kissing me all the time, showering me with countless, passionate kisses...

Those were the first woman's kisses I had ever known and they were the best, for all those that followed cost me terribly dear and brought me practically nothing.

"Come on now, don't cry, silly! I'll fix you up tomorrow if you've got nowhere to go..." I heard her soft, reassuring whisper as though in a dream...

We lay there in each other's arms till dawn...

And when it was light, we crawled out from under the boat and set off for town... Then we bid one another a friendly farewell and never saw each other again, though for six months I searched every tavern for the sweet Natasha with whom, one autumn, I spent the night I have described...

If she is already dead—and what a good thing that would be!—then may she rest in peace! And if she is still alive—then peace be unto her just the same! And may her soul never wake to a sense of her degradation—for that would cause her needless suffering and do nothing to improve her life...

1895

Maxim Gorky / CHELKASH

The light blue, southern sky was so clouded by dust that it looked murky, while the sun blazed down on the greenish sea as if through a thin gray veil. It found almost no reflection at all in the water that was churned up by oars, propellers, and the sharp keels of Turkish feluccas and other craft plowing the crowded harbor in every direction. Held in check by the granite quays and crushed by the enormous weight of the vessels cleaving their crests, the waves beat against the ships' sides and the shore. Littered with flotsam, they hurled themselves again and again at both vessels and quays, roaring and foaming as they did so.

The clanking of anchor chains, the crashing of couplings on the railway trucks bringing up fresh cargo, the clanging of sheet iron falling on the cobbled roadway, the hollow banging of wood, the clattering of carts, the whistling of steamers that rose from a muffled roar to a piercing shriek, the shouts of stevedores, sailors and customs officers—all these sounds merged into the deafening melody of the working day. Surging in restless waves, they hung low over the harbor, while wave upon wave of new sound rose towards them from the earth—first with a muffled roaring that shook everything around, then with a harsh clattering that rent the dust-laden, sultry air.

Granite, iron, wood, cobbled roadway, ships and men—all lent their mighty voices to this impassioned hymn to Mercury. But the voices of mortals were barely audible in this chorus, and they sounded faint and ridiculous. And the men themselves, they who had given birth to all this uproar, seemed ludicrous and pathetic too: grimy and tattered, with backs bent under the weight of the loads they were carrying, they ran busily to and fro amid clouds of dust, surrounded by a sea of heat and noise. They were as nothing compared with the iron giants all around them, or with the mountains of cargo, the rattling railway trucks, and everything else that they themselves had brought into being. The things of their own creation had enslaved them and robbed them of all individuality.

With steam up and ready to sail, the massive ships whistled, hissed and sighed, and every sound they uttered seemed to contain a note of mocking contempt for the dusty, gray figures crawling over their decks and filling their deep holds with the products of their slavish toil. It almost made you weep with laughter to see the long lines of stevedores carrying thousands of pounds of grain on their backs and laying them in the ships' iron bellies simply to earn a few pounds of that same grain for their own stomachs. In the contrast between these sweating, ragged men stupefied by fatigue, noise and heat, and the mighty machines gleaming proudly in the sun—machines created by these same men, machines that after all had been set in motion not by steam but by the muscles and blood of those who had made them—in this contrast lay an entire poem of bitter irony.

The noise overwhelmed them, the dust irritated their noses and gummed up their eyes, and the heat scorched and exhausted their bodies, while everything around them seemed tense, as though about to lose its patience and erupt in a vast catastrophe, an enormous explosion that would clear the air so men could breathe freely and easily once more. Then peace would descend upon the earth, while this dusty uproar that exasperated, deafened and drove men into a melancholy fury would vanish. And then the air over the city, above the sea, and in the sky over their heads would be clear, still and glorious...

Twelve measured strokes of a bell rang out over the harbor. When the last brassy echo had died away, the frenzied music of toil began to subside. A minute later it was no more than a muffled murmur of discontent. Now the voices of men and the plashing of the sea were more audible. The dinner hour had begun.

I

When the stevedores stopped work and wandered off through the harbor in noisy groups to buy food from the women stall-keepers then settle down to eat it in shady corners on the pavement—Grishka Chelkash appeared. A daring, clever thief and an inveterate drunkard, this old rogue was well known to all the harbor folk. Barefoot and hatless, he wore a pair of threadbare corduroy trousers and a dirty cotton shirt with a torn collar that showed his tanned, bony chest. The tousled state of his graying black hair and the crumpled look of his pointed, predatory face showed he had only just woken up. There was a straw caught in his ginger mustache and another in the stubble on his half-shaven left cheek, while a fresh sprig of lime stuck out from behind his ear. Long, lanky and slightly bent, he strode slowly down the cobbled street, and twitching his rapacious, hooked nose, shot sharp glances around him, his cold, gray eyes glittering as they searched for someone among the stevedores. His long, thick mustache quivered incessantly like a cat's whiskers, and he rubbed his hands together behind his back the whole time, entwining his tenacious fingers restlessly. Even here, among hundreds of other down-and-outs just like him, he immediately attracted attention because of his resemblance to a steppe hawk, a resemblance suggested by his predatory leanness and his strangely purposeful gait whose apparent easy calm concealed the tense vigilance of a bird of prey.

As he came up to a group of stevedores who had settled down to rest in the shade of some coal baskets, a stocky young fellow got up to meet him. He had a stupid-looking face covered with purple blotches and several scratches on his neck, and had apparently been beaten up recently. Getting to his feet, he fell into step beside Chelkash and said under his breath:

"The warehouse guards have found there's two bales of cloth missing... They're looking for them."

"So what?" asked Chelkash, looking him up and down calmly.

"What d'you mean, 'so what'? They're looking for them, I tell you. That's all."

"And they've asked me to help find 'em, have they?"

And with a smile Chelkash looked towards the Free Fleet warehouse.

"Go to hell!"

The young fellow turned away.

"Hey, wait a minute! Who gave you those bruises? They've certainly messed your face up all right... Have you seen Mishka anywhere?"

"I haven't seen him for ages!" shouted the young fellow as he went back towards his friends.

Chelkash walked on, and everyone he met greeted him like an old friend. But though usually cheerful and full of sarcastic humor, he seemed out of sorts today and replied curtly to those who questioned him.

From behind some bales of merchandise a customs guard suddenly appeared. He wore a dark green uniform that was covered in dust, and carried himself aggressively erect. Blocking Chelkash's path, he stood before him in a challenging pose, his left hand gripping the hilt of his short sword and his right reaching out to grasp the thief by the collar.

"Stop! Where are you going?"

Chelkash took one step back, then looking up at the guard, smiled a chill smile.

The soldier tried to make his genial but crafty red face look threatening, puffing up his cheeks till they turned crimson, knitting his brows, and opening his eyes wide, but instead the whole effect was rather amusing.

"I've told you before—don't come in this harbor or I'll break your neck! And here you are again!" he shouted menacingly.

"Hello, Semyonich! Haven't seen you for ages," said Chelkash calmly, and held out his hand in greeting.

"Don't let me catch you in here again! Go on, get out!"

But he still shook the thief's outstretched hand.

"Look here now, tell me," Chelkash went on, without letting go of Semyonich's hand and shaking it in a familiar way, "have you seen Mishka anywhere?"

"What Mishka, for God's sake? I don't know anybody called Mishka! Get out of here, man, clear off! If the warehouse guard sees you, he'll..."

"The ginger-haired fellow I worked with last time on the *Kostroma*," said Chelkash, persisting with his question.

"The one you went thieving with, you mean! They've taken him off to the hospital, that Mishka of yours—he got his leg crushed by some cast iron. Now get out of here, I tell you, while you're being asked nicely, or I'll throw

247

you out by the scruff of the neck!"

"Hey, just listen to that now! And you said you didn't know anybody called Mishka... You know who I mean all right! What are you so cross about today, Semyonich?"

"Now look here, don't try to get around me! Just clear off!"

The guard was growing angry, and looking about him, tried to free his hand from Chelkash's strong fingers. Chelkash looked at him calmly from under his bushy eyebrows and without letting go of his hand, went on:

"Don't rush me. I'll say what I've got to say and then I'll clear off. Tell me now, how are you doing? The wife and kids—are they well?" And there was a twinkle in his eye as he bared his teeth in a mocking grin and added: "I keep meaning to drop in and see you, but I never seem to have time—it's the drink, you know..."

"Come on now, don't give me that! Don't try and joke with me, you lanky devil! I mean what I say, man... But perhaps you're going to start breaking into houses now and robbing folks on the street?"

"Why should I? There's enough stuff here to last you and me a lifetime, Semyonich, there really is, you know! I hear you've pinched another two bales of cloth. Watch out, Semyonich, take care! Mind you don't get caught!"

Filled with indignation, Semyonich began to shake, spluttering as he tried to say something. Chelkash let go of his hand and strode calmly away on his long legs, heading back towards the harbor gates. Swearing furiously, the guard set off after him.

Chelkash was in better spirits now; he whistled softly through his teeth, and with his hands thrust in his trouser pockets, walked slowly along chuckling to himself and cracking witty jokes to right and left as he went. The people he passed paid him back in his own coin.

"Hey, Grishka, the chief's taking good care of you today, isn't he?" someone shouted from a crowd of stevedores who had already eaten their dinner and were now lying on the ground having a rest.

"I've got nothing on my feet, so Semyonich is seeing I don't step on anything sharp," replied Chelkash.

They reached the gates. Two soldiers frisked Chelkash then pushed him gently out onto the street.

He crossed over and sat down on the curb facing the door of a tavern. A line of loaded carts came rumbling out of the harbor gates, while toward them came a line of empty ones with their drivers bouncing up and down on their seats. The harbor belched thunderous sound and clouds of acrid dust...

Amid this frenzied uproar Chelkash was in his element. He had the attractive prospect of a sizeable haul that night, a haul that required very little effort but a great deal of skill. He was sure he had the skill to do it, and narrowing his eyes with pleasure, imagined how he would go on the spree the next morning when his pockets were full of banknotes... He remembered his friend Mishka—he'd have come in very useful tonight if he hadn't gone and broken his leg. Chelkash swore, thinking he might not manage the job by himself. What kind of a night would it be, he wondered? He glanced up at the sky, then looked down the street.

Five or six yards away, sitting in the road and leaning against the curb, was a young fellow wearing a dark blue cotton shirt and trousers, bast shoes, and a tattered red cap. Beside him lay a small knapsack and a scythe whose broken handle was wrapped in straw and neatly bound with string. He was a broad-shouldered, stocky fellow with light brown hair, a sunburned, weather-beaten face, and big, blue eyes that looked amiably at Chelkash.

The thief bared his teeth in a grin and stuck out his tongue, then pulling a terrible face, stared at him with wide-open eyes.

Rather bewildered, the youth blinked in surprise, but then suddenly burst out laughing and shouted: "Hey, you're a queer fellow!" Then without getting up, he slid awkwardly along the curb to where Chelkash was sitting, dragging his knapsack in the dust and knocking the handle of his scythe on the paving stones as he went.

"Been on a fair old binge, have you, old fellow?" he asked, tugging at Chelkash's trouser leg.

"And what a time we had, young 'un, what a time!" confessed Chelkash with a smile. He had taken an instant liking to this sturdy, good-natured boy with his bright, childlike eyes. "Been haymaking then?"

"I'll say! We mowed a whole mile but we only made a few coppers. It was really bad! You never saw so many folk in your life! Some of them were starving, so they knocked the price right down. What could you do? They only paid sixty kopeks in the Kuban. It was a bad business! But in the old days, they say, they used to pay three, four or even five rubles!"

"In the old days! They'd pay three rubles just to look at a Russian! That's how I earned my living about ten years ago. You'd come into a village and say 'I'm a Russian!' And straightaway they'd start looking you up and down, feeling you and marveling at you—and they'd give you three rubles for a start! Then something to eat and drink as well. And you could stay there as long as you liked!"

As he listened, the round-faced youth opened his mouth wide in bewildered delight, but then, realizing Chelkash was making it up, he smacked his lips and burst out laughing. Chelkash kept a straight face, hiding his smile in his mustache.

"You're a queer fellow all right! You sound as if you're telling the truth and I'm listening and believing you... But really, you know, in the old days they..."

"Well, isn't that just what I'm saying? I'm telling you, in the old days they used to..."

"Go on with you!" said the youth, waving his hand at Chelkash in amusement. "What are you, a cobbler or something? Or a tailor? What d'you do for a living?"

249

"Me?" asked Chelkash, then thought for a moment and said: "I'm a fisherman..."

"A fisherman? You? So you catch fish, do you?"

"Why does it have to be fish? The fishermen around here don't just catch fish, you know. It's mostly dead bodies, old anchors, boats that have gone down—all kinds of things! There's special hooks for that..."

"You're lying, you're lying! I bet you're one of those fishermen who sing:

We cast our nets
Upon dry shores,
Over sheds and over stores!"

"Have you ever met any fishermen like that?" asked Chelkash, glancing at him with a grin.

"No, where d'you think I could have seen them? I've heard about them though..."

"D'you like them?"

"Fellows like that? 'Course I do! They're not bad at all. They're free and they can do just what they like..."

"But what's freedom to you? D'you really like it?"

"What d'you mean? 'Course I do! When you're your own boss, you can go wherever you like and do what you want... 'Course I like it! If you can keep yourself in good order and you've got no ties—that's the main thing! Go your own way and do what you like, so long as you keep God in mind..."

Chelkash spat contemptuously and turned away.

"Now look what a fix I'm in..." said the young fellow. "My father's dead, the farm's only small, my mother's old now, and the land's sucked dry—so what can I do? You've still got to live. But how? Nobody knows. I could marry into a good family. That'd be fine if only they'd give the daughter her share. But oh no! Her father won't do it, the old devil! So that means I'll have to work myself into the ground for him..for a long time...years and years! So you see how bad things are! But if only I could get hold of about a hundred and fifty rubles, I'd be on my feet straightaway and then that Antip would get nothing out of me! 'Will you give Martha her share?' I'd say to him. 'You won't? Right, don't then! Thank God she's not the only girl in the village.' And I'd be quite free, you see, I'd be my own boss... Yes!" He heaved a sigh. "But now there's nothing I can do except marry his daughter. I thought to myself: right, I thought, I'll go off to the Kuban and make a couple of hundred rubles—that'll be enough! Yes sir! But it didn't work out. So I'll just have to be a farm hand instead... I'll never do any good running my own farm, never! So there you are!"

The youth had not the slightest desire to marry under these circumstances. As he spoke, his face became dismal and pale, and he began to fidget.

"So where are you off to now?" asked Chelkash.

"What d'you mean, where am I off to? Home, of course."

"Well how was I to know? You might've been going to Turkey for all I know..."

"To Tur-rkey!" exclaimed the youth slowly. "What honest Christian would ever want to go there? What a thing to say!"

"You really are a fool!" murmured Chelkash, and turned away from his companion again. This sturdy country boy had awoken something in him...

An obscure, slowly growing feeling of irritation was stirring deep inside him and preventing him from concentrating on what he had to do that night.

Stung by Chelkash's words, the youth muttered something under his breath and threw him a sidelong glance. Puffing up his cheeks in an amusing way and pouting, he blinked his narrowed eyes at a ridiculous speed. He evidently had not expected his conversation with this bewhiskered ruffian to end so rapidly and in such a hurtful way.

But the ruffian was no longer paying any attention to him. Whistling thoughtfully, he sat beating time on the curb with his dirty, bare heel.

The boy felt like getting even with him.

"Hey you, fisherman! D'you often get drunk?" he was about to say, but just then Chelkash turned to him and asked:

"Listen, young 'un! D'you want to do a job with me tonight? Tell me quick!"

"What kind of job?" asked the youth distrustfully.

"What d'you mean, 'what kind'? Whatever I ask you... We'll go fishing, and you can row..."

"Oh, I see... All right, why not? I don't mind work. It's just that... I wouldn't want to get into any trouble. You seem a bit suspicious to me...kind of shady."

Chelkash felt a burning feeling in his chest and muttered in a voice full of chill malice:

"Don't talk nonsense about things you don't understand, or I'll give you one on the head, and that'll make things a bit clearer for you..."

Leaping up from the curb, he tugged at his mustache with his left hand and clenched his right into a hard, sinewy fist, his eyes flashing.

The boy took fright. Glancing swiftly around him and blinking timidly, he leapt up too. Looking each other up and down, the two men stood there without saying a word.

"Well?" asked Chelkash sternly. He was trembling with rage, seething at the insult from this young puppy whom he had despised while talking to him but for whom he now felt sudden hatred because of his clear, blue eyes, his healthy, sunburned face, and his short, sturdy arms. He hated him because he had a village somewhere with his own house in it, because a well-to-do

251

peasant had asked him to be his son-in-law, and because of his whole life, both past and future, but most of all because he, a mere child in comparison with himself, dared to love freedom—freedom he could not appreciate and did not need. It is always unpleasant to discover that someone you consider your inferior loves or hates the same things as you do and therefore resembles you.

The boy looked at Chelkash and recognized in him a master.

"I don't...really mind, you know..." he began. "I'm looking for work, you see. It doesn't matter who I work for, you or somebody else. I only said that because you don't look like a working man—you're so...er...untidy, you know. But that can happen to anybody, I know. Good Lord, d'you think I haven't seen drunks before? Oh, I've seen dozens of them!.. And some were a lot worse than you."

"All right, all right! So you're willing, are you?" asked Chelkash again, though less harshly now.

"'Course I am!.. With pleasure! What's your price?"

"That depends on the work. What it's like, I mean, how big the catch is... You might make about five rubles. All right?"

Now that it was a question of money, the peasant wanted to be exact and demanded the same from his employer. Suspicion and distrust awoke again in the boy's mind.

"That's not good enough for me, friend!"

Chelkash entered into the part.

"Wait a bit, we needn't talk about it right now! Let's go to the tavern!"

And walking side by side, they set off down the street, Chelkash twirling his mustache with the important air of a master, and the boy wearing an expression that showed complete readiness to obey but mistrust and fear at the same time.

"What's your name?" asked Chelkash.

"Gavrila!" replied the boy.

When they reached the smoke-blackened, dirty tavern, Chelkash went up to the counter and with the familiar air of an habitué ordered a bottle of vodka, cabbage soup, roast beef and tea. Then, after totting up what he had asked for, he said curtly to the barman: "On my tab!" to which the man replied with a silent nod. This instantly inspired Gavrila with respect for his master, who despite his dubious appearance evidently enjoyed considerable confidence and respect.

"Well now, we'll have a bite to eat and talk things over. You sit here for a minute and wait for me. I'll be right back."

He went out and Gavrila looked around. The tavern was in a basement; it was damp, dark and full of the suffocating, acrid smell of stale vodka, tobacco smoke and pitch. Facing Gavrila at another table sat a ginger-bearded drunk wearing a sailor's uniform that was covered in tar and coal dust. Hiccupping continually, he grunted a song composed of disjointed, broken words that were furiously sibilant one minute and raucously guttural the next. He was evidently not a Russian.

Behind him sat a couple of Moldavian women. Black-haired, swarthy and ragged, they too were wheezing a drunken song.

Then more figures loomed up out of the darkness, all of them strangely disheveled, half-drunk, garrulous and agitated...

Gavrila felt very frightened. If only his master would come back! The various noises of the tavern merged into one, and it sounded as if an enormous beast with a hundred different voices was roaring in blind exasperation as it vainly tried to break out of this stone pit... Gavrila felt a distressing intoxication pervading his body, making his head spin and his eyes grow hazy as they darted fearfully over the tavern...

Chelkash came back and they began to eat and drink, chatting as they did so. After his third glass of vodka Gavrila was drunk. He felt very gay and wanted to say something agreeable to his master who—splendid fellow that he was!—had treated him to such a good meal. But though they surged in waves into his throat, for some reason the words would not come off his tongue, for it had suddenly become very heavy and unwieldy.

Chelkash looked at him and said with a mocking smile:

"Had a drop too much, eh?.. Oh, you fool! And after only three glasses, too! How are you going to work tonight now?"

"Old friend!" babbled Gavrila. "Don't worry! I'll see you're all right! Come on, let me give you a kiss!"

"That's enough now! Here you are, have a drop more!"

Gavrila went on drinking, and eventually reached the point at which everything around him began to sway in undulating, rhythmic movement. It was unpleasant and made him feel sick. He had a foolishly ecstatic expression on his face, and whenever he tried to say something, he smacked his lips in a ridiculous fashion and mumbled incoherently. Watching him intently, Chelkash seemed to remember something, and twirling his mustache, smiled gloomily the whole time.

Meanwhile the tavern resounded with a drunken roar. The red-haired sailor was asleep now, slumped on the table.

"Right then, let's go!" said Chelkash, getting up.

Gavrila tried to get up too but could not manage it, and swearing richly, burst out laughing in the inane way drunks do.

"You're finished!" said Chelkash, sitting down again facing him.

Gavrila kept on laughing, looking at his master with glazed eyes. And deep in thought, Chelkash watched him intently. He saw before him a man whose life had fallen into his wolfish clutches. He felt within him the power to do whatever he liked with that life, to turn it this way or that. He could rip it in two, like a playing card, or help establish it once and for all in the solid framework of peasant existence. Sensing he was master of another man's destiny, he reflected that this youth would never drink a cup as bitter as the one

253

fate had given him... And he both envied and pitied this youthful life, despising it yet grieving for it when he thought how it might fall again into the hands of someone like himself... And in the end all his feelings merged into one, becoming protective and paternal. He felt sorry for the young fellow but he needed him all the same. Then Chelkash took hold of Gavrila under the arms and nudging him gently from behind with his knee, pushed him out into the yard of the tavern. There he laid him on the ground in the shade of a pile of logs, then sat down beside him and lit his pipe. Gavrila tossed about for a while then mumbled a little and fell fast asleep.

II

"Ready then?" asked Chelkash under his breath as Gavrila struggled with the oars.

"Just a minute! This oarlock's loose—shall I bang it in with the oar?"

"No! No! Don't make any noise! Press down harder on it, and it'll go in by itself."

They were both wrestling silently with a boat that was tied to the last of a whole flotilla of sailing barges loaded with oak staves and big Turkish feluccas carrying palm and sandalwood and thick cypress logs.

The night was dark, and heavy banks of ragged storm clouds drifted across the sky, while the sea was calm, as black and thick as oil. It gave off a damp, salty odor and splashed softly as it lapped against the ships' sides and the shore, rocking Chelkash's boat a little. Out on the distant expanse of water offshore the dark shapes of vessels loomed up out of the darkness, their sharp masts topped by multicolored lights thrusting into the sky. The sea reflected their lights and was strewn with scores of yellow patches that shimmered beautifully on the matt black, velvet water. The sea was sleeping the deep, sound sleep of a workman worn out by the day's toil.

"Let's go!" said Gavrila, dipping the oars into the water.

"Right!" said Chelkash, and with a powerful thrust of the steering oar he sent the boat out into a gap between the barges. It floated quickly away over the smooth water which glowed with pale blue phosphorescence under the oars, and gleaming softly, a long ribbon of fire streamed out in its wake.

"How's your head then? Does it ache?" asked Chelkash affectionately.

"Like hell! It's banging away like a hammer... I'll douse it with water in a minute."

"What for? Here, wet your guts instead, then you might come around a little quicker," said Chelkash, holding out a bottle.

"Huh? Good Lord!"

There was a soft, gurgling sound.

"Is that better? Hey! That's enough!" said Chelkash, stopping him.

The boat scudded away again, silently weaving its way between the other vessels... Suddenly it shot out from among them, and the sea—boundless and mighty—opened out before them, stretching away into the dark blue distance where mountains of clouds rose from the water into the sky. Dove-gray and lilac they were, fringed with yellow down, or greenish, the color of sea water, or the dull, leaden hue of storm clouds that cast such oppressive, dreary shadows over the earth. They drifted slowly by, first overlapping then mingling, merging their colors and shapes before dissolving and rising once more in new forms that were grimly majestic. There was something fateful in the slow movement of their inanimate masses. It seemed as if there was an infinite number of them far away on the edge of the horizon, as if they would climb forever with immense indifference into the sky, having maliciously resolved never to allow the heavens to shine again upon the sleeping sea glittering with its millions of golden eyes—the multicolored stars shimmering in reverie and arousing exalted desires in men to whom their pure radiance is so precious.

"Isn't the sea marvelous?" asked Chelkash.

"It's all right! Just a bit frightening, that's all," replied Gavrila, pulling strongly and rhythmically on the oars. Still shining with the warm, pale blue glow of phosphorous, the water gurgled faintly and splashed.

"Frightening? You really are a fool!" muttered Chelkash mockingly.

He loved the sea. Ebullient, restless and always avid for new impressions, he could never look enough on this dark expanse that was so boundless, mighty and free. And he felt hurt by such an indifferent reply to his question about the beauty of something he loved. Sitting in the stern, he furrowed the water with the steering oar and gazed calmly ahead, filled with a desire to sail on and on, far away over this velvet-smooth expanse.

Whenever he was on the sea an expansive, warm feeling always rose within him, enveloping his soul and cleansing it of life's filth. He treasured this feeling and liked being here best, amid waves and fresh air, where thoughts of life always lose their poignancy and life itself loses its value. At night the soft sound of the sea's sleepy breathing floats smoothly over the water and the immensity of the sound fills man's soul with peace, tenderly subduing its wicked impulses and giving birth to mighty dreams...

"But where's the fishing tackle?" asked Gavrila suddenly, looking around the boat anxiously.

Chelkash gave a start.

"The tackle? It's here, in the stern."

But he felt ashamed to lie to the young fellow, and he regretted the thoughts and feelings that the boy had destroyed with his question. He grew angry. The familiar, burning feeling in his chest and throat convulsed him with pain, and he said to Gavrila reprovingly:

"Now look here, just sit and keep quiet! And don't go poking your nose into other people's business! I hired you to row, so row! But if you start talking rubbish, things'll be bad for you. Understand?"

255

For a moment the boat quivered and came to a halt. Trailing in the water, the oars churned it to foam, and Gavrila shifted uneasily on his seat.

"Row!"

A harsh oath rent the air. Gavrila raised the oars hurriedly and the boat seemed to take fright, leaping away with nervous jolts and cleaving the water with a rushing sound.

"Steady!"

Without letting go of the steering oar, Chelkash stood up for a moment in the stern and his cold eyes probed Gavrila's pale face. Leaning forward and crouching, he looked like a cat ready to spring. Gavrila could hear the fierce gnashing of his teeth and the faint cracking of his knuckles.

"Who's that shouting?" came a stern cry from the sea.

"Come on now, you devil, row! Be quiet, or I'll kill you, you bastard! Come on, row! One, two! Make one more sound and I'll tear you to pieces!" hissed Chelkash.

"Holy Mary... Mother of God..." whispered Gavrila, shaking and almost fainting with exertion and fear.

The boat swung around and turned back towards the harbor, where the ships' lights clustered in a multicolored throng on masts outlined against the sky.

"Hey! Who's that shouting?" came the cry again.

But the voice was further away now, and Chelkash felt reassured.

"It's you who's shouting!" he cried in the direction of the shouts and then turned to Gavrila who was still whispering a prayer.

"Well, young 'un, you're in luck this time! If those devils had chased us, you'd have been done for. D'you understand? I'd have fed you to the fish straightaway!"

Seeing Chelkash was talking calmly now and was apparently in a good mood, Gavrila begged him:

"Listen, let me go! For Christ's sake, let me go! Put me off somewhere! Oh! I'm done for! Come on, for God's sake let me go! What am I to you? I can't go through with it! I've never done this kind of thing before... It's the first time... God, I'm finished for sure! How did you take me in, you devil? It's a sin! You're destroying your own soul, you know! Oh, what a business!.."

"Business?" asked Chelkash abruptly. "Come on, what business, eh?"

The lad's fear amused him, and he took pleasure both in witnessing it and in thinking what a ferocious fellow he was.

"Shady business, my friend... Let me go, for God's sake! What am I to you, huh? Be a good fellow..."

"Come on now, shut up! If I hadn't needed you, I wouldn't have brought you along. Don't you see? So shut up!"

"Lord!" sighed Gavrila.

"Come on, that's enough, you fool!" said Chelkash sharply.

But Gavrila could no longer control himself, and sobbing softly, he

256

wept, sniffing and squirming about on his seat. But he rowed with a strength born of despair, and the boat flew on like an arrow. Once again the dark hulls of ships loomed up ahead and the boat was lost among them as it spun like a top through the narrow stretches of water between the vessels' sides.

"Hey you! Listen! If anybody asks you anything, then keep your mouth shut if you want to stay alive! Understand?"

"Oh!" sighed Gavrila in despair, adding bitterly: "I'm done for!"

"Stop whining!" whispered Chelkash harshly.

At the sound of this whisper Gavrila lost the ability to think and went numb, seized by a chill foreboding of disaster. Mechanically he dipped the oars into the water and threw himself backwards as he pulled on them. Raising then lowering them again and again, he stared fixedly at his bast shoes.

The somnolent plashing of the waves was dismal yet terrifying. Now they were in the harbor... From beyond its granite wall came the sound of voices, the splashing of water, shrill whistling and singing.

"Stop!" whispered Chelkash. "Let go of the oars! Push on the wall with your hands! Keep quiet, damn you!"

Clutching at the slippery stones, Gavrila pulled the boat along by the wall. It moved without a sound, its gunwale sliding over the slime that covered the stones.

"Stop! Give me the oars! Give them here, I tell you! Now where's your identification? Is it in your bag? Give me the bag then! Come on, hurry up! That's so you won't run off, young 'un... You'll not try it now. You might've managed it even with no oars, but you won't dare go without your I.D. Now just wait here! And watch out, because if you make a sound I'll catch up with you even if you're at the bottom of the sea!"

And then, suddenly catching hold of something, Chelkash rose into the air and disappeared over the wall.

Gavrila gave a start... It had all happened so quickly. He felt the accursed heaviness, the fear that filled him in the presence of this lean, bewhiskered thief, falling from him and slipping away... He'd escape now! Heaving a sigh, he looked around him. To his left towered a black hull without masts. It was like an enormous coffin, deserted and empty... Every time a wave struck its side it echoed with a hollow, booming sound that resembled a heavy sigh. To his right, rising out of the water, stretched the wet, stone wall of the quay, lying like a heavy, cold serpent uncoiled upon the sea. Behind him more dark hulls were visible, while ahead, through the gap between the quay and the side of the coffin, he could see the sea, silent and deserted, with black storm clouds banked above it. Oppressive and vast, they drifted slowly across the sky, shedding terror in the darkness and threatening to crush mere mortals with their immense weight. Everything was cold, black and sinister. Gavrila felt afraid. This fear was even greater than the fear inspired in him by Chelkash. It gripped his chest in a powerful embrace, reducing him to a lump of timid flesh and riveting him to his seat...

257

But all around everything was silent. There was no sound but the sighing of the sea. The clouds drifted across the sky just as slowly and drearily as before, but more and more of them were rising from the water, so that looking at the sky, one might have thought it too was sea, only a choppy sea turned upside down over its fellow that was so drowsy, calm and smooth. The clouds looked like waves whose curly, gray crests were plunging towards the earth, like abysses from which those waves had been torn by the wind, like newborn rollers not yet covered with the greenish spume of fury and wrath.

Gavrila felt overwhelmed by all this somber silence and beauty, and wanted to see his master again. But what if he didn't come back? Time was passing so slowly, more slowly even than the clouds drifting across the sky... And the longer he waited, the more ominous the silence grew... But then there was a splashing, a rustling and a whispering on the other side of the breakwater. Gavrila felt as if he were about to die...

"Hey! Are you asleep or something? Here, catch this!.. Steady now!" came the muffled sound of Chelkash's voice.

Something heavy and square was lowered from the harbor wall. Gavrila took it into the boat. A similar bundle followed. Then the lanky figure of Chelkash climbed over the wall, the oars appeared, Gavrila's knapsack fell at his feet, and breathing heavily, Chelkash took his seat in the stern.

Looking at him, Gavrila smiled shyly with gladness.

"Are you tired?" he asked.

"A bit, young 'un! Come on now, get rowing! As quick as you can! You've made yourself a tidy little sum, you know! Half the job's done now. All you've got to do is get through right under those bastards' noses, then take your cash and go back to that Mashka of yours. You've got a Mashka, haven't you, young 'un?"

"N-no!" replied Gavrila, pulling on the oars for all he was worth, his chest working like a pair of bellows and his arms flexing like steel springs. The water gurgled under the boat, and the pale blue ribbon running out in her wake was wider now. Gavrila was covered in sweat but he kept on rowing with all his might. Having felt terror twice that night already, he had no wish to feel it again and desired only one thing: to get this damned job over with as soon as possible, set foot ashore, and escape from this man before he really did land him in jail or kill him. He made up his mind not to talk to him or contradict him and to do everything he was told, and if he managed to get away from him safely, he promised to say a prayer to St. Nicholas the Miracle-Worker the very next day. And indeed, an impassioned prayer was ready to pour forth from his breast that very moment. But panting like a steam engine, he held it back and remained silent, shooting distrustful glances at Chelkash from under his brows.

Meanwhile, the long, lean thief sat hunched up like a bird about to take to the air. Staring into the darkness with his hawk's eyes and sniffing the air with his predatory, hooked nose, he grasped the steering oar with one tenacious hand while with the other he tugged at his mustache that quivered as his thin lips curled in a smile. He was pleased with his success, pleased with himself and this young fellow whom he had terrified and made his slave. Watching Gavrila rowing as hard as he could, he suddenly felt sorry for him and wanted to reassure him.

"Hey!" he began softly, with a grin. "Got a good fright, did you, huh?"

"It's all right!" breathed Gavrila with a grunt.

"Now go steady with those oars. That'll do. We've just got one more place to get past now... Have a rest..."

Obediently Gavrila stopped rowing for a moment, wiped the sweat off his face with his shirtsleeve, then dipped the oars into the water once more.

"Now row quietly. Don't make a noise with the oars. We've got to get past some locks here. Quietly, quietly... These folks mean business, young 'un... They might just start fooling around with their guns, and you'll have a hole in your head before you know it."

Now the boat was gliding along almost without a sound. The only sign of its movement was the blue glow of the water dripping off the oars, and where the drops fell into the sea a blue patch flared for a moment. The night grew more and more dark and silent. Now the sky no longer looked like a restless sea—the clouds had spread across it and covered it with an even, heavy curtain that hung low and motionless over the water. And the sea had become calmer and blacker still, smelling more strongly of warm salt and not seeming as boundless as before.

"Oh, if only it'd rain!" whispered Chelkash. "Then we'd get by behind it like a curtain."

To the left and right of the boat great shapes rose from the black water. They were barges—motionless, somber and black too. On one of them a light was moving—someone was walking about with a lantern. Lapping against the vessels' sides, the waves made a muffled, plaintive sound, and the hulls responded with a hollow echo, as if arguing about something and reluctant to give way to the sea.

"It's the cordon!" said Chelkash in a barely audible whisper.

From the moment Chelkash had told him to row quietly, Gavrila was filled again with a painfully acute feeling of apprehension. As his whole body strained forward into the darkness, he felt as if it were being stretched out. His sinews and bones drew taut with a dull pain, his head—filled as it was with a single thought—was aching, the skin on his back quivered, and sharp, cold needles seemed to be piercing his feet. His eyes ached with the strain of peering into the gloom, and any moment he expected someone to loom up and yell at them: "Stop, thieves!"

Now, when Chelkash whispered, "The cordon!", Gavrila gave a start: a searing thought flashed through his mind and grated on his taut nerves—he wanted to cry out, call for help... He had already opened his mouth and half

259

risen from his seat, thrusting out his chest and taking a deep breath with his mouth wide open, but suddenly, stricken with terror that stung him like a lash, he closed his eyes and slumped into the bottom of the boat.

Ahead, far away on the horizon, a huge sword of pale blue fire rose from the black water. Cleaving the darkness, its sharp point slipped over the clouds and fell upon the sea in a wide, blue ribbon of light. There it lay, and in the radiance of its beam the shapes of ships, hitherto invisible, came floating out of the gloom, black, silent and shrouded in the abundant darkness of night. It was as if these vessels had lain on the sea bed for many years, swept away there by the force of a mighty storm. Now they had risen from the depths at the behest of this fiery sword born of the sea—risen so they might look upon the sky and all things above the waves... The rigging entwined around their masts looked like clinging seaweed that had risen from the deep with these black giants entangled in its coils. Then once again the terrible blue sword rose from the depths. Glittering, it clove the night and fell once more on the sea, but in a different direction this time. And where it fell, once again the shapes of vessels, hitherto invisible, came floating out of the darkness.

Chelkash's boat came to a stop and rocked on the water as though bewildered. Gavrila lay on the bottom, covering his face with his hands, while Chelkash kicked him and hissed in quiet fury:

"It's the customs cruiser, you fool! That's its searchlight! Get up, you fool! They'll throw the light on us any minute! You'll destroy both of us, you devil! Come on!"

Finally, when the heel of Chelkash's boot delivered a particularly painful kick to Gavrila's back, he leapt up, and still afraid to open his eyes, sat down on the seat. Feeling for the oars, he seized them and began to row.

"Quiet! Or I'll kill you! Come on, keep quiet! What a bloody fool you are, damn you! What are you frightened of, eh? You ugly devil! It's just a light, that's all! Quiet with those oars, blast you! They're looking for smugglers, but they won't catch us with it—they're too far out. Don't worry, they'll not see us. Now we're..." Chelkash looked around in triumph "we've done it, we're out of danger now! Phew! Well, you're lucky all right, even if you are a bloody fool!"

Gavrila said nothing and rowed on, breathing heavily and looking askance towards where the fiery sword still rose and fell. He simply could not believe Chelkash when he said it was only a light. There was something inexplicable about this chill blue radiance that clove the darkness and made the sea shine with a silver brilliance, and he was gripped once more by hypnotic, wretched fear. He rowed like an automaton and sat hunched up all the time, as if expecting a blow from behind. He was now devoid of all thought, all desire, for he was soulless and empty. The agitation of this night had drained him of everything human.

But Chelkash was triumphant. Accustomed to such strain, his nerves were already relaxed. His mustache twitched voluptously and there was a gleam in his eye. He felt magnificent, and whistling softly through his teeth, he filled his lungs with the moist sea air, looking around and smiling genially whenever his eyes came to rest on Gavrila.

The wind sprang up and roused the sea, making it break into swift ripples. The clouds seemed to become thinner and more transparent, but they still covered the whole sky. The light wind was blowing freely now, but the clouds were motionless, as though engrossed in tedious, dreary thoughts.

"Come on now, young 'un, get a grip on yourself! What a sight you are! You look as if you've had all the wind knocked out of you, and there's only a bag of old bones left! It's all over now. Hey!"

Gavrila still found it pleasant to hear a human voice, even though it was Chelkash speaking.

"I can hear you," he said quietly.

"That's it! You damned coward... Come on now, sit in the stern and let me row. You must be tired!"

Mechanically Gavrila changed places with him. As he moved to take the oars, Chelkash glanced into the boy's face and noticed that his legs were shaking and that he was swaying. Feeling sorrier still for him, he patted him on the shoulder.

"Come on now, young 'un, don't be afraid! You've done a good job, you know, and I'll pay you well for it. How'd you like a twenty-five ruble note, huh?"

"I don't want anything. Just put me ashore..."

Chelkash waved his hand in a gesture of hopelessness, spat and began to row, flinging the oars far back with his long arms.

The sea was awake now. It frisked with countless little waves, giving birth to them, decorating them with fringes of foam, then running them into each other and breaking them up into fine spray. The foam hissed and sighed as it melted away, and the air was filled with melodious splashing. The darkness seemed more alive now too.

"Tell me," began Chelkash, "you'll go back to your village, get married, start working the land and sowing wheat, and then your wife'll bear you some children. But there won't be enough to eat, so you'll spend all your life working yourself to the bone... Well, what d'you think about that? How much fun is there in living like that?"

"None at all!" replied Gavrila timidly, with a shudder.

Here and there the wind tore rifts in the clouds, and through them showed light blue patches of sky with one or two stars in them. Reflected in the playful sea, the stars danced over the waves, first vanishing then appearing again in all their brilliance.

"Keep more to the right!" said Chelkash. "We'll soon be there now. Yes, the job's finished! A nice piece of work it is, too! D'you see how it's done? Just one night and I've made five hundred rubles!"

"Five hundred?" asked Gavrila slowly in an incredulous voice, but then immediately took fright, and giving the bales in the bottom of the boat a

261

kick, asked quickly:

"But what's this then?"

"That's very expensive stuff. If I sold it at the right price, it'd fetch well over a thousand. But I won't ask too much for it... Smart, eh?"

"Is that right?" asked Gavrila. "If only I had money like that!" he sighed, immediately remembering his village, his wretched farm, his mother, and all those distant yet dear things for whose sake he had gone in search of work and worn himself out that night. He was overwhelmed by a flood of memories—his little village on the side of a steep hill that ran down to a river hidden in a grove of birches, willows, rowans and birdcherry... "Oh, that'd be great!" he said with a sad sigh.

"I'll say! I suppose you'd jump straight on a train for home... And wouldn't the girls go mad over you, oh my! You could choose whichever one you liked! You could build yourself a house, though I suppose there's not quite enough money for that..."

"No, that's true...there's not enough for a house. Timber's expensive in our parts."

"Well, all right then. You could fix up the old house instead. And what about a horse? Have you got one?"

"A horse? Yes, I've got one, but she's very old, damn her."

"Right, so you'd buy a new horse, a really good one! And a cow... And a few sheep... And some poultry too, eh?"

"'Course I would! Oh, Lord! I'd set myself up fine!"

"Yes, young 'un, that'd be the life all right... I know a bit about things like that myself. I had a place of my own once... My dad was one of the richest men in the village..."

Chelkash rowed slowly. Rocking on the waves that lapped playfully against its sides, the boat hardly moved forward at all over the dark sea now growing more and more sportive. The two men sat there dreaming, rocking on the water and looking pensively around them. Chelkash had reminded Gavrila of his village in the hope of cheering him up a little and reassuring him. To begin with he had been laughing softly into his mustache as he spoke, but then, as he provoked a response from his companion by reminding him of the joys of peasant life—a life he himself had long ago grown disillusioned with, a life he had forgotten and only remembered just now—he gradually became carried away. Instead of questioning the boy about his village and its affairs, almost without realizing it he began to say to him:

"The main thing about being a peasant, young 'un, is the freedom! You're your own boss. You've got your own house—it might not be worth much—but it's yours just the same. You've got your own land too—it might only be a small plot—but it's still yours! You're king on your own land! You've got your own identity... You can command respect from anybody... Isn't that right?" asked Chelkash fervently.

Gavrila looked at him with curiosity and he too felt inspired. In the course of their conversation he had already managed to forget who this man was, and now saw in him nothing more than a peasant just like himself, bound to the earth forever by the sweat of many generations and by the memories of childhood—a peasant who of his own free will had cut himself off from the land and from concern for it, and who had therefore been duly punished.

"That's true, brother! Oh, how right you are! Just look at you now—what are you without land? The land, my friend, is like your own mother, and you can't forget it for long."

Chelkash began to have second thoughts about what he had said... He felt the irritating, burning sensation in his chest that he always got when his pride—the pride of the reckless daredevil he was—had been injured by someone, especially if it was someone he considered worthless.

"You're talking rubbish!" he said fiercely. "Perhaps you thought I meant all that seriously... You'll get nothing by waiting, you know!"

"Well, you're a queer fellow all right!" said Gavrila, feeling timid again. "Did you really think I meant you? After all, there's hundreds like you! Oh, what a lot of unhappy folk there are in the world! Homeless wanderers, all of them."

"Here, take the oars, you fool, and row!" ordered Chelkash abruptly, for some reason holding back the torrent of passionate abuse that swelled in his throat.

Again they changed places, and as he climbed over the bales into the stern, Chelkash felt a powerful urge to give Gavrila a kick and send him into the water.

Their short conversation had come to an end, but now, even in Gavrila's silence, Chelkash felt the breath of the village wafting over him... He became so absorbed in thoughts of the past that he forgot to steer the boat, and carried away by the swell, it drifted out to sea a little. The waves seemed to know that it had lost its sense of direction and they played lightly with it, tossing it higher and higher and flashing under the oars with their soft, blue fire. In his mind's eye Chelkash saw swiftly-flitting pictures of the past, the distant past now separated from the present by the barrier of his eleven years as a down-and-out. He saw himself as a child, saw his native village, his mother, a plump, red-cheeked woman with kindly, gray eyes, and his father, a stern-faced giant of a man with a red beard. He saw himself as a bridegroom and saw his bride, the black-eyed Anfisa who was always so soft and gay with the long plait hanging down her back. Then he saw himself again, a handsome young soldier in the Guards. Then his father again, gray now and bent with toil, and his mother, grown short and wrinkled. He saw the way he was greeted by the whole village when he came home from the army, and remembered how proudly his father had shown off his Grigory to everybody, this strong, handsome soldier with his fine mustache... Memory, that scourge of the unfortunate, brings even the stones of the past to life, and to the bitter venom drunk long ago it adds a few drops of honey...

Chelkash felt as if a soothing, tender breath of native air were wafting over him, bringing to his ears the gentle words of his mother and the earnest remarks of his peasant father. With them came many other forgotten sounds and the strong, rich scent of mother earth that had just thawed and been plowed, and was now covered with the emerald sheen of winter crops... He felt uprooted and lonely, cast out forever from the way of life that had produced the blood flowing in his veins.

"Hey! Where are we going?" asked Gavrila suddenly.

Chelkash gave a start and glanced around with the alert, uneasy look of a bird of prey.

"Look where we've drifted to, damn it! Row a bit harder..."

"You were miles away, weren't you?" asked Gavrila with a smile.

"I'm tired..."

"We won't get caught now with these things, will we?" Gavrila asked, giving the bales a kick.

"No...don't worry. I'll hand them over in a minute and get the money... Yes!"

"Five hundred?"

"At least."

"My, what a sum! If only I had that much, poor devil that I am! Oh, I'd sing a song with that lot all right!"

"A song about being a peasant?"

"You bet! Right now I'd..."

And Gavrila took flight on the wings of a dream. But Chelkash said nothing. His mustache was drooping and his right side was soaking wet where it had been drenched by the waves, while his eyes were sunken and had lost their brilliance. Everything predatory had gone out of him, effaced by a submissive pensiveness that was apparent even in the folds of his dirty shirt.

He turned the boat sharply and steered it towards a black shape that rose from the water.

Clouds had covered the sky again and a fine, warm rain began to fall, pattering merrily on the crests of the waves.

"Stop! Keep quiet!" ordered Chelkash.

The boat's bow bumped against the hull of a wooden barge.

"Are they all asleep or something, the bastards?" growled Chelkash, catching with the boat-hook at some ropes hanging over the side. "Let the ladder down! And it's raining now too! A pity it didn't start a bit earlier! Hey, you fools! Hey!"

"Is that Selkash?" came a soft, purring voice from up on deck.

"Come on, let the ladder down!"

"Kalimera, it's Selkash!"

"Let the ladder down, you black devil!" roared Chelkash.

"What a temper he's in tonight! Oh my!"

264

"Climb up, Gavrila!" said Chelkash to his companion.

A minute later they were on deck, where three dark, bearded figures jabbered excitedly to one another in a strange, lisping tongue as they looked over the side into Chelkash's boat. A fourth man, wrapped in a long cloak, went up to Chelkash and silently shook his hand, then eyed Gavrila suspiciously.

"Keep the money till morning," said Chelkash to him briefly. "I'm going to get some sleep now. Come on, Gavrila! Are you hungry?"

"I'm tired..." replied Gavrila, and five minutes later he was snoring loudly. Sitting down beside him, Chelkash tried on a pair of secondhand boots, and spitting thoughtfully, whistled sadly through his teeth. Then he stretched out beside Gavrila with his hands under his head and lay there with his mustache twitching.

The barge rocked gently on the choppy water and a plank creaked plaintively, while the rain fell softly on the deck and the waves lapped against the side... It was all very sad and sounded like the lullaby of a mother who has no hopes for her son's happiness...

Baring his teeth in a grin, Chelkash lifted his head and looked around, then muttering to himself, lay down again... Lying there with his legs spread wide, he looked like a giant pair of scissors.

III

Chelkash was the first to wake. Looking around uneasily, he immediately felt reassured and glanced at Gavrila, who was still asleep. The boy was snoring sweetly and smiling at something in his sleep with all his sunburned, childlike face. Chelkash heaved a sigh, then climbed up the narrow rope ladder. Through the open hatch above the hold a leaden patch of sky was visible. It was light, but the day was dull and gray, as it so often is in autumn.

Chelkash came back about two hours later. His face was flushed and his mustache twirled up in a jaunty fashion. Wearing a stout pair of high boots, a short jacket, and leather trousers, he looked like a hunter. The clothes were shabby but they were well made and suited him, making him look broader, concealing his bony frame, and lending him a military air.

"Hey, young 'un, get up!" he said, giving Gavrila a kick.

Gavrila jumped up, and not recognizing him because he was still half asleep, stared at Chelkash with frightened, bleary eyes. Chelkash burst out laughing.

"Just look at you!" said Gavrila finally with a broad smile. "You're quite the dandy now!"

"It doesn't take me very long. But you really are a coward, aren't you? How many times did you nearly die of fright last night, huh?"

"But just judge for yourself—I'd never done anything like that before! I could've destroyed my soul forever, you know!"

"Well, would you do it again, eh?"

"Again? But you see, it's...what should I say? What would I get for it? That's the point!"

"Well, what if you got a couple of beauties?"

"Two hundred rubles, you mean? All right... I might do it..."

"But wait a minute! What if you destroyed your soul?"

"Well, yes, but perhaps... I wouldn't destroy it after all!" said Gavrila with a smile.

"You wouldn't, and what's more you'd be made for the rest of your life," said Chelkash with a merry laugh.

"Well, all right then! That's enough joking. Let's make for the shore..."

And there they were in the boat again, with Gavrila rowing and Chelkash steering. Above them was the sky, gray and evenly banked with clouds, while the dull green sea played with the boat, tossing it up on the little waves and flinging gaily bright, salty spray against its sides. Far ahead, beyond the bow, could be seen a strip of yellow sand, while behind them the open sea stretched away to the horizon, furrowed by legions of waves adorned with magnificent, white foam. And over there, far away in the distance, many ships could be seen, while off to the left was a whole forest of masts and the heaped, white buildings of the town. From that direction a muffled rumbling came drifting over the sea, a dull roaring that together with the splashing of the waves made fine, stirring music... And over everything hung a thin shroud of ash-gray mist that veiled the expanse around them...

"My, it's going to be bad tonight, all right!" said Chelkash, nodding towards the open sea.

"Will there be a storm?" asked Gavrila as he plowed vigorously through the waves. He was already soaked from head to foot by wind-blown spray.

"I'll say!" Chelkash affirmed.

Gavrila looked at him searchingly...

"Well, how much did they give you then?" he asked eventually, seeing Chelkash was not going to broach the subject.

"Here!" said Chelkash, taking something from his pocket and holding it out to the boy.

Gavrila saw a bundle of multicolored notes and everything took on brilliant, rainbow colors before his eyes.

"Oh! And there I was thinking you'd lied to me! How much have you got there?"

"Five hundred and forty!"

"Very smart!" whispered Gavrila, watching avidly as Chelkash put the money back in his pocket. "Oh my! If only I had money like that!" he said, heaving a dejected sigh.

"You and me'll go out tonight, young 'un!" cried Chelkash in delight.

"Oh, we'll have a few drinks all right... Don't think I won't give you your share, boy... I'll give you forty! Right? Is that enough? I'll give it to you now if you like."

"All right then, if you don't mind. I'll take it now!"

Gavrila was trembling all over with a feverish anticipation that emptied his chest of air.

"Oh, you bloody fool! 'I'll take it!' he says. Then take it, young 'un, go on! Please take it, I beg you! I just don't know what to do with so much money! Do me a favor and take some of it. Here!"

Chelkash held several notes out to Gavrila. Letting go of the oars, the youth took them with a trembling hand and began to hide them in his shirt, narrowing his eyes greedily and gasping as though he were drinking something burning hot. Chelkash watched him with a mocking smile. Then Gavrila seized the oars again and began to row with nervous haste, looking down all the time as though afraid of something. His shoulders and ears were quivering.

"You're a greedy devil! And that's bad... But what can you expect? After all, you're a peasant..." said Chelkash thoughtfully.

"Just think what you can do with money!" exclaimed Gavrila, suddenly blazing up with passionate excitement. Then hurriedly, jerkily, as if outstripping his own thoughts and catching at words in passing, he began to talk about what life was like in the village when you had money and when you hadn't. Respect, prosperity and merriment!..

Chelkash listened to him attentively with a serious look on his face and narrowed his eyes thoughtfully. From time to time he gave a contented smile.

"We're there!" he said, interrupting what Gavrila was saying.

A wave lifted the boat and drove it neatly onto the sand.

"Well, young 'un, it's over now. We've just got to pull the boat up a bit more so it doesn't get washed away. Then somebody'll come for it. And now you and me must say goodbye! It's about five miles to town from here, so what'll you do? Go back into town again, huh?"

Chelkash's face shone with a goodnatured, crafty smile, and the whole of him had the look of a man who had thought up something extremely pleasant for himself but totally unexpected for Gavrila. Thrusting his hand in his pocket, he rustled the notes.

"No... I'm...not going... I..." said Gavrila breathlessly, choking with something.

Chelkash looked at him.

"What's eating you?" he asked.

"Nothing..." But Gavrila's face turned red then gray and he kept shifting from one foot to the other as if he wanted to fling himself on Chelkash or felt profoundly agitated by some impossible desire.

Chelkash was rather taken aback at the sight of the boy's agitation. He waited to see what would happen.

Gavrila broke into strange laughter that sounded more like sobbing. He hung his head, so Chelkash could not see the expression on his face, but he saw Gavrila's ears turning first red then white.

"Oh, to hell with you!" said Chelkash, waving his hand in a hopeless gesture. "Have you fallen in love with me or something? You're just like a stupid girl! Or does it make you feel bad to say goodbye to me? Come on, young 'un, tell me what's wrong, or I'll go!"

"Are you going?" cried Gavrila in a ringing voice.

The deserted, sandy shore reverberated with his cry, and the yellow dunes washed up by the waves seemed to stir. Suddenly Gavrila leapt up and flung himself at Chelkash's feet, embracing his legs and pulling them close. Chelkash swayed then sat down heavily on the sand, and clenching his teeth, swung his long arm with its hard fist through the air. But he did not have time to hit Gavrila, for he was stopped by the boy's pleading, timid whisper:

"Dear friend!.. Give me that money! Give it to me, for Christ's sake! What is it to you? Look, in just one night, one single night... But it'd take me years and years... Give it to me, and I'll pray for you! All my life, in three churches, I'll pray for the salvation of your soul! You see, you'll only throw it away...but I'll put it into the land! Oh, give it to me! What's it to you? What would it cost you? One night, and you're rich! Do someone a good turn! After all, you're done for... You've got no future... But oh! I'd... Give it to me!"

Dumbfounded and filled with resentment, Chelkash sat on the sand, leaning back and trying to push Gavrila away. He sat there without a word, staring in horror at the boy who had his head pressed against Chelkash's knees as he whispered his breathless entreaties. Finally Chelkash pushed him away and leaping to his feet, thrust his hand in his pocket and flung the notes at Gavrila.

"Here! Take it!" he cried, trembling with agitation, loathing and pity for this greedy slave of a man. And having flung the money at him, Chelkash felt like a hero.

"I was going to give you some more anyway. I felt sorry for you yesterday when I remembered my own village... I thought to myself: I'll help the boy. I was just waiting to see what you'd do, whether you'd ask for it or not. But you... Oh, you soft devil! You beggar! How can you torment yourself like that just for money? You fool! You're a greedy lot, you peasants! You lose your heads... You'd sell yourselves for five kopeks!"

"Dear friend! May Christ save you! D'you know what I am now? I'm... rich!" squealed Gavrila in delight, trembling all over and hiding the money inside his shirt. "Bless you, my friend! I'll never forget you! Never! And I'll tell my wife and children to pray for you!"

As Chelkash listened to Gavrila's howls of joy and looked at his radiant face distorted by ecstatic greed, he felt that he—an idler and a thief who was estranged from everything he could call his own—could never be so greedy, so base, so lacking in self-respect. No, he'd never be like that! This thought and the feeling that went with it and filled him with the awareness of his own freedom, made him linger there beside Gavrila on the deserted shore.

"You've made me so happy!" cried Gavrila, and seizing Chelkash's hand, he pressed it to his face.

Chelkash bared his teeth like a wolf but said nothing. Gavrila went on giving vent to his feelings:

"And d'you know what I was thinking? On the way here... I thought to myself... I'll give him one with the oar...bang!...take the cash and chuck him in the sea... Who'd miss him, I said to myself. And even if they do find him, I thought, they won't start trying to find out what happened or who did it. He's not the kind of fellow they'd kick up a fuss about! Nobody needs him! Who'd worry about him?"

"Give the money here!" roared Chelkash, seizing Gavrila by the throat...

Once, twice, Gavrila tried to break free, then Chelkash's other arm coiled around him like a snake... There was the sound of a shirt tearing—and then Gavrila was lying on the sand, his eyes staring wildly, his fingers clutching at the air, and his feet flailing desperately. Erect, lean and rapacious, Chelkash bared his teeth in anger and laughed a harsh, sarcastic laugh, and his mustache quivered nervously on his angular, pointed face. Never in all his life had he been so insulted, never had he felt so offended.

"Well, are you happy now?" he asked through his laughter, and turning his back on Gavrila, set off towards the town. But before he had taken half a dozen steps, Gavrila arched his back like a cat, sprang to his feet, and swinging his arm wide in the air, hurled a round stone at him, shouting spitefully:

"Take that!"

Chelkash groaned and clutched his head, then staggering, turned towards Gavrila and fell face down on the sand. Terrified, Gavrila stood stock still and stared at him. Chelkash moved one leg and tried to lift his head, then stretched out, quivering like a string. Then Gavrila took to his heels, fleeing into the distance where a shaggy, black cloud hung over the dark, misty steppe. The waves roared as they ran up onto the sand, melting into it then running up again. The foam hissed and the air was full of spray.

It began to rain—lightly to begin with, then quickly becoming a heavy downpour that flooded from the sky in slender streams. They wove a web of watery threads that immediately enveloped the expanse of steppe and sea. Gavrila vanished behind it. For a long time nothing could be seen but the rain and the long figure of the man lying on the sand at the water's edge. But then Gavrila appeared again, running out of the rain like a swooping bird. Reaching Chelkash, he fell on his knees beside him and tried to move him. His hand touched something warm, red and slimy. He gave a start and shuddered, his face wild and pale.

"Get up, brother, get up!" he whispered in Chelkash's ear to the sound

269

of the rain.

Chelkash came to and pushed him away, saying hoarsely:

"Clear off!"

"Brother! Forgive me! It was the devil who..." whispered Gavrila, trembling and kissing Chelkash's hand.

"Go away... Clear off..." wheezed Chelkash.

"Take this sin from my soul! Forgive me, brother!"

"For... Get away! Go to hell!" shouted Chelkash suddenly, and he sat up on the sand. His face was pale and angry, while his glazed eyes kept closing as though he was very tired. "What more d'you want? You've done what you wanted...so go away! Clear off!" And he tried to give the grief-stricken Gavrila a kick but could not manage it. He would have collapsed again if the youth had not stopped him by holding him up by the shoulders. Chelkash's face was level with Gavrila's now. Both were terrible and white.

"Pah!" said Chelkash, and spat into his companion's wide-open eyes.

Gavrila meekly wiped his face with his sleeve and whispered:

"Do what you like to me... I won't say a word. Forgive me, for Christ's sake!"

"You bastard! You can't even play your filthy tricks like a man!" cried Chelkash contemptuously, and reaching inside his jacket, he ripped a piece off his shirt. Silently gritting his teeth, he began to bandage his head. "Did you take the money?" he asked grimly.

"No, I didn't, brother! I don't need it! It only brings trouble!"

Chelkash thrust his hand in the pocket of his jacket, and pulling out the bundle of money, put one colored note back, then flung the rest to Gavrila.

"Take it and clear off!"

"I won't take it, brother... I can't! Forgive me!"

"Take it, I said!" roared Chelkash, rolling his eyes terribly.

"Forgive me! Then I'll take it..." said Gavrila timidly, and he fell at Chelkash's feet on the wet sand that was so abundantly flooded by the rain.

"You're lying, you will take it, you bastard!" said Chelkash confidently, and pulling up Gavrila's head by the hair, he pushed the money into his face.

"Take it! Take it! You didn't work for nothing! Don't be afraid, take it! Don't be ashamed just because you nearly killed a man! Nobody'll bother you for killing someone like me. They'll even thank you when they find out. Here, take it!"

Gavrila could see Chelkash was joking, and he felt better. He grasped the money tightly.

"Will you forgive me then, brother? Will you, huh?" he asked tearfully.

"Dear friend!" replied Chelkash mockingly, getting to his feet and swaying. "What's there to forgive? Nothing! Today you got me, and tomorrow I'll get you..."

270

"Oh, brother, brother!" sighed Gavrila sorrowfully, shaking his head.

Chelkash stood before him with a strange smile on his face. The bit of rag around his head was gradually turning redder and beginning to look like a Turkish fez.

It was raining cats and dogs now. The sea murmured with a muffled roar and the waves beat in savage fury against the shore.

The two men were silent for a while.

"Well, goodbye!" said Chelkash mockingly as he turned to go.

His legs shaking, he staggered and held his head in a strange way, almost as if he was afraid of losing it.

"Forgive me, brother!" begged Gavrila once more.

"All right!" replied Chelkash coldly as he set off on his way.

Off he went, reeling and resting his head on the palm of his left hand the whole time, while with his right he tugged gently at his brown mustache.

Gavrila watched him until he disappeared in the rain that was pouring more and more heavily from the clouds in fine, endless streams and enveloping the steppe in impenetrable, steel-gray gloom.

Then Gavrila took off his wet cap and crossed himself. Looking at the money in his hand, he heaved a deep sigh of relief and hid the notes in his shirt. Then with long, firm strides he set off along the shore in the opposite direction to that taken by Chelkash.

The sea roared as it hurled great, heavy waves on to the sand and smashed them into foam and spray. The rain lashed both water and land in its zeal, and the wind howled... The air was filled with roaring, howling and rumbling... Because of the rain neither sea nor sky were visible.

Soon the rain and the sea-spray washed away the red stain where Chelkash had lain, washed away the footprints of Chelkash and the youth on the sand... And on the deserted shore there was nothing left to recall the little drama enacted by these two men.

1894

There were twenty-six of us, twenty-six living machines shut up in a basement where from morning till night we kneaded dough to make pretzels and crackers. The windows of our basement looked out onto a pit lined with bricks that were green with slime. The windows were covered on the outside with fine wire netting, and the sunlight could not reach us as the panes were coated with flour dust. Our boss had put up the netting to stop us giving a crust of his bread to beggars or to those of our comrades who were starving because they were out of work. He called us all swindlers and cheats and gave us bad offal for dinner instead of meat...

It was airless and cramped living in that stone box with its oppressive, low ceiling covered with cobwebs and soot. It was unpleasant and sickening being trapped between those thick walls stained with patches of dirt and mold... We would get up at five in the morning without having had enough sleep, and at six, full of lethargy and indifference, were already sitting down at the table to make pretzels from the dough prepared by our comrades while we were asleep. And all day long, from first thing in the morning until ten at night, some of us sat at the table shaping stiff dough and rocking gently to and fro so as not to grow numb, while others kneaded flour with water. And all day long the boiling water in the cauldron where the pretzels were cooking sang its pensive, melancholy song, and the baker's shovel scraped swiftly and angrily against the hearthstone as it flung lumps of slippery cooked dough onto the hot bricks of the oven. From morning till night the wood burned on one side of the oven, and the ruddy glow of the flames flickered on the basement walls as though in silent mockery. The huge oven resembled the hideous head of some fantastic monster rearing up from beneath the floor, its gaping maw ablaze with brilliant fire, breathing sultry heat upon us and watching our ceaseless toil through the two sunken, black air vents above its brow. Those two deep cavities were like eyes—the pitiless, impassive eyes of a monster. They stared at us with the same somber look the whole time, as if weary of watching slaves of whom nothing human could be expected, and despising us with a chill contempt born of infinite wisdom.

Day in, day out, amid flour dust and the mud we brought in on our feet from the yard, we kneaded dough and made pretzels, wetting them with our sweat as we stifled in the fetid, close heat of the basement. We hated our work with a bitter hatred and never ate what our own hands had produced, preferring black bread instead. Sitting at the long table facing one another—nine men down each side—we moved our hands and fingers mechanically for hours on end, growing so accustomed to the work that we no longer even watched our movements. And we grew so used to looking at each other that

273

we all knew every wrinkle on our comrades' faces. We had nothing to talk about—we were used to that—and kept silent all the time apart from when we swore, for there is always something to swear at a man for, especially if he is a comrade. But we rarely swore at each other—how can a man be to blame for something if he is half dead, if he is like a zombie, if all his feelings are crushed by oppressive toil? Silence is agonizing and terrible only for those who have already said all there is to say; but for people who have not yet begun to speak, keeping silent is simple and easy... Sometimes we would sing, and our song would start like this: hard at work, someone would suddenly heave the deep sigh of a weary horse, and softly begin to sing one of those long drawn-out songs whose plaintively tender melody always lightens the heavy burden of sadness weighing on the singer's heart. One of us would start to sing, and at first the others would listen in silence as his solitary song faded and died beneath the oppressive ceiling like the little light of a camp-fire glimmering in the steppe on a wet autumn night, when the gray sky hangs low over the earth like a roof of lead. Then a second voice would join the first, and the two would float softly and sadly through the stuffy air of our cramped pit. And suddenly all at once several voices would take up the song—and growing stronger and louder it surged like a wave and seemed to force back the dank, oppressive walls of our stone prison...

Now all twenty-six of us are singing; loud, long-practiced voices fill the bakery with sound. The song feels cramped in the basement, and moaning and weeping, it beats against the stone walls, cheering the heart with softly stirring pain as it reopens old wounds and arouses yearning in the soul... The singers heave deep, painful sighs; one of them suddenly breaks off and listens to his friends for a long time, before adding his voice to the general wave of sound once more. Another cries "Oh!" in a melancholy voice and sings with his eyes closed. Perhaps the deep, broad wave of sound seems to him like a road bathed in brilliant sunlight that leads off somewhere into the distance—a wide road with himself walking along it...

The flames in the oven still flicker, the baker's shovel still scrapes over the bricks, the water still bubbles in the cauldron, and the glow of the fire still dances on the wall in silent mockery... And with words that are not our own we sing of our aching sorrow, of the painful yearning of living creatures deprived of sunlight, the sad longing of slaves. And so we lived, twenty-six of us, in the basement of that big stone building, and so heavy was life's burden that it seemed as though all three stories of that building rested on our very shoulders...

□□□□□

But apart from our singing we had something else that was fine and good, something that we loved and that perhaps took the place of the sun for us. On the first floor of our building there was a gold embroidery workshop,

274

and among the many girl seamstresses in it was a sixteen year-old housemaid called Tanya. Every morning her little pink face with its merry blue eyes would press against the small window cut in the bakery door from the passage, and her sweet, ringing voice would call to us:

"Hey, prisoners! Give me some pretzels!"

At the sound of that clear voice we would all turn around and look joyfully and kindly at the pure, girlish face that smiled so sweetly at us. It gave us great pleasure to see that nose pressed to the windowpane, and those little white teeth gleaming between pink lips parted in a smile. Jostling each other, we would rush to open the door for her, and then—looking so charming and gay—in she would come. Holding out her apron, she would stand before us, cocking her little head on one side and smiling the whole time. A long, thick plait of auburn hair hangs down over her shoulder and lies on her breast. Grimy, coarse, ugly men that we are, we look up at her—the threshold is four steps above the floor—look up at her with uplifted eyes, and wish her good morning with some special words that we use only for her. When we speak of her our voices are softer and our jokes more mild. Everything we do for her is special. The baker takes a shovelful of the crispest, ruddiest pretzels out of the oven and tosses them neatly into her apron.

"Mind the boss doesn't catch you!" we warn her. She gives a mischievous laugh and shouts gaily to us:

"Goodbye, prisoners!" and vanishes as swiftly as a mouse.

And that's all... But for a long time after she has gone we talk pleasurably about her—saying just the same things we said yesterday and the day before, because she and we and everything around us is just the same as it was both yesterday and the day before... It is very painful and hard for a man to live when nothing changes around him, and if his soul is not destroyed, the longer he lives the more painful everything around him becomes... We always talked about women in a way that sometimes made us feel disgusted with ourselves for saying such shamelessly crude things, but that was understandable, since the women we knew perhaps did not even deserve to be spoken of in any other way. But we never said anything bad about Tanya. None of us ever allowed himself to touch her, or even make an improper joke when she was there. Perhaps this was because she never stayed very long, merely flashing before us like a falling star then vanishing. Or perhaps it was because she was small and so very beautiful, and because all that is beautiful inspires respect, even in rough, coarse men. Besides, though our drudgery did turn us into dull, ox-like creatures, we were still human beings, and like all human beings we could not live without something to worship. We had no one finer than Tanya, and no one but she paid any attention to us in our basement— no one at all, though there were dozens of people living in the same building. Lastly—and this was probably the main reason—we all regarded her as something that belonged just to us, something that only existed, it seemed, because of our pretzels. We considered it our duty to give her hot pretzels, and this became our daily sacrifice to an idol, almost a sacred rite that brought us closer and closer to her with every passing day. Apart from the pretzels, we gave her a good deal of advice as well—to dress warmly, not to run too fast down the stairs, and not to carry heavy bundles of firewood. She listened to our words of advice with a smile, answered them with a laugh, and never obeyed us, but we did not take offense, for we only needed to show we cared.

She often asked us to do things for her, like open the heavy door into the cellar or chop some wood—and we would gladly do it. We would do anything else she wished too, even taking a kind of pride in what we did for her.

But when one of us asked her to mend his one and only shirt for him, she gave a scornful snort and said:

"Whatever next! Catch me doing that!..."

We had a good laugh at the silly fellow, and none of us ever asked her to do anything for him again. We loved her—and that is all there is to say. A man always wants to bestow his love on someone, though he sometimes sullies or crushes the other with his affection, and may even poison the life of his dear one, because in loving he does not respect the object of his love. We had to love Tanya, for there was no one else we could love.

Now and then one of us would suddenly begin to talk like this:

"Why is it we make such a fuss over the girl? What's so wonderful about her, huh? We go to a hell of a lot of trouble for her, you know!"

But whoever allowed himself to say things like that was put swiftly and sharply in his place—we had to have something to love and had found it. We loved it, and the thing loved by all twenty-six of us had to be unassailable to each of us individually, like a sacred object, and anyone who opposed us in this was our enemy. Perhaps we did not love what was truly good, but there were twenty-six of us, and so we always wanted what was dear to each of us to be held sacred by all the others.

The love of men like us is no less serious than our hate...and perhaps that is why some proud fellows claim that our hatred is more flattering than our love... But if that is so, why then do they not shun us?

□□□□□

Apart from his basement where pretzels were made, our boss had a bakery too. It was located in the same building and separated from our pit only by a wall. But the bakers—there were four of them—kept aloof from us, considering their work cleaner than ours. Thinking themselves better than we were, they never came to our workshop, and made fun of us in a scornful way when they met us in the yard. We did not visit them either: the boss had forbidden us to do so for fear we might start stealing bread buns. We disliked the bakers because we envied them; their work was easier than ours, they got better pay, they were better fed, they had a light, spacious workshop, and they were all clean and healthy—so we found them offensive. We, on the other hand, were all sallow, with gray faces. Three of us suffered from syphilis and several others had scabies, while one was completely crippled by rheumatism. On holidays and during time off the bakers wore jackets and boots that squeaked. A couple of them had accordions, and they would all go out for a stroll in the park. But we wore dirty, ragged clothes and down-at-heel shoes or bast sandals, and the police would not let us into the park. So how could we like the bakers?

Then one day we heard that their head baker had started drinking and had been fired. But the boss had already taken on someone else, apparently, and the new man was an ex-soldier who went about in a satin waistcoat with a watch and gold chain. We were curious to have a look at this dandy, and one after the other kept running out into the yard in the hope of seeing him.

But he came to our basement himself. Kicking open the door, he stood smiling on the threshold, and said to us:

"Hello there! How d'you do?"

Bursting through the door in dense, smoky clouds, the frosty air billowed at his feet, while he stood looking down at us from the threshold with his big yellow teeth gleaming under his neatly twirled, blond mustache. His waistcoat really was rather special—it was dark blue and embroidered with flowers, and the whole of it shone somehow, while its buttons were made of little red stones. It had a gold chain too...

He was a handsome fellow, that soldier, tall and strong with ruddy cheeks and big, bright eyes that had a fine look in them—tender and serene. On his head he wore a stiffly starched, white cap, and beneath his spotless apron could be seen the pointed toes of his highly polished, fashionable boots.

Our baker asked him politely to close the door. He did so without any hurry and then began to ask us about the boss. Vying with each other, we told him the boss was a skinflint, a swindler, a crook, and a tormentor—all the things we could and should have said about him but that cannot be printed here. Twirling his mustache as he listened, the soldier examined us with his soft, bright eyes.

"You've got a lot of girls around here..." he said suddenly.

Some of us laughed politely, and others pulled sugary faces, while somebody explained that there were nine girls in the building.

"D'you have a good time with 'em?" he asked with a wink.

Again we laughed, but not very loudly and in a rather embarrassed way... Many of us would have liked to make him think we were bold fellows just like he was, but we could not do it. Not one of us could do it. Someone confessed as much, saying quietly:

"How can we..."

"Well yes, it's hard for you lot!" he said with self-assurance, examining us intently. "You're not quite...up to it... You haven't got the confidence...

the decent appearance...the looks, you see! Looks is what a woman likes about a man! She likes a good body...everything just right! And then she likes to see a bit of strength... Likes a man's arm to be like this!"

He pulled his right hand out of his pocket and showed us his arm with his shirtsleeve rolled up to the elbow... The arm was strong and white, and covered with shining, golden hairs.

"Your legs and chest—everything's got to be nice and firm... And then a man's got to be dressed right...well turned out, you know, so he looks good... Take me now—the girls really go for me. I don't go after 'em or encourage 'em—they just throw themselves at me half a dozen at a time..."

He sat down on a sack of flour and told us at length how the girls loved him and how bold he was with them. Then he went away, and when the door had squeaked and closed behind him, we remained silent for a long time, thinking about him and his exploits. And then suddenly somehow everyone began to speak at once, and it immediately became clear that we had all taken a liking to him. He was such a nice, simple fellow—he'd just come in, sat down for a bit, and chatted with us. No one ever came to see us, no one ever talked to us like that, in such a nice, friendly way... And we kept on talking about him and his future triumphs with the seamstresses, who when they met us in the yard either pursed their lips in distaste and gave us a wide berth, or walked straight towards us as if we were not there at all. But we always just feasted our eyes on them when they were crossing the yard or walking past our windows, with their pretty little fur coats and bonnets in winter, and their flowery hats and brightly-colored parasols in summer. But among ourselves we talked about them in a way that would have filled them with shame and indignation if they had heard us.

"But what if he goes and... messes up our little Tanya!" said our baker suddenly in an anxious tone. Struck by his words, we all fell silent. We had somehow forgotten about Tanya—it was as if the soldier's large, handsome figure had screened her from us. Then a loud argument began: some said she would not stoop to that and others maintained she would not be able to resist him, while the rest proposed to break his neck for him if he started pestering her. In the end, we all decided to keep an eye on the soldier and Tanya, and warn her to beware of him... That brought the argument to an end.

□□□□□

About a month passed. The soldier baked bread rolls, went out with the seamstresses, and often dropped in to see us, but never said anything about his conquests. All he did was twirl his mustache and lick his lips with relish the whole time.

Tanya came every morning for her pretzels and was as charming, affectionate and gay as ever. When we broached the subject of the soldier, she called him a "goggle-eyed calf" and other funny names, and that reassured us. We felt proud of our girl when we saw how the seamstresses made up to the soldier. Tanya's attitude towards him raised all our spirits somehow, and as though guided by her example we began to treat him with scorn. But we grew fonder still of her, greeting her in the mornings in an even more joyful, kindly way.

But one day the soldier came to see us when he was a little tight. He sat down and began to laugh, and when we asked him what the joke was, he explained:

"Two of 'em have had a scrap over me—Lidka and Grushka... What a mess they've made of each other! Ha-ha! One of 'em grabbed the other by the hair and threw her on the floor in the passage, then she got on top of her... Ha-ha-ha! They scratched each other's mugs...tore their clothes...did I laugh! Why is it women can't fight fairly? What do they have to scratch each other for, huh?"

He sat on the bench looking so clean and strong and cheerful, just sat there laughing all the time... We did not speak. This time for some reason we found him objectionable.

"Why do I have such luck with the girls, huh? It's killing! I just give 'em a wink, and that's it!"

He lifted his white hands covered with their shining hairs and slapped his knees hard. And he looked at us with pleasant surprise, as if genuinely perplexed by his success with women. His plump, ruddy face shone with self-satisfaction and he kept licking his lips with relish...

Our baker scraped his shovel angrily on the hearth and suddenly said mockingly:

"It doesn't take much to chop a little fir tree down, but you try felling a pine..."

"What? Are you talking to me?" asked the soldier.

"Yes, you..."

"What did you say?"

"Nothing...it's only a joke!"

"No, wait a minute! What are you talking about? What pine tree?"

Our baker did not reply. His shovel moved swiftly inside the oven, tossing in boiled pretzels then gathering up those that were ready and flinging them noisily to the floor where boys sat threading them on bast strings. He seemed to have forgotten about the soldier. But the latter suddenly became very agitated. He stood up and walked towards the oven, running the risk of being struck in the chest by the shovel handle as it jerked through the air.

"Look here, tell me what girl you mean! That's an insult...turn me down? There's no one would refuse me, oh no! And you go and insult me like that!..."

He really did seem genuinely offended. He probably had nothing to respect himself for apart from his skill in seducing women. Perhaps that was

279

the only living thing about him, the only thing that enabled him to feel like a real human being.

There are people for whom the finest and most precious thing in life is some sickness of the body or soul. They are obsessed with it throughout their lives and live for it alone. While suffering from it, they are nourished by it, complaining to others about it, and so attracting the attention of their fellow human beings. Because of it they elicit sympathy from others, and have nothing else in life but this. Deprive them of this sickness, cure them of it, and they will be miserable, because they will lose their *raison d'être* and their lives will become empty. Sometimes a man's life is so wretched that he is forced despite himself to set much store by his vice and make it the reason for his existence. And so it might be said that people are often depraved out of sheer boredom.

The soldier had taken offense and kept hanging around our baker, whining at him:

"No, tell me who you mean!"

"D'you want me to tell you?" said the baker, suddenly turning to him.

"Yes, come on!"

"D'you know Tanya?"

"Yes, why?"

"Well there you are then! Just try and..."

"Me?"

"Yes, you!"

"Her? Pah—that's nothing!"

"Well we'll see!"

"You'll see all right! Ha-ha!"

"She'll..."

"Give me a month!"

"You're a real boaster, aren't you, soldier!"

"Two weeks then! I'll show you! Who d'you say? That Tanya? Pah!..."

"Come on now, get out of here...you're in our way!"

"Two weeks—and that's that! Oh, you..."

"Get out, I said!"

Our baker suddenly became angry and brandished his shovel. Astonished, the soldier stepped back, looked at us all for a moment without a word, then said softly in an ominous voice: "All right then!" and went out.

Intrigued by it, none of us had said a word during the argument. But when the soldier had gone, we all began to chatter loudly in our excitement.

Someone shouted to the baker:

"It's a bad business you've started, Pavel!"

"Get on with your work!" he replied furiously.

We knew that the soldier was stung to the quick and that Tanya was in danger. We knew it and yet at the same time were all seized with pleasurable, burning curiosity as to what would happen. Would she hold out against him?

280

And almost all of us shouted confidently:

"Little Tanya? She'll resist him all right! She's no pushover!"

We were terribly anxious to put our little idol to the test, and kept trying to convince each other that ours was a steadfast idol who would emerge triumphant from this confrontation. In the end we even began to wonder whether we had provoked the soldier enough, thinking that he might forget about the quarrel and that we really ought to injure his pride once and for all. From that day on we began to live a peculiar, excitingly tense kind of life—something we had never known before. We would argue for days on end, becoming cleverer somehow and growing more talkative and eloquent. We seemed to be playing a game with the devil, and our stake was Tanya. And when we heard from the bakers that the soldier had started "running after little Tanya," our life became so thrilling and full of interest that we did not even notice that the boss had taken advantage of our excitement by adding another five hundred pounds of dough to our daily quota. We did not even seem to grow tired of the work any more either. Tanya's name was on our lips all day long. And every morning we waited for her with a special kind of impatience. Sometimes we imagined that she would no longer be the same Tanya as before, but different somehow.

But we said nothing to her about the argument that had taken place. We never asked her any questions and treated her in the same kind, affectionate way as before. But something new had already crept into our relations with her, something that was alien to our former feelings for her. That something was keen curiosity, sharp and cold as the blade of a knife...

□□□□□

"Well! Time's up today!" said the baker one morning as he began work.

We were all well aware of it without being reminded, but we gave a start all the same.

"Have a good look at her...she'll be here in a minute!" he suggested.

Someone exclaimed ruefully:

"As if you can tell anything just by looking!"

And once again a loud, heated argument began. Today at last we would find out just how pure and inaccessible to filth was the vessel to which we had entrusted all that was best in us. That morning, for the first time somehow, we suddenly realized that we really were playing a game with high stakes, and that this test of our idol's purity might destroy it for us. For the past few days we had heard that the soldier was pursuing Tanya both persistently and importunately, but for some reason none of us had asked her what she thought of him. She kept coming punctually every morning for her pretzels and was just the same as always. That morning too we soon heard her voice:

"Hello, prisoners! I've come..."

281

We hurried to open the door for her, and when she had come in, contrary to our usual habit we greeted her with silence. Staring hard at her, we did not know what to say or what to ask her, and just stood before her in a silent, somber crowd. She was evidently surprised by this unusual reception—then suddenly we saw her turn pale, become uneasy and begin to shuffle somehow. Then she asked in an unnatural voice:

"Why are you all...like this?"

"And what about you?" flung out the baker in a gloomy voice, not taking his eyes off her.

"What d'you mean—me?"

"Oh, n-nothing..."

"Well come on then, be quick and give me the pretzels..."

Never before had she tried to hurry us...

"You've got plenty of time!" said the baker without moving, his eyes still fixed on her face.

Then she suddenly turned and disappeared through the door.

The baker picked up his shovel and turning to the oven, said quietly:

"So that's that! The soldier's done it! The bastard!"

Jostling one another like a flock of sheep, we went shambling back to the table, silently took our seats and set limply to work. After a short time someone said:

"Perhaps she hasn't..."

"Come on! Don't give me that!" shouted the baker.

We all knew he was a clever man, much cleverer than we were, and his shout told us he was convinced of the soldier's triumph. We felt uneasy and sad...

At twelve o'clock, during our lunch break, the soldier came in. He was as spruce and dandified as ever and looked us straight in the eye as he always did. But we felt uncomfortable looking at him.

"Well now, good people, d'you want me to show you what a soldier can do?" he said with an arrogant sneer. "Just go out into the passage and look through the cracks in the wall...d'you get my meaning?"

We went out and, leaning on one another, pressed our faces to the chinks in the plank wall of the passage that led out into the yard. We did not have to wait long... Soon Tanya came quickly across the yard with a preoccupied look on her face, jumping over the puddles of melted snow and mud in her path. She disappeared through the door into the cellar. Then, without hurrying and whistling softly as he went, the soldier crossed the yard and followed her inside. His hands were thrust in his pockets but his mustache was twitching...

It was raining, and we could see the drops falling into the puddles and making them ripple. The day was wet and gray—a very dull, tedious day. Snow still lay on the roofs, while dark patches of mud had already appeared on the ground. And the snow on the roofs was covered with a grimy, brown crust too. The rain fell slowly with a dismal, dripping sound. It was cold and uncomfortable waiting in the passage...

The soldier came out of the cellar first. He set off slowly across the yard, with his mustache twitching and his hands in his pockets—just the same as always.

Then Tanya came out too. Her eyes...her eyes were shining with happiness and joy, and her lips were smiling. And she walked as if in a dream, swaying with unsteady steps...

We could not take this calmly. Rushing to the door, we all leapt out into the yard and began to whistle and yell at her in furious anger.

When she saw us she gave a start, then stood stock still, her feet in a patch of mud. We surrounded her, and full of malicious joy abused her without restraint, cursing her with obscenities and shouting foul oaths at her.

We did this steadily and without hurrying, seeing that she was surrounded by us and could not escape, and realizing we could jeer at her to our heart's content. I do not know why, but we did not hit her. She stood surrounded by us, turning her head first this way then that and listening to our insults. And more and more fiercely, more and more violently, we flung our venomous, filthy words at her.

The color drained from her face. Her light blue eyes, so full of happiness just a moment ago, were wide and staring, while her breast heaved and her lips trembled.

Surrounding her, we took vengeance on her, for she had robbed us. She had belonged to us and we had given our best for her, and though that best was only the crumbs of beggars, there were twenty-six of us and only one of her, so no punishment we inflicted could match her guilt! How we insulted her!... She did not say a word, but just stared at us with wild eyes, shaking all over.

We laughed, we roared, we snarled at her... More people came running up to join us... One of us pulled at the sleeve of her blouse...

Suddenly her eyes flashed fire. Without hurrying, she lifted her hands to her hair, and said in a loud but calm voice right into our faces:

"Oh, you poor prisoners!..."

And she set off walking straight towards us, simply set off as if we were not standing there blocking her path at all. And that is why none of us actually stood in her way, but let her pass.

When she was clear of our circle, without turning around she added just as loudly in a proudly contemptuous voice:

"Oh, you filthy swine...you scum..."

And off she went—erect, beautiful and proud.

And we were left standing in the middle of the yard in the mud and rain, under a sunless, gray sky...

Then we walked silently back to our damp, stone pit. As before, the sun never looked in at our windows, and Tanya never came to see us any more...

1899

283